Straw Horse

Book Two of the Kat Wilde U.P. Mysteries

TERRI MARTIN

Modern History Press

Ann Arbor, MI

Straw Horse: A Kat Wilde U.P. Mystery

ISBN 978-1-61599-465-6 paperback
ISBN 978-1-61599-466-3 hardcover
ISBN 978-1-61599-467-0 eBook

Published by
Modern History Press
5145 Pontiac Trail
Ann Arbor, MI 48105

www.ModernHistoryPress.com
info@ModernHistoryPress.com
Tollfree 888-761-6268 (USA/CAN)

Distributed by Ingram Book Group (USA/CAN/AU)

To my publisher and proofreaders,
who likely now need therapy.

And he who strives to touch the stars,
Oft stumbles at a straw.

—Edmund Spenser

1

"Are you okay?"

I heard the words but couldn't answer.

"Susie, call 911!" Nikko said.

911?

"How will they get her out of here?" Susie asked.

"They'll need to know we're on the trail about a half mile from Big Lake Road, and they'll wanna bring a portable stretcher. Kat, can you hear me?"

"I got no bars," Susie said.

"Mine's satellite. Use it."

Big Mac!

"She blinked! She's trying to say something."

This observation came from Nikko Olsen, whose face was strangely out of focus. Nikko was my sort-of boyfriend and a Michigan Department of Natural Resources (DNR) conservation officer, or CO for short. He was assigned a couple of counties away, but his roots were in Peshekee (Pah-Shee-Key) where I happened to live.

"Big Mac!" I shouted. At least I thought I had shouted it.

"She's mumbling something," Nikko said. "Where the hell is the ambulance?"

"It's only been, like, two minutes since I called. I think she was asking about Big Mac."

This last string of words sounded like someone talking underwater, but I still recognized the voice as Susie Koskinen's. Susie is a college girl with a lot of ambition.

"It's been more than two minutes," Nikko said. "Kat! Can you hear me?"

I nodded. The entire county could likely hear him. Maybe the ambulance could follow the bellowing. Kat is short for Kathryn. My last name is Wilde. People love to tinker with my name. Very annoying people.

"Big Mac!" I said.

"She's wondering about Big Mac," Susie said.

Big Mac was the Belgian draft horse I had been riding. Susie, Nikko, and I had been cantering through the woods when something caused my horse to bolt. Mac is a rescue horse I have been fostering through an equine rescue nonprofit called Four Hoof Rescue, or 4HR. He's a big fella, but generally solid as a rock. Susie was the reason I had been out riding Big Mac. We were testing him out for his suitability for special needs children to ride. Susie was studying to become an equine therapist and had wrangled me into her plans.

"I expect he's headed back to the barn," Nikko said.

"Nope," Susie said. "He's right over there. Got no bridle."

"Huh?" I said, running my hand over my face. When I took my hand away, there was blood. Nikko had pulled my helmet off and was dabbing at my face.

Great. Just call me Scarface. Another gash on my face. It would be added to the talon slash across my cheek, delivered by a territorial eagle during my zipline escapade, which had been Nikko's idea of an adventure. The current disaster was my doing and had been meant to be a simple ride in the Crystal Lake Wilderness, which abutted my land.

Branches snapped. Voices.

Some might call me accident-prone. But it wasn't until I "inherited" my uncle's horse operation, Wildwood Stables, that my physical wellbeing had seemed to be in constant peril. Since taking ownership, I have suffered a torn meniscus (knee injury), been nearly defaced by the aforementioned eagle, endured an apocalyptic storm during a kayak adventure, barely escaped a live cremation (courtesy of a couple of baddies who had been blackmailing my uncle), and now find myself seeing stars and apparently bleeding to boot. Well, life isn't dull.

"Over here!" Nikko shouted.

Next thing I knew, I had a bandage slapped on my face, a contraption put around my neck, and then, they carefully lifted me onto a stretcher. Someone put a blanket over me and secured their handiwork with several straps.

"Is he okay?" I asked.

"I'm fine," Nikko said.

"She means Big Mac," Susie said. "I got him. He's fine, but the bridle is toast. Don't worry, Kat; he'll follow Shadow and Rusty back to the barn."

Shadow and Rusty were Susie and Nikko's mounts.

On the count of three, the first responders hoisted the stretcher.

"I swear to God," one of them muttered. "I'm getting too old for this."

Nikko leaned over me. "I'll get to the hospital as soon as we get the horses back to the barn."

* * *

The person who pulled the curtain back was the same incredibly handsome doc who had treated me during my last visit to the emergency department at Peshekee Memorial. His ID badge featured a name that was long and complicated. He smiled.

"Hello. I'm Dr. Zahid Sulaimankhel," he said with a trace of a Middle Eastern accent.

"Me again," I said. "Nice to see you Dr. ah...."

"Call me Dr. Zee. I remember you. You're the horse person!"

"Uh huh."

"My wife has *three* Arabians now. I will never be able to retire."

This made me smile. It was true. Horses were a money pit. My late Uncle Phil, from whom I had indirectly inherited Wildwood Stables, had been deeply in the red before he passed away from cancer. So far I wasn't doing a whole lot better financially than Uncle Phil and still had to keep my part-time pity job at Wilde Accounting, which was owned and operated by my father, Gary Wilde. My mother handled payroll and benefits.

"So, you had a fall. Laceration on your left cheek." He looked at it. "No sutures needed. It will heal well with the butterfly bandages we put on. X-rays came back okay. I understand you were wearing a helmet, but the EMTs indicate you were dazed."

"Uh huh."

"How are you feeling now?"

"Ridiculous," I said, sitting up. "I'm fine."

It was a lie. The room took a spin, and I grabbed the handrails of the bed.

"Perhaps a mild concussion, in spite of the helmet," he said. "No other apparent injuries."

Someone said, "Thank you, nurse." The curtain swished open, and my mother, the one and only Clara Wilde, bustled into our cramped space.

"Kathryn Wilde!" she bleated. "What on earth—oh, hello, doctor, er...."

"Dr. Zee," I said. "Same one who saw me when I messed up my knee."

The knee injury had occurred during a tussle with the now deceased Scott Summers, who had claimed ownership of Wildwood Stables. His twisted scheme involved a secret marriage to Uncle Phil's caregiver, Sasha, who posed as my uncle's love child from his military days. Sasha had been the first dead body found at Wildwood Stables. Scott Summers had been the second. Both were homicides. We're trying to live it down.

Dr. Zee shook Mom's hand and gave a 100-watt smile. "Your daughter will be fine. I do have to ask, however, was she accident-prone as a child?"

"Let's just say she didn't have tea parties and play with dolls," Mom replied.

"Hey, Mom," I snapped. I wasn't keen on my mother recounting my unorthodox childhood. Mom found my preference for "boys' toys" over girlie things troublesome.

"Hello, darling," she said, bending over to give me a peck on the cheek. "How are you?"

"I'm okay, and Nikko will be here soon to take me home," I said, giving Dr. Zee a hopeful look.

"Nikko called me, dear. I'm here to take you home. He said he's having the vet out to look at some horse—Max? Apparently a cut on his leg."

"Oh no!" I said. "Mac, not Max. I've got to get out of here. Can someone put this rail down? Where are my clothes?"

Dr. Zee placed a hand on my shoulder, blocking my futile attempts to push down the bedrail.

"Now Miss Wilde, no need to worry. I'm sure your horse will be fine. In any event, I intend to discharge you so long as you don't drive for at least forty-eight hours, and you cannot be alone tonight. Also, no horseback riding for a few days. I don't want your brain bounced around right now, and we need you to watch for symptoms of a concussion. The nurse will give you instructions, and if your condition worsens, which I don't expect, please give your regular doctor a call or come back to the emergency department." He turned to a laptop attached to a rolling apparatus and began briskly typing.

"Oh dear," Mom said. "I can take her home, but her father and I are leaving tonight for a conference."

"Nikko..." I said.

Mother gave me a penetrating look. Nikko staying with me overnight was clearly not an option.

"I mean for a while," I said. "Aunt Lin will be around tonight. I'll be okay so long as she doesn't try to poison me with one of her tea concoctions."

The click of computer keys halted and Dr. Zee looked up from his laptop.

"Kidding," I said. Aunt Lin is what some would call eccentric. I call her a lifesaver for the help she is at Wildwood Stables, and all for a paltry wage. Plus, she can cook, though mainly vegan, and keeps our cat, Jupiter, mellow on catnip. Aunt Lin is my only and thus favorite aunt. She is Mom's much younger sister and more like an older sister than an aunt to me. She lives with me in a modular home—the mod—at Wildwood Stables along with Jupiter, who I swear is part raccoon or ocelot or both. Aunt Lin is beyond eccentric, and I love her, in spite of her determination to play the lyre and push strange herbal tea on everyone.

"Well, I suppose Lindsey will have to do, though I'd rather have you home."

Lindsey was Aunt Lin's full first name. To Mom, the mod was where I lived and home was where I grew up.

"Well, then, that will do fine," Dr. Zee said, snapping his laptop shut. "The nurse will be in shortly."

* * *

Mom dropped me off at the mod with strict instructions to "take it easy." Fortunately, she was in a hurry to go home to do some laundry and pack for her and my father's trip to Chicago for some kind of accountants convention. While the CPAs would be inundated with deadly PowerPoint presentations and handouts featuring esoteric bullet points and colorful Venn diagrams, Mom would be hitting the shopping district in the Loop. Neither activity remotely appealed to me.

Wildwood Stables is located at the end of Horse Camp Road, a rutted, washed-out dirt monstrosity that keeps out the riffraff and gives welcome visitors second thoughts about coming. Aunt Lin's Subaru was not parked at the mod, so I wouldn't be facing any questions or medicinal tea from her. I had to admit it rankled me a bit that Aunt Lin's Subaru used to be *my* Subaru. The vehicle betrayed me and developed a multitude of expensive problems. I sold it to Mike's Auto to be sacrificed to a bunch of teenagers enrolled in a program to learn by "doing" under the mentorship of a supervisor. Once the Subaru was in tip-top shape, it was raffled off. Aunt Lin purchased the winning raffle ticket for $25. Some people just had all the luck.

My aunt had many things on her plate, including a meditation class, vegan cooking, and music lessons on the lyre. For the latter, she was mainly self-taught via YouTube since there weren't many local opportunities for professional lessons on ancient Greek musical instruments.

I slipped just inside the door and watched Mom pull away. The moment she moved out of view, I hustled to the barn to check on Big Mac. When I got there, the vet had already left and Mac was quietly munching hay in his double-size stall. Susie and Nikko were giving Rusty and Shadow their post-ride rubdowns.

"How is he?" I asked, rushing over to Mac's stall and sliding the door open.

"He's fine," Nikko said, coming over to me. "How are you? Hey, sorry. I couldn't come to get you. What's the word from the doc?" He pushed my hair away from my face and looked at the crusty cut on my cheek, then gave me a chaste kiss on my cracked lips.

My hair, on a good day, could best be described as an overgrown shrub. On a bad day, it had a zip code of its own. My mother claimed it was our Hungarian blood. That, combined with the Irish side of the family—being Dad's—caused my hair to somehow get caught in a deranged genetic battle. Having Hungarian hair combined with my 5'9" height made me a bit of an outcast during my high school years. While being tall was handy when assigned a top locker, it tended to be intimidating to boys who had not yet reached their final growth spurt.

"I'm fine," I said. "Just have to take it easy for a day or two. Can't ride or skydive. I can go to work tomorrow, though. Yippee. What about Mac?"

Susie came over to join us. "His leg was cut from the brush you guys got into. I mean, it was a bramble bush. Dr. Jukkila did some stitches in his hind leg and gave us this ointment to put on the other cuts. There's, like, a million of them."

I went into Mac's stall, looked at the damage, and petted his neck. Mac, being a cold-blooded horse, was generally calm and steady. The term cold blood to describe a horse has nothing to do with the actual blood but relates to the earlier breeds coming from arctic regions. Draft horses are generally referred to as cold bloods for their steady work ethic and quiet, dependable temperaments, in contrast to the hot bloods, such as Arabians and Thoroughbreds. Mac looked over at me and stopped chewing his hay.

"What was that all about?" I asked him. It just wasn't like Mac to spook and bolt as he had in the Crystal Lake Wilderness. He had run blindly into the bramble thicket, somehow losing his bridle and throwing me into Br'er Rabbit's habitat.

"He seems calm now," I said. "But something sure set him off out there."

"Maybe a deer?" Nikko said.

"Are you kidding?" I said. "Deer are all over the place here, and he never bats an eye."

"Maybe something blew across the trail," Susie said.

"Yeah, but there wasn't a breath of wind," I said.

"Do you think he smelled a bear or maybe a moose?" Nikko asked. "A moose would spook anything. They're beyond weird looking."

"Shadow didn't spook," Susie said. "Wouldn't he and Rusty have smelled or seen something too? And Shadow will freak at a gum wrapper on the trail."

"Could be poachers," Nikko said. "Not my district, but I can still check it out."

CO Nikko Olsen: always on duty.

Mac gave me a benevolent look, sighed, and shook his head as if to tell us we were on the wrong trail.

2

I reported for "duty" at Wilde Accounting at exactly 8 a.m. the next morning, thus thwarting any reprimand from the office overlord, Rose Gustafson. I wasn't sure if it was okay to drive or not, but I did anyway. I felt okay; just looked a wreck.

"Morning," I said.

Rose glanced at the clock and looked at me. "*Now* what happened to you?"

"Took a spill. I'm fine."

Of course Rose had not asked if I was okay, but I put it out there anyway. A kind person would describe Rose as "retro," with her outdated hairstyle, which may still contain backcombing and hairspray from the sixties. I had no idea where she found clothes, unless it was someplace called "Dowdy Duds for Drudges." She wore a pair of half glasses, which hung from a rhinestone chain around her neck. Rose made it a point to be at her desk and on duty before anyone else. She had a pullout writing table with a piece of paper taped to it that featured several columns, one for each employee. When one of us committed a transgression, Rose made note. We called it the Nasty List. Currently, regular office personnel only consisted of Rose, her son Gerald "Gussy" Gustafson, my father, sometimes Mom, and me. There wasn't much material for the Nasty List since Dad's right-hand associate, Char Houle, had left under less-than-ideal circumstances.

The only other so-called employee was Raymond Leblanc, who was strictly freelance and kept us technologically up to speed and out of trouble with both our clients and the IRS. Raymond was Anishinaabe, or Ojibwa, and stayed close to his Native American heritage. He lived mostly off the grid in a cabin on the reservation, which abutted a corner of Wildwood's back forty. Raymond managed to have electricity in his cabin via solar panels and a generator, but there was no indoor plumbing. He snowshoed in and out in the winter.

What amazed all of us was that Raymond seemed to show up when we needed him. In spite of his remote location, Raymond had rigged up Wi-Fi at his cabin and through that had cell service, thus making him reachable. Usually. Nobody quite knew the scope of Raymond's employment. That included Dad and gave Rose little to work with for assigning him demerits. Raymond and Aunt Lin were "seeing" each other. That relationship was as much of an enigma as his job description.

Gussy came out of his office and grinned. "Hey, Kat, what does the other guy look like?" He emitted an off-putting snort.

"Hey, Gussy," I said. "Lookin' mighty spiffy in your khakis."

"Er, thanks," he said, looking down at his nicely creased pants as if seeing them for the first time.

Gussy was firmly tied to his mother's apron strings. He had finally completed his coursework to become a certified public accountant and was now working his way through the testing. Dad had given him a boost in status after Char left and moved him from a modest cubicle to her vacated office. This rise in his status gave Rose a boost as well since she lived vicariously through her son.

Gussy's promotion created an opening for his old position along with his former cubicle. I was not in the running for the job and doomed to be a file clerk for all eternity. My circa 1950s metal desk was squeezed into a cubby between a file cabinet and the stairs leading up to Dad's office.

"Anyway," I said, "the *other guy* was a thornbush that my horse dumped me into."

Rose clucked her tongue and shook her head. "Honestly, I don't know why you Wildes feel it necessary to deal with those animals."

Sometimes I didn't know why either.

Dad would not be in that morning since he and Mom had taken off for Chicago. That left the three of us to hold down the fort. I found it unsettling since it was two Gustafsons against one Wilde. I decided to slide into my diminutive nook and keep my head down.

"There are boxes to go into the attic," Rose said. "Gerald will help you."

One of my jobs as lowly file clerk was to shift and purge files. We had started keeping things on flash drive sticks but still maintained hard copies of almost everything. "Always good to have a two-tier system," Dad had said, "in case of a catastrophe."

Turned out that a flash drive stick *was* a catastrophe in Uncle Phil's life when a former employee, Justin Wright, used one to store photos of Uncle Phil and him in compromising positions. We found out after Uncle Phil died that he had been a closet gay, and Wright used the photos to extort money from him. Currently, Wright, along with his ditzy partner in crime, Melinda Swift (aka several other names), are serving jailtime and awaiting appeal. Swift had also extorted money from my uncle through a caregiver she employed, Sasha Saari-Summers, who claimed to be my uncle's lovechild, which was a total fabrication. When things began to unravel for the Wright/Swift combo, they kidnapped Char Houle, then bound her up and locked her in a remote, abandoned bunkhouse at Wildwood Stables. Nikko and I stumbled upon the situation and soon found ourselves duct-taped with Char inside the cabin, which our captors then set on fire. An unexpected rainstorm saved the day. I prefer to think of it as divine intervention.

While all the horror of the past still haunted me, the drudgery of everyday life was front and center, namely, shuffling boxes of files up to the storage attic. Wilde Accounting occupied a converted two-story house in the Village of Peshekee. Dad's suite was upstairs along with a conference room and a marvelous view of Lake Michigamme. Another small and steep stairway led up to the attic where the old files and other office paperwork were stored. I spent a good deal of my time up in the musty, cramped space assembling Bankers Boxes and purging files.

Before Wildwood Stables came charging into my life, Rose and I had an unofficial contest to see who could arrive at the office the earliest and leave the latest. She did it for power, I did it to annoy her. But the petty competition had gotten squeezed out once Wildwood Stables came front and center. As my responsibilities grew at the stable, my time management skills deteriorated. In a way, I was simultaneously living the dream and a nightmare.

I booted up my laptop and began scrolling through emails, sorting the good from the bad when my cell whinnied at me. I love my whinny ringtone because it always startles Rose and makes her look around, momentarily confused, before she gives me a poisonous look.

I didn't recognize the caller, so answered in my professional voice, "Wildwood Stables, Kat Wilde speaking."

"Hi, Kat. It's Marjorie VanderVeen from Four Hoof Rescue. How ya doin'?"

"Marjorie! Wonderful to hear from you." I decided not to mention Big Mac's and my close encounter with the thornbush, unless there was a repeat performance. "Things are going well. Big Mac is thriving."

"Great!" Marjorie said. "So far, the only interest I've had in him is for a kiddie park that has wagon rides. I know Mac was an Amish plow horse, but not sure how he'd do pulling a wagon full of hyper kids around. Plus, I need to check the place out."

"Oh," I said. This would be the hard part of fostering horses—giving them up to permanent situations. My hope was to retain Big Mac for Susie Koskinen's ambitious plan to start up an equine therapy camp for special needs kids. But so far, nothing much had moved forward on that.

"So anyway," Marjorie said, "I've got a couple of more horses for you, if you want to take them."

"Wow! Really?"

"Yup. They're largely untrained youngsters we rescued from an auction. Because of their poor condition, only the meat buyers had bid on them until I derailed that."

"You say largely untrained?"

"They're three-year olds that have been handled very little. They have great bloodlines, or so I'm told, but failed to spot out as Appaloosas. So the breeder dumped them at auction."

An Appaloosa is largely valued through its unique coat pattern. Typically they develop either a white blanket of hair mottled with spots on their rump, or, even better, a base color overlaid by a spotted pattern, or "leopard." Thus, like a racehorse that won't run or a dog that won't hunt, those that don't spot diminish in value.

Of course I said yes. Somehow I'd find time to gain the trust of the two and let them know they were safe and loved. The generous monthly stipend for their care would not hurt the bottom line at Wildwood Stables either.

"How about Saturday afternoon?" Marjorie said.

"Wow, that's quick," I said.

"Well, it's almost as far for me to trailer the horses back to Four Hoof than to just head to your place. We have temp quarters for a couple of nights, need a vet check, then Saturday we'll load the rascals up and head for the bridge."

The bridge was the Mackinac Bridge, which spans the Straits of Mackinac and connects Upper and Lower Michigan.

"Okay, then; see you tomorrow afternoon," I said.

After I hung up, I saw Rose peering at me over her cheesy glasses. The Nasty List drawer rumbled open.

I felt a rush of adrenaline. Two more horses—largely untrained at that—would put more on my already full plate. There was no question that Aunt Lin and I needed help. I had posted a sign at Pete's General

Store a couple of weeks prior, and the only person who had so far responded was someone who wanted weekends off and preferred to work remotely.

I sighed and opened up my in-progress project, the July e-issue of the *Wilde Words of Wisdom* newsletter. Of course it was already mid-July, so it was going to be the July/August issue. While most of us think of April as tax time, many businesses have a different fiscal year, so the *Words of Wisdom* from Dad was ongoing. My phone dinged and I saw a message from Nikko. Somehow a stupid text from him made my heart speed up just a tad. I wasn't sure where our relationship was headed, but unquestionably it was an amazing if not tumultuous journey.

Ready for adventure?

Here we go again, I thought. Nikko's adventures were why I was bearing physical and emotional wounds that still gave me nightmares.

What kind of adventure? I texted back.

Just a little side by side.

I answered with an emoji with a question mark over its head.

I'm coming home tomorrow and bringing a surprise. Actually, I have two surprises. When's your next day off?

I don't get any days off, but I don't work at the office on the weekend.

See you at 9 sharp Sat.

≠ 3 ≠

"So where is he taking you this time?" Aunt Lin asked as she stirred some concoction that was bubbling on the stove.

"I have no idea," I said. "He just said he had a surprise. Well, two surprises, actually."

"I'll bet."

Aunt Lin was clearly a holdover from days past. When she wasn't wearing her barn chore clothes, she dressed like she was headed to a love-in. Her hair had been a rainbow of unnatural colors since she came back into our lives a few months back. She wore muumuus and clattering beads and earrings that could serve as wind chimes. Much of her life was seeing to her health through meditation, diet, and weirdness. In spite of her peace-loving facade, Aunt Lin had a dirty mind along with a sarcastic streak. On those occasions when Nikko and I "got it together," Aunt Lin always seemed to know. Add clairvoyance to her many attributes.

"Yow!"

This comment belonged to the feline Lord of the Manor, Jupiter. He was a pathetic creature that Mom had taken in as a stray during a frigid polar vortex. Somehow he had become my responsibility and Aunt Lin's by association. Jupiter was missing most of one ear and one of his eyes squinted more than the other, looking like a perpetual wink. His somewhat kinked tail sported spiral rings, which inspired Mom to name him Jupiter after the planet. Unfortunately, the planet with rings is Saturn, but Mom felt that changing the name would only add to the cat's identity crisis. Truth was, Jupiter did not respond to his name or any other name, but graced us with an appearance when and where he felt like it. Though he did make various disturbing noises, his entire vocabulary consisted of one word: Yow!

That morning, as with all mornings, Jupiter strolled in and plunked himself next to his food dish, which still bore the crusty remains of the previous evening's repast. Aunt Lin, a vegan, found cat food repulsive. Hell, I found it repulsive, but not so much for its animal content as the vile smell and viscous texture. I picked up his dirty bowl and dropped it in the sink to soak, then pulled a clean dish out of the kitty cupboard along with a can of Bon Cat-étite that proclaimed to be *In A Class All Its Own!* I popped open the can, scraped the food into the bowl, and placed it before him. Jupiter reverted to his feral instincts and circled his bowl as if stalking his prey, all the while emitting a low, guttural noise that made the hair on the back of your neck stand up. Once he had successfully subdued his imaginary quarry, he dug in and made a humming noise as he ate.

I changed his water and went back to the kitchen table to contemplate the day that had started a couple of hours earlier. That morning, as with all mornings, I rose at 5:30 a.m., grabbed a cup of coffee (set on an automatic timer), threw on my barn coveralls, stepped into my muck boots and headed to the stable where my charges awaited their breakfast and daily turn-out into various paddocks or the pasture. I gave the horses a sweet feed grain mixture in their stalls and, weather permitting, their hay in racks outside. Once the gang had been turned out, I mucked the stalls, swept the aisle, prepared the grain for the next day, checked the outside water troughs, and did a quick inspection of everyone and everything. If there were no issues, this took about an hour.

Once back in the mod, it was time for more coffee and food. If I was going into the office, I'd grab a shower, throw on some jeans, and head out. But that morning bore the mystery of a new adventure with Nikko, who would be arriving in a few minutes. Whatever he had in mind, I needed to be back at Wildwood by midafternoon to welcome my two new rescue charges.

"Want some oatmeal?" Aunt Lin asked, dishing up a bowl.

"Sure, thanks," I said. When Aunt Lin turned her back, I snuck my spoon into the sugar bowl and loaded up the oatmeal. I went to the fridge, pulled out the milk carton, and poured some in.

"There are chia seeds if you want to add something actually healthy," Aunt Lin said.

"I'm good."

"So, I see you're wearing jeans. No water adventure today?" Aunt Lin asked.

"I'm just going with the jeans, tennies, and a jacket. If I need scuba gear or a parachute, Nikko will have to bring it."

After finishing my doctored-up oatmeal, I rinsed the bowl and put it in the dishwasher. I refilled my coffee cup and went outside to wait for Nikko. I sat in one of Uncle Phil's decrepit web chaise lounges on the tiny mod porch and soon spotted something coming down Horse Camp Road. Even a distance away, I could hear it clatter and bang along the ruts and potholes. I stood and held a hand over my eyes to shade the sun as I watched a SUV approach, towing a utility trailer with some sort of machine on it. The vehicle was the familiar Olsen Tahoe. Nikko's father, Ollie Olsen, owned the vehicle, but let Nikko borrow it when he came home to visit. Ollie, whose real first name was Marion, was the sheriff of Peshekee County and had been reelected ever since I could remember. His wife, Freida, and he lived in town and were close friends of my parents. All four parental units were less than subtle in their hope that Nikko's and my relationship would move beyond adventure into commitment.

The vehicle and trailer circled and came to a shrieking stop in front of the mod.

Now what? I thought.

Nikko opened his door and got out, then turned and lifted his dog, Tobey, out and set him on the ground. The pooch raced over to me barking madly and jumped up against my legs, nearly knocking me off balance. It was good to be loved unconditionally, even if it was by your boyfriend's dog.

"Hey there, Tobey," I said, squatting down and vigorously scratching the squirming dog. "How ya doin' boy? Bet your daddy brought you along to chaperone, eh?"

Tobey was a pit bull terrier, or "pittie" for short. Nikko had found him wandering in the woods one day, emaciated and terrified. The Olsens had taken him in and nursed him back to health. The dog bore scars from horrors of the past. Truth was, Tobey was just a big love muffin who would only get aggressive if one of his humans was in danger.

Nikko came over to me and pulled me into him for a promising kiss. Promising what, I wasn't sure, but it was beyond a peck on the cheek. Nikko was one of those guys who looked good no matter what the situation. Whether slicked up or caked with mud, he seemed to exude sexuality. The come-hither smile and practically perfect kissing didn't hurt either. Fortunately, in spite of Nikko's father being on the short side and his mother being average, Nikko had managed to grow to a height slightly in excess of six feet, which worked well with my being "tall for a girl." Nikko's dark blond hair was in a perpetual state of chaos, which somehow added to his outdoors man appearance.

Well, he was an outdoors man, as evidenced by our next adventure that likely involved the gnarly-tire machine perched on the trailer.

"What's this contraption you've got here?" I asked, walking around the trailer.

"Bobcat," he said. "A side-by-side utility terrain vehicle, or UTV."

"Side by side?"

"Yup."

"And this involves me how?"

"We sit side by side instead of front and back. Cozy except probably Tobey will be in the middle. This is really my dad's Bobcat. He got it cheap at a police auction. Drug dealers used it to transport stuff offroad. Got confiscated in a bust and auctioned off."

"So your dad, the sheriff, owns a druggie buggy," I said, smirking at my cleverness.

"Very funny. I like it, though—the Druggie Buggy. Anyway, I thought we could take it for a ride and check out a few things."

"No offense, but I'd really rather ride a horse than this—Bobcat."

"Well, you can't ride horses right now because of your fall, remember? Plus, I'm actually on official duty and need to check out an abandoned vehicle on one of the fire roads in the Blueberry Plains State Forest."

"Official duty?" I said. "Blueberry Plains abuts the wilderness tract along with Wildwood, and it isn't your district. How come you have to investigate—and on your day off?"

"Well, that's my second surprise!"

"What, working on your day off?"

"No, the surprise is I've been transferred."

I felt a lump in my throat. Was he moving away—maybe downstate?

"Oh," I said, trying to sound casual. "Where?"

"Here, Kat," he said, waving his arms around. "I put in to transfer to the Peshekee District, and it got approved about three days ago. Effective immediately. Russ Harper, who was the CO here, transferred downstate a month ago. I applied to replace him, but didn't want to say anything until it was a done deal. Anyway, I'm gonna give up my apartment in Ontonagon and move in with my folks until I can get a place here."

I was pretty sure this was good news. Though I had to digest it. Meanwhile, I knew the response Nikko was expecting.

"Hey, that's great!" I said. "I'm really happy for you."

Nikko looked at me and smiled. "We can see each other more than every ten days or so. Can you handle that?"

I smiled back. "You know, I think I can."

Tobey barked enthusiastically while whirling his tail in a circle.

* * *

I clutched a handle on the doorframe of the Bobcat as we bounced down a poorly maintained two-track through the Blueberry Plains. The UTV had an enclosed cab and the engine noise reverberated inside to the point where we had to shout to be heard.

"Tell me again why I'm coming along on the investigation," I yelled. "And I'm not so sure this road is doing my possible concussion any good."

"Well," Nikko yelled back, swerving and barely missing a large branch halfway across the road, "you're coming because I wanted to put some adventure in your life!"

"Uh huh."

"And, well, I need a witness, and I'd rather have you than Dad or try to round up someone else from the DNR. Like you said, Blueberry Plains, Crystal Lake Wilderness, and Wildwood Stables share some boundaries. I'm not sure if the abandoned vehicle is actually on state land. That's what the off-road riders said. However, if it was in the Crystal Lake Wilderness or on Wildwood land, they would have been illegally riding and, of course, might have altered the truth a bit. In any event, in case it is on Wildwood land, I want you along."

"I see."

"Technically, I should be using a DNR vehicle, but I don't have one assigned yet, so I thought Dad's...ah...Druggie Buggy would be just the ticket." He looked at me and grinned. "Plus, I wanted to see you."

I smiled. Okay, he finally got the right answer, though the bone-jarring ride in the Bobcat did not encourage a lot of romance. We were into our long, hot summer days in the U.P. and I was roasting. Dinner and maybe a movie in an air-conditioned theater would have been nice. However, Nikko was not a traditional boyfriend, and for that matter, I wasn't your run-of-the-mill girlfriend. Perhaps we went together like that mismatched pair of socks tucked in the back of the underwear drawer.

A sparkling lake came into view and Nikko pulled the Bobcat over. He turned off the engine and put the gearshift into park. We were instantly engulfed in blessed silence.

"Are we there?" I asked. "I don't see any abandoned vehicle. Or are you pulling the ol' out-of-gas ploy?"

"We're not there, and we have plenty of gas. But I think Tobey should go for a walk."

Tobey had been asleep between us, which was a good thing. When awake, and especially when even moderately excited, Tobey panted nonstop and made a maddening clicking noise with each breath. He lifted his head and gave a look as if asking, "Wussup?"

"And I need a break driving this thing," Nikko added.

"What lake is this?"

"Birch Lake. Pretty, isn't it?"

"Yeah, it is kind of nice. I've never ridden a horse back this way. I usually stick to the Crystal Lake area where there aren't any motor vehicles."

The three of us got out and Nikko snapped Tobey's leash onto his collar. We walked down to the lake and sat on a bench that provided a spectacular view. White Birch and cedar trees lined the shores of the pristine lake. The bench bore a plaque stating: "In Memory of Ed, who loved this spot."

"Gee," I said, slapping at a mosquito. "I guess we're sitting on some sort of memorial."

"Yeah," Nikko said. "It was Ed Heikkinen. He worked for the DNR for like forty years, and when he died, he was cremated and had his ashes scattered in this lake."

I stared at the water for a moment, trying to imagine the ceremony. It all seemed a bit macabre. "I love the way the ripples sparkle in the sun," I said, trying to lighten the mood. "Reminds me of diamonds." I slapped another mosquito. "Got 'em. I seem to be a mosquito magnet."

Nikko put his arm around me and I scootched closer. He turned to look at me and pulled me into a kiss.

A deafening shot exploded in the air, causing us to leap off the bench and crouch down. Tobey barked frantically and Nikko pulled him into a tight grasp. "It's okay, boy. Nobody's gonna hurt you."

"What in hell was that?" I shrieked. "Did someone set off a stick of dynamite?"

"Sounded like a shotgun blast to me," Nikko said. "Probably a twelve-gauge. Close."

"How close?"

Nikko stood and I reluctantly stood as well, pressing myself to him and Tobey, who was still in Nikko's grasp.

"Came from that way. Might be poachers, or just someone shooting for the hell of it."

"People do that? Shoot for the hell of it?"

"Sure, but they have to obey the rules."

Nikko was quiet for a moment as if trying to make a decision.

"I should probably take you back to your place and head back out to see if I can find anything naughty going on."

I took a deep breath. "You're not taking me home. They could be on Wildwood land, and I want to check it out with you. Plus, you need some backup."

Nikko looked at me. "Please tell me that you're not hiding a gun somewhere."

"Well, no, but I can be feisty. You said so."

"Actually, I called you plucky."

"Whatever. Are we going or not?"

All three of us climbed back into the Bobcat and rumbled along a two-track fire road in the general direction of the shot. That's when the second shot went off, vibrating the cab of the Bobcat.

4

"Well, that was closer," Nikko said. "I think this road leads to some private land, but private or not, you can't hunt out of season. There're some fresh tracks here from ATV tires."

"ATV?" I said.

"Yeah, an all-terrain vehicle. I can tell by the size of the tires."

Then the third shot went off. By now we were less startled, or perhaps numb with PTSD.

"Tracks cutting off here," Nikko said, steering the Bobcat around a corner onto a barely-there trail. Sure enough, deep tracks meandered through the trees. Eventually, we came to a small clearing.

Nikko braked. "Shell casing," he said, pointing to the side of the trail.

The only thing I saw was moss, leaves, rocks, and a rotting log. Nikko got out, pulled a disposable glove from his pocket and snapped it on, then picked up something red from the leaf litter.

"When the poacher says he wasn't in the area, if we can match the casing to his gun or even get some prints, we got 'em."

"Wow," I said. "Really?"

"Sure, if it was used in a murder. In this case, it would be used as a bluff."

Nikko climbed back in and continued to follow the tracks. The trail opened up into a larger clearing. We stopped and all got out.

"Okay, here're casings number two and three." He walked around a while, looking at the ground, crouching down and brushing leaves away and so on.

I began randomly walking through the tall weeds, pretending to look at things. "Hey?"

"Yeah," Nikko said.

"What am I looking for?"

"Blood, tufts of hair, feathers—something to indicate an animal was shot."

Tobey and I roamed aimlessly for a few minutes, then he started pulling on the leash and heading into the brush with great purpose.

"Whatcha got there, fella?" I asked.

Tobey barked and pulled harder, then almost dragged me into a tangle of brush. He ran excitedly in circles and continued barking. If he had been able, I think he would have pointed, but alas, he was bred for illegal dog fights rather than hunting. I bent over and looked at a spot where the brush had been crushed down a bit.

"Hey, Sherlock!" I yelled over at Nikko, who was on his hands and knees taking a picture of something with his phone.

"You're hilarious!" he yelled back. "What?

"Well, it's not blood or guts, but I found—or rather Tobey found—some sort of thingamajig."

Nikko stood and brushed off his pants. "Is it disgusting? Tobey likes disgusting stuff."

"Just get over here and look at this," I said.

Nikko joined Tobey and me and peered into the brush.

"Well, I'll be..." Nikko said and started to reach for the object.

Engine noise caused us to turn our attention to someone approaching. A person barreled toward us, riding what looked like a four-wheel motorcycle on steroids.

The ATV pulled up to us and skidded to a stop.

"Hey!" the rider yelled, jumping off. "What are yous—oh."

Nikko faced the man who could best be described as grizzly. He sported an unkempt beard and wore a crushed felt hat and clothes that likely had never seen the inside of a washing machine.

"Woods cop," the man said.

"CO Nikko Olsen," Nikko said, reaching out to shake the man's grubby hand.

"Leevi Waddaga," the man said. "I own this land yous are on."

"We heard some shots," Nikko said.

"That woulda been mine," Waddaga said, climbing off his machine and joining us at the edge of the thicket.

"Not much open for hunting right now, Mr. Waddaga," Nikko said.

"Call me Leevi. Mr. Waddaga was my pa's name. Anyway, I weren't huntin' no critters."

"That so?"

"Yup."

"Just shooting for fun?"

"'Course not. I was shooting down one of them flying saucers that been going over here and everywheres else."

"Flying saucers?"

I looked back at the thingamajig in the thicket.

"Well, it wudint actually a saucer, but she was flyin'. Some kinda UFO, I'm thinkin'. I don't take to folks spyin' on me."

"UFO?" I said.

"Yup," Leevi said. "Unwelcome flying object. Say, that's a nice pup yous got there. He hunt?"

"Well, he does hunt for, er, *unidentified* flying objects, I guess," I said.

Nikko looked in the thicket. "Well Mr.—er, Leevi, looks to me like the UFO that you shot down is a drone."

"A what?"

"A drone," Nikko said. "Kind of a flying robot that can be remotely controlled or programmed by a computer to perform a function."

I said, "I think Amazon delivers packages with drones."

"I didn't order no package from Amazon," Leevi said. "Anyway, they've been flying all over the place. This is the first un I got."

Nikko pulled the drone out of the brush. It was severely damaged, with only one propellor left and part of the body of the thing clean gone, but some writing on the side had survived the assault. The unit was red and not terribly large. It had—or used to have—four arms jutting out where, presumably, the now mostly missing propellers had been attached. The front looked diabolical with two round bolts or some kind of hardware emulating eyes. I suspected the tidy little mechanism under the "eye" bolts was a camera. All in all, a somewhat innocuous-appearing device, now mortally wounded by buckshot.

"U-S," Nikko said. "There on the side."

"Like the US of America?" Leevi said. "So, it is the gov'ment spying on me."

"Well, the forestry industry does use these things for surveying the land," Nikko said.

"Oh," Leevi said. "Never thought of that. But they shouldn't be over my land looking at trees. They ain't for sale."

"True," Nikko said. "I'm curious where they stage it. I've gotten no notice of such a thing. Could be the U.S. Forest Service doing some surveying, not the DNR. Still, they should have notified me, or my supervisor. And U-S may not stand for the USA. Might be some company that they outsourced a job to."

"There's some smaller words under U-S," I said. "I think it says Uni Sur."

"You-nee what?" Leevi said.

"Maybe united something," Nikko said.

"Survey?" I said.

"We have a winner!" Nikko said. "Only I bet it's unified—Unified Survey. I've heard of it. Not the company, but a unified survey means, like, a multi-faceted approach to a problem, product, or venture."

"Wow," I said. "You learn that at CO school?"

"Maybe," Nikko said, grinning.

Leevi gave a snort. "Well, she ain't gonna be venturing around here no more."

I asked, "You say this is the *first* one you got, Leevi?"

"Yup. Seen one the other day—but maybe it was the same one what's in the brush there. One I saw before was red too."

"Would that have been about two days ago?"

"Believe so. Dang thing went outta my range, so I never got a shot off."

"I think I know what Big Mac spooked from," I said. "Big Mac is a horse I was riding," I added when Leevi scrunched his face into a question.

"Well, Leevi," Nikko said. "Good shootin' anyway. But if this device was legally doing some surveying, you might be in hot water for, ah, taking it down."

"But it didn't have no right!"

"I tend to agree," Nikko said. "Tell you what. I'll look into this a little and if I can, I'll avoid mentioning how it got in the scrub brush here. These things do crash on their own, after all."

"I may have missed it this time too," Leevi said, pulling off his hat and scratching his head. "I was just braggin'. I thought it was some Chinese thing spying on me, like with them balloons. Or maybe our own gov'ment."

"I don't care for it going over my place either," I said.

Leevi squinted at me. "Say, ain't you that Wilde woman what's taken over Phil's place?"

"In the flesh," I said, reaching over to shake his scaley hand. "Guess we're neighbors."

"Well, pleased to meet ya, miss. Your uncle was one of the best. I'm real sorry about his passing."

"Thank you."

Nikko loaded the drone into the bed of the Bobcat. He, Tobey, and I bid my rustic neighbor farewell and climbed into the cab. He started up the engine, put the machine into gear, and we headed back down the rugged trail.

"Do you think this drone is legit?" I asked.

"I think I smell a rat," Nikko said.

"That might be Tobey's breath," I said. The dog had started briskly panting, making his signature clicking noise.

"Ha ha," Nikko said.

"You know, I heard that horses never look up," I said. "Not sure if it's true, but we were in thick woods, so I doubt Mac actually saw the drone, yet I'd bet the farm that's what spooked him." I thought about this for a moment. "I didn't hear anything, but we were galloping with the wind in our ears and hooves thudding, which may have drowned out any noise the drone made. But horses have a very keen sense of hearing. Maybe Mac heard the buzzing. Could be that the other two horses weren't bothered, but with Mac, maybe it triggered some sort of memory of a bad experience. He's been through a lot."

"If only horses could talk," Nikko said.

"They do, in a way. You just have to listen."

Nikko nodded.

"Now what?" I asked.

"Still got to check out the abandoned vehicle," he said. "After that, I'll make some phone calls. Then maybe you and I can do something."

"Such as?"

"I'll think on it."

5

We backtracked for a while, then cut off on a marginally improved two track, which Nikko somehow knew was fire road number seven. Originally, the road was likely used by logging trucks for harvesting timber. Restrictions applied to motorized vehicles, along with hunting, trapping, and other activities in the Blueberry Plains. Dispersed camping was allowed so long as the rules and regs were followed.

"Tell me again what we are doing," I said. "I'm cooking in here. Doesn't this thing have air conditioning?"

Nikko reached forward, pulled a lever, and pushed the front windshield open. "Presto! Air conditioning for her ladyship. And what we are doing, besides investigating random gunplay and UFOs, is looking for an abandoned vehicle. Got a report that a van's been parked off a ways from this road. Been there almost a week according to some guys riding their four-wheelers back here."

"Could they just be camping?"

"Could be, but the reporting person said it looked to be abandoned, like someone just dumped a junker out in the woods."

"Why would someone do that?" I asked. "I mean, the scrap dealer will give you a couple hundred bucks and pick up the car to boot."

"Could be that the vehicle died on the owners back in the toolies, and they walked out or snagged a ride with someone and haven't been able to deal with getting the thing moved. My job is to verify and report. Then we'll probably see if we can convince Mike to tow the thing out."

Mike's Auto was the local tow and repair shop and sketchy used car dealer. He also rented ATVs in the summer and snowmobiles in the winter. He had a couple of rusty trailers for rent as well.

Tobey sat up and began to whine.

"What's with him?" I said.

"Could be he has to whizz," Nikko said. "We should be getting near according to my info. Keep your eyes peeled for a vehicle stashed along here. Likely in a clearing."

We jounced along for what seemed an eternity with Tobey alternating between pant/clicking and whining.

"There!" I said, pointing. "Something flashed."

"Good eye," Nikko said, pulling the Bobcat over to the side of the road.

The flash I saw was a reflection off an outside rearview mirror. The vehicle, a Volkswagen camper, was tricked out with psychedelic retro hippie décor, including rainbows, flowers, and paisley swirls. Strange appendages sprouted from the roof.

"No wonder the damn thing quit," Nikko said. "VW hasn't made this style of camper for decades. And the original models were a nightmare to drive and maintain."

"Yeah, but it's totally, like, far out," I said.

"Sure, groovy," Nikko said.

Tobey's whine intensified.

We all got out and moved toward the camper.

"What are those things on the roof?" I asked.

"Not sure," Nikko said. "Maybe solar panels. No place to plug in out here."

"Or one hell of an extension cord," I said.

Nikko laughed and we all moved closer.

"Hello! Anybody home?" Nikko yelled.

When we knocked on the door, Tobey went ballistic.

"Oh God, no," I said.

"Yeah," Nikko said. "I smell it too."

* * *

Repulsed, I backed away. Nikko tried the side door, which was unlocked and slid open with a rumble. The smell of death wafted out and sent me to the bushes where I lost my morning oatmeal. Tobey came over to explore.

"Really, Tobey?" I said. "You are—"

The pooch licked my face and whined. I picked up his leash and found a log to sit on.

Nikko pulled a handkerchief out of his pocket and held it over his nose, then stepped into the vehicle. Within two minutes, he came back out and joined Tobey and me on the log.

"Two of them," he said. "Sitting at the little table in the thing. Well, slumped over."

I looked up. "Someone killed them?"

"Not sure. The place is a mess, but that could just be their lifestyle. They're not tied up or duct-taped, just positioned at the table with cups in front of them, like having a spot of tea."

"Suicide?" I said. "Maybe they drank some magic Kool-Aid or something? Or maybe they concocted up some weird potion that was supposed to be the fountain of youth, like Aunt Lin is always doing, and it, er, didn't agree with them."

Nikko shrugged and reached over to scratch Tobey, who was full-bore panting. "I didn't want to contaminate the scene," he said, "so did very little exploring. I did check to make sure they were dead. They most surely were. Maybe for a few days. I mean, the heat in there. And flies. I always wonder how do they get in? Man oh man."

"So now what?"

Nikko pulled out his phone, called the sheriff's department, and talked to his dad who in turn would call the state police. "They'll send someone—or multiple people."

"Is Sheriff Olsen—your dad—coming?"

"Yeah. He can lead the way."

We sat quietly on the log and swatted at biting insects for a few minutes.

"Hungry?" Nikko asked. "Got some granola bars."

"Uh, no. But I could use a drink."

"Well, we only have tepid coffee or water, your choice. Anything stronger will have to wait."

"Water for me and probably Tobey too. He's panted so much his tongue should be worn-out."

Nikko brought back a couple bottles of water and a Sierra cup for Tobey to drink out of. We sat a few more minutes. Then I started to giggle.

"You okay?" Nikko said.

I tried to suppress my mirth, but that only made me snort, and unfortunately, snot came out. Nikko handed me the handkerchief he had held over his face when he entered the camper.

"Uh, no thanks, I—er, I…"

My chortling mysteriously transformed into blubbering. "Ah I, ah ca-can't fu-frick this. Believe ca-an't be-believe this. Wha-what am I? Th-the Grim Reaper or something."

Nikko offered the handkerchief again. This time I took it.

"What the hell," I said. "It's not like those people were someone I knew. It's like somebody opened a door and let out my demons."

"A little PTSD, maybe," Nikko said. "Your life hasn't been what one would call boring lately. And the good news is that it's on public property this time and likely had absolutely nothing whatsoever to do with you, your Uncle Phil, or Wildwood Stables."

I took a deep breath and blew my nose. "Shit. Guess I better call Aunt Lin and let her know she may have to handle the delivery of those two horses from Four Hoof Rescue." Nikko handed me his phone and I made the call. I told Aunt Lin that Nikko and I were unavoidably detained. I didn't give her the details. Let her think what she will.

"Okay at the stable?" he asked.

"Yeah. Aunt Lin said, 'You two kids have fun. I'll handle things here.' She thinks we're—you know...."

Nikko put his arm around me, and Tobey climbed up into my lap.

"I wish," Nikko said, pulling me closer. Tobey tucked his jughead under my arm.

"My two fellas," I said.

* * *

Sheriff Olsen's caravan of assorted emergency vehicles arrived about forty-five minutes later. Hanging out with corpses made it seem longer, and in spite of a heavy dose of DEET, the deerflies relentlessly orbited Tobey and me. Besides the sheriff's black and white, two state police squad cars, a fire rescue vehicle, ambulance, and a civilian vehicle lurched down the rough road toward us. Some had their light bars still flashing from their time on the highway. Sirens were muted.

Sheriff Olsen got out of his car first and walked briskly over to Nikko.

"They're in there," Nikko said, pointing at the camper.

"Yeah, I kind of figured that," Sheriff Olsen said. "I'll let the staties handle things at this point. I was just the guide. Troopers are used to paved roads with lots of road signs pointing the way."

A familiar state trooper emerged from one of the cruisers. Before she shut the door, she leaned back into the cruiser, said something to her partner, and the overhead lights shut down. She walked over to me, and her partner slid out the passenger door and went over to join Sheriff Olsen.

"We have to quit meeting like this," she said.

"I'd like to say it's nice to see you again, Sergeant Witz," I said.

Sergeant Witz had been involved in the two homicide investigations that occurred earlier that year at Wildwood.

"You have a new partner?" I asked.

"Oh yeah. Iggy transferred back downstate to be closer to family. He and his wife had a kid, and they want to be close to the grandmas."

Iggy was the nickname of her previous partner—short for Ignatius. His last name eluded me.

"This one's a cub—a rookie," she said, nodding toward her new partner. "Trooper Sam Klaus. He's riding with me and going to have a glorious day experiencing his first body."

"Actually, bodies," I said. "Klaus? As in Santa?"

Witz gave me a mischievous look. "Spelled with a K, but still wide open for ridicule. The bodies I suspect are pretty ripe in this heat."

"I'd say so," I said. "Nikko had the honor of checking things out. But the smell...."

"Vicks VapoRub helps," she said, pulling out a little jar, dipping her finger, and applying a glob to each nostril.

Tobey began to sneeze violently.

"I'll keep that in mind," I said, reaching down to pet the dog.

"Strong stuff," Witz said and walked toward Klaus.

Even from a distance, I could tell Trooper Klaus was quite pale. I figured it was just a matter of time before he tossed his cookies. Not that there was any shame in that. A man got out of the civilian car and headed over to the VW camper. Two other troopers had gotten out of their cruiser and joined the man. I noted he was carrying a black bag and recognized him as one of the doctors from Peshekee Memorial. Today, he was the medical examiner or ME. Lucky him. Morbid curiosity got the best of me, so I tied Tobey to a tree and walked over to join the conclave.

Nikko turned to me and frowned. "You don't need to see this."

I shrugged and watched the ME go into the camper, accompanied by Sergeant Witz. A few minutes later, the two emerged. I discreetly moved closer to the two, hoping to get some nuggets of info. Witz turned her attention to an approaching vehicle.

"Damn, he found us," she said.

"Who?" I asked.

"Spiller."

Lieutenant Spiller was the Grand Poohbah of the local state police post who could make the Dalai Lama confess to the Seven Deadly Sins. I had experienced my share of Lieutenant Spiller in various "interviews" during the homicide investigations at Wildwood. Spiller could have been mud wrestling an alligator, and would still emerge with a crisp, clean shirt, polished brass, and perfectly creased uniform pants. My presence at yet another corpse fest was likely to earn more unwelcome attention from him. Even though the unusually high annual homicide rate in Peshekee County was not my fault, it was undeniable that I was smack dab in the thick of it all. And when it came to Spiller, there was no escape, but I didn't need to draw attention to myself either. I slunk over to Tobey and untied him, then we quietly climbed into the sweltering Bobcat and attempted to merge with the interior.

The lieutenant strode purposefully over to Sergeant Witz. Witz and he chatted a bit. She pointed at the camper. He pointed to the new guy, Klaus. Witz spoke to Klaus, who came scurrying over. More chit chat and Klaus went to the cruiser, opened the trunk, and retrieved a camera, which he hung around his neck. He returned to his superiors and the ME joined them. The guys lingering by the rescue fire truck got something that looked like a black tarp out of one of the compartments and carried it toward the VW camper. Klaus followed and they all disappeared into the camper. The other troopers began processing the scene, taking photos, and looking at the ground, I suspect, for tire tracks or footprints. Of course, there were plenty of both now that a veritable cavalcade of vehicles had contaminated the area, along with footprints from assorted law enforcement and medical personnel.

By and by, Klaus and the EMTs, along with the ME, emerged from the side door of the camper, struggling awkwardly with what I knew damn well were fully loaded body bags. Klaus dropped his share of the load and headed for the bush.

"Too bad. He almost made it," I said to Tobey, who let out a low woof.

Witz went over and picked up the slack, and the two victims were loaded in the back of the ambulance for transport. No question there'd be an autopsy—autopsies.

Eventually the scene was processed and Mike's Towing showed up with his wrecker. He hooked onto the camper and headed off. The various vehicles followed, driving past Tobey and me. Lieutenant Spiller was one of the last in line and stopped next to the Bobcat. I waved weakly and gave what I hoped was a serious, grieving expression. He rolled down his window and looked at me.

"Hello Lieutenant."

"Miss Wilde. How nice to see you again. I trust all is well at the ranch?"

"Um...."

Spiller craned his neck to get a look at the demolished drone in the back of the Bobcat.

"What have we here?" he asked.

"Oh, something we're hoping to, ah, get fixed. Picked it up from a friend."

I was not a smooth liar, and why did I feel the need to lie? I tried to remind myself that I had done nothing wrong.

"I see. Well, good luck and I'm sure we'll be talking soon," he said. His window slid up and he drove away.

Nikko, who had been chatting with his dad, finally got in the Bobcat and turned to look at me. "That was very nasty business. I need a drink."

"I could go for a cheap bottle of wine," I said.

"We'll stop at the corner store before I take you home."

"Oh God, I have the two new horses to contend with. I hope Aunt Lin will still be speaking to me. I'm dead meat if she missed a lyre lesson or had bad vibes during meditation."

"We'll get two bottles of wine," he said and jammed the Bobcat's lever into gear.

≠ 6 ≠

There was a lot going on at Wildwood when Nikko and I rolled in. We had stopped along the way and picked up a couple of convenience store sandwiches and energy drinks, foregoing the wine and any idea of romance for the time being.

The vehicular activity included a two-horse trailer and tow vehicle, a truck camper, Aunt Lin's Subaru, and a beater sedan of undetermined species. The human activity included Marjorie VanderVeen from Four Hoof, Aunt Lin, Raymond, and an unknown man slouching by the truck camper. Lastly, I suspected two "largely unhandled" equine youngsters were thumping around in the horse trailer.

"Kat!" Aunt Lin yelled. "Thank God you're back. Marjorie needs some help with the horses, and that guy over there wants to talk to you." She nodded toward the man leaning against the truck camper.

Raymond needed no explanation, since he was "sparking" Aunt Lin. I suspected the beater-mobile was his or a loaner from a friend.

Nikko, Tobey, and I climbed out of the Bobcat. I hurried over to Marjorie and we shook hands. Always a firm handshake from that woman.

"Marjorie, so sorry I'm late. There was a major emergency going on near my place and Nikko and I got into the thick of it."

"No problem," Marjorie said. "Runnin' late myself." She glanced over at Aunt Lin and whispered, "Thank God you got here before I had to drink your aunt's toxic tea."

"She means well," I said, looking at Aunt Lin and Raymond, who was peering into the bed of the Bobcat, likely at the battered drone. "Anyway, this is my, er, friend Nikko Olsen. You remember him, right?"

Marjorie and Nikko shook hands. "How could I forget?" she said with a wink and a smirk.

I thought I saw Nikko flinch a bit under her vise-like handshake. Then the bum winked back at her. I looked over at the man by the truck camper.

"Can I help you?" I asked.

The man took off a crumpled cowboy hat and, I swear, moseyed over to us. He wore faded jeans, a flannel shirt, and scuffed cowboy boots that peeked from beneath ragged pant cuffs. Age was difficult to determine as his face had the look of someone who spent a good deal of time outdoors. He reminded me of Paul Hogan in his younger days in the 1980s movie *Crocodile Dundee*. The man was not hard to look at.

"Clay Randall," he said, offering a calloused hand to me and nodding at Marjorie and Nikko.

"Kat Wilde," I said. I liked the guy; he didn't automatically go for the man in the group to state his business.

Loud thumping came from the horse trailer.

"Well, Mr. Randall, before you tell me what I can do for you, we obviously need to get these horses out of the trailer."

"Excellent idea," Marjorie said, heading to the back of the trailer. She unlatched the ramp and lowered it.

We all peered inside where the two horses stood, huddled together and pressed against the front of the trailer.

"I didn't tie them up inside here," Marjorie said. "But I have leads on them so we can get ahold and bring them out. The leads are short enough that they won't step on them, but something we can grab onto. If I get the one, the other will follow, and you can get hold of the lead." She climbed under a padded chain across the back of the trailer and approached the horses.

Then things got interesting.

"Whoa!" Marjorie shouted, jumping back just in time as one of the horses reared and struck out a hoof at her. She ducked back out under the chain. "Guess the sedation has worn off. These two—one colt and one filly by the way—have been through so much. The colt, Oscar, is protective of the filly, Emmy."

"Like the Oscar and Emmy awards, huh?" I said.

"Yup. Barely three years old and somewhat halter trained, and Oscar was castrated, but that's it. They seem to have a dim view of humans in general."

"If someone did that to me, I'd have a dim view too," Nikko said.

This made Clay Randall snort and slap his hat on his leg. "Amen," he said.

Marjorie gave the menfolk a withering look. "We had to give the colt a mild sedation to get them both loaded. That, of course, was many hours ago, so now he's fully alert."

We all peered into the trailer at the two youngsters. They glared back at us.

"How about some grain to lure them out?" I asked.

"Worth a try," Marjorie said.

Grain didn't work. The two had no interest in the shallow rubber feed tub we pushed inside with a rake handle.

"You could just back the trailer into a paddock and leave it open. Maybe they'll come out on their own," Nikko said.

"Not a bad idea," Marjorie said, "except I needed to head back, like, two hours ago."

"Maybe we should move away," I said. "Quit intimidating them. I can make some coffee."

"Okay," Marjorie said with a sigh. "I better call the office and let them know things are delayed."

"Mind if I try?"

We all turned to look at Clay Randall who had posed the offer.

"I don't know," I said. "I have a really big deductible with my liability insurance."

"Won't need no insurance," Clay said. "I'm pretty sure I can coax the two out. Got some experience."

"Well, then, if it's okay with Marjorie, it's fine with me."

"Knock yourself out," Marjorie said.

Maybe not the best thing to say.

Clay crammed his hat back on his head and climbed under the chain, then looked back. "Best y'all just kind of move away. If them horses don't care for people, then the less of us the better."

We all slid out of view alongside the trailer.

We heard a squeal, a thump, and some mumbling. Then all was quiet. Next, we heard the chain being unsnapped and Clay and one of the horses, Oscar I thought, followed him serenely out of the trailer. The other horse, Emmy, followed, her short lead dangling free.

Oscar's neck arched into a question mark and his ears pricked forward. He gave a snort as he took in his surroundings.

"That's right little fella," Clay said. "Have a good look around. This is your new home. Looks like a mighty fine place to me."

The roundabout compliment made me swell a bit with pride. The place *was* looking better every day. I was liking this Clay Randall more and more.

"Where do you want these two?" Clay asked.

"Over here. I have an empty paddock," I said, leading the way.

We turned the pair out into a small paddock adjacent to the pasture. The other horses that had been lounging in the pasture went on high alert, heads up and nostrils flaring. Rusty—my first horse in the Wildwood venture and alpha member of the herd—led the way as he and the others marched closer to the fence for a look. Oscar gave a guttural warning and put himself between Emmy and the others.

"I have an electric wire running across the pasture fence," I said. "It will keep them from getting into Oscar's space."

Marjorie had been quiet during the process. She gave Clay a look and said, "That was impressive. How...?"

"I've always had the touch," Clay said.

"What, are you a horse whisperer or something?" Nikko asked.

"Or something," Clay said.

"Well, Mr. Randall—Clay—thank you very much," I said. "Say, we never had a chance to find out what, ah, brings you to Wildwood."

"Saw the ad at Pete's," he said. "For the job. I'd like to apply. Figure seein' is better than tellin'."

* * *

"You just hired him on the spot! But what do we know about this guy?" Aunt Lin asked. "I mean, where did he come from?"

Aunt Lin, Raymond, Nikko, and I were crammed around my table in the mod kitchen drinking Aunt Lin's homemade lemonade, which featured pulpy floaties and mysterious green leafy pieces swimming about. It was beyond sour, so we all discreetly added sugar and picked the leaf pieces off our tongues. Tobey was lying across my feet making them sweat in spite of the air conditioning going full tilt. Jupiter the cat stood in the doorway, tail lashing to show his disapproval of the Canine Enemy Intruder.

"Don't know, don't care," I said. "He was amazing."

"That so?" Nikko said. "Amazing."

"Yeah, *amazing*!" I said, enjoying a touch of jealousy from my wandering-eye boyfriend who saw no problem flirting with any woman who gave him a second look. When Nikko manages to make the move from his old apartment in Ontonagon to Peshekee, I'll need weaponry to fend off the female groupies.

"Your Aunt Lin is right," Nikko said.

"Thank you," she said, then added, "About what?"

"Hiring a total stranger. I mean, he could have some issues."

Actually, someone who came out of nowhere in a truck camper wearing cowboy regalia most likely would not have a sparkling resumé. So long as he hadn't committed any major felonies, I was good with a sketchy past.

"And where will he live?" Aunt Lin asked, plunking down a plate of crackers and a tub of her homemade hummus.

Raymond reached out, smeared some of the bean dip on a cracker, and popped it in his mouth. I saw him grimace, but he chewed and swallowed dutifully. Aunt Lin thought garlic was a cure for everything, and I could smell it emanating aggressively from the bean dip. I noted Tobey's head jerked up and he sniffed the air.

"In the truck camper, I guess," I said.

"What!" Nikko said. "You're going to have this guy—this, this unknown guy living here? At Wildwood?"

"Well, yeah," I said. "That's what stable hands do."

"In spite of what we saw in the woods?" he said.

"Could I have some water?" Raymond asked, struggling to swallow. "What about the woods?"

"Yeah," Aunt Lin said. "What did you see in the woods?" She put a glass of water in front of Raymond, who grabbed it and took a swig.

"Ah, well..." Nikko said, realizing he had blabbed out of line.

"Oh, just a couple of bodies," I said. "You know, same ol', same ol'."

Raymond turned away abruptly and water spewed out of his mouth, spraying Jupiter, who had edged closer to the Canine Enemy Intruder. The cat levitated and shot out of the room.

* * *

Of course we had to tell the entire story of our day's experience, swearing all parties to complete secrecy. We all speculated on the cause of death, with Aunt Lin suggesting voluntary ingestion of something fatal. "You know, like the Electric Kool-Aid Acid Test from the sixties. Of course, that was way before your time."

"Ah, but I had a Cult History elective course in college," I said. "So I'm up on the counterculture of the sixties."

"Seriously?" Aunt Lin asked. "They teach that stuff in college?"

"Sure. I got an 'A'."

Nikko said, "The boomers are always talking about the so-called good old days. How could we *not* know about it?"

"And there's no question that the retro VW camper reflected that era," I said, looking at Nikko. "Did the couple look like a couple of hippies?"

"Well, now that you mention it—and of course I was more concerned about whether or not they were still alive—he had longish hair—"

"Hey," Raymond said. "What's wrong with long hair on a guy?"

"Nothing, sweets," Aunt Lin said, reaching over to stroke Raymond's glossy black hair, which was fastened into a nape ponytail.

"But he didn't look, er, Native American," Nikko said. "The hair was blondish and the woman had long graying hair with a headband. I think there was some fringe on it."

"So," I said, "maybe the couple decided to have a transformational experience—you know, the Kool-Aid thing—and drank some kind of hallucinogen. Maybe LSD is making a comeback."

"Or meth, or fentanyl, or any number of street drugs these days," Nikko said.

"Or, maybe asphyxiated in their camper," Raymond said. "Perhaps running it to recharge something and got a snootful of carbon monoxide."

"It wasn't running when we got there," I said. "But maybe it ran out of gas, you know, after a day or so."

"Except," Nikko said, "it was an all-electric vehicle, except the gas stove and furnace. Pops figured that out first thing. I don't think EVs emit toxic fumes. Of course it was plenty *toxic* when I opened the door."

My stomach took a quick flip as the smell of death erupted from my memory.

"Anyway, I'm sure the autopsy will show the cause of death," Nikko said. "Suicide by toxic tea, drug, and alcohol abuse, or victims of a disgruntled lover inflicting something not immediately obvious, such as—"

"Or with the candlestick by Colonel Mustard in the conservatory," I said.

Morbid and disrespectful, but it made everyone laugh.

"Will your dad be in on that—the autopsy?" I asked.

"Oh yeah. Pops is like a dog with a bone."

"So candlesticks and poison potions aside, maybe just accidental?" I said.

"I'm leaning toward an accident," Nikko said. "I wasn't in there long, but other than the place being a mess, I didn't see any sign of a struggle with the two. I mean, they were just sitting there, well, kind of slumped over, but...ah, anyway, I still don't like some unknown guy living here with two women."

So we had circled back to my hasty hiring spree.

"Oh please," Aunt Lin said. "Give me a break."

This was good. Nikko had insulted Aunt Lin's ability to guard and protect, which nudged her over to my side.

"Well, I mean—"

"Stuff it," Aunt Lin said.

Raymond cleared his throat.

"You got somethin' to say?" Aunt Lin asked, glaring at him.

"Nope."

"*Anyway,*" Nikko said, "I think you should at least do a background check. You can get his specifics and run it through a program available online to employers."

I had to admit that it was a sensible suggestion.

"I'll send you the link," Raymond said. "You'll need the guy's full name, DOB, DL, and Social Security number to start. There'll likely be more than one Clay Randall, but the Social Security number will pin it down."

"Okay, thanks," I said. "By the way, I would like to note that I have 200 bales of hay coming in a few days and frankly need some muscle to put it in the hay barn. So, Clay Randall will be put to the test right off the mark." I looked around at the others.

"I'm tied up all next week," Nikko said. "You know, duty calls. Really. Unless it comes in the evening."

"The hay will come when the farmer gets it on the wagon, and it will be Wednesday afternoon. It's supposed to rain Thursday, so we gotta get it in the barn if it kills us."

"We?" Aunt Lin asked.

"All hands on deck," I said.

"I'll see if I can get the afternoon off," Nikko said.

Aunt Lin gave Raymond a steady look.

"Okay, I'll be here," he said. "Probably. Anyway, I'm wondering how that busted-up drone out in the Bobcat ties into the dead hippies."

We retold the shotgun blast investigation.

"Hmm," Raymond said. "So ol' Leevi took it down, eh?"

"Well at first he was proud to admit it," Nikko said. "But then when I suggested he might be in trouble, he backpedaled and said he was sure he missed, and we kind of did a consensus that it came down on its own and crashed."

"Funny how there's some double-aught buck in it," Raymond said.

"Yeah. Have no idea how that would have got there. Maybe some animal," Nikko said, trying to suppress a grin.

"Sure. Buckshot always makes good nesting material," Raymond said.

"So what do you think the drone was doing flying out there?" Aunt Lin asked, smearing a cracker with her death-by-garlic hummus.

"Probably some kind of surveying," Nikko said.

"Whatcha gonna do with it?" Raymond said.

"Haven't a clue. Guess turn it over to the Sheriff's Department or maybe check with the U.S. Forest Service and see if they're missing one."

"Or," Raymond said, "I could check it out. The cops'll just stick it in a lost and found room somewhere, and I'd like to know what the thing was doing out there."

"Me too," I said.

"Ditto," Aunt Lin said.

"Far as I'm concerned, it's just some broken piece of junk. Have at it, Raymond, and let me know what you can find out."

"Yow!" Jupiter slunk into the room, giving a wide berth to the Canine Enemy Intruder.

"Cat has a built-in clock for suppertime," Aunt Lin said, going to the kitty cupboard where she pulled out a can of food and peered at the label. "Well, at least this one is fish and not ground-up cow or chicken."

"Holy smokes!" I said, jumping up. "Time to feed the gang."

"I'll help," Nikko said. "Unless your hired hand is coming back."

"Nope, he's gonna start on Monday. Got business to take care of."

"Humph," Nikko said.

7

Nikko and I headed to the stable to get things organized before we brought the horses in to eat.

"So, how many horses do you have here now?" Nikko asked.

"Well, let's see. There's my first and favorite, trusty Rusty. Then the Koskinen horses, Shadow and Misty, Big Mac the Belgian, and now Oscar and Emmy. So, six. Six mouths to feed and poop to clean up. I don't even have time to ride."

"Maybe you should quit your job at the office," Nikko said.

"What? And give Rose the satisfaction? Hah! Plus, I need the medical insurance and a supplemental income. At least I'm down to two days a week. But this is why I need to hire Clay Randall—to help out. Aunt Lin is pretty good about doing basic chores, but there is more to horses than just throwing some hay out in the pasture."

"So I'm finding out," Nikko said.

I walked down the stable aisle and began sliding open stall doors. Except for the two new ones, the horses would head into their assigned stalls from the pasture. I had fashioned a gate and fencing to create a passage to funnel the horses into the barn. From there they would plod into their appropriate stalls and be rewarded with sweet feed and hay. Due to time constraints, I had to feed their morning hay in racks located in the pasture and paddocks. However, for the evening repast, I fed hay in their stalls to avoid the inevitable dickering about who had dibs on where to eat.

"I think I'll put the two newbies together in this larger one," I said, sliding open the door to a double-size stall.

I stepped in to inspect the quarters. I had put down shavings earlier but needed to add grain and water buckets. "Someday I'll have automatic waterers. I—hey!"

Nikko had snuck up behind me and pulled me against him. He began to explore my neck, which frankly had to be a bit ripe with well-earned sweat.

"What do you think you're doing?" I asked, glad he couldn't see me breaking a smile.

"Oh, just giving you some support," he said, turning me around. "You have wood shavings in your hair."

"No I don't," I said, reaching up absently.

"Oh, my apologies. I meant that you *need* some wood shavings in your hair."

"That so? May I ask why?"

"You may," he said. "I find it, well, hot."

"Hot."

"Memories. You know, over there in that stall when we first—"

Nikko was resurrecting our passionate doings during a major spring blizzard, during which we were snowed in at Wildwood.

"Just stop," I said. "There are people—"

"They're all gone."

"Aunt Lin—"

"Went with Raymond."

"Oh," I said. "Now with that established, perhaps you could quit distracting me and help—if that's not too much trouble."

"I'm not sure," Nikko said, sliding his hand under my damp T-shirt. "I mean, I would expect some sort of payment."

"Okay," I said. "Here's the deal. You help me, and I won't tell on you."

"Tell on me? To whom?"

"Maybe your mom, that's to whom."

"Ma thinks I can do no wrong, and she adores you. In fact, she—"

"Your mom knows you're ah—she adores me? Really? Anyway, so okay, my mom and dad, and Aunt Lin—"

"Your folks are away and Aunt Lin knows."

"But she is sworn to protect me!"

"Just shut up," Nikko said, pulling me into a kiss, his hand fumbling around the back of my bra, obviously searching for hooks.

I started to laugh, which abruptly ended the kiss.

"What?" Nikko asked.

"It's a sports bra. There are no hooks."

"Ah—well, that explains—"

"The master is humbled! Don't feel bad. These things make the corsets of yesteryear look like child's play."

"I'm sure I can overcome," Nikko said, moving in for some follow-up activity.

"Duty calls," I said, reluctantly pulling away. "I always take care of the horses before my own needs. It's the horsewoman's creed."

"Hmm. Sounds promising."

"I am not making any promises, except I can guarantee that the present venue—being the barn—is not an option."

"I see," Nikko said. "And would there be a more favorable—ah—venue?" He nodded in the direction of the mod.

"Maybe. But first, I must judge your worth. I'm thinking poop patrol."

"You drive a hard bargain," Nikko said as he picked up the manure fork and bucket. "I expect significant payment—in kind, if you get my drift."

I pushed a wheelbarrow containing sweet feed down the aisle and began filling the feed buckets. "Oh, I get your drift. Loud and clear."

* * *

I was hunched over my laptop at the office when my phone dinged. I glanced over at Rose who was peering at me over the top of her cheaters. Rose opposed texting and the use of cell phones in general. She soundly rejected Dad's offer of a smartphone for those rare times when she wasn't glued to her desk, preferring—actually insisting—to use the outdated landline phone system, which featured a bank of assorted buttons that only she understood.

"There are still boxes to go in the attic," said her ladyship.

"Yeah, yeah," I muttered. It was probably 90 degrees up there, and I was waiting for the cold front to come through on Thursday to do the chore.

Rose was not pleased with my insubordination. I could hear her calculating whether or not my disobedience was sufficient to warrant an entry on the Nasty List.

"I'll do it Thursday," I said, hoping for clemency.

"See that you do."

I was on very thin ice indeed, but as things were going in the right direction at Wildwood, I was undergoing an attitude modification in the office. Mom often referred to it as my sassy side, or perhaps she would say I was being "fresh"—an old-fashioned way of saying I was lippy and better zip it.

I heard the door swish open and Dad's voice. He was followed by Raymond and a young woman I didn't recognize.

"Hey, everyone," Dad said. "This is—ah...."

"Mii Waagosh," Raymond said.

Rose looked over her glasses and nodded at the woman.

Gussy came out of his office and his mouth fell open.

The young woman was a beauty. Raven hair flowed over her shoulders. She had high cheekbones, flawless latte skin, huge brown eyes, and the build of a triathlete.

"Right," Dad said. "Mii—ah...."

"You can call me Mia. My Ojibwa name is Mii Waagosh, which means Little Fox. My spirit animal."

"Mia is my sister," Raymond said. "She has all the brains in the family."

"Wow!" Gussy said. "Nice to meet you."

"It sure is," I said, reaching out to shake hands with her. "I'm Kat Wilde. I work part time doing filing and such."

"So, same last name as Mr. Wilde. You must be related?" Mia said.

"Guilty as charged," I said. "He's my dad."

Dad moved over to Rose's desk. "This is Rose, our office manager and indispensable team leader who holds it all together."

This brought a smug upturning of Rose's lips.

"Over there is Gussy, who recently was promoted to accounting assistant."

"Hey!" Gussy said.

"Hey," Mia said.

"Where has Raymond been hiding you?" I asked.

"Right now she lives with our Aunt Lucy," Raymond said. "She has been working hard at the tribal college, getting her degree in business and getting straight A's. Gonna graduate soon."

"Mia is our new intern," Dad said. "She will be filling the slot Gussy left when he was promoted."

Gussy reached up to straighten his slightly askew tie. I saw him glance quickly at his crotch, presumably to make sure his fly was not open. At least that was what I hoped.

"I really appreciate this opportunity," Mia said, smiling. "I'm so excited to get going!"

"Well," Dad said, "I do have to head out—"

"I'll show her around!" Gussy said.

"How sweet of you," Mia said, smiling at Gussy. "I hope I can live up to working here. Everyone in my class is positively green with envy that I got this job."

Rose smiled wickedly, then pulled open the drawer with the Nasty List. She pulled out her ruler and added a new column.

A new potential transgressor was among us. *Welcome to Wilde Accounting.*

After things settled and Dad and Raymond left, I finally got to open the text, thinking—okay, hoping—it would be Nikko. Turns out it was from Susie Koskinen, and it also turned out to be even *better* than Nikko.

WE GOTT THE GRANT! For the childrens theripy camp!

Then she had an emoji of a horse and a child in a wheelchair. The emojis were good, but her spelling and punctuation needed work.

Excellent! I texted back with a couple of celebratory emojis of my own. *How much?*

Like, lots. The drecktor send me a email.

I figured she meant director. "Lots" to Susie could be five hundred or ten thousand dollars.

Forward me the email please.

OK Buy.

Buy what? Oh, she meant bye. I made a mental note to suggest Susie sign up for a basic comp class when she returned to her college classes in the fall. Within seconds, an email popped into my inbox from Willamina Moss, director of the Magic Stirrup Foundation for special needs children and also head of the equine therapy certification program that Susie was enrolled in.

The gist of the message was that Willamina, aka Willie Moss, had applied for a grant with the State of Michigan for a horse camp for children with physical and mental disabilities. While it wasn't a done deal—there were certain additional requirements—a five-year grant ranging comfortably in the six-figure range was provisionally awarded. Wildwood Stables was the location apparent. Willie Moss had done a good deal of work on the grant, citing need, and a plan for renovating the old horse camp at Wildwood into an accessible facility. The budget included *payment* to Wildwood Stables for the camp, which was bucks upfront plus ongoing lease income.

"Well, hot diggity damn!" I shouted, jumping up.

The Nasty List drawer rumbled open.

8

I was still flying above and beyond cloud nine when I pulled into Wildwood's parking area. Things had not been idle while I was away. The first thing to catch my eye was the sight of my new handyman, Clay, working with one of the newbie horses, Oscar. The colt, a gray with black mane and tail, or blue roan, was larger than his lady friend, Emmy. The filly, a strawberry color with cream mane and tail, or red roan, was lounging in the loafing shed seemingly unconcerned about Oscar's whereabouts. While neither had produced Appaloosa markings, which led them to their downward spiral in value, I thought they were both gorgeous. They just needed a little TLC. Okay, a lot of TLC.

Clay had Oscar on a lunge line in a small circular paddock that Dad and I had rigged up, which was designed to work horses from the ground. The lunge line is a long, nylon-webbed rope training device hooked to a swivel on the halter. The twenty-five to thirty-five feet of line allow sufficient slack for the horse to walk, trot, and even canter around the trainer. The horse is encouraged to move forward and circle the trainer who gives voice commands and cues with a lunging whip. The lunging whip—a long, slender device—is designed to give the horse visual guidance, not strike or intimidate the animal. Eventually, the horse will move forward and realize he must travel in a circle because of the lunge line restraint.

So far, Oscar seemed befuddled at the request and first tried to pull away, then when encouraged to move out, he stopped and faced Clay as if to point out the ridiculousness of the whole thing. Clay continued to encourage the youngster, giving a voice command of "walk" and touching the ground beside Oscar with the whip. Oscar tossed his head, exhibiting a small act of disobedience and confusion.

Clay continued to patiently give voice commands while I watched from the truck. I was still driving Uncle Phil's old beater truck, which had come with Wildwood. The vehicle lacked bells and whistles, but did provide the basics: go, turn, and stop. Being that it was July and the truck had no air conditioning, the cab was heating up even with the windows open. I climbed out and walked over to the lunging session.

"How's it goin'?" I asked. Truth was, I hadn't been sure when Clay was going to come onboard, or for that matter, if he would show up at all. In any event, I'll admit to feeling a wave of relief that help had arrived—and in time for the load of hay coming the next day.

Clay turned around and nodded at me. He walked up to Oscar and scratched his jowl, which is the large cheek area on a horse's head. Oscar dropped his head, and his lower lip drooped and quivered, making him look a bit dopey.

"I think he's in love," I said, climbing through the paddock railing and walking over to them.

"Nah, but I don't think he's quite so jumpy," Clay said, slipping some kind of treat to the horse.

"So, ah, the other one, Emmy, isn't fussing?" I asked.

"She was at first. So was he, but they gotta be able to separate without a hissy fit. It's okay for horses to have buddies, but not so's they cause trouble when we ask them to earn their keep."

"I guess they just had each other for a while," I said.

"Yup."

"So, anyway, ah, welcome to Wildwood. Sorry I wasn't here when you came. Duties at the office and all, you know."

"Sure. No problem," Clay said, patting Oscar's neck. "Lady in the house told me where I could park the camper before she took off. I couldn't see just sitting around bein' idle, so I got this fella out to see where he was at."

"Well, good. Um, I'm just going to run into the mod and change into my barn clothes and get started on chores. Is there anything you need to get settled?"

"No, Miss. I got the truck camper pulled 'longside the stable there and plugged in. The camper has holding tanks, so I filled it with water for the shower and such, and I'll go to the county treatment plant when I need to empty things out."

"Okay, then," I said. "And please call me Kat. Maybe someday we can build a bunkhouse, especially before winter. Oh, and you are welcome to have meals with Aunt Lin and me. She's a—well, a different kind of cook, and I'm hopeless. But somehow we survive."

"That's real kind of you. I'm a pretty good cook myself. I can whip up a meal or two."

"Sure," I said. "I should warn you that Aunt Lin is a vegan and repulsed by about anything a normal person would eat."

"Noted," Clay said, then scowled. "Just one question."

"Sure."

"What's a vegan?"

Oh boy. I see the bad moon rising.

* * *

Aunt Lin made it home from one of her touchy-feely classes in time to watch Clay and me muck out the stalls. The horses had been fed and were turned out to pasture for the evening.

"Hey, Clay, I see she's got you starting off with the dirty work," Aunt Lin said.

Clay nodded at Aunt Lin and gave a puzzled glance at her outfit, which was a fusion of yoga and flower child.

"So, sorry I'm late," Aunt Lin said. "I'll go start dinner. Do you like tofu, Clay?"

"Toe-what?" he asked.

"You'll love it! Oh, Kat, a guy stopped by."

"A guy?"

"Yes. Um, let me see, he left his card and I put it somewhere. I think his name was Allen, no, Helix? Something like that. He mentioned history. Maybe a teacher or a history buff. I really didn't look his card over closely. Anyway, he was looking for you. Like I said, his card is somewhere."

"A history teacher is looking for me?"

"I know. Sorry. I'll look for the card."

"What did he want?" I asked.

"Not sure. He said he'd like to talk to you about—let's see, how'd he put it? Ah, a purely mutually advantageous proposition."

Well, that piqued my curiosity. Rarely did I get a so-called *purely mutually advantageous proposition*—or any proposition, except from Nikko, whose ideas were not pure.

"He said he'd stop back in a day or two."

"Okay, thanks." I said.

Clay, seemingly uninterested in the mystery visitor, had wheeled a load of soiled bedding from the barn to the manure pile off in the woods. When he returned, he wiped the sweat off his brow with a ragged kerchief and looked from me to Aunt Lin.

"Sorry Clay," I said. "I would have gotten that."

"Mind if I make a suggestion?" he asked.

"Not at all," I said.

"You need to get a spreader and a conveyor for cleaning out the stalls."

"Yeah, I know," I said. "There were those things here at one time, but they got sold off when Uncle Phil had to close the place down. Now I wish we had hung onto them."

"Well that manure pile ain't goin' nowhere but up. Just sayin'," Clay said.

"Or we can have lentil soup!" Aunt Lin piped up.

I couldn't fathom how Aunt Lin's mind journeyed from manure disposal to dinner choices.

"No," she said. "It's too hot for soup. Don't worry; I'll think of something."

Clay watched her head toward the mod, then looked at me.

I shrugged. "If we're lucky, it will be sandwiches and maybe some vegan mac salad. Aunt Lin might let us have bologna if she doesn't have to touch it or smell it. Probably she'll smear her gluten-free bread with bean curd."

"I don't mind beans," Clay said.

"Keep that thought."

* * *

I couldn't breathe. I swear, the humidity was a million percent and the air rivaled a sauna.

"Why did you pick the most humid day to put up hay?" Nikko said between gasps. "And the next question is why did I volunteer to help? And," he added to anyone who would listen, "why can't I have a normal girlfriend that likes doing her nails and going to the spa?"

"And why can't I have a boyfriend who doesn't whine about a little manual labor?" I snapped.

Nikko, Raymond, Clay, Aunt Lin, and I were all schlepping fifty-pound bales into the hay barn. The farmer had delivered three loaded wagons, each piled to the heavens. We were on the last one. Everyone was sweating rivers. Hands grew raw in spite of sturdy gloves, and muscles and tendons screamed in protest. At least mine did, and I assumed others were experiencing similar discomfort. Clearly my hair was the worst victim of the ordeal, and had sprung from its restraints transforming into a giant puffball sufficient to block the sun. We were all beyond ripe and mottled with hay chaff that had stuck to our every nook and cranny.

Except Clay. He was a machine. Granted, he did sweat, but his breathing did not come in desperate gasps, and I never saw him stagger under the weight of the bales. This did not go unnoticed by the other manly men in the group. Nikko scowled every time he and Clay bumped shoulders. Raymond, perhaps more secure in his masculinity, simply grunted and occasionally winked at Aunt Lin. I suspected they had entered some kind of deal. We womenfolk saw no need to compete with one another. There was no shame in stopping to guzzle water and lament over a broken nail.

Eventually, the hay was in the barn and we all sat slumped on the empty wagon, wheezing like steam engines. The farmer said he'd retrieve the wagon before dark. I couldn't imagine the labor involved in baling the hay and getting it stacked on the wagons. It made hot tarring a roof in August seem like a breeze.

"Lemonade anyone?" Aunt Lin asked.

We all thought about Aunt Lin's lemonade, devoid of sugar and infused with unidentifiable floaties.

"Naw, just a fresh bottle of water," Raymond said.

We all muttered our agreement, but nobody moved.

"Actually," Clay said. "I could use a beer."

That perked everyone up—or most everyone.

"Got some brewskies in the camper," Clay said, jumping down from the wagon. He returned a few minutes later and passed around some cans beaded with condensation.

Aunt Lin declined. "You know alcohol will dehydrate you even more."

We all glared at her and watched her slide off the wagon to strut righteously toward the mod.

I held the cold can up to my forehead, then popped the tab and took a slug. Nikko and Clay were already halfway through theirs.

"Somebody's not gonna get any lovin' tonight," Nikko said, looking at Aunt Lin as she entered the mod and slammed the door.

Raymond grunted and smiled, then took a swig of beer. "It's not like that. You white men are so defiling."

That made Clay snort beer out of his nose.

"Hey, you're wasting good brew!" Nikko said.

Men could be so base. But I was glad to have their help unloading hay.

"So, Romeo," Nikko said, looking at Raymond, "what's the verdict on the drone?"

"It's broken."

"No shit," I said.

"My, such talk for a lady," Raymond said.

"Bite me," I snarled. I was sweaty and prickly from hay stems poking me everywhere and in no mood for a lecture on acceptable female etiquette.

"What drone?" Clay asked.

I filled him in.

"And for the record," I said, "I can hold my own with salty language with any man sitting right here on this miserable hay wagon."

"I've no doubt," Raymond said.

"The drone! Spill it," Nikko said.

"Busted—can't be fixed. Still looking at some things with it, but I'd say it isn't any hobby drone you can buy online. Best I can tell, it's an A52 Lite DJL Pro model with HDR video, thermal, and sonic capabilities max range drone."

"You could tell all that?" I asked.

"Sure," Raymond said.

"Not the government," Nikko said. "I remember there was some name on the side—"

"Unified Survey. I did some looking into the company. They obviously survey from the air, using drones. It saves bushwacking through the wilderness on foot or ATVs."

"Surveying what?" Clay asked.

"For lumber, maybe?" Nikko asked.

"Nope. Don't think so," Raymond said. "I think the thing is equipped with a magnetometer."

"A magna-what?" Clay asked.

"Magnetometer."

"For what?" I asked.

"Surveying."

Nikko threw his empty beer can at Raymond but missed. "You people talk in circles."

"We people?" Raymond said.

"Yeah!"

"Uh oh," Clay said. "We gonna have a race war?"

"I meant techies—not, ah, Native Americans," Nikko said. "Why does everything have to be about race?"

Raymond laughed and threw the empty can back at Nikko, hitting him in the forehead.

"Hey, that's gonna leave a mark," Nikko said, rubbing his forehead.

"Serves you right," I said. "You're so impatient."

Raymond nodded at me.

"So, back to the magna-whatever..." I said.

"Used to detect metals or maybe minerals," Raymond said.

We all digested that for a moment.

"Such as...?" I asked.

"Ore, gold, silver, nickel. Depends. All that stuff is found in the Canadian shield. Even diamonds."

"The Upper Peninsula is part of the shield," Clay said. "Precambrian."

We looked at him.

"Hey, I went to college."

"Me too," I said. "But I didn't take geology."

"What's Precambrian?" Nikko asked.

"Really, really old, dude," Raymond said. "The Creator was just getting started with organizing the heavenly bodies."

"Back to the magna—thing," I said. "What was the thing looking for?"

"Dunno," Raymond said. "But it wasn't hunting for the nearest dollar store."

"That doesn't add up," Clay said. "I say they were looking for gold or maybe copper."

"I don't like it," I said. "I mean, according to Leevi Waddaga, it was over his land when he, ah, saw it come down."

"Well, doesn't mean it was actually surveying anything," Nikko said. "I mean it could have been a test run or just getting from point A to point B."

"I'm with Kat," Raymond said. "You've got private land, the reservation, and the Crystal Lake Wilderness. I'm gonna see if I can get more info on where the drone came from. But for now, if you'll excuse me, I have to go drink some damn lemonade so that my lady will, uh, play the lyre for me."

"Sure hate to spoil the beer buzz with lemonade," Nikko said.

"It's worth it," Raymond said, sliding off the hay wagon.

"Want another?" Clay asked. "Beer that is, not lemonade or—whatever. I got a few more in the camper. Maybe you could sneak it into the house."

"Nah, thanks," Raymond said.

"Suit yourself," Clay said, taking the last swig of his beer and crushing the can with a mighty squeeze.

Nikko watched him and looked down at the empty that had bonked him in the head. I could read his mind; he was contemplating the same mindless manly act.

"You know, you can't get your deposit back if you crush the can," I said.

"Wouldn't want that," Nikko said, jumping down from the wagon.

He reached up and took my hand, and I slid down on watery legs. "Oh man," I said. "I've turned to Jell-O."

A low, ominous growl rumbled from a distance.

"Oh damn," I said. "A storm is coming."

"Yup," Clay said, looking at the dark, crouching cloud bank moving toward us. "You're lucky, Kat, to have gotten the hay when you did."

Once hay gets rained on, it's considered less desirable and cannot be baled wet due to the risk of spontaneous combustion.

"Should we put the horses in?" I asked.

Nikko took out his cell phone and tapped at the screen. "Severe storm warning. Lightning, heavy rain, and gusty wind."

"Now, if we were looking at a tornado, well, you'd wanna turn them loose," Clay said. "Last place they should be is trapped in a building that's coming apart."

Nikko looked back at his phone. "Says a fast-moving cold front. No tornado watch or anything like that. Major temp drop, though, and possible *hail!*"

"Probably best to put the critters in," Clay said.

We looked at the horses that had become agitated, moving around restlessly and tossing their heads.

A cold wind swept through us as we hurried to the pasture. All I could think of was the line from *The Wizard of Oz*, "Auntie Em, Auntie Em!" And the fact that the mod had no basement or storm cellar.

* * *

Fast moving was an understatement. The three of us barely had gotten the horses ensconced in their stalls when gusty winds drove torrential sheets of rain against the steel roof of the stable. Rafters creaked, and we had to shout over the drumming of the downpour. The day had nearly turned to night, requiring us to turn on the barn lights.

"As usual, they did not predict any severe weather when I checked early this morning," I said. "The weather report said a cold front would move through, bring cooler temps and some rain—but not until tonight."

A jarring clap of thunder shook the building, immediately followed by a strobe lightshow through the Plexiglas barn windows. I made my way down the aisle, looking in at each horse. Rusty glared at me critically. He never cared for the confinement of a stall and held me personally responsible for the inconvenience. Big Mac was foraging his stall for anything edible, and the other four were pacing nervously. Misty banged her hoof on the stall door.

"Them two are gonna get dizzy," Clay said, pointing out Oscar and Emmy who were circling their shared stall, throwing bedding against the wall.

More thunder and flashes of lightning. Then a racket began on the steel building, sounding like a massive load of buckshot.

"Hail," Nikko said.

"Wow," I said, looking around nervously.

"Anybody shut the hay barn door?" Clay asked.

"Oh crapola!" I said.

"I'll get it," Nikko said.

"Naw," Clay said. "I ain't made of sugar. I'll get 'er shut and head to my camper. Yous two can keep an eye on the nervous nellies here."

"You'll get soaked!" I said. "Take the slicker hanging in the tack room. And there's hail! You should wait."

"I think that stopped," Nikko said.

"Truth is, I think my camper windows 'er open, not to mention the roof vent. Probably too late, but I'll see."

"Great!" I said. "I just remembered that the truck's windows are open too."

"I'll get 'em," Clay said and dashed out into the deluge.

"So, I guess it's just you and me, once again riding out the storm," Nikko said, pulling me toward him.

I swear, the man never missed a beat. I may have shamelessly succumbed to his charms once in the barn, for which I plead weakness due to years of abstinence. In no uncertain terms would such an act be repeated.

"Don't get any ideas, buster. Once this storm is over, we need to assess the damage. And make sure Aunt Lin and Raymond are okay and stuff."

"Uh huh," Nikko mumbled, pulling me into a kiss.

He smelled of alfalfa hay, manly sweat, and beer—a combo sure to get a gal's pheromones humming. Nonetheless, I was going to stick to my guns.

"Not gonna happen," I said.

"What?" Nikko said innocently. "I just wanted to kiss my plucky gal."

"Will you shut up with the plucky? I don't like its rhyming potential."

"Hmm," Nikko said, sliding his hand along my sweaty back and pulling me in.

I'll admit to weakening a bit and may not have resisted sufficiently. Somehow he backed me up against a stall door and pressed into me. Okay, I weakened a lot as Nikko applied a full-court press.

Then there was a loud crack, followed by more cracks and snaps. Then the lights flickered and went out.

"Uh oh," Nikko said, removing his hand.

"Damn! I hate losing power."

"Someone up there is putting the kibosh on us."

I had to admit the timing was a bit unsettling. I gave my eyes a few seconds to adjust to the semi-darkness and did a quick visual of the horses. Best I could tell, they were all coping.

"That certainly got my attention," I said.

"Don't forget where we left off," Nikko said.

"I'm sure you'll remind me."

Nikko went over to the building's small service door and cracked it open. "Okay, I see the problem. A tree came down on the power line leading to the barn and, ah, just wondering if you have insurance on your truck."

"Oh no!" I cried. "Clay was going to shut the windows. Do you see him?"

Nikko raced out of the barn and became semi-lost in the sheets of rain blowing sideways. He sloshed through ankle-deep water to the truck and ducked under the boughs of a fallen white pine. I stood anxiously at the door, unable to see anything. Eventually, Nikko ran back to the barn, soaking wet.

"He's under there. He's conscious but probably hurt. Not sure. I can't move the branches. We need a chain saw."

"I have a regular saw and then something called, um, a re-sip—er...."

"Reciprocating. Get it. And I'll get your aunt and Raymond—and call 911."

9

We managed to cut the tree limbs off Clay and lay him on a horse blanket. Then the four of us carried him on the makeshift stretcher into the barn and out of the rain. While rural life had its perks, waiting for emergency personnel to arrive was not one of them. Clay was conscious but confused. He kept muttering that he was fine and to leave him be. I was no expert, but I knew something didn't look right with his arm and shoulder. My handyman had only made it three days before being injured. I was beginning to feel like a hex had been put on Wildwood Stables and me personally. What next? A swarm of locusts? I pushed the idea out of my mind. No reason to throw ideas into the ether.

The rain finally let up, and I slid open the main barn door. I watched anxiously and eventually saw the strobing lights of the Peshekee County Ambulance as it minced its way down Horse Camp Road.

"Finally!" I said, running out of the barn and waving frantically.

The vehicle bobbed through puddles into the parking area and backed toward the open barn door. Clay gritted his teeth and looked at me as the paramedics loaded him on the gurney.

"Just so you know, Miss Wilde, I did manage to get the truck windows shut."

I looked over at Uncle Phil's truck.

"Thanks, Clay," I said, laughing. "I'm afraid it might have a makeshift sunroof now."

The paramedics wheeled Clay toward the ambulance, dodging puddles as best they could.

One of the paramedics looked over his shoulder at me. "That's two times this month," she said. "Shall we just park an ambulance here permanently? You know, so we don't have to deal with the road coming here. I mean, we lost part of the exhaust system last time."

"Sorry!" I said. "Fixing the road is on my to-do list."

I watched as they loaded Clay into the back of the ambulance.

"Someone will meet you there!" I yelled. "At the hospital."

"Yeah," Clay said, then lifted his head and grinned. "You'll be hearing from my lawyer!" he shouted as the doors closed.

"I'll go in the mod and call the power company," Aunt Lin said. "We were smart to keep one landline hardwired."

"Guess I'll head back home, make sure everything's okay there," Raymond said. He and Aunt Lin exchanged a kiss and headed their separate ways.

I watched the ambulance drive off, sans lights or siren. I thought that was a good sign; likely the medical personnel deemed his injuries non-life threatening.

"Hope it's just his shoulder," Nikko said.

"Yeah. I wonder how bad the truck is—"

"You better watch out for that downed wire," Nikko said. "Truthfully, we should avoid standing water, so maybe wait until the power company fixes it."

"Guess we're lucky nobody got zapped," I said. "Well, someone needs to go to the hospital to help square things. Probably me, but, ah, I don't seem to have wheels. Again."

I watched the ambulance move out of sight, carrying my maintenance guy/horse whisperer.

Aunt Lin came out of the mod and rejoined us. "Power company will be here as soon as they can. They cautioned us to stay clear of the wire."

"Guess I better call Dad and let him know what's going on," I said. "Maybe he can send Gussy or someone to give Clay a ride after they patch him up. Oh, crap."

"What?" Nikko said.

"Well, hospitals don't just let you come and go without paying or having insurance."

"Should be workers' comp," Aunt Lin said. "I'll go and see if I can handle stuff. Maybe give your mom a call."

"Thanks, Aunt Lin," I said.

My mother essentially was the HR department for Wilde Accounting. She did payroll, managed insurance, and made sure labor laws were posted in a conspicuous place.

Aunt Lin went back into the mod, then returned carrying an enormous satchel, which I swear to God was her lyre case. The sun poked out, and I shaded my eyes with my hand. Just as Aunt Lin's Subaru disappeared, I spotted another vehicle making its way up Horse

Camp Road. Nikko and I watched it bump and lurch its way toward us.

"Now what?" I asked.

"Your folks?"

"No. But I better give Dad a call and fill him in."

Nikko handed me his satellite phone. "I'll go see what the mystery car is all about."

"Thanks." I punched in the office number.

"Wilde Accounting," announced Rose in a clipped tone. "How may I direct your call?"

"Hey Rose, it's Kat. Is Dad there?"

"Hello Kathryn. Yes, he's here, but he's with a client and not to be disturbed."

"Okay, sure. Hey, I have a wire down here at the stable, and unfortunately no power. But everyone's fine. Well, not exactly everyone. Clay had to be taken away in an ambulance."

"Clay who?" Rose asked.

"Randall. You know, my new handyman. Hey, is everything okay there? I mean we really got slammed with the storm."

"Everything is fine," Rose said, offering no further information. Weather-related anxiety was not in Rose's character. I envisioned the roof blowing off the building and Rose still stationed at her desk, undaunted and hair still perfectly coiffed.

"Good. Anyway, no need for Dad to worry. I'll keep him posted, but wonder, ah, about.... Anyway, I'll talk to him later."

"Very well," Rose said. "I'll tell him you called."

I was going to bring up the inevitable and obscene medical bills that would be coming along due to Clay's injuries, which clearly happened on the job. I was thinking I had some kind of worker's comp insurance for that. I hoped, anyway. Even if Rose knew, I was not about to give her the satisfaction of *knowing* when I didn't. Besides, Aunt Lin would hopefully get things on track at the hospital.

I looked over at Nikko talking through the window to the person who had driven up in a shiny black car with tinted windows. A Mercedes Benz ornament adorned the grill, and the vehicle looked as out of place as a palm tree in the Northwoods. A man finally got out of the car and headed toward me. Nikko directed him to avoid the downed wire area. The man nodded and glanced at Uncle Phil's truck, which looked a bit forlorn peeking from beneath the branches of the felled white pine.

"Can I help you?" I asked.

"Oh, I hope so," the man said, reaching out to shake my hand. His grip was on the limp side. His well-tailored suit looked as out of place as his vehicle. "Looks as if you've had a spot of trouble here." The man had an accent. Though not heavy, it was there, though I couldn't place it.

"Yes, you could say that."

"I left my card and briefly explained my business to, uh, I believe it was your aunt. I wonder if you've given any thought to my proposal."

"To tell the truth Mr.—ah—"

"Varga. Alex Varga."

"Mr. Varga—"

"Please call me Alex."

"Kat Wilde. And this is my, um, associate, Nikko Olsen."

Nikko nodded at the man.

"I am very pleased to make your acquaintance," Varga said, grinning broadly and revealing an excellent set of veneered teeth.

"I'm sorry," I said. "I have no idea what your *business* is, Mr. Varga. And I'm rather busy right now because of the storm and all. I have horses to care for and we are waiting for our power to be restored. If you're selling insurance, you can see I'm not a good risk."

The man tossed his head back and barked out a fake laugh. I noted that not a hair moved out of place. I couldn't imagine the impression my bedraggled appearance was giving. Not that I cared.

"No, no no," he said. "I'll just let you know that I'm looking to buy some land in the area, but it must be specific land. My research shows that you are now the owner of such land as I desire. You see, my father, Petar Varga, was first-generation American, and his father—obviously my grandfather—was an immigrant from Croatia and worked in the copper mines. Sadly, my father recently passed away—God rest his soul. I have come to settle things, and I want to honor him with having a 'piece of heaven' as he called the upper stretch of Michigan. Yooper, I believe he referenced."

"Yes, see, Yooper is kind of a reworking of the name of the inhabitants of the Upper Peninsula. You know, the U.P. or Yooper."

"Ah," Varga said. "So an amalgamation so to speak."

"Exactly," I said, as if I knew what amalgamation meant. Nikko looked at me and smirked.

"Well, my father says he and my grandfather, Stjepan Varga, did much in the wilderness of the Yooper, as you call it—"

"No, we people are Yoopers. The land is the U.P. or maybe the Yoop."

"Technically, Upper Michigan," Nikko said.

"You have to excuse me for my ignorance," Varga said. "You see, my mother took me back to Croatia when I was very young, so while I have dual citizenship, I am not totally versed on the ways of America, especially such a wild place as—what did you call it? Oh yes, the Yoop. But I can see why my father always held a place for this land in his soul. And, as I said, I want to revere him with the purchase of some land."

"How very honorable," I said, hoping my skepticism wasn't too obvious. "Anyway, Mr. Varga—"

"As I requested before, please call me Alex."

"Alex. Offhand, I don't know of any land for sale, but there's the Riverside View Condos just outside town that might have something for sale and a couple of realtors have offices on Main Street."

"Well, thank you for that information, but you see, Miss Wilde—or may I call you Kat?"

"Sure."

"You see, Kat, I want *this* land." He motioned his arm around.

"You mean *my* land?"

"Correct. Oh, not all of it, but just some of it. I checked at the village clerk's office and find you have much land. Surely you could spare some? I will pay you handsomely."

"Sorry, Alex. None of my land is for sale. This is my late uncle's place, and I have strong family ties as well. Plus, I need all the land to run my operation. I'm sure you can pick up a camp or some vacant land in Peshekee County. Again, you might check with the realtors—"

"I am so disappointed," Varga said. "I had my heart set on a corner of your property."

Nikko finally came to life and asked, "Which corner?"

"Oh, the one that borders the wilderness. Northwest. It is so perfect. My father talks of he and my grandfather exploring, hunting, fishing, and doing so much in the place that once had a homestead. I have reason to believe, well actually am quite certain, that it is now the northwest corner of your land."

"Well, see, I need that parcel myself because it borders the Crystal Lake Wilderness, thus allowing me and others to ride from my property to the state land."

"A small thing to negotiate," Varga said.

"Just not negotiable," I said.

"I do not give up easily," Varga said.

His smile had hardened. My scalp prickled, and I felt as if the mob had come calling.

"I believe the conversation is over," Nikko said. "Miss Wilde is not interested in selling any land."

"I believe I was talking to Kat," Varga said.

"And I'd like you to leave, *Mr. Varga*," I said. I could feel fresh perspiration prickling my underarms.

"Such a pity," Varga said. "I do hope you'll change your mind. Here is another one of my cards, should you wish to reach me."

I looked at the card, but did not take it. We locked eyes, waiting for the other to blink, until Nikko reached out and took the card.

"You know, Kat, my mother was very wise," Varga said. "She had a saying about my father. She said that he was sometimes a fool who placed his wager on a straw horse—one that held no promise of winning the race or an argument, because it was flawed. I can guarantee that my horse always comes in a winner."

"Sounds like a threat," I said.

Varga shrugged. "Take it as you will. It would sadden me if you come to regret a poor decision."

He turned and walked back to his Mercedes.

Nikko and I watched the black vehicle mince its way down Horse Camp Road.

"His story has more lies in it than a golf course," Nikko said.

"Huh? Yeah, honoring his father, my foot. But what would he want with a chunk of rugged terrain in the middle of nowhere? I don't believe for a minute he would consider a camp to honor his father—who he apparently held no strong bond with anyway. Varga strikes me as the kind of dude who would require a dozen servants in accompaniment to uncork his champagne, draw his bath, and prepare a seven-course meal."

"Maybe we can look into his father's death," Nikko said. "See if at least that part of the story is true."

"What was his name—the father—Peter?"

"Sounded like that," Nikko said. "By the way, I took the business card for a reason, not because I was capitulating."

"Well, I didn't want to get cooties," I said. "Capitulating?"

"Look it up," Nikko said, studying the card. "Says here *Aleksandar Varga, Historian, Global Consultant*. There's some writing in a foreign language—maybe a translation, a website, phone number, and email address here."

"Pretty vague," I said, taking the card from Nikko and inspecting it. "Fancy 'A' and 'V'. What font do you suppose that is—Transylvania, Gothic Revival?" I turned the card over; the back was blank.

"I'm always suspicious of consultants," Nikko said. "When they come around, it never ends well."

"I have a feeling our business with this Varga guy is not finished." I slipped the card into my back pocket. "I'm gonna check out his website soon as the power is back and I've showered and can get online."

"Speaking of unfinished business," Nikko said, placing his hands on my shoulders and pulling me toward him.

"I'm totally gross—and so are you for that matter. You've got to be kidding!"

"Never more serious," he said.

10

Sheriff Ollie Olsen took a big chomp of his burger. "I have to say I was reluctant to have some Frenchie cheese curds on a hamburger, but this thing is tasty."

Nikko and I had picked up lunch for his dad, the sheriff, from our locally famous burger joint, Bill's Burgers. The gastronomic monstrosity that the sheriff was consuming was called the Blue Burger, and featured a third pound of succulent ground beef, crumbled blue cheese, spicy pickles, sliced black olives, lettuce, tomato, and a slathering of seasoned mayo, all perched impossibly high on a kaiser roll. The burger was accompanied by homemade fries, a jumbo Coke, and rounded out with the colossal cookie *du jour*: cranberry cheesecake.

We had gathered in Sheriff Olsen's office for a lunch meeting pertaining to the two deceased persons discovered by Nikko and me when he was investigating an abandoned vehicle in the state forest. Since the investigation involved two bodies, things had been turned over to the police, but Nikko still had a report to write. A lunch meeting was suggested by Sheriff Olsen, and naturally we were expected to provide the lunch and had strict instructions of what to bring (burgers) and who *not* to tell (the sheriff's wife, Frieda).

The sheriff's office possessed not one iota of charm and likely had not been deep cleaned for decades, if ever. The cement block walls were painted a bilious institutional green that had been popular back in the sixties when it was touted to be either soothing or likely to extract confessions. From its exterior, the Peshekee County Sheriff's Department building was reminiscent of a Soviet gulag. Sheriff Olsen's workspace was a toxic wasteland. His computer monitor sported an assortment of colorful sticky notes and not one square inch of his 1950s gray metal desk had been spared from disheveled piles of paperwork, manila folders, food wrappers, empty coffee cups, and more sticky notes. One corner of the desk held a somewhat outdated framed photo of the Olsen family.

"So, have you and Lieutenant Spiller of the state police been, ah, collaborating on the deaths?" Nikko asked.

"Yup," the sheriff said. "Somewhat. Spiller's an ass but then so am I. In any event, turns out that the couple croaked from poisoning. You got any extra ketchup packets? I got some somewhere in a drawer, but it's just easier to check with you first."

"Poisoned!" I said, through a mouthful of my favorite burger, The Yooper. I handed the sheriff some ketchup packets.

"Yup. Thanks. I hate opening these things," he said, chewing on the corner of one.

"Accidental?" Nikko asked. "I mean, they were drinking something, right?"

Sheriff Olsen took a large swallow of his drink. "Your mother says I'm poisoning myself with this food. Do you know what she packed me for lunch today?"

"No, I do not," Nikko said with a sigh.

"Chicken breast on diet bread. Just chunks of cold, dry chicken and some celery. No mayo or even mustard. I mean mustard is like zero calories." He took another bite of his burger, chewed, and swallowed. He looked down at his belly, shirt buttons straining against the pressure. "Maybe I do need to lose a few pounds, but who doesn't?"

Sheriff Olsen was built like a fireplug. Though it is said that offspring inherit their height from their fathers (perhaps an old wives' tale), Nikko had been blessed with a tendency to favor his mother's side, including height.

"So, I'm wondering," I said, "you know, since Nikko and I found the two—ah—dead people, what are we talking about with poison? I mean, that's such a, I don't know, British spy Scotland Yard kind of thing."

"*Au contraire*," Sheriff Olsen said. "Poison is still very much used as a means of dispatching one's enemies. Remember the ricin incident in the eighties?"

"I wasn't born yet," I said.

"It pops up now and then. It's from castor beans. Also, one can purchase things fairly easily at the local hardware store or online."

"Like what?" I said.

The sheriff wiped his mouth with a couple of paper napkins. "Rat poison, cleaning chemicals, and whatnot. But in this case, it wasn't ricin or any of that other stuff kept under the kitchen sink."

"And...?" Nikko asked as he dipped a fry in a puddle of ketchup.

"This cookie is okay, but I prefer chocolate chip," Sheriff Olsen said.

"I'll make a note," Nikko said.

We waited while the sheriff chewed. Lunch meetings had their drawbacks. Food was such a distraction.

"Could have been accidental," the sheriff said. "Some kind of natural harvesting of plants or weeds that went awry."

"Okay, such as?" I said.

"Maybe water hemlock," the sheriff said. "Probably."

"Aha!" I said. "Didn't I mention hemlock back when we found the, um, bodies?"

"Jason Martinez and Emily Bentley," the sheriff said.

"Excuse me?" I said.

"The vics. ID'd as Jason Martinez and Emily Bentley. At least that was what the IDs said that we found."

"So, they died from hemlock?" Nikko asked. "Like a hemlock tea or something?"

"Or something," the sheriff said, noisily sucking up the last dredges of his Coke. "Found some residual digestive material during the autopsy that points to hemlock. I've done a little research and water hemlock does resemble other more palatable things, such as wild parsley, sometimes called cow parsley. It's edible."

"They did seem to be living like hippies," I said. "You know, the kind that claim to live off the land gathering nuts and berries and bathing once a month in the river."

"Yeah," Nikko said, as he slipped a few French fries under the remains of his burger bun.

"That's weird," I said.

"What, hippies?" Nikko said.

"No, fries on the burger."

"Saves time."

"Just wrong. *Anyway,* about the hippies. So, case closed?"

"Maybe," the sheriff said. "Except...."

We waited. I had righteously passed on getting a cookie and was eyeing Nikko's, wondering if he would share.

"Smells funny," the sheriff said.

"What?" Nikko asked. "The food?"

"No, son, the *accidental* part."

"How so?" I asked. "Can I have a bite?"

"Later," Nikko said, waggling his eyebrows.

"Well, hemlock—even this water hemlock, which by the way grows right here in the U.P., was found in their camper in like a tea tin.

Poisoning by water hemlock has pretty serious symptoms. Convulsions, seizures, vomiting, diarrhea, and so on."

"They looked fairly peaceful to me," Nikko said, "as far as dead bodies go, that is."

"Exactly," the sheriff said.

"I meant your cookie," I said.

Both Sheriff Olsen and Nikko looked at me.

"A bite, I...."

"Just sayin' there should have been some evidence of a rather horrific death," the sheriff said.

Nikko handed me his cookie and I broke off a piece—well about half. He mouthed, *You owe me*, then smiled.

"So, maybe someone slipped something in their beverage and the poor people went through a horrible ordeal, then died," Nikko said. "The killer then cleaned up the place, put things back in order, perched the couple at the table nice as you please, and hoped it would look like an accident. Ta-da!"

"Maybe," the sheriff said. "I'm telling you it would be hard to pull that off without a major cleanup crew. I mean soiled clothing would need to be changed, all the surfaces and objects around the place wiped down. Things may have been broken, so they'd need to be removed. There'd bound to have been some sort of residual material suggesting violent death."

"Or," I said, "maybe they died somewhere else and were taken back to their van and *staged*."

Nikko smiled and nodded. "Very perceptive."

"Still have the potentially soiled clothing, but now that you mention this, I think they were only wearing loose-fitting robes of some sort, or maybe muumuus. No underwear, which we chalked up to a lifestyle choice."

"Commando!" I said. "Maybe a guy thing, but the woman not so much."

"So," Sheriff Olsen said, "the couple is murdered for unknown reasons, at an unknown location—"

"Perhaps a rendezvous spot for something," I said.

"Drugs?" Nikko asked.

The sheriff held up his hand to silence us. "Served a lethal dose of hemlock, allowed to convulse and die, then are hosed down and dressed in some kind of old-fashioned gowns or robes. *Then* hauled back and propped up at the table in such a way as to suggest a pleasant tea party. Maybe the perp or perps even planted some of the poison plant in the tea cannister."

We contemplated the theory.

"Far-fetched, but feasible," Nikko said.

"The question is why," I said. "If we know why, then maybe it will give a lead to who—or whom."

The sheriff said, "Have you ever considered going into police work?"

"Not for a minute."

Sheriff Olsen rose from his desk and looked out the window. "We're doing a thorough workup of the camper. Of course the staties say they're in charge, but they really don't want to be. They hate things like this. They'd much rather have a nice, clean shooting at a bar with forty witnesses. Anyway, I'm in the loop, and I ain't ready to call this an accident."

* * *

When Nikko and I left the sheriff's department, we headed to Mike's Auto where my truck—my only means of transportation—had been towed after the storm's debris was cleared away. When the power company had cut away the fallen white pine to repair the broken power line, they had been nice enough to also remove the limbs and branches from the truck. While the thing would still start, the roof had a major dent—actually a hole—and the windshield had shattered into a million pieces, making it unfit to drive. I had given Mike a couple of days to inspect the damage but suspected that his verdict would not be good.

"I'm not feeling hopeful that my truck can be fixed," I said.

"Best to prepare for the worst," Nikko said.

"Well, the good news I guess is that Clay doesn't need surgery. They were able to put his shoulder back in place."

"That had to hurt like a sonofabitch."

"He should be back on limited activity pretty soon."

Nikko frowned and said, "By the way, did you ever run that employee background check on him?"

I tried to look confused and said, "On who?"

"Clay Randall. You know, Raymond gave you a link that employers can use."

"Oh, yeah, that. Well, I kinda forgot. Plus, I think it costs money."

"I'll give you whatever it costs. I don't totally buy his story."

I decided not to accuse Nikko of being jealous or threatened. Clay Randall was around my father's age, for God's sake. I decided to change the subject.

"I'm more worried about that creep, Varga," I said. "Now *his* story is obviously bogus."

"I thought about telling Pop about him," Nikko said, "but I didn't want to get him off track from our discussion about the dead people in the camper."

"I thought about that too, but the food alone was enough of a distraction."

"Yeah, Ma is always trying to get him to eat healthy. She used to cook huge meals every night. Now, not so much. Last night, we had some kind of boneless, skinless chicken—I think the leftovers ended up on Pop's lunch sandwich—and rice with green beans. No dessert. Not a cookie in the house. The sooner I can get my own place here in town, the better."

"So, who will do the cooking there?" I asked.

Nikko looked at me and smiled.

"Hey, don't look at me!"

"Probably my old friends Mrs. Stouffer and Mr. Swanson. And there's always the Peshekee Pizza Palace."

The Peshekee Pizza Palace was far from palatial, but indeed had excellent pizza, subs, salads, spaghetti, and ravioli. If Nikko ate there regularly, he would endanger the hot six-pack abs he sported.

"Or you could learn to cook," I suggested.

"Or you could."

I ignored his remark. "So, anyway, back to Varga. I did go online and try to bring up his website. I got an error message."

"That can happen for legit reasons," Nikko said.

"I googled him, too."

"Anything?"

"Not really. Varga is a pretty common name, so got a bunch of hits on similar names. For example, there is an Alexis Varga. A woman."

"Well, maybe our Varga was a gal and became a guy, or changes back and forth."

I chewed on that idea for a moment but couldn't see it. "*Alexis* sells beauty products for aging women. Guarantees that wrinkles will be gone in just a few days. Also, if you buy her vitamins, your sex life will soar."

"Well…?"

"Well, what?"

"Did you buy any of that stuff. Especially the last th—hey!"

Swing and a miss.

"So, again, back to our Mr. Varga," I said.

"Did you try the email?"

"Nope. Then he'd have my email, not that it's difficult to find. Still, the guy gives me the creeps, and I don't want to reach out to him, that's for sure."

We pulled into Mike's Auto, and I saw my truck slouched next to the service door.

"Doesn't look good," Nikko said.

"What the hell am I gonna do?" I asked. "I blew every cent I had on the three loads of hay. I've got nuthin' for repairs or even a miniscule down payment on even the most junky thing, and I really, really, need a truck."

"Well, let's see what Mike says," Nikko said.

We climbed out of the Olsen SUV that Nikko borrowed from his dad. He was almost as poor as me—still paying off his student loans—but at least had a state vehicle when he was on the clock.

Mike came out of the service door, wiping his hands on a blue shop towel.

"Hi Mike," I said.

"Hey, Kat," he replied and nodded toward the truck. "Glad you weren't in that thing when she got smushed."

"Yeah."

"How's your hired hand doin'?"

"Pretty good," I said. "He'll be in a sling for a couple of weeks. Hard thing is keeping him down."

"Yup," Mike said, glancing down at his hands. "So, here's the deal on the truck."

"Uh huh?" I said.

"She's toast."

"Damn."

"While technically the chassis is okay—and by okay I mean it wasn't messed up by the tree landing on the truck—I will mention that it's mainly rust holding it together. Anyway, the frame on the truck is what we call sprung. You got insurance? They'll total it and give you something."

I was trying very hard not to choke out a sob. "I only got PLPD. You know, for liability."

Nikko put his arm around my shoulders, as if comforting a loved one at a family funeral.

"Shame," Mike said, "though I'm thinking you wouldna' gotten more than a thousand dollars."

"Well, now what?" I asked.

"Tell you what," Mike said. "I'll give you scrap price for the truck. Runs about two hundred. I won't be makin' a penny, but your uncle was a good friend, and now you're a gal trying to save things that he cared about. Wish I could do more. Well, there is one thing—I can give ya a loaner for a week or two. Won't be much, but it'll get you around."

"Well, two hundred is fair, I guess," I said. "And the loaner would be great. Thanks, Mike."

"I'll get my checkbook, and maybe you can dig up the title for me. Gotta have that signed over before the scrap dealer will take her."

Nikko looked at me.

"We did take care of transferring ownership to me after Uncle Phil died," I said. "I know where Aunt Lin keeps the papers like that, so I'll bring it by."

Mike went into the auto building, and I went over to the truck and wrenched the door open. I removed my snow scraper, a blanket, hat, gloves, water bottle, crowbar, hammer, bailing twine, a roll of duct tape, a plastic container of breath mints, and several outdated Michigan maps.

Mike came out and handed me a check for $200 and the keys to a "vintage" Jeep.

"Thanks, Mike," I said, shaking his almost-clean hand.

"You'll need to gas up the Jeep. Registration's in the glove box. It's insured on my business policy, and if you get pulled over, you are just taking it out for a test drive, okay? Last I knew there were some things that don't work, but most of it's not important, and it's the best on the lot."

"I really do appreciate this," I said. "You're a lifesaver."

"No problem," he said. "Sorry you're having a spell of bad luck."

Unfortunately, a "spell" of bad luck seemed to be my perpetual state of being that likely wouldn't end anytime soon.

≠ 11 ≠

After assuring Nikko he didn't need to follow me home, I climbed into the loaner Jeep, put the key in the ignition, and gave it a turn. Nothing. Just for the heck of it, I jiggled the gearshift lever and the engine sprang to life. The dash lit up—partially. Interestingly, the wipers started going and the left turn signal merrily blinked to life. I flipped the turn signal lever a few times and the blinking stopped. The odometer displayed an alarming excess of 250,000 miles and a plethora of idiot lights glared at me, including the low tire warning, oil change time, and the check engine light that was in an urgent blinking mode.

I adjusted the mirrors—both cracked—and fumbled for the seat adjustment lever. Eventually, I found its broken remains lying on the floor, apparently a victim of too much road salt. Though my long legs awkwardly jutted toward my chin, I'd have to live with it. I dug the seatbelt out of the seat crack and snapped it on. Next, I tried the air conditioner. While the blower worked, nothing but musty hot air came out. The radio produced silence. I put the beast in gear and urged it into action. It lurched forward, then smoothed out a bit. The brakes ground when applied, and the steering was looser than a goose's waddle.

I did what any responsible businesswoman would do, and that was stop at the bank and deposit the check from Mike, holding back fifty dollars in hopes of getting squeezed in for an emergency hair appointment sometime within the millennium. The Jeep idled roughly while I called my stylist, Jeannie.

"Jeannie's Dreamy Dos!" she chirped.

I humbly begged for some time in the salon chair.

"You know, sweetie pie," Jeannie said, "you can make appointments ahead of time and not wait until you're suicidal."

"I know, I know. But I've had a lot happen lately and, er, I'd like to tell you all about it. You know, while you're converting me from bush woman back to ravishing beauty."

"Oooo, like what has happened?"

"Too much to tell now."

"Well, let me see. I might be able to squeeze you in after my last one this evening, say around seven? I'll need to see if my mother can watch Brianna a few hours longer."

Brianna was Jeannie's six-year-old daughter. Jeannie was a single parent who managed to graduate from high school when eight months pregnant, get her degree in cosmetology, and start up her own business. While the father of the child had remained a mystery, Jeannie's parents stood by her side and helped with Brianna. Jeannie raked in good money, but being a hair stylist was no picnic.

"Perfect," I said. "I have to dash back to the stable and meet up with someone, then feed the critters and all, and should be able to make it to town by seven. Thanks a ton, Jeannie!"

"No prob," she said. "Gotta go—got someone done processing. You better deliver on some juicy stories."

The Jeep reluctantly jerked out of the bank lot and we headed home. I hoped the miserable condition of Horse Camp Road wouldn't finish the vehicle off.

* * *

"So, ah, Ms. Moss," I said. "Thank you so much for making the trip way out here."

"Call me Willie. Ms. Moss sounds like an evil Disney character."

Willie was the director of the Magic Stirrup Foundation, which had given a preliminary commitment to transform the Wildwood Stables campground into a camp for special needs children. She had come out to do an initial inspection of the old campground along with her mentee, Susie Koskinen. The idea of converting the dilapidated horse campground into a juvenile therapeutic dreamland was Susie's brainchild.

"So let me show you around," I said.

"The place is awesome!" Susie said. "You should have seen what Kat started with. She's done, like, so much since she took over."

"Very nice to hear," Willie said. "I do see that the stable itself appears very serviceable. Shall we start there?"

After a tour of the stable, we headed out into the pasture and checked out the horses. Most were escaping the bugs by lounging in the loafing shed. We still kept Oscar and Emmy in a separate paddock, and they had sought solace in the shade of a large maple.

"Who's this fella?" Willie asked, walking up to Big Mac who had the second paddock/riding arena to himself.

"That's our rescued draft horse, Mac. He was a workhorse for the Amish, and unfortunately, when they can't work anymore, they get sold at auction. Usually for meat."

I explained my arrangement with Four Hoof Rescue.

"Yup, I've heard of them," Willie said, scratching Mac's forehead.

"Oscar and Emmy—the roans—are my latest charges. Rusty over there was kind of a local rescue and my first horse. The other two, Shadow and Misty, belong to Susie here and her sister."

"So, what horses would we use for the children?" Willie asked.

"I would trust Rusty for sure. And probably Big Mac, though he may intimidate the kids because of his size." I didn't mention he had recently dumped me into a thornbush.

"Well, you'd be surprised how brave these kids are," Willie said.

"Totally!" Susie said. "And Shadow is really well behaved. I think Misty would need to be, like, monitored."

"By monitored," Willie said, "she means several people would accompany the child riding the horse. Sometimes there is one leading and one on each side of the child."

"That's a lot of staff," I said.

"We often seek out volunteers. I note there is a tribal school in the area. That might be a good source."

"Sounds great," I said. "How many horses would we need?"

"Realistically, we could start out with two or three, but eventually I'd suggest maybe six. The number of children enrolled will likely be capped, which is unfortunate. I'd start by talking with the local schools—seek out special needs kids in the area. You will be surprised how the roster will fill up quickly. There is a lot of training before anything can happen. Lots of hoops to jump through."

"I can help!" Susie said.

Willie smiled at her, then said, "I understand there is a campground involved. Generally, our therapy programs only involve day camp. Actually, having an overnight experience is a new concept that will require a lot of logistical planning, but it does open up opportunities for children who may live too far away to come to day camp. Some require special equipment just to travel. Susie here thinks you've got just the setup."

"Well, perhaps *potential* setup. You see, I haven't been able to do anything with the campground. It was originally built as a kind of guest camp, for folks to bring their horses and camp in a rustic setting.

My Uncle Phil, who passed away last fall, took folks on trail rides and such. Once he fell ill, things simply weren't kept up."

"Understandable," Willie said.

"Should we drive back or walk?" I asked. "It's about a quarter mile down the two-track."

"Oh, let's walk by all means."

I hadn't been to the horse camp for a couple of months, and it showed. Weeds had grown rampant, and limbs had come down from the last storm, taking out most of what was left of several corrals. Clearly, nature was reclaiming the campground.

"Well..." Willie said, looking around.

"Sorry. I haven't had the time or resources to do anything with this place," I said.

Willie continued to work her way through the area, with Susie on her heels. I picked my way around, randomly removing limbs and debris from the campsites.

We all reunited in a small, weedy clearing.

"How do you feel about simply removing all the remains here and starting over?" Willie asked. "The children would need a special setup anyway, as some have mobility issues. And on a positive note, this is a lovely spot."

"I have no problem with your clearing out the old campground," I said. "And I'll mention that there are trails from here leading to the Crystal Lake Wilderness. If you think this spot is nice, the wilderness is spectacular."

"Indeed," Willie said, as she continued to look things over. "Oh my!"

"What?" I asked.

Willie was pointing off into the woods. "Do you have a horse that got loose? I think I saw one out there—just a flash...."

Susie and I looked at each other.

"The ghost horse," Susie whispered.

"Impossible," I hissed back. The so-called ghost horse Susie was referring to was something she and I had seen last spring, and was chalked up to a hologram created by Raymond for the entertainment of the campers back when the campground was still active. Raymond swore he had removed all the equipment some time ago, and suggested perhaps a residual spiritual phenomenon was occurring. Whatever it was, it wouldn't be a good selling point.

"I don't see anything," I said. It was true, nothing was there *anymore*. "Perhaps a deer? Or the sun playing on the...mist."

"What mist?" Susie asked. Big help she was.

Willie was frowning and staring off into the woods. "I swear it...well, perhaps it was a deer. Just a flash, really, of something." She took one last look around, brow furrowed.

"Are you feeling okay?" I asked. "You do look a bit, well, perhaps the heat?"

"Yes, I do have issues with the heat index," Willie said. "I've never, ah, hallucinated though."

"Stress from the heat can do strange things with our bodies," I offered. I hated gaslighting Willie, but I didn't want the whole deal to evaporate. I would be talking to Raymond posthaste.

"I can get my Jeep," I said. "We can go get something to drink at the mod—er, the house."

"No, no. I can walk. But a nice glass of water would be appreciated. That is, unless you have a cold beer."

I smiled. I really liked this woman. "One beer, coming up."

* * *

After Willie left, I headed to the barn to do chores. When I walked in, Clay had already started things and was pushing a wheelbarrow of sweet feed down the aisle to ration out in the feed buckets.

"Hey!" I said. "You're supposed to be in the camper resting. Where's Aunt Lin?"

"Not back yet from some sort of class in town. She brought me some soup a while ago. I would check to make sure the cat is still around. He may be the reason there seemed to be hair in the soup."

"I think that sometimes kale, or maybe it's celery, makes hair-like stuff in the porridge. You have to pick it off your tongue when Aunt Lin isn't looking. I'm sure it wasn't Jupiter—the cat—because Aunt Lin is a vegan."

"Well, I dumped it over in the weeds. We'll see how they like it. I made myself a sandwich. Got some bologna left if you want a bite."

"No thanks," I said. "I had a big lunch. Now, I must insist that you follow doctor's orders."

"Hell with that. All I could do not to come out when you and that woman was pokin' around."

Clay had been ordered by the doctor to restrict any movement of his left shoulder until his next appointment could assess its healing progress. The tendons and whatnot needed to be allowed to mend.

Even with a bum shoulder, he was a major asset to Wildwood. I thought about Nikko pushing me to have him checked out via the link Raymond had sent me. I wasn't keen on opening a can of worms. So what if he had bad credit or something? Likely it would come up again.

"I have to admit, you have rigged up a pretty good system for pushing the wheelbarrow with one arm," I said.

"Yup. Good thing it's a two-wheeler."

I hoisted a bale of hay into a wooden cart I'd picked up at a rummage sale that worked perfectly for transporting hay and other things around the place. Next, Clay filled the water buckets (holding the hose in one hand) and I mucked out the stalls. Lastly, we headed outside to let the horses in for their evening repast. Each one was standing at the gate, ready to get their grub.

Evening chores successfully completed, I headed to the mod to spruce up a bit before driving back into town for my hair appointment. I'd mulled over how much to share with Jeannie. There were the two dead bodies in the VW camper. That was actually old news since it was in the paper, on the local radio station, and on the local TV phone news app. However, no details, suspects, etc. had come to light with the public. And I was privy to knowing the possible cause of death. Maybe that would be a good, juicy subject to feed Jeannie, who, as was any self-respecting stylist, the core of town talk.

Another thing was the drone. Probably best to see what more Raymond could find out about its purpose. The most unsettling thing was the visit from Varga. I knew the chunk of land he insisted on buying. Totally unremarkable from all the other acreage, except perhaps its easy access to the wilderness. His story about the land's purchase being an act of respect for his late father didn't hold water. In fact, his lame reasoning pretty much fit the meaning of a straw horse—something that lacks refinement or credibility. Ironically, Varga had said his mother described his father in such a manner.

My medical mandate of "no riding" had certainly expired. After all, I had helped put up three loads of hay in the heat and humidity without passing out. A nice hack on horseback was way less strenuous. Maybe I'd mount up and take a closer look at the back forty—take Nikko with me. And maybe while I was at it, I'd take a look around the old campground to try to spot any hologram paraphernalia Raymond may have placed. He swore he had removed it all a long time ago, but *something* was still causing the manifestation.

12

"Those two dead people—I think I saw them. They came into the shop as walk-ins hoping I could squeeze them in. Sweetie pie, how long since we've given the shrub a trim?"

My stylist, Jeannie, was running her fingers through my hair, with her talon-like nails occasionally snagging on a snarl.

"It hasn't been that long," I said. "I've been really busy. Anyway, just a trim today. No time or money for color. About this couple—tell me more."

"I think I saw you last spring. Yup. The highlights are pretty much gone. But I don't have time for color either. They were weird—well, not really weird, but kind of odd. Not one to judge, but I'd say they were a little old to be acting like hippies—that's kinda what they reminded me of. He had a long stringy ponytail. I hate it when men have the long hair but don't bother to even wash it. She was wearing a retro kind of outfit—flowy skirt, vest that looked Native American. Long hair in pigtails. I mean, she looked to be like forty, and pigtails! Then I realized it was a wig. I don't do wigs!"

"So, you thought they were the dead couple?" I asked.

"I figured it was them, from the description and all I heard. I mean they sure weren't local or even your typical tourists."

"Did you tell this to the police?"

"Uh, no. Should I?"

"Well you did get to see them, ah, alive."

"Sure," Jeannie said. "But so what? I couldn't squeeze them in, but said maybe Rollo's would. Hate sending people to my competition, but then I have all the work I need. Oh, and they wanted to find that hysterical museum—"

"You mean the historical museum?" I asked.

"Yeah, that's what I said. So I pointed them the way."

"I never got a look at them, ah, when Nikko and I were checking out their camper. Sheriff Olsen told me their names: Jason someone and Emma—no, Emily, with a different last name."

Jeannie began wetting my hair down with a spray bottle. "So—do the cops know how they died?"

I contemplated just how much to share and decided to go vague. "Some kind of accident—maybe with some plants they collected to make tea."

"Seriously? I've heard of that with mushrooms. I said they were odd, but now I'm thinking stupid."

Once Jeannie was satisfied that my hair was sufficiently soaked, she worked in some kind of magic goo that transformed my hair from frizz to soft curls. Next, she attacked with scissors.

I looked at a photo of a darling yet somewhat petulant appearing little girl taped to the vanity mirror.

"Brianna's growing up," I said.

"Six going on sixty," Jeanie said as she snipped away. Ringlets of hair floated down and settled on the floor.

"I have her in daycare three days a week, and Ma watches her the other times. She is way ahead of things for her age. Already can do some arithmetic and is a good littler reader."

It had been my experience that parents generally thought their children were "way ahead" and destined to provide endless parental boasting rights.

"Can write her name in cursive, she's memorized the alphabet, and can count to a hundred. Also, she's learning some Spanish."

"Seriously?" I said.

"*Si, señorita,*" Jeannie said with a giggle.

More snipping took place, then a quick blow dry and flatiron application. Jeannie handed me a mirror and whirled my chair around. "How's that?" she asked.

"Massively improved." I said, "You are a genius. Wish I had a date tonight."

"Well, it does stay light for a while yet," she said. "Maybe you can go stand on the street corner in downtown Peshekee and score something."

I threw a comb at her, which she easily ducked.

"Now I'm gonna have to sanitize that," she said, bending to pick it up.

"I wonder why they wanted to go to the museum," I said.

"Didn't ask, of course. Maybe look for a book on edible plants or something. You're all done, honeybun," she said, untying and removing the nylon cape and giving it a shake. "Now pay up and make another appointment *in advance* so I don't have to squeeze you in."

* * *

My hair still looked pretty good when I walked into Wilde Accounting the next day. It had been a challenge to get there as the Jeep loaner tried to stall every time I came to a stop. I was forced to brake with one foot, put the vehicle in neutral, and rev the engine with my other foot so it wouldn't die. I couldn't live in denial much longer; I needed reliable transportation.

Rose looked up from her computer screen and studied the clock. I was three minutes late. A small smile curved the corner of her mouth as she slid open her drawer containing the Nasty List.

"Hey Rose," I said. "How do you like my hair?"

I said this as a distraction. Never had I asked Rose for feedback on my personal appearance, though she often expressed her opinion.

Hand still menacingly poised over the Nasty List, Rose looked up and assessed my appearance. "Very nice," she offered.

"Thank you. That's a fetching scarf you have on today, by the way. Where did you get it?"

I was having a grand time throwing Rose for a loop. We never *ever* discussed such girly things. She appeared to be abandoning the Nasty List for the moment and reached up to touch her scarf.

"Ah, well, I'm not sure," she said, clearly being caught off guard.

Gussy emerged from his office, looking quite sharp except his tie was on inside out. I wasn't sure how he'd managed that.

"Gussy, luv," I said, going over and unknotting his tie. "Who dressed you this morning?"

"Uh...."

We both knew it was usually his mother. Strange that she screwed up the Windsor knot.

Now I had both Gustafsons slightly off balance. I worked on redoing Gussy's tie while he stiffly stood at attention.

"Dad in yet?" I asked.

The swish of the front door answered my question.

"Morning everyone!" he said as he strode in.

We returned the greeting, nearly in unison, but with varying tones of enthusiasm. While my father was a true-blooded accountant, his appearance didn't fit the nerd stereotype of a bean counter. Dad preferred the rugged-guy look, often wearing jeans and a denim shirt—or flannel in the winter. His graying hair exhibited a slightly tousled style, and from time to time—much to my mother's dismay—Dad's chin sported a manly three-day beard. While Dad wore the obligatory Wilde Accounting cheater/reader glasses, no plastic pocket protector adorned his shirt pocket. Instead of a briefcase, Dad carried his paperwork in a leather duffle bag along with his workout clothes, in case he had a chance to hit the gym.

"Nice to have it a bit cooler, eh?" Dad said. "Kat. What is that *thing* parked out in your usual spot and when will the truck be fixed?"

I hadn't yet explained the death sentence of Uncle Phil's truck to dad. It seemed like calling him would be like trying to get him to fix the problem.

"It's a loaner," I said, hedging the second part of his question.

"Gussy," Dad said as he headed up to his suite. "Come on up. I have a new client for you."

"Yes sir!" Gussy bleated, and tore away from my tie-tying efforts.

"When does the new intern, Mia, come in?" I asked Rose. I was glad to see she had abandoned the Nasty List and resumed whatever she was doing at the computer.

"I believe she comes in around midday. Apparently that's how interns work. They come and go as they wish."

A great deal of what Rose enters onto the Nasty List is tardiness. If one doesn't have set hours, it puts a damper on her as overseer of such things.

"Well, she is still finishing up with some other requirements, I guess," I said.

Rose sniffed and clicked away on her keyboard, then looked at me. "You haven't forgotten the boxes, I assume. Perhaps when Gerald is done with your father, the two of you can get those things tended to."

"Right," I said, moving over to my nook and throwing my purse under my tiny desk. I booted up my computer and began my day by surfing social media. It was a way to look busy when one is actually procrastinating. Since I was meeting up with Nikko at some point soon, I thought I better do the blasted background check on Clay Randall that he had nagged me about. I scrolled through my emails and eventually found the link that Raymond had given me.

After rummaging through my satchel, I found Clay's application to work at Wildwood. It basically was a piece of paper with minimal information, hopefully sufficient to get the job done. Turns out it was. The name of the outfit that came up on the link was Employment Management or EM. I was presented with a plethora of things to navigate, starting with setting up an account, providing a charge card, certifying a lot of policy mumbo jumbo with an e-signature, proving I wasn't a robot, and verifying I had read the lengthy information of what was legal and how to avoid getting sued. Yadda yadda yadda. Nobody reads that stuff.

I moved on to a mind-boggling number of options to choose from, including drug screening, credential checks, employment verification, and so on. There were three levels of no-frills pre-employment screening options, which mainly looked for past criminal history, credit problems, etc. The first level was "Basic," the second was labeled as "Enhanced," and the third was "Pro," with prices reflecting the depth of the screening. The cost was surprisingly reasonable, especially for the "Basic," which is what I chose. Eventually, I was able to plug in Clay's particulars and finalize my purchase. Very quickly I was informed that for an extra fee, I could have an expedited report within twenty-four hours. Otherwise, I could do the routine turnaround of three to four business days. The whole thing seemed foolish and, frankly, I felt a bit underhanded checking out Clay behind his back. Unless he had an outstanding warrant for homicide, I didn't care about his past. He was the best thing that had ever happened to Wildwood, at least since I had become owner. In any event, I would be able to tell Nikko I was giving due diligence, plus all the busy work involved made me appear to be busy in Rose's eyes, which delayed dealing with the storage boxes.

I had texted Nikko the previous evening and saw that he had finally responded. I had my phone on mute so as not to give Rose a reason to revisit my morning transgression.

Nikko texted: *Next day off is tomorrow.*

Good, mine too. Let's go for a ride (horse emoji)

Another adventure?

Maybe (smiley face emoji)

Signing lease on new apartment in a.m.

Where?

Tell you later. I'll come out after.

OK

And Spiller wants to talk.

When?

Soon.

Why?

Don't know.

I did an emoji of a pile of poop.

Nikko did an emoji of a laughing face.

I waited for something more, like XXs and OOs. A heart emoji. Puckered lips.

Nada.

* * *

"So where are you taking me?" Nikko asked as he led Rusty out of the barn.

"That back forty that the creepy guy, Varga, wants so bad," I said. I had decided to take Misty out for the ride. She was Susie Koskinen's sister's mare and didn't get much trail time. Also, Rusty was smitten with Misty, so that helped minimize a horse's natural reluctance to ride away from the comforts of their barn and buddies.

"What do you think we'll find?" Nikko asked, swinging into the saddle. His skill level had improved much since the first time he'd ridden with me.

"You know," I said, "you would probably be a lot more comfortable in some English riding breeches and riding boots. Jeans and sneakers are really not kosher."

"Those stretchy *breeches* look too girly for me. Not to say I don't like what they do for you."

"They can do a lot for a guy too."

"Quit ogling me," he said with a grin. "You women are all alike."

I gave a derisive snort.

"So, to repeat my question before we got on the subject of my attire," he said, "what do you think we'll find at this place you're taking me?"

"Don't know. I do know there was a homestead there. The buildings have pretty much disintegrated over time, but I think there's still maybe a few remains to poke through. For what, I have no idea."

The weather was cooler and the humidity down, but the bugs would still be unrelenting, so we had put bug nets over the horses' eyes and ears and doused them in repellant. Likewise, Nikko and I had armed ourselves with a sufficient layer of DEET.

We had a couple of options for getting to our destination. One was to cut through the campground, pick up a two-track that spurred off with an option to head toward the old bunkhouse, then cut over to a lesser-traveled bridle trail that meandered a bit and eventually arrived at the boundary to the Crystal Lake Wilderness. Our second choice was to bypass the campground road and go directly on the bridle trail. I decided to start with the direct but slightly more rugged route, and we could pick up the campground road on our way back to do a little poking around for any evidence of the equipment used for Raymond's horse hologram.

Misty and I led the way while Nikko plodded along behind.

I turned in my saddle so he could hear me. "So, tell me about your new apartment."

Nikko grinned. "I was thinking you might ask that. Nothing special, and actually, it's a small house outside of town on Perch Lake Road. Though I'm leasing, there's an option to buy."

"I see," I said. "It's nice to have options," I added then turned back to face front. I wasn't sure how I felt about Nikko's idea of buying. What was I hoping? That we'd get married and he'd move into the mod with Aunt Lin and me? We were nowhere near that discussion.

"At least I won't be making my parents crazy by living with them."

"Yeah. Been there, done that."

Not that long ago I had been financially forced to live in my parents' basement after being downsized from my career job as grant writer for a health care organization. When Uncle Phil died and left Wildwood Stables to my dad, he convinced me to take over the defunct horse stable, which was my ticket out of the basement and into a life of hard work, frustration, and borderline poverty. But I was the boss, usually, and I couldn't help but feel pangs of pride and growing self-esteem.

"Some of the guys are gonna help me move tomorrow," Nikko said. "You want to help?"

"I've got to go into the office tomorrow. Sorry. Hey, are you going to take Tobey?"

"Not sure. Ma loves that dog, and I'm gone a lot. Sometimes I pull twelve-hour shifts. I might just get ol' Tobes on my days off."

"Kind of like visitation," I muttered. Obviously the conversation was not going to amount to anything particularly revealing in the Kat/Nikko relationship. Which was fine.

There was a substantial ravine ahead, chock full of roots and rocks.

I turned around again to face Nikko. "Hey, I'm thinking we should dismount and lead our horses down this steep spot. Let them concentrate on picking their footing."

We got off the horses and led them down the gnarly trail. We stopped at the bottom to take a breather and gulp or two of water.

"You've got a dead mosquito or something on your nose," Nikko said.

I reached up and swiped at my nose. There was a little blood residue on my hand.

"And maybe another on your neck," he said. "Let me check."

I had bound my hair with a scrunchie before putting on my riding helmet. Nikko moved the ponytail aside, presumably to examine my neck.

"Must look closer," he said, moving in and nibbling a bit.

"Hey!" I said. "What are you doing?"

"Checking for parasites."

I turned to face him and he regaled me with a jazzy grin, then moved in for a kiss. Unfortunately, our riding helmets collided and caused the kiss to land a little off center.

"So..." he said.

"So..." I said. "Ah, I guess we should move on."

"Move on as if...?"

"To the, ah—"

Nikko had managed to press me against Rusty, while still holding the horse's reins.

"Property, homestead place," I concluded.

Rusty began pulling away to reach some greenery, which threw Nikko off and broke our embrace.

"Hey there fella," Nikko said.

"Rusty has always been my protector," I said. "He's been known to inflict serious injury on people if he thinks I'm threatened."

"That so?"

"You betcha," I said, gathering Misty's reins and preparing to mount.

"Let me give you a leg up," Nikko said just as I had my foot stretched into a stirrup. Before I could bounce into the saddle, Nikko gave a sturdy boost via my backside.

"Always trying to cop a feel," I said.

"Just being helpful."

≠ 13 ≠

It was hard to spot anything remarkable at the homestead site. Nature had mostly reclaimed the area, and all that really remained was a tumbledown chimney and a few knotty apple trees in a nearby clearing.

We dismounted and secured our horses to a nearby tree. We had put halters under the horses' bridles before hitting the trail so we could tie them up safely with lead ropes, not reins. Only cowboys in Western movies tied horses by the reins.

"I haven't been here since I took Wildwood over," I said. "Uncle Phil took trail rides through here and on into the Crystal Lake Wilderness. I do remember stopping here and poking around, trying to imagine the immense challenges of trying to scratch out a living."

I wandered around a bit, thinking about life at this place. Nikko followed me.

"A lot of rocks," he said. "I'd say a glacier left a lot of boulders behind during its Ice Age journey. Not good farmland, even if you cleared the forest."

We walked back to the chimney ruins. "It was a lot more open when I last saw it," I said. "Back when I was a kid. Really grown over now. I think whoever lived here probably tried to make a go of farming and eventually moved on to some other means of making a living, such as lumberjacking or working in the mines, like Varga claimed his ancestors did."

"Can't imagine why Varga wants this piece of land," Nikko said.

"There is a nice little stream nearby. I think there's brookies in it. but I don't think Varga is interested in fishing."

"Do you know the name of the family who once lived here? Do you think it was someone related to Varga?"

"I don't have any idea," I said. "Maybe I can research it at the register of deeds' office."

Nikko got his phone out and took some photos of the area. "Just trying to figure out what is so special about this place."

"Yeah. Maybe he was telling the truth. You know, family ties."

"Maybe," Nikko said. He walked over to the dilapidated chimney and took another picture.

I joined him and walked around the area where the cabin would have stood. You could still make out the faint footprint of the structure. A disorganized array of rocks suggested the general outline of the cabin.

"Do you think these were used as a foundation?" I said, kicking a boulder with my toe.

"Probably," Nikko said. "Homesteaders used what they could find to scrabble a living and build what they needed."

"I suppose we should head back," I said. "I'd like to check out the campground for something."

"Okay."

"We can water the horses at the little stream I mentioned that's around here—somewhere. I remember it when Uncle Phil took me back here."

We returned to the horses and untied them. I noticed Rusty had managed to gnaw some of the bark off the tree he had been tethered to.

"I'm surprised this horse has any teeth left," Nikko said, giving Rusty's muzzle a scratch.

"Well, when you've been nearly starved to death, you tend to obsess over any potential food. Even bark. If we're quiet, I bet we can hear the stream and find our way to it."

We stood silently, hearing the occasional buzz of an insect and slight whisper of a breeze to break the silence.

"I think I hear it," Nikko said. "This way."

We led the horses and headed in the general direction of the faint rushing noise. The noise grew louder, and soon we saw the stream. We picked our way over and the horses lowered their heads to drink.

"I wonder if it has a name," I said.

"Probably," Nikko said. "I'll get my topo information app going later and we'll see."

"Or we could just name it."

Nikko looked at me and smiled. "What did you have in mind? Hey, how about Wild River?"

"I get the double meaning. Very clever, but it's not exactly a wild river, more of a meandering stream or even a babbling brook."

"Things look—disturbed," Nikko said.

"Huh?" I asked.

"Like somebody's been through here. Look, broken branches and still some ruts."

"Ruts from what? And don't animals break branches?"

"Not like this. As far as the ruts, not sure, since the rain probably washed out the details, but likely an ATV."

I walked over and looked. I had to admit Nikko had excellent tracking skills because I really didn't notice the so-called disturbed area until he pointed it out.

"Hmm," I said. "Wonder if he or she was coming or going. Either way, I think they were trespassing."

"*And*, even if they were a little off course, no motorized vehicles are allowed anywhere near here, except for fire or emergency situations."

"And look there," I said, pointing off onto the other side of the stream. "An orange tag. Do you think it has to do with forestry management?" I asked, feeling a bit smug at noticing the marker first.

"Nope," Nikko said. "Usually spray paint is used, not a ribbon, and usually blue, though other colors can come into play. Besides, before any logging would be done, they'd have to build a road, not to mention getting permits to log in a designated wilderness."

"Somebody was marking a spot to cross the stream."

"Our nameless stream," Nikko said, moving next to me and draping his arm across my shoulder. "By the authority vested in me as an employee of the Michigan Department of Natural Resources, I hereby dub thee *Nameless*."

"Cute," I said.

* * *

We rode the different route back, heading past the old bunkhouse and into the derelict campground. I dismounted and began scanning the trees. Nikko followed suit.

"I give," he said, looking up. "What are we looking for?"

"Not sure," I said. "You know the ghost horse thing that I kept spotting last spring?"

"Yup. Something to do with a hologram that Raymond was a party to."

"Yeah. Well, I saw it again. Well, actually it was Willie who saw it first."

"Willie?"

"The woman who is in charge of the Magic Stirrup Foundation that is going to refit the camp into an equine therapy place for special needs kids."

"So, this Willie saw the hologram—or whatever it is? Can I quit looking up? I have a crick in my neck."

"No, keep looking," I said. "And yeah, she saw it, but I'm ashamed to say I feigned ignorance. I thought we were done with Raymond's little tricks."

"And have you asked Raymond about it?"

"No. He'll deny it. I want to find the equipment, remove it, and shove it in his face."

We continued to look around.

"Any idea what we are actually looking for?" Nikko said.

"Something that doesn't belong."

"You do sometimes sound like a cop."

"Not plucky?"

"Oh, that too."

"Maybe I can get Aunt Lin to wheedle some info out of him," I said with a sigh.

"And you're devious, too," Nikko said. "Wish I had a secret for you to wheedle out of me."

"Oh, you do have your secrets, Nikko Olsen. I just don't have the energy to do any wheedling right now."

"Later?" he asked, rubbing the back of his neck.

I gave him an icy look.

"Got a crick in my neck. You could massage it."

"No time for that," I said, looking at my watch. "Chores to do. Wanna help?"

"Oh, gee, I'd love to, but I better go pick up the U-Haul for moving day tomorrow."

"Right."

"Oh, and don't forget that Spiller wants to see us tomorrow too. I think he said at like three. Maybe you should call and check."

"Me? Hey, if he wants to see me, he can call *me*."

"Well, see, I told him I'd make sure you were there. I imagine it's just routine and all because of that hippie couple."

"I sat in the Bobcat the whole time!"

Nikko shrugged and we got on our horses and headed back to the stable.

"He has it out for me, Spiller, and I don't know why," I said.

"Maybe because of the bodies that keep piling up. You really need to find a new hobby besides this compulsion for collecting cadavers."

"But they weren't even on my property!"

"Close enough."

* * *

There's nothing that gets a horse owner out of bed quicker than someone yelling, "The horses are out!"

Clay was banging on the mod door while delivering just such a report. I threw on some sweats and rushed to open the door. Clay was there, arm still in a sling, wearing jeans and boots, no shirt.

"Guy drove up the road here and woke me up. Asked if we had any horses because he saw a bunch of them running down Big Lake Road."

"But how...?" I asked.

"No idea," Clay said. "I haven't even checked to make sure it's true."

We had decided during the hot weather, so long as no storms were in the forecast, to turn the horses out to pasture and paddocks for the night. They could graze, roll in the dirt, and do their business outdoors without being subjected to the baking sun or swarms of flies.

"That pasture fence is solid, high tensile wire and the gate double latched," I said as we hurried across the parking lot. It was dark, but the sodium light provided enough light for us to see the area.

"Don't see anything out in the pasture. Looks like those three are gone," Clay said, shining a flashlight across the pasture.

"Oh God!" I said.

"What's going on?"

"Aunt Lin! You about scared me to death. The horses are out."

"Not all of them," Clay said. "Mac is still here in his paddock, and Oscar and Emmy are in theirs. Must be the main pasture that the others escaped through."

"So Rusty, Misty, and Shadow are running around out there in the dark!" I said. "Where did the guy tell you they were?"

"Big Lake Road, heading east," Clay said.

"I'll get my keys and head out to look," Aunt Lin said.

"I'll take the damn Jeep. Clay, you come and bring some halters and lead ropes and maybe a shirt. Everyone bring your cell phones and hope we will have enough service to communicate."

Clay hurried into the barn and returned carrying several halters and lead ropes along with a handful of horse treats. Because of the sling, he had only managed to put one arm in a hoodie leaving the other sleeve flapping behind him. He scrambled into the passenger seat and barely shut the door before I floored it. We tore down Horse Camp Road and squealed onto Big Lake Road, heading east. Unfortunately, one headlight on the Jeep was blinking on and off, and the other seemed pretty dim.

"How long you gonna drive this thing?" Clay asked.

I didn't answer him because I had no idea. We drove about a mile, then came to the Little Mountain Road intersection. Aunt Lin was right behind me.

I picked up my phone and sent her a text.

I'll go right. You keep straight.

Okay (thumbs-up emoji)

I tore around the corner and then decided that since I had no idea where I was going, I should slow down. A car approached from the other way and began flashing its lights. When we came side by side, we stopped and rolled down our windows. A teen couple sat in the other car.

"Did you see any horses?" I blurted.

"Yeah, I mean I guess," said the boy. "Something scary in the road ahead, man. Whew. I almost hit one. I thought they were maybe some moose."

"I tol' you they were horses," said the girl.

"Where were they heading?" I asked.

"Don't know," said the boy. "I was too damn scared to notice."

"They headed up the road, then veered off," said the girl. "I was gonna call the sheriff and report it, but—"

"No need. We'll round them up," I said. "Thanks."

I took off while Clay shone his flashlight around the side of the road. "Hey—look out in that hayfield. I think I see something," he said.

I screeched to a halt, the old brakes shrieking in protest, and jumped out of the car. "Yeah, there they are, the brats."

I took a halter, lead rope, and one of the horse treats and stumbled through the stubby hayfield. "Hey fella," I said, approaching Rusty. "Wanna treat?"

Rust snorted and moved away.

"It's me," I said. "Be a good boy. Let's go back to the barn."

Rusty watched me approach as if trying to figure out who or what I was. He snorted again. I kept talking and he lowered his head and let me approach. I slipped him an apple treat and worked the halter over his head. Clay had approached the other two and managed to get a halter on Shadow.

"So, now what?" I asked Clay.

"I guess we head home. Misty will follow."

"It's miles to walk!" I said.

"Who said anything about walking? I brought extra lead ropes. We can attach two to the halters and use them as reins."

"And hope that the horses don't realize that we really don't have any control," I muttered. I'd never ridden without a bridle. Or a saddle, for that matter. "*And* there's the Jeep," I added.

"Leave the keys in it; maybe someone will steal it."

Clay gave me a leg up onto Rusty and maneuvered his way onto Shadow, grabbing the mane with his non-sling arm.

I pulled out my phone to text Aunt Lin.

Got 'em. Riding home. Please come and follow.

On my way. (surprise emoji)

14

"This is where they got out," Clay said, bending over to look at some broken fence wire.

"How did that wire just break?" I asked. "It's galvanized twelve-and-a-half gauge. Takes, I don't know, a couple thousand pounds of pressure."

"Didn't break," Clay said. "It was cut. See here, how the wire is crimped a bit where the cutters compressed it? Broken wire would show some fraying. Cut wire is cleaner."

"But who...?"

"Yeah, who and why," Clay said, standing up. "Sometimes kids will do these things on a dare or as an initiation. Prove they are badass."

"But someone could have been killed, or one of the horses could have been injured. This isn't like stealing a mailbox or draping toilet paper on somebody's shrubs."

"Yeah, well, it's been my experience that kids don't think about consequences, just the adventure. The lucky ones somehow survive. Others might end up rolling a car in the ditch or visiting the ER with drug or alcohol poisoning. Or maybe do some time in the juvie."

"I sort of remember those days—not the juvenile hall. Really the wildest thing I ever did was something we called a musical chairs fire drill where a bunch of us all crammed in a car, stopped at a red light, then jumped out and switched seats before the light turned green. If someone didn't make it, we pretended to take off and leave them behind. Of course people in other cars honked at us, which we thought was a show of support. Oh, and once one of the girls mooned some people in the car next to us and it turned out to be her granny and a carload of her church lady friends. Boy, did she get it."

"You were pretty wild and crazy all right," Clay said with a chuckle. "I won't mention what I did as a youth since it's been so long ago it would have involved dinosaur tipping."

We looked at the sprung fencing and sighed in unison.

"Normally, I could repair this on my own," Clay said, "but since I've only got one good arm...."

"Hey, no problem," I said. "I'll help. I just need to call the office again, and instead of being late, now I'm going to have to take the day off."

I hated the satisfaction it would give Rose when I begged off. She'd keep track of things to make sure I made up the hours or casually mention to Mom when she did payroll that I (once again) was short of the paltry hours I normally work. As if I'd cheat my own father!

By the time Clay and I got the fence stretched and repaired, it was getting close to two in the afternoon, and Nikko and I had the command appearance with Lieutenant Spiller at the state police at three. I just had time to shower before Nikko picked me up for the inquisition.

As I stepped out of the shower and began towel drying my hair, my phone dinged. I picked it up and an alert of a new text flashed across the screen. Nikko.

Hey Kat. Got a problem.

You? I had a midnight adventure!

What?

I'll explain later. Picking me up?

Can't. Got called into work. Some kind of illegal animals to round up.

Illegal animals?

Yeah. Wild pigs.

Wild pigs?

Not kidding.

Cancel Spiller?

No, you go. Routine. No worries. I let him know I'll meet later.

Since I couldn't find an emoji flipping him off, I used a less controversial angry version of the quintessential smiley face. It had smoke pouring out of its ears and its face was red.

He responded with an emoji of a laughing smiley face. Again, no hearts, XXs, or OOs. The jerk.

Fortunately, I guess, nobody stole the Jeep, and Aunt Lin had given me a ride to pick it up before she left or her yoga class. I glanced over at the rust bucket. It seemed to be glowering, maybe pissed off that I'd left it unattended on the side of the road. I hoped it was up for the journey into town. Spiller didn't seem like the type to forgive tardiness. Why was I so worried? It wasn't like I'd done anything wrong. Yet, being called into Spiller's lair was like being sent to the principal's office. Nothing good ever came of it.

* * *

"Thank you for coming, Miss Wilde," Spiller said, rising from his gleaming, compulsively clean desk. He reached out to shake my hand.

Lieutenant Spiller was the epitome of spit shine. His hair was buzzed, his face close shaven, his uniform pressed to perfection, and the polished brass accoutrements adorning his shirt stood at attention in their various assigned spots.

"Sure, no problem," I said, returning the handshake. I half-expected him to use some of the hand sanitizer from the pump bottle on his desk after we shook. Nevertheless, we seemed to be off to a cordial start, which was good.

"Sorry. Nikko got called on—ah—an animal emergency," I said, lowering myself into the impossibly uncomfortable plastic-molded guest chair.

"Yes, I did get a message of sorts about his unavoidable conflict."

"Pigs," I said.

Lieutenant Spiller frowned and gave me a glacial look. "I beg your pardon."

"Wild pigs—sorry, I wasn't implying—I mean they don't still call you that, do they? Pig, I mean?"

The lieutenant simply stared at me.

"I guess that was what you call a Freudian Slip," I said, forcing a fake chuckle.

"Really?"

"I mean, you know, a slip of, er...."

"Shall we move on from psychoanalysis to the reason I asked you to come in?" Spiller asked.

So much for a cordial start.

"Sure. If this is about those people in the camper, I really didn't even see them. I mean I saw them—well, in the body bags. Ah—"

"Actually, I *am* curious about how you happen to be around whenever we encounter a suspicious death, but—"

"Suspicious? I thought it was accidental."

"—as I was saying, you do seem to be in the thick of things when bodies are found, but the dead couple is not why I asked you to come in." Spiller frowned down at his desk and rearranged the stapler, tape dispenser, and a letter opener.

I couldn't imagine why else I was being called in. Surely he hadn't heard about the horses getting out. No, Nikko and Spiller had set up the meeting (without consulting me) before the Wildwood roundup. And the Jeep, well, it was a menace on the road, but nobody had pulled me over. All those things were not Spiller's concern anyway and would be left to a lowly trooper to investigate. I decided not to prompt the lieutenant to spill it—that made me smile, Spiller spilling it. I hoped he didn't notice me trying to suppress a grin.

Desktop accessories in order, Spiller looked up and said, "I understand you have—or had—possession of a drone."

"Drone? Oh! The drone that, um, crashed. I think earlier it had spooked my horse and I took a spiller—ah, fall—and later, yeah, Nikko and I heard the—a crash and went to investigate."

"A crash? Or maybe a shot?"

"Maybe," I said. "Not sure." Of course I was sure, but being vague seemed the best answer.

"And you two went to investigate?"

"Sort of," I said. "Do you mind telling me what this is all about? I mean, a drone was flying over Crystal Lake, my place, and other private property. Nikko said he had no info on any surveying going on."

"I see," Spiller said.

"So," I said, "what's the deal?"

The lieutenant sighed. "Apparently, a legitimate organization was doing some surveying and a representative of that organization reported that they believed the drone was intentionally shot down. A complaint has been filed. There may be criminal charges or at the least a demand for restitution."

"Uh huh," I said. Now I was frowning. "Maybe there was something unauthorized going on with that thing. We noticed some writing on it. U-S or uni-something. Survey. We figured Unified Survey."

I looked at the lieutenant for confirmation. His stoney expression revealed nothing.

I charged on, "I'd sure like to know what they were surveying on my land and Leevi Waddaga's land too. And the Crystal Lake Wilderness for that matter!"

I was doing my best to play the outraged citizen, but clearly, I was no match for the lieutenant, who fixed me with a cold stare. I don't think he even blinked or took a breath. Apparently, I wasn't supposed to demand answers.

"I'm actually not certain what they were surveying," Spiller finally said. "I imagine it has to do with mining or forestry in the area."

We were at an impasse. I was certain Spiller had an idea of what the Unified Survey company was doing. While it may have been legal, it likely wouldn't have been popular, whether mining or lumbering or searching for Sasquatch. And as far as the demise of the drone, I wasn't going to throw Leevi under the bus for shooting down the thing.

"I guess I'm wondering what this all has to do with me," I said.

"Really quite simple. The owner wants to salvage the drone, and it seems you and Officer Olsen took possession of it. Didn't it occur to you to turn it in?"

"Well, Nikko did some checking and nobody seemed to know why there was a drone in the area or whose it was. We, ah, decided to have it analyzed. You know, to track down the owner."

"Really?" Spiller said. "I thought Olsen was a conservation officer who normally looks for poachers and such. And I don't believe you are in law enforcement, are you? When property like that is found, it stands to reason somebody might be looking for it."

"True," I said. "However, I'd sure like to know exactly what this outfit is doing flying a drone over those areas. I think a lot of people would like to know. I mean, it wasn't a hobby drone."

"And you know this because?" Spiller said.

"As I said, somebody's looking at it—somebody who knows this stuff."

"Does this somebody have a name?" Spiller asked.

"I'll tell you when you tell me the purpose of the drone surveying," I snapped. Nikko was right. I could be plucky.

Spiller's nostrils flared a little. "I will ask you then to get ahold of this *somebody* and have them deliver the unit to the authorities—namely, me."

I was pretty sure at that point that the boxing match was over and I was against the ropes. Nikko was in deep, deep trouble right now. Some boyfriend, throwing me to the wolves—or wolf. Wild pigs, my ass.

"I'll see what I can do," I said.

"By tomorrow."

I refrained from any more snappy retorts and nodded.

* * *

I went into the office on Friday to make up for missing work the day before. By some small miracle the Jeep coughed to life and I was successfully transported to Wilde Accounting—on time. I bid Rose a good morning and she gave a little grunt in return. Rose was difficult to read, but I suspected she was not happy about something, and I soon figured out it had to do with Gussy, who was lurking around our cute new intern, Mia. I heard Mia giggle and Gussy snort. Rose bristled and pinched her mouth into a tiny knot.

"Well, those two seem to be getting along," I said, intentionally stoking the fire. I slid into my nook and tossed my purse on the ugly 1950s metal desk. I decided I'd do a little online research to find out ownership of the old homestead land Varga was determined to get. When Nikko and I checked it out, it seemed pretty unremarkable. If I had time, I was going to go to the Peshekee County Register of Deeds after work to see if they could offer any information.

I booted up my computer and glanced at my inbox. I was surprised to see a response from Employment Management telling me my pre-employment report was available for downloading. *That was quick,* I thought. I decided I needed a shot of coffee before I could deal with deciphering Clay's background check. I headed for the coffee pot and heard more giggling and snorting. Then Mia said, "Ohmygod! That's hilarious."

"Snork snork. Like she saw a ghost!" Gussy said. "Oh wait she—"

"Shh."

One could only guess what was worthy of an omigod, two snorks, and a shush. I went to the coffee pot and noted it bore the dregs of the previous day's brew. Things were definitely amiss at Wilde Accounting. I grabbed the pot and headed to the sink in the restroom to rinse and fill. I heard the front door swish open, followed by a mixture of voices. Dad, Mom, and Raymond all entered together. I measured coffee into the filter, poured water into the reservoir and hit start. Gussy scooted out from Mia's cubicle and headed to his office. Raymond gave him a poisonous look and went back to make sure his sister had not been violated. I wondered what it would be like to have an older brother to protect me from predators, namely boys, then later men. Of course I had Dad who was very proficient at sniffing out the intentions of any guy who came calling.

"Hello Kathryn," Mom said, giving me a light peck on the cheek. "Hello everyone. It's your favorite day. Payday!"

"Yay!" Mia said from behind her cubicle wall. "My first ever payday."

"Congratulations," I said.

Dad grabbed a cup of coffee before it was done dripping. Fortunately, the coffeemaker had an auto-pause feature. "So, Kat, what's this I hear about the horses getting out?"

I told him my tale of woe. The recounting of the precarious ride back with only lead ropes and a halter, and of course Clay with one arm in a sling and Aunt Lin following with her four-way flashers blinking. This triggered laughter and snorking from behind Mia's partition.

"So, you think vandalism?" Dad asked.

"Yeah, probably kids. I'll have to keep the horses in at night, I guess."

"Well, glad you and Clem got it fixed."

"Clay," I said.

"Right. Clay," he said, taking a swig of coffee and grimacing.

Dad went up to his lair and Raymond headed back into the lobby.

"Hey, Raymond," I said. "So, about the drone."

"Yeah?"

"Lieutenant Spiller of the state police says we gotta turn it in."

I saw Rose's antenna go up, figuratively speaking, although there could *literally* be an antenna within Rose's towering hairdo.

"Found property and all," I said, waving Raymond over to my area.

"Say, I want to take a look at that Jeep you're driving," Raymond said, nodding toward the door.

Raymond and I went outside, away from inquiring minds.

"So, the UAV—"

The what?" I asked.

"UAV. Unmanned aerial vehicle—the drone," Raymond said, "has what is called a magnetometer."

"Which is...?"

"Used to detect things. Sometimes minerals. But it's possible it can be used to find other things."

"Such as?"

"Such as anomalies in the earth."

"Anomalies?"

"Something abnormal. Something that doesn't exist naturally. It could be a new technological development still in the testing stage."

"Well, the owner of the thing wants it back and has filed charges," I said. "Spiller is being pretty close-mouthed about what the thing was doing flying over the area."

"Spying, looking for something, testing. Who knows?" Raymond said. "It could even be military cloaked as a private enterprise."

"This is getting more and more curious," I said.

Raymond shrugged. "I can drop it off at the state police post if you want me to. My buddy and I went over it, and we don't have any way of telling what was actually being surveyed or recorded. The images or signals would have been sent back to its handler."

"Or the mother ship!" I said.

Raymond smiled. "We could always start a rumor about space aliens. It would give everyone something to talk about besides the price of eggs. And probably the police would get a lot of crackpots reporting things. That's always fun."

"Probably not a good idea," I said, thinking about how Nikko's dad, the sheriff, would not appreciate a bunch of UFO sightings being called in. Not to mention Spiller, who would look for a way to blame me, possibly rightly so.

"Anyway," I said, "I'd appreciate it if you did deliver it to Spiller. But I'm not done trying to find out what's going on. I mean, what if they plan to start mining in Crystal Lake Wilderness, or worse yet, try to steal my land!"

"There is a lot of nickel in the area," Raymond said. "I will do some checking around with the tribe. See if they've caught wind of anything."

"Thanks," I said.

"Trust me. If they plan on trying to get something going under the radar, I guarantee there will be trouble."

After Raymond left, I returned to my computer, which had gone into semi-sleep mode. I awakened it with a mouse jiggle and went back to my inbox, where I found the Employment Management email and clicked it open. There was an attachment, which I opened, and "presto" a report of Clay Edward Randall, DOB 05/15/1960, appeared. It verified his last known address, which was in Wyoming, his Social Security number, his gender (male), and race (Caucasian). I waded my way through the document and learned Clay had no outstanding warrants, an excellent credit report, and a rap sheet. Okay, not a long rap sheet, but an arrest and misdemeanor conviction three years prior for destruction of property. I was pretty sure my jaw hit the desktop and I must have said, quite loudly, "SONOFABITCH!" because office noise ceased for a moment and Rose gave me the evil eye before the Nasty List drawer rumbled open.

15

No matter what may be flying in the air or lurking underground, or for that matter, what nefarious deeds a stable hand may have committed, some things remain unchanged, such as the need to eat, sleep, relieve oneself, blink, breathe, bathe, and, of course, do chores. When the sputtering Jeep shuddered to a stop in Wildwood's parking area, I noted that Clay was lunging the other newbie horse, Emmy. She was being a brat, but as usual, Clay was showing infinite patience and persistence, even with only one good arm. Oscar was standing at the fence one paddock over, whinnying every ten seconds or so, which probably wasn't helping things.

"Hey, how's it goin'?" I asked, approaching the ring where Clay and the filly were working. The man was a wonder with horses, and I saw no need to derail the workout session by pouncing on him with a demand for answers to questions I should have asked in the first place. Eventually, I'd get to it; I just had to figure out how and when. And one thing was for certain—I wasn't going to bring it up with Nikko.

"Oh, not too bad for a first time. She hasn't been worked much, that's for sure. I'm almost done here."

"How's the arm?" I asked.

"Actually, doing pretty good. I take this thing off when I'm not active. I get an MRI tomorrow, and if things are doing okay, I may be able to lose the damn sling altogether."

"I'll be back in a little bit to help with chores," I said.

"Sounds good."

I entered the mod to find Aunt Lin in the kitchen, vigorously chopping some greenery. Jupiter was observing, crooked tail snapping back and forth like a metronome.

"Yow!"

"Hey Kat," Aunt Lin said. "I'm making a shredded veggie casserole. You can add cheese to your portion."

"And meat," I said. *And flavor.*

"Yow!"

Jupiter came over to me and rubbed against my leg, then headed to the cupboard where his Bon Cat-étite canned food was stored.

"Would you mind?" Aunt Lin asked.

I got a can of Savory Salmon out of the kitty cupboard, snapped open the top, and plopped the food into a clean dish. Jupiter circled my legs as I made my way over to his feeding area and plunked down the dish. He did his usual guttural predatory noises, circled the dish, and dug in, humming contentedly.

"God, that stuff stinks," Aunt Lin said. "The casserole will bake about forty minutes, then we can eat." She slid the bilious glop into the oven. "I made gluten-free biscuits and we have sugar-free jelly."

"Sounds great. I'll just get changed, help with chores, and we can, ah, give the casserole a try."

Nikko had an uncanny sense of timing when he texted me. I had just stripped off my work clothes and was down to my undies when I heard a bling on my phone. It felt intrusive, as if someone had barged into my changing room at the clothing store. Even though we weren't on video chat, I grabbed a robe before I opened my text messages.

Sorry I missed Spiller.

Yeah, you are on my Nasty List.

Nasty List? You mean like Rose.

Worse!

Sorry. Pig emergency.

Can't wait to hear.

Want to see my new digs?

Can't. Have chores and L has dinner.

Pizza ordered.

I sent a "thinking" emoji.

1527 Perch Lake Road. 3rd house on right. Yellow with green trim. I have beer.

I'll be over after chores.

I got cocky and added an emoji heart. Nikko could take it how he wished. Probably he'd think it was because he offered pizza and beer, and probably something special for dessert. And he could be right.

* * *

I pulled into the miniscule driveway of Nikko's new residence. After I squeezed the Jeep next to his DNR truck, I got out to look the place over. The house was a small ranch painted a buttercup yellow with sage-green trim. Very cute. A postage-stamp-size front yard that needed mowing had a small cement walk leading to a miniscule porch. A couple of overgrown shrubs threatened to take over the porch steps. Next to the front door stood an empty flower planter that appeared to have been abandoned for some time. The house was squeezed between two similar neighboring houses with barely enough room between to fit a garden hose.

The front door opened before I could knock. Tobey came streaking out and leapt against my kneecaps. I squatted down and gave the pooch a vigorous scratch along his spine. He wiggled and set his tail into helicopter mode.

"Welcome to my castle!" Nikko said. "Come on in."

The cuteness of the place abruptly ended when I stepped inside. I could only describe the decor as "Desperate Bachelor." I had never been in Nikko's apartment in Ontonagon but wondered if it had been worth the trouble and expense to move his paltry possessions, which even the most undiscerning dumpster diver would probably reject. The living room accoutrements included a beanbag chair, card table with two lawn chairs, a couch that likely harbored the next pandemic, a sixty-five-inch television perched on a board supported by cement blocks, a foosball game, and an enormous wooden spool-cum-coffee table, which held a dozen or so empty beer bottles. While there was a lamp, it had no shade and was sitting unplugged on the floor. I felt as if I had entered a homeless encampment or an opium den.

During the tour, I was shown where the "powder room" was located (no shower curtain, one towel, and no soap in sight) and then the "master" bedroom, which had a mattress on the floor with a rumpled blanket and no sheets. A dog bed sat next to the mattress and looked slightly more inviting that the human bed. The closet door was open, revealing a few of Nikko's neatly hung uniforms. The rest of his clothes were folded in sloppy piles and stacked in a corner of the room. Naturally, there were no curtains or decorator pillows to be found, though there was one framed photo sitting on the floor featuring Nikko kneeling next to what was presumably a dead deer. He was holding the head up to show off the animal's rack. The buck's tongue hung out, making the creature look drunk. Lastly, Nikko showed me the second bedroom, which he called his computer room. Indeed, there was a laptop in there sitting on top of a small, pressboard computer stand. Boxes of papers and God-knows-what were stacked everywhere. A couple of shotguns stood in the corner, barrels pointing up. I wondered what Freud would have to say about them. Tobey sniffed around enthusiastically and found something that apparently he deemed edible. He scarfed it down before Nikko could stop him.

"Probably left over burger bun or something," Nikko said. "I bought a bag of burgers for the guys who helped me move."

Before I could ask how the burger bun or whatever found its way into the computer room, Tobey hurled up whatever it was onto the one rug in the room.

"Hated that rug anyway," Nikko said, rolling it up and carrying it toward the outside door.

Dog barf notwithstanding, the whole place gave a robust smell of cheese, pepperoni, and mushrooms. My favorite.

"I put the pizza in the oven to keep it warm," Nikko said as we came back inside and headed to the kitchen. "Do you want a beer or a Coke? I have both."

"Beer would be great," I said, looking in the cupboards for plates and such.

"Ah, I usually just use paper plates. I haven't gotten around to getting much for the kitchen."

"I see that," I said, finding the stack of paper plates and a roll of paper towels.

"Ma is coming over tomorrow. She and I are going to the thrift store or maybe Walmart to, you know, get a few things. Wanna come?"

I twisted the cap off the beer he handed me and took a swig, which bought me a little time to figure out how to wheedle my way out of the invitation. I wasn't quite ready to help my so-called boyfriend set up housekeeping. He hadn't proclaimed his love for me or even put a heart emoji on his texts. Besides, I'd barely been able to get my own house in order, and of course I did have a lot of help from my mom just like Nikko was doing. I guess we were both still loosely tied to the apron strings.

"Oh, gee," I said after two or three more swigs of beer. "I'd love to, but I'm gonna go to the Peshekee Historical Society Museum and check some things out."

"Since when are you interested in the historical society?" he asked, pulling the pizza out of the warm oven. A little grease had seeped through the cardboard, but it smelled heavenly.

We headed into the living room, with Tobey at our heels. Nikko looked at the dog and gave the command to sit. Tobey lifted a paw and barked.

"He gets his commands a little mixed up," Nikko said. "But he's a good boy. Who's a good boy?"

Tobey threw himself on his back, paws sticking up in the air.

"Anyway," I said, "I went to the register of deeds today, you know, to find out about that old homestead, and the lady there said while they would have records of all land transactions, she suggested I check with a woman named Elsie Tuttle at the museum, who knows a lot about the early homesteading in the area and so on. Also, the clerk at the register of deeds said it was too close to closing time to set up the microfiche thingy that would need to be used for research. I guess they're working on digitizing things, but most stuff is still either in books or on microfiche. It's much less tedious to check out what this Elsie with the Peshekee Historical Society has to say. The museum where she volunteers has limited hours and is only open Mondays, Tuesdays, and Saturdays, so I need to go tomorrow."

"Okay, too bad. Ma likes you and thinks I'm an idiot. You two could have a great time emasculating me."

"Tempting," I said. "Maybe when you're ready to visit a furniture store I can help you pick out a new couch."

"What's wrong with my couch?"

We looked over at the saggy, stained, derelict unit crouched against the wall.

"Well, okay, I admit I got it off the curb on trash pick-up day."

"Ugh," I said.

"Food's getting cold. Let's eat."

We sat at the rickety card table and tucked into the pizza. While the ambiance sucked, the cuisine was superb. I snuck Tobey a chunk of crust under the table.

"I saw that," Nikko said. "No feeding the dog at the table."

"Yeah, okay," I said. I had no intention of depriving Tobey of his dog-given right of begging. I changed the subject. "So, Officer Olsen," I said, "tell me all about the pig roundup. And this better be good."

16

I arrived at the Peshekee Historical Society Museum at the stroke of nine. Even though I'd grown up and lived in Peshekee most of my life, I had never visited the museum. A set of enormous red logging wheels sat in the yard along with a couple of horse-drawn farming implements. The building itself was a log structure with a black steel roof and green trim. It had a covered wooden porch with a few old items sitting on it, including a washtub and butter churn and a couple of things that were a mystery to me. I stepped up to the door just as someone flipped the sign on it from closed to open. A woman swung the door open and let me in. She was wearing period clothing that reminded me of the old TV series, *Little House on the Prairie.*

"Hi," I said.

"Good morning," she replied with a smile. "I'll just get some lights switched on and my coffee going, and then you can let me know how I can help you."

Fluorescent lights flickered on, and I browsed the photo-laden walls, taking in the sepia pictures of stone-faced men and women during various phases of history in the area. Some were simply standing in front of a cabin or store. There were multiple shots of miners wearing carbide lamp hats. The men looked dirty, tired, and glum. Photos of logging through the years lined a good deal of one wall. There were also artifacts enclosed in cases, some upright, some in table form. All items were protected with glass covers and many had interpretive signs describing the museum items. I worked my way down and around, checking out pictures of downtown Peshekee in its infancy. Pete's General Store was in one of the photos, and I thought it nice that it hadn't changed much over the decades. Another photo showed men standing on a rocky cliff over a deep ravine. Some people were down in the ravine with pickaxes and shovels.

"That's a photo depicting the hardships those men endured building the Peshekee Grade Railroad," the museum woman said. "My name's Elsie, by the way."

"Kat Wilde," I said, offering my hand.

I took a closer look at Elsie's old-time clothing. The dress was made of a floral material with a long, full skirt, long sleeves, and a high neckline. A full-length apron was tied around her waist. She wore a bonnet and her gray hair was pulled into a bun at the nape of her neck. Her face had a few wrinkles and not a bit of makeup, but her eyes sparkled and her smile seemed warm and sincere.

I reached out to shake her hand and said, "I love your outfit. It's amazing."

"Why, thank you. I admit I ordered it online. I'm not much of a seamstress."

"I can't even sew on a button," I said.

We shared a laugh and looked back at the photo.

"This is very interesting," I said. "I did learn that only one train ever went on those tracks."

"Yes, the first and last train to go on those tracks derailed and fell into the Peshekee River. They called it the two-million-dollar scam," Elsie said. "I think it was just a case of poor planning. *Really* poor planning and underfunding."

I moved farther down the wall to a photo of a stout, stern-faced woman and skinny man wearing droopy overalls standing in front of a crude log cabin. Four raggedy children of varying heights formed a line in front of their parents.

"Amazing that people lived up here like that, isn't it?" Elsie said.

"Yeah," I said. "I can't imagine how they made any kind of a living."

"Well, logging and mining brought a lot of folks to the area. It was actually pretty prosperous at one time. Still a lot of loneliness and hardship, though. Should I just let you browse, or do you have something specific you're looking for?"

"As a matter of fact, Elsie, I am curious about homesteading in the area. See, I now own my late uncle's place, Wildwood Stables, and there's an old homestead, which borders the Crystal Lake Wilderness. I am curious about its history before my uncle owned it. The lady at the register of deeds said you were very knowledgeable."

"Oh my, how nice of her. And I did know that your uncle passed last fall. Please accept my deepest condolences. I do hope you're planning to keep the place intact and aren't letting some slick land developer chop it up. So many things in Peshekee County have already been ruined."

"I'm doing my best," I said. "I have no plans to sell off anything."

"I imagine it's a challenge for a young woman such as yourself to manage things," Elsie said. "I am curious about your plans—if you don't mind my asking."

"Not at all," I said. "Actually, I've not publicized much at this stage, but I do foster neglected and abused horses. I board some horses, and eventually we'll do some training and have riding lessons. But the big plan is to start a riding therapy camp for special needs children."

"You teach these children to ride?" Elsie asked.

"Well, what they are learning is self-confidence along with riding skills. They learn to care for horses and build self-esteem."

"My, that does sound marvelous. I do wish there had been such a thing when my Frankie was little."

"Your son?" I asked.

"Yes, he was what you now call special needs. Back when he was a boy, they called him retarded or slow-witted. Even when he became an adult, people taunted and teased him."

"I'm so sorry," I said.

"He really is very clever with his hands. My Frankie can fix anything."

"Uh huh," I said. It seemed fruitless to try to get things swung around to my reason for visiting the museum.

"He's been...gone, and I'm so pleased to have him back home. I don't know what I'd do without him. He helps me out so much. I lost my husband many years ago."

I muttered some condolences and didn't venture asking more about Frankie, hoping we could move on. I did feel bad for people being maligned because they didn't fit in. I'd had a taste of that since I was tall and towered above most of my classmates—female and male.

"Do forgive me for going on," Elsie said. "I believe we were talking about your place—Windwood is it?"

"Close—Wildwood. So anyway, as I mentioned when I came, I'm trying to find out some things about Wildwood land."

"Of course," Elsie said. "Exactly what are you hoping to learn about it?

"I have a person determined to purchase a particular piece of land, which has the remains of an old homestead. The person—his name is Alex Varga—claims his interest is to honor his father. I am skeptical of this person, to say the least."

"I see," Elsie said. "More likely fibbing about that. Probably one of those scammers trying to buy up property to develop and turn a profit.

They can be very sneaky and look for vulnerable landowners. I suspect that at some point your acreage was owned by a logging company—as was a lot of land around Upper Michigan. Probably your uncle purchased it from that company."

"That's what I understand. I know he said he got the land very cheap at the time. I didn't pay a lot of attention to the details when he talked about it. I was young and just there to ride the horses. Wish I had paid attention."

"Well, we all do wish that of our family history. Once they are gone, we've lost it unless someone writes it down."

"We've got a deed somewhere in his personal effects, but that doesn't help me understand why the man who visited me wants to purchase the property, unless as you say, he was prospecting for land to buy up for development. But why just that forty acres? Why not something with better terrain and closer access to utilities, roads, and other improvements?"

Elsie looked thoughtful for a moment. "I suppose there could be some kind of family connection that your gentleman is looking into. But I have to agree, it smells fishy."

"He said his family came from Croatia. His grandfather worked in the mines. But he didn't claim that any ancestors lived on that chunk of land—just fished and camped there. And frankly, the man was quite aggressive."

"Oh my," Elsie said. She looked thoughtful for a moment. "Upper Michigan was not very heavily sought after for homesteading. Most were interested in heading out West. People were allowed to acquire up to 160 acres—"

"That's how many acres I have at Wildwood," I said.

"Interesting," Elsie said. "Usually, the acreage doesn't stay intact. It's likely your uncle's land—now yours—was subject to homesteading, in that it was considered unowned, which was obviously a requirement. Of course, they didn't take into account the Indigenous people who were occupying any of it. But don't get me started on that!"

I nodded. Though a good deal of Peshekee County was still part of the Ojibwa Indian Reservation, much had been taken over by logging, mining, homesteading, and general sprawl.

"As I said," Elsie continued, "Upper Michigan was considered a true wilderness with not much to offer, so there wasn't the competition like down below or out West. But we did get some settlers who were used to incredible hardships and harsh weather, such as the Finnish immigrants who were seeking to become citizens of the United States. It is unfortunate that it was very difficult to make a go of farming or other endeavors, especially here in the U.P. However, there were jobs in logging camps and mining. Also, unfortunately, the Homestead Act was subject to a lot of issues."

"Such as?" I asked.

"Fraud. Some by land grabbers and developers, logging companies, railroads, and such. Often the homesteaders simply didn't have the means to purchase what they needed to build even a cabin, let alone a barn, livestock, tools, seeds, and so on."

"I noticed the old apple orchard at the homestead at my place," I said.

"Yes, they did try some orchards, but they took a while to bear fruit. And of course, insects, hungry wildlife, blight, and so on were always concerns."

"So, what about here in Peshekee County? I mean, was the homestead on my place, do you think, originally settled during the Homestead Act?"

"I'd say so," Elsie said.

"Wish I knew who—who was the first to settle it."

"Well, my research has shown that it all started with one person here in Peshekee County."

I perked up. Maybe I could make some sense of everything—Varga's intense demand for those acres—if I had a starting point. What was so damn special about it? I didn't believe for one minute that Varga was on the up and up.

Elsie looked thoughtful; her brow furrowed. "You know, I must say, there is a bit of a coincidence here."

"What?" I said.

"Well, I had a couple come in here a while back asking about homesteading in the area."

"Maybe a teacher or college student doing research?" I asked.

"They didn't say, but they didn't seem to be either. Truthfully, these people reminded me of aging hippies. They didn't claim to be teachers and seemed too old for the traditional college students. They said they were doing research on homesteading. The woman was working on writing a book, and the man said they were thinking of homesteading in the sense that you live off the land, don't have modern conveniences such as electricity and running water. People are all caught up in the simplicity of it all until winter hits. Then chopping firewood and melting snow for water becomes quite troublesome."

I nodded. I wasn't a fan of power outages or frozen water pipes.

"Anyway, the couple seemed to be stuck in the sixties. I remember those days," Elsie said wistfully. "I went to college downstate and it was all about love and peace, except it wasn't. There were a lot of not so good things that went on. Drugs for one."

"Still a lot of those around," I said.

"Oh, I know. But most of us boomers have grown up and moved on, for heaven's sake. Of course, folks could say that *I'm* caught in a time warp, with my obsession for the past. But it's strictly academic. I have no desire to live in the so-called good ol' days. Those two just seemed to be, I don't know, not authentic, with their outrageous hippie clothing. Don't get me wrong. They were nice and polite, but something about them was a bit off kilter."

We only had one pair of aging hippies I could think of, and they were now dead.

"How so?" I asked, hoping Elsie could be more specific.

"Well, for one thing, the man's facial hair looked fake. I mean, the moustache was crooked. And I swear the woman was wearing a wig with the long pigtails hanging down. A little bit of hair was leaking around the edges. It was like they were playing a role, like in that musical *Hair*. Oh my, that one caused a scandal!"

Elsie had a knack for wandering off track, but eventually I was getting some information. I found it interesting that Sheriff Olsen didn't mention the apparent disguises. Of course Lieutenant Spiller would not have reason to bring it up. Mainly he was focused on getting the drone back, not delving into the deaths of the couple—at least not with me.

"I don't suppose you saw what they were driving?" I asked.

"As a matter of fact, I did! One of those old VW campers, all fixed up. It was very nice. I just love old, preserved things. I suppose that's obvious," she said, sweeping her hand around, indicating the artifacts throughout the museum.

"Do you recall what they may have been looking at when they were here?" I asked.

"Well, I don't usually discuss other folks' business," she said. "I probably shouldn't have mentioned the coincidence of all the homestead questions, but I did find it interesting, and I just felt unsettled with their visit."

"I understand your concern," I said. "However, I'm quite certain that those two people are now, ah, deceased, and figuring out what they were doing here at the museum might provide a connection."

Of course, their deaths seemed likely to be accidental by ingesting water hemlock, but Lieutenant Spiller did let slip that their deaths were *suspicious*. And the sheriff had a similar view.

"Oh my!" Elsie said. "Of course. I did read about—it was *you* and that conservation officer who found them. Oh dear. I never made the connection at all. There wasn't much in the paper. That must have been a horrifying experience to come across their—remains."

"I'll admit it was pretty awful," I said. "So, I guess we are back to my wondering what they were looking into or looking at—you know, with them having passed away and all...."

"By all means. It's one of the most treasured things a museum can have. A journal. As I said, when people die, their stories die with them, unless they write them down. That couple asked about a journal involving a certain family. How they knew it would be here is a little bit of a mystery, but they said that during their research, the trail led here."

I nodded encouragingly. "Did they take this journal—check it out?"

"Oh, my, no," Elsie said, shaking her head vigorously. "We don't allow anything to leave the museum except for special loans to other museums or maybe for a school or college. But we always accompany the items and bring them back."

"So, would you mind...?"

"Of course," she said. "I'll get if for you. As I said, it all started with a single person—a woman."

"I beg your pardon?"

"A single woman started this journal. Her story is ordinary and extraordinary at the same time."

"Really?"

"Yes. Please come this way."

Elsie pulled some cotton gloves out of her pocket and put them on. "For some items we wear gloves so that the oils from our hands don't damage the artifact."

We walked over to a cabinet, and she removed some keys from her pocket. She slid one into the lock, opened the door, and pulled out a very old, tattered book with a green cloth cover. She cradled it as if it were a delicate piece of China.

She turned to me, still clutching the book. "An interesting thing about the Homestead Act is that single women who had come of age were legally allowed to homestead. It was a rare opportunity for women to strike out on their own rather than simply get married and depend on their man to support them. Often the men died in horrible accidents, leaving widows with children. Those widows were also allowed to homestead."

Elsie turned and led me to a very old wooden table. "I'll get you some gloves, and you are free to look through this journal and take photos or notes, but of course as I said, you can't take it with you. Please be mindful that the pages are very old and brittle, so due care is essential."

The door jingled, and a very large man lumbered in and looked around. He was wearing baggy shorts and a T-shirt a couple of sizes too small, and he had a lot of tattoos on his biceps. The man wore a cap over an apparent bald head and sported a goatee. He looked vaguely familiar, but that wasn't unusual in a small town. He looked around the museum and spotted Elsie talking to me. He gave me a hard look and scowled.

What was that all about? He continued to stare at me, so I smiled and waved. Elsie scurried over to her desk where she got some gloves out of a drawer and brought them to me.

"Now, if you'll excuse me, that is my son, Frankie. He's going to do some yard work, and I must get him keys to the maintenance shed."

"Thank you, Elsie," I said. "You've been beyond helpful."

She beamed. "I'm so pleased. Though I am sorry about that couple and their passing. I will include them in my prayers."

The journal was about eight by twelve inches in size. Its cloth cover was blank and had begun to unravel at the corners. A faded ribbon hung out of the bottom of the journal and likely served as a bookmark or maybe a keepsake. I carefully opened the cover to the first page, which simply said: *Property of Helvi Paavola Huntington.* The ink had faded, and the last part of the name, Huntington, appeared to be slightly darker. If I were a detective, I'd say it was inserted later; perhaps Helvi married and added it. On the inside of the front cover was a crudely drawn diagram of a family tree. I took my phone out and snapped a picture so I could decipher it later. I continued to carefully page through the journal, pausing briefly at the entries and taking more photos. At a glance, they appeared to be a recounting of ordinary events, such as the purchase of laying hens or the concern of frost on the vegetable garden. Helvi expressed great excitement when she wrote of gaining the position of salesclerk at "the Mercantile," which I believed might later have become Pete's General Store. It would take time to read all the entries. I took as many photos as possible, but it became obvious I would be making a few trips back to the museum. About halfway through the book, I found a very old photo tucked between the pages, which featured a tall, thin woman. Unlike the women in most photos of the era, Helvi Paavola Huntington wore baggy trousers, sturdy-looking boots, and a blousy shirt. And she was smiling.

17

Pounding and yelling jolted me out of my REM sleep. I leapt out of bed and rushed into the living room. More pounding on the front door.

"Whaaa—who's there?" I yelled.

"It's Clay. Fire! Call 911."

I yanked open the door and saw huge tongues of fire reaching for the sky.

"What's going on?" Aunt Lin asked as she stumbled into the living room.

"Fire—call 911," Clay repeated and hurried away. "I'll get a fire extinguisher."

I ran to my bedroom, grabbed my cell phone, and punched in the emergency number.

"911," said the dispatcher. "What's your emergency?"

"Fa-fire at the Wildwood Stables! Horse Camp Road." I struggled to get the words out.

Aunt Lin had thrown on some clothes and raced out the door.

In a calm voice, the dispatcher said, "Could you please tell me what kind of fire—kitchen? Grass fire—"

"Barn! The barn!" I said. "Oh God, the horses are in." I tore out the door, feet bare, still clutching my phone to my ear.

"You said a barn fire. Is it occupied?"

"Yeah, no—wait," I said.

As I approached the blaze, I could see that the flames were not coming from the barn but rather engulfed the Jeep.

"Car fire," I panted into the phone.

"A fire engine is being dispatched," she said. "Is the car occupied?"

"No—no, it was parked. It's—it's going down. The fire. Clay is spraying it with a fire extinguisher."

"Okay, ma'am. We'll have the truck there in a few minutes. Do you need an ambulance? Are there any injuries?"

"No—we're all fine. Omigod," I said. I was beginning to hyperventilate. I staggered toward the blackened frame of the Jeep but was knocked back by the intense heat. The air was acrid with the smell of melting steel, incinerated upholstery, and burning rubber. Thick, black smoke billowed from the destroyed interior of the Jeep. In no uncertain terms, the Jeep was toast.

"Would you like me to stay on the phone with you?" the dispatcher asked.

"No—but thanks. Gotta check on the horses."

I hurried over to Clay, who was still holding the fire extinguisher.

"Fire department's on the way," I said. "God. I really can't thank you enough for putting that—that inferno out before it spread to the barn."

"Mostly out," Clay said. "Fire extinguisher ran out of juice." He looked down at my feet. "Did you know you're not wearing shoes?"

"I need to check on the horses," I said. I could hear a siren off in the distance.

"Your aunt's in there. Maybe you should, ah, go get some shoes and other stuff on."

I realized I was wearing only a thin T-shirt that showed pretty much everything and baggy shorts that were sliding down. I hurried back into the mod, threw on a jacket, and stepped into my muck boots, not bothering with socks. I could hear the siren come closer, then drop off. Likely they had reached our road. I hurried back out to see the fire truck wheel into the parking area and a couple of firemen jump out and start pulling a hose off the truck. A third fireman—a woman—went over to the side of the truck and turned on the pump. The hose filled and came to life, and the two holding it directed the robust spray toward the smoldering remains of the Jeep. They also doused the area around the vehicle, presumably to avoid any grass igniting from stray sparks and flaming debris. The Jeep remains hissed with steam, and eventually the fire appeared totally extinguished.

I hightailed it to the barn and saw Aunt Lin rubbing Rusty's nose. The smell of smoke was present but not overpowering. I turned on a large exhaust fan positioned in the peak of the barn. Since the incident with the cut pasture fence, we had been keeping the horses in the barn at night. I was beyond grateful that the fire hadn't set the building on fire.

Aunt Lin turned to look at me. "Rusty's the most upset. The others seem okay."

"Thanks," I said, hurrying over to Oscar and Emmy's stall. They were huddled in the corner, nostrils flared, but not panicky. Big Mac had his head hanging over the stall door, calm and quiet. Maybe he would make a great horse for the therapy camp. Misty and Shadow nickered loudly, probably wondering what the fuss was all about and hoping it was feeding time.

I joined Aunt Lin at Rusty's stall. He was relaxing; his lip drooped a little. She looked at me and frowned.

"I know," I said. "This was no accident—or bored kids up to mischief."

Clay came in and joined us. He looked at me and said, "One of them out there wants to talk to you."

My mind was still spinning from the adrenaline rush. It was beginning to look like someone was sabotaging Wildwood. It was true Clay was the first one on the scene, but then that was really no mystery, since he was camped out near the stable. And who would do such a thing? Alex Varga popped into the forefront.

I headed outside and saw the firemen reeling the hose back into the truck. The firewoman came over to me, holding a clipboard. She wore a nametag that said *Robertson.*

"Everything appears to be out," she said.

I saw the headlights of a vehicle bounce down Horse Camp Road toward us.

"Looks like the police are here," Robertson said. "Anyway, sometimes hot spots will reignite. Keep an eye out and call us back if needed."

"Thank you so much for getting here so quickly," I said. "I—I can't imagine if the barn…." I felt a sob coming on. I hated that—when my voice got all warbly and a giant lint ball seemed stuck in my throat.

"We're just glad nobody was hurt and that you didn't lose any livestock," Robertson said.

The approaching vehicle was a state police cruiser. It pulled up and stopped. I recognized the trooper—it was Sergeant Witz. She spoke into the microphone clipped to her shirt and then headed over to Robertson and me. Witz looked at the smoldering remains and formed a silent *wow* with her mouth.

Witz and Robertson greeted each other, then Sergeant Witz looked at me. "We meet again," she said.

"Truthfully," I said, "I'd like to stop meeting this way."

She turned to the firewoman and said, "So, what we got here?"

"Car fire," Robertson said. "Just starting to question the witness."

"That would be me," I said. The bobbing headlights of another vehicle made their way down Horse Camp Road.

"More company," I said. "I wonder..." Then I noticed the car as the Olsen SUV. Nikko. I felt a little jump in my chest.

"I'll just need some information," Robertson said. "And if Sergent Witz here has questions...."

"I'll need to do a report, too," Witz said.

"Fire away," I said.

Both women looked at me, clearly suppressing laughter. Okay, bad choice of words. Nikko pulled up next to the other vehicles, threw open the door of the SUV and jumped out. He looked around and saw the Jeep rubble, then spotted me with Robertson and Witz and hurried over.

"Are you all right? The car—what happened?" he asked.

"This is my friend-who-is-a boy, CO Nikko Olsen," I said by way of introduction to Robertson and Witz.

Nikko gave me a puzzled look.

"Well, boyfriend sounds so—middle school," I said.

"So does friend-who-is-a-boy. Anyway, is anyone gonna tell me what's going on?"

"Well, a fire—" I began.

"I *know* there is—was a fire. Dad heard it on the police radio he keeps on all the time and called me. He said the staties were going to respond since the sheriff's department only has one cruiser on tonight, and it's way at the other end of the county. But I thought I'd make sure, you know, that you were okay."

"I'm okay now," I said. I gave Nikko a quick synopsis of the night's events while Robertson and Witz jotted down some notes on their clipboards.

"So," Robertson said, "if you could just give me—us," she added and nodded toward Sergeant Witz "—some information, we'll go ahead and wrap things up."

"Sure."

First, she got my particulars, such as name, address, contact info, and so on, then said, "Of course the vehicle is a total loss. What make was it?"

"A Jeep."

"Do you know what year and model?" Sergent Witz said.

"Well, no, it was old, though, and in rough shape. It actually belongs—belonged to Mike's Auto. It was a loaner."

"Okay, well you can tell Mike he can get a report for insurance purposes," Witz said.

I had doubts that insurance would be of much help in this case. Mike had loaned me transportation and it was now a twisted pile of rubble.

Sergeant Witz looked at me and said, "Do you have any idea how the fire started? Had you been having issues with the vehicle, say with the fuel pump or a gas leak?"

Nikko chuckled. "Kat here is the queen of bad luck when it comes to cars."

I glared at him and he forced his smirk into a straight face.

"It had a lot of issues," I said, "but it's not like I was driving it when it caught fire. I got home from work and an errand and parked it there around suppertime. How could it just—combust?"

"Do you suspect arson?" the firewoman asked.

"You mean like vandalism?" *Or sabotage*, I thought.

"Did you say there might be insurance on the vehicle?" Sergeant Witz asked. She gave me a steady look.

"Hey," I said. "I know what you're thinking. But, look, the Jeep was a proverbial piece of shit. It wasn't worth more than a couple of hundred bucks as scrap. Probably Mike has a big deductible on the cars he sells—if he has insurance at all, so I don't see insurance fraud as what is going on here."

"Okay then," Witz said. "I think we will put this fire down as suspicious and ask for an investigation. We'll cordon off the area for now until the fire marshal can get with our crime scene gang and take a look."

"Okay," I said. "Thanks."

Aunt Lin and Clay came over and joined the group. Witz and Robertson got Clay's name and asked him a few questions, since he was the one who discovered the fire. Clay said he saw nobody. He awakened when he heard an explosion and bright lights filled his camper.

"I never heard any explosion," I said.

"Well, it was more like a loud pop," Clay said, "then a whoosh."

"Gas tank, maybe," Nikko said.

"Once a car fire gets started," Robertson said, "it can be quite a spectacle. Often things pop and even explode when they expand from the heat."

"But how would it—just start like that?" I said.

"That's what we need to find out," Sergent Witz said. "But for now, just please stay clear of the, ah, Jeep, and we'll be looking into things in the next few days."

Eventually Robertson headed to the pumper. She and the waiting crew climbed in and the fire truck lumbered away. Witz handed me her business card and asked me to call if I noticed anything suspicious. Hell, the *whole* thing was suspicious. I contemplated whether I should have mentioned Varga. I continued the mental debate as I watched her head to her patrol car and drive off.

"This stinks to high heaven," Aunt Lin said. "Literally and figuratively."

"Wasn't any kids that did this," Clay said, looking over at the wreckage.

"I don't think it was kids that cut the fence, either," I said. I looked at him. "I wonder if the two things are connected."

"Hard to believe they're not," Clay said.

"I don't like this one bit," Nikko said. "What's next?"

We all chewed on that thought for a moment.

"We need security," Aunt Lin said. "I'm calling Raymond and seeing how much cameras and stuff would cost. He has connections."

We checked on the horses one more time; then Clay went to his camper.

"I'll make tea," Aunt Lin said, heading to the mod.

"Alone at last," Nikko said, pulling me into him.

I clung to him, taking in the warmth and comfort of the embrace. Night sounds took over the silence: crickets, an owl, and the distant yip of a coyote. For a moment I felt it was all a dream and I was at peace, then an annoying sob worked its way into my reverie. In a flash, I was blubbering into Nikko's shoulder.

"Hey," he said. "It's okay. We'll get to the bottom of this."

I pulled away and looked at him. "Varga?"

"Maybe," Nikko said. "But why and how? I mean, the man didn't strike me as someone who would want to soil his hands and fancy suit by starting a fire—"

"Or crawling around in the dark, cutting fence wire," I added.

We were thoughtful for a moment.

"Maybe he has somebody do his dirty work," I said.

"I hate to mention this, but your stable hand there, Clay, seemed to have come around about the time Mr. Varga braced you."

"So? Oher people have come around too."

"Such as?" Nikko asked.

"Well, Willie Moss, but she's legit with the Magic Stirrup Foundation, and we had an appointment and all. Otherwise, it's just Aunt Lin, Clay, and me."

"So, back to Clay…we don't know much about him," Nikko said. "I'm wondering if you ever did that background check."

"As a matter of fact, I did," I said, infusing my tone with indignation.

"And…?"

"Still, ah, waiting." It was partly true. I was waiting to talk to Clay. "Besides, I don't for a minute think he was involved. I mean, why would he? What possible motivation could he have to cause me trouble?"

"Just leaving no stone unturned," Nikko said. "He seems like a solid guy to me, but he is a stranger who just showed up. And it is a bit of a coincidence that Varga came from under his rock about the same time."

"Well, Clay answered my ad, so there is that. He didn't really just *show up*."

"True. So, we're back to Varga," Nikko said. "The vandalism—or sabotage—happening shortly after his visit, and he does have a motive, although a bit vague. Maybe you need to mention Mr. Varga to Sergeant Witz. I'm pretty sure they suspect arson with the Jeep. And it's obvious that neither you nor Mike gained a thing by the vehicle being torched. Arson is a felony and I don't think they will brush you off."

"It all seems so dramatic," I said. "I mean, Varga *did* give me the willies, but what would he or anyone accomplish by sabotaging Wildwood?"

"Hoping you'd throw in the towel, maybe. Cave and sell him that piece of land so that the unfortunate incidents quit."

I thought for a moment and felt my figurative hackles stand up. "That blowhard can go back to Croatia on a leaky boat. If he's behind this, we're gonna find out. I will admit, I'm on edge, though, wondering what will be next. Okay, I'll get in touch with Sergeant Witz. I just don't want to talk to that lieutenant. He will find a way for me to feel guilty about coloring my hair."

"You color your hair?" Nikko said.

"Sometimes, when I have extra money," I snapped. "Anyway, that's between my stylist and me, so butt out."

Nikko held up his hands as if warding off potential punches.

"Sorry," I said. "I'm a little on edge."

"Sure, I know, you've had a rough night. So, are you doing okay?" he asked, putting his arm around my shoulder. "Do you want me to stay?"

"No, I know you have to work tomorrow. So do I, for that matter. Horses still gotta be taken care of. We'll be fine." I had to admit it was tempting, but the idea of needing protection from the boogeyman didn't sit right. "Don't you have wild pigs to hunt down?"

"That I do," Nikko said, dropping his arm to his side. "Turns out they're actually domestic, not wild. They are Russian boars and quite aggressive."

"Russian boars! Cripes, I don't want to run into one of them."

"Yeah. They escaped from a farm raising them—well, it's really a hunting outfit. The animals are enclosed and people come in and shoot them along with whitetails and elk."

"That's disgusting!" I said.

"The place is owned by Cam and Valerie Jesson."

"I went to high school with Val. Well, it was Kline then. Yeah, Valerie Kline. She was a stuck-up bitch."

"I think I dated her," Nikko said with a grin.

"I'm sure you did. Okay, she was gorgeous and athletic. I admit she kicked ass on the volleyball court. Homecoming queen and all. After graduation, we all thought she'd go on to college and set the world on fire. As I recall, Valerie Kline got married because, as they used to say, she *had to*. It happened. Now she's running a game ranch."

"So, shotgun weddings aside," Nikko said, "the Jesson piggies apparently burrowed under the fence and escaped into the wild. Cam suspected someone sabotaged the operation by bending up the chain link and digging out some dirt to give a means for the critters to escape."

"A lot of sabotage going on in Peshekee County," I said.

"Probably not connected," Nikko said. "*And* there is a question of the legality of the porkies themselves, since they're considered an exotic species. Yet they're really domestic animals so we can't just shoot them. Like I told you before, they're messing up the ecosystem, rooting things up, decimating nests and so on. They need to be rounded up and sent back to the farm. The whole thing is a cluster that will be tied up in court."

"And here I thought you were just a fish cop," I said.

"I wish."

I looked again at the burned-out Jeep and shivered.

"Sure you don't want me to stay?"

"Yep—I mean, nope. I'm good. I'll go have some tea with Aunt Lin."

Nikko kissed me goodbye, climbed in the SUV, and drove off. I watched the vehicle work its way down the road, then I headed for the mod. There was no point in trying to go back to bed. I slumped at the kitchen table while my aunt conjured up some tea. I wondered how I'd break the news of the incinerated Jeep to Mike. And to Mom and Dad, for that matter.

Jupiter entered the kitchen and looked at his empty food bowl. I swear he looked at the clock, shrugged, and strutted off. The cat could tell time.

"You have a way with motor vehicles," Aunt Lin said, handing me a cup of her concoction. "This is the third one under your care that got, shall I say, rendered immobile. Too bad Uber doesn't come out here."

I took a cautious sip and decided the tea wasn't too bad.

"And I got no wheels. Again," I said with a sigh.

"Well, you can borrow mine until you figure something out."

There comes a time when a girl must admit defeat in her quest for independence and humble herself before her parents, seeking help. There was no shame in that, was there?

18

I borrowed Aunt Lin's Subaru and drove it to Mike's Auto Sales and Service and hunted him down. He was in the service bay under a car perched high on the lift.

"Hey!" he said. "That the Subaru my gang of kids fixed up?"

"Yeah," I said. "Sure is. Aunt Lin lent it to me."

"So, Jeep died on ya did it?" Mike asked. "Want me to bring the wrecker?"

"Oh, well, no need. I mean, yeah, it's definitely dead and eventually you might need to haul it off on, I don't know, maybe a trailer or something."

I told him my tale of woe about the fire and how the Jeep was now a mere puddle of melted waste. Mike stood there for a moment with his mouth gaping while wiping his hands on an oily rag.

"I'll pay you for the loss as soon as, ah, maybe next payday. How much do you think it was worth?"

Mike furrowed his brow, calculating its worth.

"I figure twenty bucks," he finally said.

"Twenty bucks! I know it is—or was—worth more than that as scrap."

"Yeah, I suppose, but it gets embarrassing sending too much stuff to the scrapyard. Makes it look like my lot is full of a bunch of junkers."

I looked around. His lot *was* full of a bunch of junkers.

"Are you sure?" I asked. Maybe I wouldn't have to beg my parents for help after all. Or at least not to quite the degree I had imagined.

"Oh yeah, I'm sure. You got a photo or anything?"

"Can you get insurance? I do have a photo!"

"Insurance? Hah. Too big a deductible, and even if it was worth making a claim, my rates would just go up. Nope, twenty bucks will buy me a burger and maybe a beer. Now I wanna see what she looks like."

I pulled out my phone and scrolled to one of the photos of the fiery aftermath. Mike whistled and started to chuckle. "Can yous send me that? I want to show the fellas at Carl's." He pulled a phone out of his pocket and gave me his number.

Carl's was the local bar and grill where the locals went for the Friday fish fry, beer, pool, and to listen to live music on the weekends. I shot Mike a text with the attached photo and pulled a twenty out of my purse.

"You made my day, Kat. You need to borrow another car? You have a reputation to keep up, you know? Maybe I can get some bets going on how long the next one will last. I could make a bundle, eh?"

I was mortified. A bet as to when my next vehicular annihilation would occur was humiliating. However, one must sometimes swallow her pride in the name of pragmatism.

"Whatcha got?" I asked.

* * *

After chores the next morning, I called the state police post and asked for Sergeant Witz. I was told she was on days off and would be back for third watch on Tuesday. The dispatcher assured me she'd take a message and see that the sergeant got it.

The Jeep carcass was even uglier in daylight. Yellow crime-scene tape surrounded it, and a hideous halo of scorched earth made a near-perfect circle around the auto carcass. I assumed somebody from either the fire department or state police would be coming out to go over things at some point, so the eyesore would likely be with me for a while. I was no expert, but I couldn't imagine that there would be any evidence left in the ashes and twisted metal. If the arsonist used gasoline to start the fire, so what? The Jeep had half a tank when I parked it. Obviously, fingerprints and tiny hair or fabric samples would have been vaporized. So, unless the culprit was really stupid and dropped something or was spotted making his or her getaway, we had nothing.

Even though it was Sunday, chores still needed to be done, so there wasn't the option of lingering over coffee and the gluten-free cinnamon buns Aunt Lin had made. They actually weren't bad, especially smeared with my secret stash of butter.

Clay and I had turned the horses out into the pasture and were mucking out the stalls when I heard the crunch of gravel from a car pulling in. I went out to find Raymond and Gussy getting out of Gussy's beater car. Gussy went over to the decimated Jeep and made a whistling noise.

"Lin says yous need some security cameras," Raymond said. "I got several motion-activated ones here from the electronic repurpose pile at the recycle center. They're good for inside or outdoors. I suggest one on each corner of the barn on this side, one down the aisle, and maybe another pointing toward the road or where you got the horses out there. They don't have a real long range, but the resolution is pretty good."

"Wow," I said. "That was quick—you getting some equipment. Those locations for mounting them seem good to me." I let out a big sigh. "Things have been, well, a little crazy around here."

"I see that," Raymond said, nodding toward the burned car. "Gussy here is interested in learning about technology, so I brought him along."

"Great," I said. "Hi, Gussy."

"Hey," Gussy said. "Man, I've never seen anything like that burnt-up car. Can I take a photo?"

"Sure."

"Sweet!" I hadn't seen him that chipper for a long time. I suspected a cute young intern was the reason.

"So, Raymond," I said, "did you drop off that drone to Lieutenant Spiller?"

"Yeah. Well, actually I left it at the front desk and told the trooper there that the bossman wanted the thing. You should have seen the look on that guy's face. Guess they weren't expecting a two-hundred pound Indian to come in bearing gifts."

"Bet that was a hoot."

"Yeah, it was rich," he said.

"Oh, and you were going to check around with the tribe about any rumors of mining or logging."

"I put my feelers out, but so far I'm coming up with zip. I'll let you know if I get anything."

"Okay, well the mystery continues. Thanks for everything. We'll pay you for your time here with these cameras."

"Nah, I got this. Don't like Lin and you being the targets of whatever is going on at this place. Once we get things installed, it'll be rigged so that the video can go wireless to your laptop. You can review the recording each day, or whenever you want."

"I can't thank you enough," I said. "Things have been, well—"

"Damn scary." He looked at the melted car, then at the rust bucket Mike had lent me.

"I see yous got something new to drive," Raymond said.

"New would not be how I'd describe it; more like better than nothing. Barely."

The replacement vehicle was a 2007 Ford pickup with rusted-out bed, dismembered tailpipe, oxidized hood, missing tailgate, cracked windshield, and bald tires. According to Mike, who lent me the truck, it was disposable, so I needn't worry if I went over a pothole and the chassis snapped in half or the exhaust system bit the dust.

Gussy came over and said, "Got all the stuff out of the car. Hey, Kat, any idea how the fire started?"

"Maybe," I said, dodging the question.

If I said anything in front of Gussy, it would soon be shared with Rose and, ultimately, the entire village of Peshekee, and I didn't want to have to deal with that just yet. It was bad enough breaking the news to Mom and Dad. Both—especially Mom—suggested I consider moving back home. Of course that wasn't even a remote option. There was Aunt Lin and Clay and a growing herd of horses to consider. Nope, I was in for the long haul at Wildwood Stables. I had wisely withheld any mention to my parents about Alex Varga's offer that I "couldn't refuse." It wouldn't be long, however, before that info got leaked. If things got any dicier, I would buy a gun. Dad had taught me something about shooting when I was a tween. I thought it was totally cool but had no desire to go hunting with him, which ended the firearms lessons.

I told Raymond where to get the extension ladder and to let me know if he needed a hand. By the time I got done with Raymond, Clay had finished up barn duty and was putting the wheelbarrow away.

"So, Clay," I said. "How's the shoulder?"

"Good as new," he said, rotating his arm. "Probably shouldn't do any weightlifting, though."

I told him about the motion cameras, and he headed for his camper as I went back to the mod for a second cup of coffee and another cinnamon bun. Nikko and I were going to take another ride out to the homestead later that afternoon. Meanwhile, I was going to bring up some photos I took of Helvi Paavola Huntington's journal and see if there were any clues about the old homestead.

Just as I sat at my laptop, my cell phone neighed at me. I loved that ringtone. The readout said MSF and wasn't local. Magic Stirrup Foundation?

"Hello," I said.

"Hi Kat. Willie Moss here from Magic Stirrup."

"Willie, hello. How are things going?"

"Well, first I want to apologize for acting so damn spacey there at the campground. I mentioned to my shrink that I'd seen a ghost horse and she said that stress can cause hallucinations and suggested I take a break from work and go someplace peaceful. Hah!"

I felt a twinge of guilt for not being straight with Willie. Time to fess up. "Ah, Willie, I do apologize for your experience. I think what you may have seen was a hologram."

"A what?" she asked.

"A hologram. It's created with a projector, mirrors, maybe a laser—I don't know. I looked into it and found that at one time a hologram show was used to entertain back there at the campground when families with kids were camping. I've talked to my techie friend and all. So, no worries about hallucinations. What you saw was probably something residual, er, from whatever was rigged up there."

The last part was a total fabrication on my part. I doubted there was such a thing as a *residual* hologram. I sounded about as convincing as a traveling salesman selling snake oil. I had seen the images myself back in the spring, and at that time, Raymond had said there had been a hologram setup at the campground, but the equipment had been removed for months. Still, Raymond was a little dodgy about the whole thing.

"Well, thank God for that!" Willie said. "Now I can tell my shrink I've solved my own problem and demand a refund. She charges a fortune."

"Well, again, so sorry to have concerned you."

"Oh, I love it. Life is a collection of stories, isn't it? *Anyway,* I'm calling for a reason."

My heart picked up a few beats. Was the whole deal for the kids' camp going down the tube? No, she sounded way too upbeat for bad news.

"We got final approval for funding what I'm calling the Magic Stirrup Camp, and the renovations can begin. I expect a crew to visit your place in the next week to assess what needs to be done. It will be a process and take the rest of summer and well into the fall, I'm sure, but we'll get there! Plus, I'll have a lease payment for you by the end of the month."

Music to my ears! The end of the month was just around the corner. "Hey, Willie, that's fantastic. Thanks so much. Wait 'til I tell Susie."

"Yes, do tell that go-getter that her vision will become a reality. Hey, we'll talk later. I gotta go, but wanted to let you know that the proverbial check is in the mail. *And* I am relieved I'm not hallucinating."

Things were once again looking up. Since the good times were rolling, I decided to transfer my photos of Helvi's journal to my laptop and see what they had to offer. The museum volunteer, Elsie, had said it had all begun with one woman. Elsie seemed to be offering me a jumble of puzzle pieces to put together. And it started with Helvi Paavola Huntington.

The first photo I brought up was of a somewhat crudely sketched family tree. Those things always confused me once we got into third and fourth generations, but I studied it anyway. Helvi was the daughter and apparently only child of Eero and Kaija Paavola—clearly Finnish names, with birth and death dates written beside their names. I wondered if they had immigrated to America or if Helvi was the first generation to make the journey. Her date of birth was September 14, 1876, and no date of death was recorded, which made sense, since it was her personal journal.

A line connected Helvi to the name of William Edward Huntington with a date of June 26, 1905. I figured this to be their wedding day. Helvi would have been the ripe old age of twenty-nine years or so, likely considered past her prime for marriageability.

There was no recording of William's parents. Helvi and William had four children, two boys and two girls. They all had what I considered biblical names: Sarah, Matthew, Luke, and Ruth. The four children came into the world from 1906 to 1912. Of the Huntington offspring, Matthew, Luke, and Ruth married and had children. Sarah, the oldest, had no indication she was married, but she did have a line leading to a child, "baby boy," but no name or date of birth was listed. I suspected that Sarah's child was born out of wedlock, or maybe stillborn or adopted. Unfortunately, the family tree ended with Helvi and William's grandchildren. I surmised by the mid to late-1900s, Helvi Paavola Huntington had aged or even passed away. Folks were lucky to make it into their sixties in those days.

Somewhere within the Huntington timelines, Word War I took place, followed by the Great Depression. I wondered if William served in the First World War, which started a couple of years after the last child was born. The next generations would have brought them through World War II, Korea, Vietnam, and the baby boomer/hippie counterculture, and eventually into the twenty-first century.

Other than Sarah's child, everything seemed in order in the Huntington family. As far as I could tell, the name Varga was not in the mix. Of course, according to Alex Varga, the connection to the homestead parcel on my land was simply a special place to go, which didn't hold much water in my bucket. Also, I wasn't sure exactly where in Peshekee County that Helvi Paavo Huntington staked her claim under the Homestead Act. I would need something that would tie the Huntington family to Wildwood land. Simply having a stream nearby or an old apple orchard wasn't enough. Peshekee County had dozens of streams and rivers, and abandoned apple orchards were abundant.

I was hoping more research into Helvi's life as a pioneer woman would enlighten me as to its specific location and the timelines when the Huntington family occupied it. At some point, they would have moved or passed away. I wasn't thrilled at the idea of going back to the Peshekee Register of Deeds office and rooting around in the dusty county building basement trying to decipher the microfiche records.

And of course, no county records would reveal why Alex Varga wanted that land. When Varga fed me his tale, he probably figured I'd be more interested in dollar signs than his flimsy story. But he had miscalculated, and I highly suspected he was moving on to plan B: sabotage. I needed to figure out what Varga was really after, and I was sure it wasn't a trip down his family's memory lane.

19

I read a few more photo pages from Helvi's journal while I waited for Nikko to show up and join me for another horseback ride to the old homestead. I had also invited Susie Koskinen, who had exploded with excitement when I told her about the final approval of the Magic Stirrup Camp.

The early pages of the journal related to Helvi's life as a single woman in a rugged and harsh land.

I feel truly blessed to be granted this parcel of land, but fear that with winter approaching and no real shelter, I must seek a temporary situation within town. With only the tent and water from the stream, I do not see the future I had hoped for. While I still have a small amount of cash, it will not be sufficient to build even the most humble structure. My provisions are low and to replenish is beyond my means. I turn to God and ask for His guidance.

And I thought I had it rough, running a horse stable by the seat of my pants. At least the pantry was stocked and I had a furnace for heat and others to help me. I moved to my next journal page photo. Things were looking up a bit for my Helvi.

Oh blessed day! I have secured a situation with the Mercantile in town. The kindly owner Samuel Huntington and his wife Mary offered me a clerking position and living quarters located above the store. I shall be content for the winter to live within town and among others, for it is surely lonely in the wilderness with only the pines and flowing water for companions. I thought there would be others staking their claims, but it would seem not.

Aha! I thought. The Huntington name again. And according to Helvi's journal entry, she was the only one likely to have homesteaded in the area. It was just as Elsie from the museum suggested: It all started with one person. But while that built a strong case for Helvi being the homesteader on my back parcel, it did not give me a clue as to what was in it for Varga, and why he came all the way up into the Northwoods to acquire it.

I scanned a couple of pages, reading about the progress of Helvi Paavo's life. I was curious about her marriage to William—how they met and what made her abandon her life as a single woman for marriage and children.

I was introduced to the nephew of Mr. and Mrs. Huntington who planned an evening of a social sort for us. His name was William Edward Huntington and he had come to visit his aunt and uncle, who had done much to raise him because his parents perished of the consumption. It was a tragic story, indeed. However, I wasn't terribly interested in being courted by Mr. Huntington, but thought it polite to socialize so as not to seem ungrateful. But I came to find William a dear and gentle man, who showed complete devotion toward his aunt and uncle. I was quite taken by him and felt my heart warm.

Oh boy, now it was getting interesting. She gave me a little more information on how things panned out for her and William. While she had acquired the standard 160 acres of land via the Homestead Act, William apparently made no land claim. He did, however, have a fair amount of inherited wealth and was able to substantially contribute to the development of Helvi's acreage by building a *sturdy and spacious cabin*, as she called it. They were also able to build a barn, purchase livestock, plant crops, and basically make a viable farm. It sounded like the perfect union.

I was dying to know if Helvi continued to be her own woman, in spite of having wifely and motherly duties. Unfortunately, I hadn't photographed the pages that would have revealed those years of her marriage and raising a brood of youngsters, as was the norm of the day. I'd have to go back to the museum and check out that part of the journal I'd skipped over. I was getting more enthralled with Helvi's life story than finding out what was so special about that hardscrabble chunk of land she owned.

I had only one journal photo left in my collection. In it Helvi spoke of the rocky soil, which made it difficult to till. She mentioned a giant boulder with what she described as white and gold streaks, which I suspected to be quartz and pyrite. Helvi wrote: *I call it my spirit rock. The brilliant white gleams with the purity of our Lord Jesus and the gold reflects the richness of his love. I go there to ask God for favors and thank Him for His many blessings.*

I was touched by this woman and felt a jolt of resolve being infused into my life from her. How did my setbacks even remotely compare to the grit and reverence of Mrs. Helvi Paavola Huntington, who found spirituality in a rock?

* * *

After shutting down my computer and pulling on my riding breeches and boots, I headed toward the barn and saw a vehicle working its way down Horse Camp Road. I figured it to be either Nikko (on time for once) or Susie. But as it drew closer, I recognized the fancy Mercedes mincing its way toward me.

Crap. I only knew one person who drove a Mercedes. And for the moment, I was solo at the stable, since Lin had run into town with Raymond and Gussy to get some items from the hardware store before it closed. Clay had taken off earlier as well to empty the waste tanks in his camper at the local campground dump station. The Mercedes purred into the parking lot and glided to a stop. Varga stepped out of the car and smiled.

"Good afternoon, Miss Wilde," Varga said.

I didn't answer.

Varga turned his attention to the Jeep remains and clucked his tongue. "Oh my, what happened here?"

"Why don't you tell me?" I asked, trying to sound badass.

"I beg your pardon?"

"Before I call the police to have you removed from my property, I'll ask you nicely to please leave."

He looked at me, then up at the video camera mounted on the corner of the barn.

"Well, well," he said.

I took out my cell phone and Varga held his hands out as if pushing something away. "If you'll just hear me out, Miss Wilde...perhaps I can explain."

"I'm listening."

"I haven't been quite honest with you."

* * *

After Varga left, I went back to the mod, popped open a can of beer, and took an enormous pull. I heard an approaching vehicle and went out on the mod porch, swigging my beer. I was still not certain if I should believe Varga's latest story. And there were large gaps he promised to fill in when he could. Meanwhile, the offer to purchase the property remained.

Nikko pulled up and swung the SUV around to the porch where I was standing. He got out and looked at me. He still wore jeans, but I noticed he had swapped his tennis shoes for cowboy boots.

"Howdy partner," I said, pointing at his boots. "Did y'all bring yer ten-gallon hat?"

"Little early for booze, isn't it?"

"Nope. Ish five ah cluck shum wahr...."

"How many have you had?"

"Just this one," I said, laughing. "I was pranking you—y'all. Ready to ride? Oh, and I had another visit from Varga."

"What! Did he threaten you? When—"

"Relax, your plucky gal sent him packin'. But now there's a new story. I'll tell you on our ride out to the homestead."

My phone dinged and I looked at the readout. It was a text from Susie.

Cant come to ride. Miss Moss needs me to do somethin for camp

Ok Good luck (emoji of crossed fingers)

"So, I guess it's just you and me—partner," I said. "Who do you want to ride?"

"Which horse is cleanest?"

"None of them."

* * *

"So Varga admitted that his lame story about his grandfather and father finding respite on the parcel with the old homestead was bogus?" Nikko asked.

"Yup. Varga said he thought I'd buy it and be happy to get a few bucks for a little chunk of land that really isn't worth anything. His words, not mine."

We had saddled up Rusty and Mac and were plodding along the trail toward the homestead. Mac was a very sweet horse, but an awkward mount because of his height and width. I had to duck low-hanging branches. The weather was warm, but not blistering hot, and the humidity was decent. Had it not been for the deer flies orbiting our heads, the day would have been perfect for a ride. We veered off the single-file trail onto a two-track and were able to ride side-by-side, which made talking easier.

"Like I said, Mr. Varga admits his story about some sentimental value of the old homestead was total fabrication. Guess he thought if he bullied me and waved a few grand under my nose, I'd quake in my boots and part with a few acres."

"Got that wrong," Nikko said, grinning. "But what's his game?"

"Well, the mystery continues. He swore his interest was legit and thrilling—his words—but couldn't become public because of the risk that others not so honest as he—again, his words, not mine—might make things difficult. He assured me that once some things were verified, he would make his mission known, and it is something that will greatly benefit mankind."

"Sounds like a load of bull to me," Nikko said, swishing a deer fly off Rusty's neck. "Is he from some federal or state agency?"

"Varga would not say who or what exactly he represents, but did say he was *not* from the government. And he swears he had nothing to do with the cut fence or car fire. He may have been lying—he's very good at that, but did say he was offended that I would accuse him of such tactics."

"Well, what were you supposed to think?"

"Exactly. And he did take note of the cameras Raymond and Gussy put up."

"So what have you found out about the homestead?" Nikko asked.

"I'm reading parts of a journal by a woman who, according to the volunteer at the museum, started the whole thing. That's how she put it."

"A woman?"

"Yup," I said. "Hear us roar."

"Oh, I hear you," Nikko said.

"The volunteer at the museum, Elsie Tuttle, has a son I guess we'd call an adult with special needs. Something about him seemed familiar and made me a little uncomfortable when he glared at me."

"Glared at you?"

"Yeah, I figure because I was tying up his mother and he was impatient. She said he had been gone a while, but I didn't pry."

"Tuttle, you say?"

"Yeah. A big bruiser of a dude; his mom called him Frankie."

"Frank Tuttle," Nikko said. "Guess he's out."

"Wait...out?"

"Yeah, prison. Don't you remember him from high school?"

We stopped our horses and I looked at Nikko. "Mr. Frank," I said. "The janitor? That's why something seemed familiar. He had hair then. I didn't even know his last name in school. Mr. Frank made himself a peephole to spy on the girls' shower room. The creep cornered me once and—and, well, he said he liked my hair. Major yuck!"

"Yup. He also poaches—or did, I hear. I think he also worked at the scrapyard."

"But Mr. Frank was just kind of, well, doughy and had long stringy hair. Elsie's Frankie has a shaved head and some muscle and a lot of tattoos."

"Prison will do that," Nikko said.

"The kids called him Franken-sped."

"Franken-sped?"

"Yeah. Sped stands for special ed."

"Harsh."

"I thought it was mean to call him that. But, of course, I wanted to fit in so didn't say anything. Guess I'm glad I can make amends with this riding therapy camp for kids."

"We all change—grow up, I guess," Nikko said. "I wasn't up for any virtue awards when I was in high school either."

"So I recall," I said, smirking at him. "Mr. *Jock*. But back to Mr. Franken…er, Frank. He got fired and all for supposedly making moves on girls, but nothing came of it."

"Oh, he was doing a lot more," Nikko said. "He was selling weed, smack, snow—you name it—to minors. A kid died. I very clearly remember it because my dad was deep into the investigation."

"Jimmy Hanson," I said. "I remember that he died but heard it was a problem with medication."

"Yeah, an overdose of fentanyl. His parents were devastated, and the family moved away."

"Wow," I said.

"I think the deer flies have found us," Nikko said.

"Yeah, let's get going."

I urged Mac into a trot, then we broke into a canter. I was pleased with Nikko's progress in horsemanship. He had decent form and was grinning ear to ear. Then the idiot said, "Race ya!" and urged Rusty into a gallop.

I didn't have much chance of winning a race riding a lumbering draft horse, but asked Mac to give me what he had. Surprisingly, he gave a little buck and took off like a shot, catching up with Rusty and Nikko.

"Eat my dust!" I yelled, pulling ahead.

We rounded a corner, and dead ahead was a downed tree over the road. There was no time to pull up, and I pointed my horse toward an opening between some gnarly branches. Mac's ears pricked forward. He took an enormous stride, then launched over the tree, allowing at least a couple of feet clearance. Another buck and we shot on down the trail. I heard a whoop, then a yelp, and glanced back over my shoulder. Well, maybe Nikko still needed some more hours in the saddle before we tried jumping. He and Rusty had parted ways, and Nikko was on his hands and knees at the side of the road. I caught Rusty and led him over.

"You okay?" I asked.

Nikko stood and brushed himself off, then muttered something. He remounted and didn't say a word as we resumed our ride at a sensible walk.

"Not speaking?"

Nikko had sustained a couple of nasty scratches, probably from the branches on the fallen tree. He dabbed at them with a bandana.

"Are you sure you don't want me to look at those cuts."

He shook his head.

"You know you need to fall off a horse regularly to join the club," I said. "There is no shame—in fact there is glory in a spectacular fall."

Nikko didn't answer and cast me a dirty look.

"I mean, at least you didn't land in a thornbush and get your head bonked like I did."

Nikko smiled.

"Or have to be hauled out on a stretcher through the thicket with the guys moaning and groaning about your weight."

Now Nikko laughed.

* * *

The day was getting on when we arrived at the homestead. We rode the horses to the little nearby stream and let them drink. The ripple of the water always mesmerized me and somehow drowned out daily worries. I could hear the Peshekee River from the mod if it was running fast, and there was no better elixir for a good night's sleep. That was so long as there were no loose horses gallivanting across the countryside or car fires lighting up the night sky.

"See any new tracks anywhere?" I asked.

"I don't see anything fresh," Nikko said.

"Marker ribbon is still tied to the tree over there," I said, pointing.

Rusty started pawing at the water, splashing Nikko's legs.

"Hey," Nikko said.

"Better get him out of the water," I said. "When they paw like that, they tend to be thinking about dropping and rolling."

We left the stream and went over to the homestead ruins. After dismounting and tying the horses to a tree, we walked around, looking for clues to sprout out of the earth and tell a story.

"How do you know your gal, whatshername—"

"Helvi," I said.

"Helvi actually lived here? Maybe this is just the remains of a logging cabin."

"I don't know for sure, but I do know that Helvi Paavola homesteaded in Peshekee County. I guess I need to go back to the register of deeds and try to find the title or whatever they had at the time."

"Yeah, if you can decipher it," Nikko said. "Usually it's a description involving sections, ranges, measurements, and such."

"Maybe if I compare it to the deed we have now for Wildwood," I said. "Or hire someone who can translate."

We walked around a bit more. I was sure this was where Helvi Paavlo homesteaded, married, and raised a family. Maybe when the children grew up, they divided the 160 acres into smaller parcels. I was eager to get back to Helvi's journal to dig deeper.

"Should we have a snack before we head back?" Nikko asked. "I brought some granola bars and water." He headed toward a huge boulder that appeared to be flat on top. "This is a perfect place to sit."

I joined him as he brushed leaves and twigs off the surface. "Milady," Nikko said, gesturing toward the boulder.

"Omigod!" I said. "It's *the* rock."

"Huh?"

"The rock in the journal. Look, there's the quartz and gold veins—pyrite. It's Helvi's spirit rock."

"Lots of rocks around here," Nikko said. "What's a spirit rock?"

I looked closer. "She described it in her journal."

"Okay, but like I said, there's lots—"

I peered closer at the smoothed-out surface. "But this one has been etched."

We both squinted at the faded words carved into the boulder.

"Spirit—I see the word spirit," I said.

"Ro?" Nikko asked.

"Rock! Spirit Rock," I said. "That's it. Helvi called a special rock her spirit rock. She said it had white and gold in it, just like this one."

"Well, not to crush *your* spirit," Nikko said, "but there are probably a lot of other boulders around here with those mineral veins running through them."

"Yeah, but not engraved. I know this is it."

I stood and looked around. "Now, Helvi Paavola Huntington, tell me what is so special about this place."

20

When we returned to the stable, I was surprised to see Clay riding Oscar. As far as I knew, the horse had never been ridden. I watched as Clay urged Oscar to move forward, sideways, halt, stand. He reached down and patted his neck, then dismounted.

I also dismounted and led Mac over to Clay and Oscar. "Wow. This your first time on him?"

"Yup," Clay said, slipping Oscar a treat. "He's still pretty young as a three-year old, so I don't want to get carried away, but we were both getting bored with the lunge line. When I first got on, he seemed a little confused, but not particularly upset. They're usually pretty good if you go about it the right way. Few more weeks and he'll be green broke."

Green broke was an equine term for barely broke and prepare to die. In nicer terms, there was still a long way to go before a horse is reliable and trustworthy.

"Raymond, Gussy, and your aunt left," Clay said, "but Raymond wanted me to tell you he'd be back to show you how to get the cameras activated into your computer—or something along that line."

"Okay, thanks," I said.

Nikko and I went into the barn to untack and rub down our horses. "Almost feeding time," I said.

"Yup. 'bout time to put on the ol' feedbag," Nikko said, looking at his watch.

"What's with the cowpoke lingo?"

"Well, little lady, just sayin' I could do with some vittles."

"Little lady? I'm not little and rarely a lady."

"Quit being so literal. I'm trying to be a delight here," Nikko said. He bent over, lifted one of Rusty's hooves, and used a pick to clean it.

"Oh, you're a delight, *pahtnah*," I said, grinning. "And I see you remembered your training."

Nikko straightened and looked at me. "Yes, I remembered to clean out his hooves. And what I was getting at is that it's almost time for us to eat dinner, and I wondered if you wanted to come to my place for some takeout. I can stop on the way home."

I vividly recalled the disastrous bachelor pad he called home; he read my mind.

"I think you'll approve of what I've—well, we've done with the place. Ma helped a lot, and so did Pop. I'm officially inviting you over, and my parents will be there."

"Really?"

"Really."

"Is this a date?"

"It can be whatever you want," Nikko said, waggling his eyebrows.

"I'll play it by ear. What time, what are we having, and what can I bring?"

"As soon as you get there, probably pizza again, and you can bring some beer."

Nikko headed home, and Clay and I started chores.

"Colt's gonna be a good horse. Smart," Clay said. "I'll get to the filly in a few weeks."

"Thanks for everything, Clay. I sure don't have the time or the ability to break horses. Those two would probably have just languished, which would have made them unadoptable."

"What I'm here for. Gotta say it's good to be back in the saddle."

"You know," I said, "I never really asked where you, ah, came from, what you did or have done. You know, like out West somewhere on a ranch?"

"Spent most of my working life assembling cars at GM. After thirty years, I got my pension and bought me the truck and camper. Decided to see the world. But all my life I've been pretty attached to horses. Like you, learned to ride as a kid and just kept my toe in the water best I could. Did some wrangling out West for a couple of years after I retired from GM. But that didn't work out."

"Interesting," I said. I decided this was as good a time as any to try to get to the bottom of the malicious destruction of property charge that popped up on the pre-employment search. "You sure have a way with horses. Glad you came onboard…um…."

"Uh huh," he muttered and looked at me. "Somethin' on your mind?"

"Well, yes. You know like I said, I'm really glad you came here and all. But things going on around here are, well, troublesome."

"Sure," Clay said. "Loose horses, arson. Got me on edge a bit too."

"So, anyway, I won't lie. I did a pre-employment check on you. I should have done it right off the bat, but I really didn't…what can I say? It mentioned some kind of trouble—malicious destruction of property? You don't seem…I mean, what the hell, Clay?"

He gave me a steady look that could have frozen a lava flow. "You think I had something to do with the troubles lately?"

"No! No, not at all. I mean, why would you?"

"I wouldn't," he said, reaching over and patting Oscar on the neck. "I guess you got a right to check out some old cowpoke that comes looking for a job. What I can tell you is that what I did was somethin' you'd have done yourself in a heartbeat. Because we both love horses and wanna give them a good life."

"Now you've really got me curious," I said, wishing I'd just procrastinated indefinitely on the whole conversation.

"And I can also tell you I'd never do anything to make trouble for you or anyone else around here. In fact, I'd go so far to say that I'd give a lot of grief to anyone who did."

I nodded. "I do believe that."

"I promise I'll give you the whole story soon. I think it will put you at ease. But meanwhile, I know your boyfriend will be waiting for you, so we'll take this up later, if you don't mind."

"Sure, whenever you're ready," I said. "No worries."

"Find anything else on that report about me?"

"Yes! You have an excellent credit score. Oh, and no outstanding warrants or garnishments or anything."

"Well, that's a relief," he said. "I expect if you had to garnish my wages, there wouldn't be anything left for my beer."

"That would be tragic!" I said, laughing.

"Yup," he said, then turned and led Oscar toward the stable.

* * *

"You're such a badass," I muttered to myself. "Whenever you're ready," I said mockingly. "No worries. Yessir, that really put the thumbscrews to the guy. Watch out, Kat Wilde is on the case!" I bellowed, directing my proclamation toward Jupiter, who had pushed his way into the bathroom where I was getting ready for a quick shower.

"Yow!"

After showering, throwing on some clothes, and slapping on some makeup, I made my way to the kitchen where an indignant Jupiter impatiently waited next to his dish. I fed the feline Lord of the Manor, then headed out to the derelict loaner truck. After a few tries, it reluctantly turned over. Clearly the battery was well beyond its warranty. I hoped that when my ship came in from the Magic Stirrup Foundation, I'd have a decent down payment for a car that wasn't gasping its last breath.

After a stop at the gas station for a fill-up, along with a twelve-pack of medium-priced beer and a low-end bottle of wine, I headed out Perch Lake Road to my friend-who's-a-boy's house.

Both Olsen cars were in the miniscule driveway, so I parked on the street. The truck chugged a while after I turned it off, then finally coughed and shut down. Nikko was standing at the doorway when I walked up. I could hear classical music playing, and better yet, I smelled something wonderful, and though the aroma of garlic engulfed me, I didn't think it was pizza.

Tobey raced out of the open door and leapt against me, barking madly.

"Hey there, Tobey," I said. "Sorry my hands are full, and you'll have to wait for me to scratch you behind your stubby ears."

"We always believe in a hearty greeting," Nikko said. He grabbed Tobey by the collar and leaned forward to kiss me. We connected slightly off kilter but it was better than a handshake.

"I see you have a respectable supply of adult beverages," Nikko said, reaching out to take the beer and wine from me. "Ma and Pop are here, so come on in and see what we've done.

He led me to the kitchen and put the beer and wine in the fridge. I was completely gobsmacked. Something smelled wonderful and the place positively gleamed. A matching set of dishes had been set out on the counter along with real silverware and nicely folded paper napkins. The kitchen countertops were decked out with such things as a toaster, coffeemaker, cannisters, and some kind of gizmo that didn't look familiar. I went over and looked at it.

"Air fryer," Nikko said. "Ma got it for me from the thrift store."

Tobey was glued to my leg and I bent down to give him proper attention. "Have you been a good boy?" (tail wag) "Have you missed me?" (turbo tail wag) "Do you want a treat?" (sharp yip and enthusiastic jumping up and down). I pulled a dog biscuit out of my purse and gave it to him.

"It's one of those heathy things," I said. "Cleans their teeth."

"Yeah," Nikko said, "if he took time to chew it."

I heard Sheriff Olsen talking loudly from the next room, presumably on his cell phone.

Frieda Olsen came into the kitchen and said, "Don't mind Ollie. He never takes a day off and there's been some kind of an accident. Anyway, hello, Kathryn dear."

"Hello, Mrs. Olsen."

"Oh for heaven's sake, call me Frieda."

"I'll try, ah, Frieda," I said. She was always Mrs. Olsen and the sheriff was always Sheriff Olsen. "Something smells great!"

"Yeah," Nikko said. "Ma cooked us a pan of lasagna. And we've got garlic toast."

"And a salad," Frieda said. "I had the lasagna in the freezer, so figured that now was as good a time as any to pull it out."

We all went into the living room where the shock and awe continued. The disgusting couch was gone and replaced with something that appeared much newer and cleaner, with an end table and lamp beside it. In addition, there were two armchairs with an end table between them and another lamp. The giant wooden spool was gone and replaced with a tasteful coffee table. A bona fide dinette set with two folding leaves and four chairs was positioned in the dining area. I didn't ask for a tour of the bedroom or bathroom, but hoped they had undergone similar transformations.

"All I can say is I love what you've done with the place!" I said, looking directly at Frieda.

She smiled and said, "Well, it was time to get some new things at home, and so when the furniture store delivered them, we just had them bring my old furniture here."

"And I paid them to haul my old stuff to the dump," Nikko said.

"And I'm in hock now for the next decade," blurted out Sheriff Olsen. He was still holding his cell phone to his ear. "I'll never get the furniture store paid off."

"Oh hush, Ollie, and get off the phone," Frieda said. "Let's eat."

Nikko smiled and whispered in my ear, "We may have to wait for dessert."

I tried to look reproachful, but my ear tingled and I felt a little twitch at the corner of my mouth. "You're just bad," I muttered.

"You betcha, little lady."

I gave him another look over my shoulder as I followed Frieda into the kitchen to help bring out the food. We all sat, and after a brief thanks to God, dug in. I periodically slipped Tobey a piece of crust from my garlic bread. Nobody told me I couldn't. After all, what was a dog without his bad breath?

"So, Pop," Nikko said, "where was the accident?"

"A rollover on Ravine Road. Rescue is there and Tori responded. We'll see about injuries. I may have to take my food to go."

Tori was Sergeant Tori Haapala, who became the first female deputy for Peshekee County about a decade ago and was more recently promoted to sergeant.

Just as I was contemplating a third helping of lasagna, Sheriff Olsen's cell phone ringtone played a tune from the hit show of the sixties, *Hawaii 5-0.*

"Yeah," the sheriff barked. "Aw, no. Shit. I'll be right there. And call the staties. You know the routine."

I quit chewing and looked at the sheriff. His face sagged and he looked around the table.

"Fatal," he said.

"Oh dear!" Frieda said.

"Do you know who yet?" Nikko asked.

"Probably," the sheriff said. "A local gal. I think you two might have gone to school with her."

I could feel the blood drain from my face. I plunked my fork down and took a deep breath.

"Now don't be blabbing anything yet," Sheriff Olsen said, "but the ID with the deceased says it's Jeannie Usitalo. Since Tori knows—knew her, positive ID will just be a formality."

"Oh my word! No!" Frieda gasped. "She's my stylist."

"Mine too," I said. "Jeannie? She has a little girl. She...was she...?"

"Best I know is it was only Jeannie Usitalo involved, not the child."

Nikko reached over and squeezed my arm. And then came the signature Kat Wilde blubber-fest.

* * *

"Morning," I muttered desolately when I arrived at work the next day.

Rose looked up from her computer and nodded. It was the most subdued I'd ever seen her. Dad and our intern, Mia, weren't in yet, and I assumed Gussy was behind the closed door of his office. Gloom hung in the air like a thick fog. We had lost one of our own and the grieving was palpable, even for those who didn't know Jeannie well. We always wonder why a fair and just God would take someone we care about. It is the biggest test for our faith. I threw my purse under my desk, sat down, and booted up my computer. I went to the local news outlet to check out any information on the accident and what arrangements were to be made. There wasn't much yet. It did say arrangements would be announced and that the accident was under investigation.

Under investigation. While I had never ridden in a vehicle with Jeannie, I couldn't picture her driving recklessly or under the influence. Her whole world was her daughter, Brianna, and Jeannie would never take unnecessary risks of any kind. Maybe she had fallen asleep behind the wheel. Jeannie worked hard and was always on the run. I wondered what would happen with Brianna. I knew she was often cared for by Jeannie's mom and dad, but they had to be getting to an age where raising a youngster might be too much. I remembered Jeannie had a brother who had never married, so not likely much help there. I had no idea what to do. When my grandparents had passed away, I was very young and not expected to do much of anything except behave. Should I stop by the Usitalo house? Bring a covered dish? I needed to ask Mom.

The front door swished open and Dad came in with Raymond and Mia in his wake.

"Mornin' all," Dad said. Not his chipper self at all. He looked at me and said, "How you holdin' up, Kat?"

"Okay, I guess," I said, feeling not okay at all.

Mia gave me a sympathetic look and said, "I'm so sorry, Kat. I mean, I didn't really know her, but...."

"Thanks, Mia," I said.

Gussy popped out of his office and smiled. Mia looked at him and smiled back. Rose looked at both of them and frowned. Raymond looked at Gussy and glowered. Dad shook his head and muttered something under his breath about trouble ahead.

Raymond grabbed a chair from the client waiting area and pulled it over to my desk.

"So, really, you okay?" he asked.

"Yeah. I mean, we weren't besties, but what with everything happening lately, it's kinda shaken my world."

"I hear ya," Raymond said. "Stinks—all of it."

"I'm just not feeling good about all the bad things that've been going on lately. Cut wires, loose pigs, the Jeep going up in flames, dead hippies, and now a deadly car accident. Probably not related, but it still feels like an ominous shift in the Peshekee way."

"The Peshekee way?" Raymond asked. "And I won't even ask about loose pigs."

"The Peshekee way, you know, safe, secure, leave our doors unlocked and a bag of cash sitting on the seat of our car with the keys still in it."

"I get it."

And, I thought, there was still the unresolved issue of the homestead. Until I knew why Varga wanted it so badly, I would have no peace. His evasive explanation and lame assurances did nothing to make me trust him. I decided the only path forward was with the Helvi Paavola Huntington journal. I planned to visit the museum right after work.

"So," Raymond said, "let me show you how the video recording works."

"Now? You mean I can do it on my laptop here in the office, even though...."

"Right you are. And from your phone. Your Aunt Lin is already set with her phone. Just like people watch their front porch for package delivery or their pooch in case he decides to chew up the couch, you can check out the goings on at Wildwood anywhere you have cell or Wi-Fi."

"Awesome!" I said.

Raymond spent the next few minutes navigating technical difficulties and then, bingo, a fairly clear picture of the Wildwood parking lot came into view.

"That's amazing!" I said.

"And we can change cameras like this. And things will be recorded. You'll need to delete the videos regularly."

"Hey, there's Rusty rolling in the dirt. Hey, Rusty!"

"He can't hear you, but we could probably incorporate speakers at some point."

"That would be great," I said.

Gussy slid out of his office and headed back to Mia's cubicle. Rose watched out of the corner of her eye, as did Raymond.

"Hey, Big Brother," I said. "Gussy is really a good guy and your sister is a big girl. You might just let things, you know, take their own course."

Raymond scowled. "It's not Gussy. Couldn't ask for a better dude. But can you imagine having Rose as a mother-in-law?"

"I see your point. However, they are just office, ah, friends, not planning nuptials—at least not yet."

"Yeah, I gotta chill. It's just that, well, I'm her big brother and I gotta make sure she, well...well, there are a lot of bad things out there."

"I get it," I said. "She's turned out splendidly. Way to go bro."

"Thanks," he said, sighing. "Gotta go. I told your dad I'd show him how to sort his email. He has over 3,000 in his inbox and doesn't know what to keep and what to dump."

"Typical man," I said. "Won't ever throw anything out. Ask my mom."

"You never know when you might need—whatever it is that you want to keep," Raymond said with a laugh. He put the borrowed chair back and headed upstairs to Dad's office. I took another look at the various camera angles. All was quiet on the Wildwood front. I had to admit it was about as interesting as watching the dust settle.

21

When I pulled up to the Peshekee Historical Society Museum, I noticed Frankie on a ladder perched against the eaves. It appeared he was cleaning moss off the roof.

"How's it goin'?" I asked.

It seemed to startle him, and he just looked at me and mumbled. So much for chit chat.

I went inside and the door gave a jingle. Elsie was in the far corner of the building, squatting down. It looked as if she were either dusting or praying.

She looked up and said, "Oh, hello. May I help you?"

"Hi Elsie. Looks as if you're working hard."

"Well, you wouldn't believe the dust in this place," she said. She grasped a chair and brought herself upright.

"Not my favorite thing to do—dust," I said. It sounded lame; I never was much for small talk.

"So, dear, what can I do for you?"

"I'd like to go over Helvi's journal some more today. I'm learning a lot, and guess I've been bitten by the history bug." I thought that was a nice touch, even if a fib.

"Oh, indeed, once bitten..." Elsie said. "I do apologize; I don't recall who you are. You say I allowed you to look at a journal?"

This took me by surprise. I was just in the museum, and we'd had a fairly lengthy conversation. Dementia?

"Sorry," I said. "As you recall, I stopped in a few days back, wondering about homesteading in the area. You gave me a journal to look over. It was very interesting."

Elsie smiled and nodded.

"I'd like to see it again."

"Oh, I can't allow that."

"But—"

"Who'd you say you were again?"

"Kat Wilde. I have Wildwood Stables. Might have a homestead on it?"

"Very well. Tell me what you learned. If it seems appropriate, I suppose I could let you look at it. I'm not sure how many more times I can let people paw through these things. They're irreplaceable, you know. Again, I need to know what you learned. I shan't ask again."

This conversation was crazy. Had Elsie Tuttle been tipping a few?

"From the journal," she prompted.

"Oh, you know, marriage, family, chickens, crops. But I'm pretty excited about actually verifying that it was Helvi who homesteaded the place. There's a special engraved boulder that Nikko and I found that matches one described in Helvi's journal."

Elsie didn't exactly scowl, but neither did she clap her hands with joy.

"Anyway, ah, I'd like to do a little more exploring," I said.

"What? Oh, I do apologize. My mind wandered a bit there. I was pondering who this Nikko was. Does he own land?"

"Ah, not exactly," I said. I wondered if I should give it up for the day.

"Well, no matter. Let me get the key and some gloves, and we'll get you fixed up. I thought you were asking for the restroom. So many of the public think they can just come in here for the facilities. My hearing, you know...."

"Thanks." I felt as if I'd been having a crazy dream, but perhaps Elsie Tuttle was a little "touched," as they said in the olden days. Or hard of hearing, or off her meds, or overmedicated, or afflicted with God knows what. In any event, she seemed to come around.

Helvi's life captivated me. I was most interested in events after she married and had a family. Though I couldn't imagine what treasure or secret the humble Huntington homestead would have, I hoped for enlightenment from the journal. It was curious that Helvi had entries telling of her children's marriages and the many blessings of grandchildren, but entries involving the oldest, Sarah, seemed to dry up. Perhaps there was a falling out. Maybe Sarah married and they lost touch, though folks wrote letters in those days.

After scanning a page about the proper way to can pickles, I found something much more interesting.

An unusual discovery occurred when William and our eldest boy, Matthew, were digging a posthole. They were working on building a pen for a cow we were going to purchase. The soil was strewn with rocks, some very large. The younger children helped carry the stones and rocks off and put them in a pile. Ruthie picked something up and brought it to me and said, "Mama, I found a special rock." Indeed it was special, and didn't look like anything found in nature.

My heart picked up a beat. First off, I remembered seeing a large pile of rocks at the old homestead when Nikko and I rode there. They were moss-covered and even had a tree growing up through them. I turned the page for the rest of the story, but it wasn't there. The next page spoke of the new milk cow they named Matilda. She was expecting a calf and everyone was quite excited. But what the heck did Ruthie bring to her mother? Perhaps it was just an animal bone or a special shiny rock. But no, Helvi said it was something not found in nature. Maybe something from an Anishinaabe village, such as a weapon or tool.

Then I noticed something. The last few pages of the journal appeared to have been removed. The inside of the spine showed the remnants of pages no longer there. There were no jagged edges to indicate they had gotten fragile and fell out or were torn out to use for some other purpose such as letter writing. I could see distinct, straight cut lines with three remnant stubs still attached in the binding. I would swear when I thumbed through the journal the previous week, there were no missing pages. I must have been frowning intensely enough to have Elsie come over.

"Did you find something useful, dear?"

"Well, I don't know," I said, moving the journal across toward her. "But I see some pages have been cut out of the end of the journal. I don't think they were missing last week when I was here. I want you to know I would never deface something so valuable as this. Did someone else come in after me—look at it?"

"Oh my, what a travesty," Elsie said, peering at the page remnants. "After when?"

"The first time I was here. Last week," I prompted.

Elsie frowned. "You looked at it without my permission?"

Here we go again, I thought.

"You mentioned that the, ah, hippie couple looked at Helvi's journal," I said, hoping to get things back on track.

"Yes, well, that's true. However, it was you who said they were dead. I don't see how they could do such a thing, now could they?"

"I swear—"

"I'm sure you do. But I'm afraid you'll have to continue your research another way," Elsie said, picking up the journal.

"But...I would never...I take photos and notes. Are there other volunteers that run the museum who may have allowed a review of the journal?"

"No. However, the Peshekee Historical Society does help organize and display new things, restock the literature rack, clean, and so on," Elsie said, walking over to the cabinet and locking the journal inside.

"Maybe you should check with them," I said.

"Perhaps," Elsie said. "Now if I can be of no further assistance, I suggest you might check with the people at the county building for more information. I must insist you don't return to the museum."

I was certain my face had flushed crimson and my ears burned. Her accusation was outrageous.

"Elsie, why would I bring this to your attention if I did it?" I asked.

She glared at me, her lips pinched into a thin line, and said, "I can have Frankie escort you out, if you wish."

No way did I want creepy *Mr. Frank* escorting me anywhere. I stood, scraping the chair back loudly, picked up my pad for notes, and strode out with as much dignity as I could muster. Frankie was still up the ladder and I was certain he watched me get into the truck. I sat a moment, my hands shaking with anger.

"That woman is a whack job and her son's a direct descendant of Neanderthal Man," I muttered to the dashboard.

I turned the key and, thank God, the engine turned over. I drove off, spraying gravel onto the freshly-mowed grass.

* * *

I was just stepping into the shower the next morning after chores when I heard the ping of my cell phone telling me I had a text.

"Now what?" I muttered.

After a quick towel dry, I threw on some jeans and a tee, then grabbed my phone. The text was from Willie Moss.

Crew arriving at 9

I looked at my watch—that was in about fifteen minutes. I assumed she meant by crew it was the guys who were going to bid on the reconstruction of the horse camp.

Ok

I'll be in touch.

(thumbs-up emoji)

Texting was great so long as you didn't have a million questions, which I did. I ran a brush through my hair and glanced in the mirror.

"Good enough," I said to my reflection.

I was still thoroughly pissed about my banishment from the museum. I debated whether I should go to the village council and make a complaint. Elsie had turned from a sweet little old lady to a nasty, accusatory shrew with a thug for a son. I knew for certain it wasn't me who had cut out the pages of the journal, so who did? Since the thing was under lock and key, it seemed the arrow pointed right back to Elsie. But why would she deface something she obviously thought so precious? Nothing was making any sense. And my mind turned back to the hippie couple—the only other ones who likely had recently looked at the journal. Yet the pages were definitely there *after* their death. Besides, if they wanted to keep track of something, they could do what I was doing and just take photos, probably with their phone camera.

I heard the plinking melody of Aunt Lin's lyre. She had her bedroom door shut, but the eerie noise filtered out like a bout of tinnitus. I went to the kitchen to grab a last cup of coffee. Jupiter was sitting on the kitchen counter with his tail pointed up, forming a question mark. It amazed me he could do that. The vet said it was related to an injury from one of the many cat fights he had engaged in during his carousing years. I reached over and scratched him under the chin. He must have been in a good mood because while he didn't purr with delight, neither did he clamp his jaws down on my hand.

"Hey, buddy," I said. "Has your day been satisfactory so far?"

He squinted his eyes into slits. I knew that meant something in cat lingo but couldn't recall what. Contentment? Disgust? Disinterest? All three?

"The phone!" I said, looking at Jupiter. "Maybe there's stuff on their phone."

Jupiter opened his eyes and yawned. Then I swear he nodded before jumping down off the countertop and padding to his favorite napping spot in the sun.

I grabbed my cup of coffee and headed to the mod porch. I would have loved to get ahold of the hippy couple's phone, if they had one. I wondered if things like that had been turned over to the next of kin or somehow became evidence. The chance of finding out anything from Lieutenant Spiller about the phone or anything else in the evidence room was as likely as the moon being made of green cheese. But there was Sheriff Olsen, whose son I happened to be—doing whatever it was we were doing.

I took a swig of my coffee, which had turned bitter with age, and saw a procession of vehicles coming up Horse Camp Road. It looked as if the entire Village of Peshekee was paying a call. I stood and squinted into the morning sun, trying to make out the identity of my visitors. The first vehicle was a large work truck with some lettering on the side: *Kusch Construction, LLC.* Behind that truck was a state police car, then a dark blue vehicle with a mini light bar on top.

A couple of guys jumped out of the work truck and looked around. I stepped off the porch and walked up to them.

"Hello," I said.

"Hi, ah, we're here to take a look at a campground," one of the guys said. He looked to be about thirteen years old. His partner had walked over to the Jeep remains.

"Yup, Willie told me you'd be here. My name's Kat."

"Josh Kusch and the idiot over there gawking at—whatever that is, er, was, is my brother Nathan. We're here to take some photos and measurements for our boss."

"I see that your name is on the truck. I take it you're a family outfit."

"Right. The boss is my dad. Hey, Nate—get your ah, get over here. Anyway, Dad will be out in a couple of days and we'll get an estimate together in a few days for Ms. Moss."

I pointed them in the right direction, then turned my attention to Sergeant Witz, who got out of the police cruiser. She went over to the sedan where a man got out and they shook hands. Witz pointed to the erstwhile Jeep. I walked over to them.

"Hey, Miss Wilde," Witz said. "This is the fire marshal, Joe Ragstaff."

We all nodded at each other and muttered assorted social pleasantries.

"We're here to look over the scene," Witz said. "Have you got anything to add to your statement since the night of the fire? I heard you called the post on my days off."

"Well, yeah, I did," I said. I debated whether or not to bring up Varga. I opted to stall while I decided. "I wasn't sure when to call. They said you were off 'til tonight, and I go to bed pretty early."

"I thought I was too, but things got changed," she said, looking at Ragstaff.

Varga was still not in the clear in my mind. All he had done was fess up that his family had no sentimental connection to my land. He still hadn't told me *what* was so damn important with the parcel. I decided it was best to come clean. Hiding my suspicions would likely backfire.

"It's kind of a tangled situation," I said. "So, maybe after you're done with whatever you need to do here, we can go inside and I'll tell you about a few visits from a Mr. Alex Varga."

"Varga, huh?" Witz said. "Okay, we'll let you know once Joe here has deemed this as arson, which is pretty obvious."

Ragstaff shrugged. "Says you."

22

Just as the fire marshal and Sergeant Witz were leaving, a couple of cars approached. It seemed Wildwood was a popular place. I recognized the first car as belonging to Dad. The second was a DNR pickup truck, which I assumed was piloted by Nikko. I went back to the mod porch, sat in one of Uncle Phil's lawn chairs, and reunited with my coffee mug. The brew was barely lukewarm, but I drank it anyway. I could still hear the faint strains of Aunt Lin's lyre. She was in the zone.

Both my parents had come, which was an ominous sign. They tended to unite when readying for battle. I wondered if Nikko's appearance was a coincidence or if he was joining my folks for some kind of intervention. All three got out, and I could hear them exchanging greetings. Mom and Dad went over to the burned-out Jeep. Nikko came on the porch and sat in the other lawn chair.

"Hey, honey bun," he said.

"Honey bun?"

"Sure, you know, sweet and, ah, sticky. I'm trying to find something to call you besides plucky."

"I see. How about just calling me by my name, or maybe one of the regular endearments that are socially endorsed."

"Such as?"

"Figure it out," I said, finishing off the dregs of my coffee. "I guess I better go inside and make a fresh pot."

I got up and went inside with Nikko following me. I grabbed the carafe and rinsed it out. When I turned to get the coffee can, I found myself facing Nikko.

"Excuse me," I said.

Nikko continued to block my way and managed to back me into the counter.

"What are you doing?" I asked, as if I didn't know.

"Oh, just saying hello to my, ah...."

"Friend who is a girl?"

"Sure," he mumbled and pressed against me.

"You know Mom and Dad will be in any moment, and Aunt—"

Nikko moved in for a kiss, which was very promising had it not been for my entire family being on the premises.

"How about you come over to my place tonight—without my parents."

"For dinner?" I was thinking about the leftover lasagna.

"Sure."

The mod door opened and Nikko backed off a little. "I'll get that for you," he said, pretending to reach a high cupboard. Thing is, I could reach all the high cupboards, but my parents didn't gasp with horror. The lyre plinked on.

"Kathryn!" Mom said. "This is just horrible."

"Hi Mom. What's horrible?"

"That—that burned-up mess out there. You could have been killed."

"I wasn't in it," I said. "Hi Dad. What's up?"

Dad came over and gave me a peck on the cheek. "I could ask *you* that," he said, looking at Nikko, who was arranging some coffee mugs on the countertop.

"Oh, same ol', same ol'," I said.

We all sat at the kitchen table and listened to the coffee pot gurgle and wheeze. The unit beeped, and I got up and poured everyone a cup.

"I am so shocked about Jeannie Usitalo dying in that car crash," Mom said, blowing on her coffee.

"Have you heard anything yet about the arrangements?" I asked.

"I took over a casserole and Alice—you know, Jeannie's mother—said the service will be next Saturday at Shute's Funeral Home. Visitation is that morning."

"How is Mrs. Usitalo doing?" I asked.

"Not well at all. The child keeps asking when Mommy is coming home. She asked *me* if I had seen her mommy. It nearly broke my heart. I wasn't sure how religious the Usitalos are, so I didn't say anything about God or heaven. However, I think they attend the Lutheran church, so maybe the pastor there will be giving some guidance in that area."

I nodded. "Hard not to fall back on the same ol' platitudes. I—I wondered what I could do. Should I take something over?"

"No, Kathryn. I think Alice mentioned having to freeze a lot of the dishes people have dropped off. I think they ask for donations for little Brianna's college fund. They're setting up an account at the credit union. Maybe that's what we should do."

I nodded, feeling a knot forming again in my throat. We all sat quietly, with only the faint plink plunk of Aunt Lin's lyre floating in.

Dad cleared his throat and said, "I see the police and another emergency vehicle were driving out as we came in."

"Yeah, they're doing a routine investigation," I said, relieved to move back to The Burning.

"Standard procedure for suspected arson," Nikko said.

"Arson!" Mom shrieked. "I assumed that, well, it just.... I thought maybe you were smoking again or something, and some gas had leaked...."

"I have never smoked!" I said, feigning indignance.

"Oh, Kathryn, how stupid do you think your mother is? I could smell the smoke wafting from the attic a mile away. The fan you used just made it worse."

"Ah, well," I muttered. "That was high school."

Nikko grinned at me. "I'm sure the authorities will get to the bottom of it."

"I certainly hope so," Mom said.

"*Anyway,*" Dad said, "we're here for a reason besides admonishing you for your high school antics."

"Okay," I said, steeling myself for some kind of ultimatum.

"Your mother and I are going to purchase a decent vehicle for you, as a kind of early birthday present."

"Wow! Really?" I asked. "Hey, that's too much, I mean, besides my birthday isn't until next month. Plus, the down payment for the mod was my birthday present."

"Okay," Dad said. "Then an early Christmas present."

"I—I have a loaner."

I heard Nikko snort. I gave him an icy look. "And I'm getting a check soon, from the foundation, which I'll use for a down payment."

I admit I was torn between asserting my independence and caving to my parents bailing me out. Again.

"Kat," Dad said. "We insist. Please, so your mother can sleep at night and, in turn, I can sleep at night."

"Not every day that parents beg their daughter to accept a new car," Nikko said. "You guys want to adopt me?"

We all laughed, easing the tension.

"We picked out something we think will be perfect," Mom said.

"So...you picked it out already?"

"A nice truck at the Chevy dealer," Mom said. "I think it's a demo."

"Repo," Dad said. "So a very good deal. It's clean and in good mechanical shape. But it will be a few days for the paperwork to be completed, since it was repossessed by the bank and all. But you can look at it, test drive it if you like. Your mother and I can give you a ride to the dealer, if you have the time right now."

"It's a very lovely powder blue," Mom said.

"Powder blue?" I said. "That's unusual."

"Yes, it was a custom color. Only one like it around." Dad said. "Just like you—unique."

Okay, the cave-in was complete. I got up and gave them both a hug. "You're the best parents a gal could have. Thank you so much. I personally love powder blue."

"Well, I want my baby to be safe," Mom said.

"And I want your mother to quit worrying," Dad said.

Nikko stood and took the last swallow of his coffee. "I gotta go, but you and I can go look at it later today, Kat. I get off at two-thirty, so I can pick you up around three and we can head over to the Chevy dealer."

"I'd have to be back by six for chores," I said.

"We'll work it out," he said.

"Okay, then," Dad said, standing up. "Your mom and I need to get to the office. I'll let you and Nikko check out the truck."

My parents left, and I walked Nikko to his DNR truck. He smiled and pulled me toward him. We looked at each other for a minute, then kissed. I heard the sound of a horse approaching, and Nikko and I watched Clay lead the filly, Emmy, past us.

"Busy place," Clay said, nodding at us.

"Sure is," I said. "So, you're gonna put the filly to the test?"

"Yup. Just a little lead line and lunging."

"Good luck," Nikko said. "Fillies can be fickle."

Clay and he laughed. I gave Nikko an elbow in the ribs.

"Ow! See what I mean."

Clay gave a rare smile and headed toward an empty paddock.

"Hey, that's gonna leave a mark," Nikko said.

"Good."

"Anyway, I should get off on time today, so long as nothing major comes up."

"Okay. Any clues on the loose pigs?"

"Well, the Jessons are sure it was sabotage."

"Yeah, speaking of sabotage, a strange thing happened at the museum."

"That sounds like the title to a good book," Nikko said.

I told him about my falling out with Elsie Tuttle over the missing journal pages.

"Maybe Frank Tuttle told her that you were a mean girl in high school," Nikko said.

"Maybe, but she seemed so delightful and then, bam! She turned on me at the blink of an eye."

"Maybe she has something to hide about this Helga woman—"

"Helvi," I corrected.

"—Helvi woman. You're pretty sure she's the one who homesteaded on your land?"

"Yeah, the Spirit Rock clinched it for me. Plus a few other things. I wish I had kept my mouth shut about the missing pages, and also wish I'd gotten photos of those pages before they disappeared. I was originally interested in the family tree and establishing that Helvi was the one who laid claim to the land. I have a pretty strong feeling the missing pages would have led me onto something that would have answered other questions."

"Such as what Varga is trying to pull?" Nikko asked.

"Right. Which leads me to a favor I need to ask you, which is to ask your father for a favor."

I told him about wanting to see if there was a phone anywhere from the personal effects of the deceased couple that might have photos from the journal.

"I know it's a longshot, but I'd still like to keep poking away at this," I said.

"Sure, Pop will do anything—short of corruption, bribery, or murder—for junk food, especially pizza from the Pizza Palace."

"Isn't that bribery?"

"Not with family, unless we're Italian. You know, like The Mob. I'll arrange something for lunch with the old man and let you know."

"That would be great!" I said, giving him a kiss.

"I expect something in return," he said, doing his signature eyebrow waggle.

"How about I give you free riding lessons," I said. "You know, to teach you to stay in the saddle and not kiss the ground."

"Hey, you said taking a fall was part of joining the club." He made finger quotes around the word "club."

"So I did. But there is a proper way to jump something. And it would seem that you lack that knowledge."

"We'll negotiate later," he said, climbing into the cab of his truck. "See you around three."

* * *

I watched Clay and the filly, Emmy, for a while, then went back to the mod to see if Aunt Lin had emerged. I was excited to tell her about my new wheels. When I stepped inside, I saw my aunt on the landline.

"Oh, here she is right now," she said, offering me the telephone.

I mouthed the word *who* and she shrugged.

"Kat Wilde speaking," I said.

"Oh, Miss Wilde, I'm so glad I caught you." It was a woman's voice, somewhat familiar.

"Okay, and who am I speaking to?" I asked, hoping it wasn't another fundraising call for something or other.

"My apologies," said the woman. "This is Elsie Tuttle from the museum."

"Yes, Elsie, I already told you I had nothing to do with the missing pages, I—"

"Oh my yes, I realize that. I have called to apologize to you for making such a terrible accusation. You see, these artifacts are like my—well, my children, and you know how protective mothers can be. Well, maybe you don't, but we are."

I couldn't make a connection between a dusty old journal and a child, but whatever. "Okay, apology accepted," I said magnanimously.

"Wonderful!" Elsie said. "And while I still have no idea what happened to those journal pages, I do have some other information that might interest you. I keep it in my office in the back and got to thinking that maybe I could make up for my poor behavior by inviting you over for a look."

"What are we talking about?" I asked. "Photos, another journal?"

"It's difficult to describe and best that I just show you."

She had piqued my curiosity.

"I could stop sometime after work, I guess," I said.

"That would be a possibility," Elsie said, "or, perhaps on Saturday."

Jeannie's funeral was Saturday, but I didn't intend to make a whole day of it. "Saturday is good, but I'll be attending Jeannie Usitalo's service."

"Oh yes, that is so terribly sad. Anyway, the museum is open 'til five on Saturdays this time of year. Perhaps you could just give me a call when you are headed this way."

"Fine," I said.

She gave me her personal cell number and we hung up.

"Well, that was unexpected," I said to Aunt Lin, who was stirring something strange-smelling on the stove.

"What?"

"That woman from the museum kicked me out the other day, accusing me of defacing something, and now she wants to kiss and make up."

Jupiter strolled in and jumped up on the countertop next to Aunt Lin.

"You're not supposed to be up here," she said.

"Yow!" he replied. He could put inflection in his yows, and this one told Aunt Lin to shove it.

"I admit I am really curious about what Elsie wants to show me."

"You know what they say," Aunt Lin said, "about curiosity killing the cat."

"Yow!"

* * *

Nikko was only a few minutes late picking me up. He had Tobey in the SUV with him. I could see the pooch's face mashed against the glass, looking at me. The vehicle stopped and the driver's door opened. Tobey leapt out and galloped toward me, tail whirling like a helicopter.

"There's my favorite fella," I said, vigorously rubbing his ears.

"I thought I was your favorite fella," Nikko said, walking over to the two of us.

"When you pant at the sight of me and whirl your tail, I'll consider it."

"Is there a hidden meaning to that?" he asked.

"Maybe," I said, boosting Tobey into the front seat, then climbing in and hooking up the seatbelt. Tobey generally rode shotgun, so we had to share the seat.

Nikko climbed in and we headed out with the air conditioning going full blast, a luxury my loaner truck lacked. Tobey commenced panting, which was accompanied by the rhythmic clicking noise with each intake of air—or exhale of air. Nikko said the vet attributed it to a deviated septum due to poor breeding practices. Surgery might be in Tobey's future.

We pulled into the lot. It wasn't hard to spot the truck of my parents' choosing. It gleamed garishly from a small hill by the side of the road, an eye-catching curiosity for certain. Nikko and I got out and gave it a look. It had a crew cab backseat and a short bed, with nary a scratch.

"This was no work truck," I said, looking at the pristine bed.

"Probably used for other cargo," Nikko said. "I'd say it was a pimpmobile."

"I thought those were usually luxury sedans."

"This is the U.P.," Nikko said, walking around it. He kicked one of the tires. "Vice vehicles are different."

"Vice vehicles?" I asked.

"Yeah, vice. You know, moonshine, drugs, sex trafficking."

"So you think this was a vice vehicle? And do people still make moonshine?"

"Yes I do. And yes, they do." He stuck his head inside the cab, then looked at the door panel. He walked around and looked underneath the truck and above the wheel wells.

"What are you doing?" I asked. "Shouldn't we open the hood or something?"

"Hmm, yeah," he said, reaching under the steering wheel and popping the hood.

We looked at the truck's innards as if they made sense. I recognized the battery, the oil dipstick, and the washer fluid reservoir. Everything else was a complete mystery.

A guy came out of the Chevy building and approached us. We made introductions. His name was Rick and he looked like he was still in high school. Rick spent a lot of time telling me what a clean vehicle the pimpmobile was. I've never understood what "clean" means in car lingo.

"So, can I test drive it?" I asked.

"You betcha," Rick said. "I know your father, and we have a deal where you can take it home and drive it as a demo until we get the paperwork in order."

"Hey, great," I said.

"Just wondering about the truck's history," Nikko said. "I understand it's a repo."

"Yeah, we ordered this thing special for a guy. He got a loan from the credit union and then defaulted. We're helping with the resale."

"And you get a cut, don't you?" Nikko said.

"Well, sure," Rick said. "Anyway, best I know the guy was into some kind of import business."

"Imports?" I said.

"Yeah. That's why he needed a truck," Rick said. "Apparently he's in jail right now—well, prison, so obviously missed a few payments."

"Uh huh," Nikko said. "We're a long way from Mexico."

"But not far from Canada," I said. "Maybe they were importing maple syrup."

That brought a few chuckles from everyone.

"Well, so long as drug dogs don't come sniffing around, I'm good with trying this thing out," I said.

"I'll get the fob and a plate," Rick said, hurrying off.

"Pimpmobile," I said.

"Yup," Nikko said. "Don't be surprised if you get pulled over a lot in this thing."

"I'll keep that in mind."

23

I parked the pimpmobile next to Nikko's family SUV, and we both got out and headed to his bungalow.

"So, how do you like your new truck?" Nikko asked.

"It's...well, I have no idea how to work half the stuff in it. It had a map showing me where I was going, it played smooth jazz on the sound system, the air conditioning was awesome, and the seat automatically adjusted to me. To start it, I just pushed a button. I guess the fob tells the truck I'm not a thief."

We walked into the house, which smelled vaguely of lemon furniture polish. I looked around and everything was tidy and appealing.

"So where's the foosball game?" I asked.

"In the computer room," Nikko said. "Ma said it shouldn't be the main focus of the place."

"And where's the pooch?"

"My folks'."

I nodded.

"Just the two of us," he added.

I nodded again.

"You okay?" he asked.

"Well, yeah, it's just that a lot of things have happened lately. That woman at the museum acting bizarre. And I just can't get over Jeannie Usitalo in that car wreck. Do they have any idea what happened?"

"Pop said it looked like her brakes failed. There were no skid marks, but there were a few drops of some kind of fluid going off the pavement leading to the rolled vehicle. If it had been the air conditioner condensation, it would have evaporated. This fluid did not evaporate. They've been looking into that. Probably just bad maintenance. And with that said, I'm glad you have something besides a death trap to drive."

"Yeah, me too. Now if you'll excuse me, I need to visit the powder room."

When I walked into the bathroom, I was amazed at the transformation. A shower curtain had been installed. Matching towels hung from racks, and there was a fancy soap dispenser next to the sink, which I swear had been polished with wax. Fluffy rugs dotted the floor, and the toilet paper end was folded into a V. When I turned to leave, Nikko was blocking my way.

"Wanna see the bedroom?" he asked.

"Maybe," I said. "Is it still disgusting?"

"Check it out for yourself."

We went down the short hall, and he opened the door to his boudoir. The nasty mattress had been removed and replaced with a real bed. Next to it was a nightstand with a cute lamp. A dresser stood against one wall and a chair with a reading lamp sat in a corner. The windows had curtains that matched the bedspread and two decorator pillows.

"Wow!" I said as I gawked at the room from the doorway. "Your mother, right?"

"Pretty much," he said, draping his arm across my shoulder. "So, when do you have to be back for chores?"

"Well, actually, I have the night off," I said. "Clay and Aunt Lin will handle it tonight. I wasn't sure I'd be back in time."

"Really?" I felt the arm tighten around me, then his hand moved under my shirt.

"I do need to be home early in the morning, though. The farrier is coming."

"The who?"

"The farrier. The guy or gal who trims horses' hooves and shoes them, if they're shod. His name is Spud Maki."

"Spud?"

"Yeah, a nickname. He won't tell anyone how he got it. Anyway, Spud's coming to do Oscar and Emmy. We aren't sure how long since they've been done, or how well they'll behave."

"Behaving is no fun," Nikko said, moving his hand from back to front.

"I thought you were supposed to feed me dinner," I said, turning to face him.

"Maybe later," he murmured, pushing me backwards into the bedroom. "Much later."

* * *

The next morning, I managed to make it back to Wildwood about ten minutes before the farrier was due. Aunt Lin met me at the door. She was wearing a lime green and orange muumuu and Jesus sandals, and her hair was wrapped in a purple turban that made my eyes hurt.

"We got a call late yesterday," she said, "from that Sergeant Witz."

"Oh, what did she have to say?"

"That the investigation with the Jeep inferno was still open but—I think she said *inactive*. And she said we could have the eyesore hauled away. I took the liberty of calling Mike's Auto, and he'll bring a flatbed and haul the thing away for two-hundred bucks."

"Two hundred dollars!" I shrieked. For that I'll haul it to the back forty."

"No, see, he'll *pay* you. He said something about putting it on display at the lot."

"Seriously? He's paying *me* for his vehicle that he lent me that I, ah, destroyed?"

"Seriously. I confirmed it with him."

"This might be my lucky day," I said.

Aunt Lin smiled at me. "Preceded by a lucky night?"

I felt my face flush. "You could say that."

"Uh huh."

Aunt Lin looked out of the mod door and whistled. "My, my, that is an interesting-looking truck."

"Nikko says it's a pimpmobile."

"I thought those were like Caddies and stretch limos," she said. "That's a badass truck."

"Nikko said this is the U.P. version of a pimpmobile."

"I see. Well, I hope insurance doesn't break you."

I hadn't given insurance a lot of thought, or any thought for that matter. Once the truck title was transferred to me, I'd have to cough up at least a few hundred bucks. Well, the check should be coming in from the Magic Stirrup Foundation soon, so there was that.

"Oh, and one more thing," Aunt Lin said. "Actually something kind of strange, I think. You might want to go over the video from last night. Something set off the motion lights around two in the morning. I looked out and didn't see anything. Probably just a deer or even raccoons, but with everything going on, well, you know."

"Okay. I'll check it out."

Spud, the farrier, pulled up at the same time Mike showed up with his flatbed tow truck. I greeted everyone and went into the barn while

Clay got Oscar out of a stall and secured him in crossties for Spud to begin work. I went outside next and watched Mike winch the twisted wreckage onto his truck, leaving behind a black circle of burnt earth that looked like a satanic ritual had taken place.

"So you're really gonna pay me for this?" I asked.

"Sure. Course it will just be a credit at the station, you know, for future mechanical needs."

"That sounds fair," I said. "But what do you want this pile of rubble for?"

"It will be a tourist attraction. I'm gonna expand my ATV rental, and that will bring them in."

I couldn't imagine a horrific burnt-out vehicle would encourage people to merrily hit the trails, but I wasn't about to point that out.

"So, I see you got that blue truck from the Chevy place. Yous don't need the loaner anymore, I guess."

"There's still some paperwork for the new truck, but I'm pretty sure things will work out. I can't tell you how much I appreciate your helping me out."

"No problem," Mike said. "I can probably kill two birds with one stone here and go ahead and tow the loaner behind my flatbed."

"Sure, good idea," I said. "I'll get the keys."

When I came out of the mod, Mike was under the truck, presumably hooking up the tow sling. He emerged and dusted off his hands.

"Funny thing here," he said. "I saw a small puddle of fluid and thought I'd check it out."

"Well, it has been leaking some oil," I said. "I've added a couple of quarts."

"Nope. This here is leaking brake fluid."

"Really? Wow, that could have been dangerous."

"And it don't look to me like corrosion so much as someone cut the line. Not all the way, mind, but partway so's the stuff would just dribble out slow."

"You can tell all that?"

"Oh sure," he said, looking at me. "Eventually yous can stomp them brakes through the floorboards, but she ain't gonna stop."

We digested the implications for a minute.

"Jeannie Usitalo may have had brake failure," I said.

Mike frowned and said, "I had that Usitalo girl's car up on the lift not that long ago for an oil change. I always do a twelve-point check. I don't know what made her miss that curve and roll the car, but I can tell you that the car was in good shape when I looked it over."

* * *

I went back into the barn to see how the hoof trimming was going. Spud was bent over, holding one of Oscar's feet between his legs. Farriers need both hands to work, so they use their legs or sometimes a special stand to hold the animal's hoof in position. It was a grueling posture that earned most farriers back issues at an early age. Spud finished the hoof and lowered the horse's leg to the floor. Oscar craned his neck as far as the crosstie would allow and Spud gave him a treat.

"He was a real good colt," Spud said. "Hooves where not horrible, but they needed a trim."

Clay took Oscar and put him in a stall, then led Emmy out for her turn. She looked a little skittish. When Clay led her over to Spud, she pinned back her ears.

"Typical woman," Spud said. "All pissed off and don't even know why."

He and Clay yukked it up.

"Hey, don't forget who's paying you," I said.

"Ya gotta sweet talk a woman," Spud said. "Give her some treats."

I watched as he slipped Emmy a horse treat, then scratched her nose. Her ears swiveled from pinned back to pricked forward.

"You like that, do ya?" Spud said. "How about you give ol' Uncle Spud one of them dainty little feet." He reached down, and Emmy did not resist him lifting her leg and bracing it with his legs.

"Do you talk to all the ladies like that?" I asked.

"Nah. Just my wife. She don't allow me to sweet talk no other gals."

I went back to the mod to grab something to eat. While Nikko had provided me with an interesting evening, which included leftover lasagna and wine, there had been no time for me to have anything more than a cup of coffee as I'd headed out the door in the morning. Aunt Lin had fed Jupiter, but he still eyed me, ever hopeful. I popped a couple of pieces of bread in the toaster and poured myself some orange juice. My laptop was sitting on the kitchen table, so I booted it up and tried to remember how to review the previous night's video cameras. There were multiple cameras and a way to fast forward so you weren't watching eight hours of absolutely nothing.

My toast popped up, and I swiped on some organic peanut butter and took a bite. I pulled up instructions to review the video Raymond had provided, and after a lot of fooling around, I got the right date. I assumed the video I'd want to review would be the one at the parking lot corner of the barn.

Eventually, a grainy image appeared. With only the sodium light for illumination, the quality was poor. However, Raymond had rigged it so when there was activity, a motion-sensitive, solar-powered floodlight would come on, giving a better picture. I fast-forwarded through the video, with the hours and minutes flying by on the bottom right of my computer monitor. I could see moon shadows moving rapidly across, and what looked like a bat flew by the camera. I took another bite of toast and finished off the orange juice just as my computer screen brightened with the motion light activation. I paused the video and squinted at the screen. I could see something or someone just caught on the corner of the screen. It looked like a person, but when I reactivated the video, the image moved out of the camera range. Eventually, things went dark again.

"Well, damn!" I said to Jupiter as I backed up the video to watch it again. The loaner truck was just out of view, but it looked like someone moved toward it—and cut the brake line.

* * *

I wished I had a locking garage to park my truck in so I wouldn't have to climb on my hands and knees with a flashlight to look for leaking fluids under the chassis. The sudden and unlikely coincidences of cut brake lines strongly indicated that someone was sending a strong "I'm not messing around" message. Someone very deranged or very devious. Or both. But who? In my case, I would suspect Varga. And although he denied stooping to any such nefarious deeds, he was a confirmed liar. Yet he just seemed too prissy to diddle with the underside of a truck. Of course, he could have a minion in the wings.

But with Jeannie Usitalo, I had no idea. She didn't even have an ex-husband or a boyfriend that I knew of. If she had been having an affair with a married man, the entire village of Peshekee would know about it. The only connection I had with Jeannie was we were friends in high school and she was my hair stylist. She was nearly every Peshekee woman's hair stylist. There would be a lot of bad hair days on the horizon until someone else set up shop.

After confirming the pimpmobile was good to go, I headed to the office to put in some of my weekly hours. A rhythmic noise filled the cab, and it took me a minute to realize the truck was telling me I had a phone call. The salesman at the dealership had given me a crash course on the mind-boggling technology that came with the truck. "Hands off" phone calls was one of the features. I wondered what else it could tell me. Maybe my blood pressure was too high or my hair was a mess. I looked at the display on the dash and it showed a phone handset and a message telling me I had a phone call. It gave the caller's number and the ringtone continued. Meanwhile, I almost went off the road three times. I wondered if the so-called "hands off" phone system was any safer than just talking on my mobile. I jabbed at a phone icon displayed on the screen and the ringtone stopped, so I said hello.

"I was just gonna give up," said a voice over my radio speaker.

"Nikko?"

"Yup. Are you driving?"

"I'm trying. This truck is like the command center at NASA. I should have a copilot."

"Oh, poor baby. Anyway, I wanted to let you know I talked to Pop about the dead couple's phone."

"Yeah?"

"He said he'd help you out. Since it's not in evidence—at least not anymore—but just their personal effects, which by the way nobody has claimed, he can probably check it out. You can't have the phone but can look at photos and pick out the ones you want texted to you. He wondered what you were doing, and I told him it was for research of the homestead."

"Fantastic!" I said. "I owe you one."

"And I intend to collect," he said. "Speaking of debts, Pop wants pizza. He suggested lunch today. Can you swing it—say around noon at the Sheriff's Department?"

"Sure, I'm only working a half day today anyway."

"Extra-large pepperoni and double cheese," Nikko said.

"Are you meeting me there?"

"You betcha. I'll bring the beverages; you bring the pizza."

"Done," I said.

When I walked into Wilde Accounting, Rose was stationed at her desk. Sometimes I suspected that she never actually *left*. Maybe she was not real, but a hologram like the ghost horse at the Wildwood campground.

"Good morning, Rose," I said, tossing my purse under my desk.

"You have a message," she said stiffly. "I don't believe it relates to the office, and I'd appreciate it if you restricted your calls to business."

I assumed Rose had already notated this breach of conduct on my heavily visited Nasty List column.

"Sorry," I said, taking the pink *While You Were Out* slip from her.

All it said was that Lieutenant Spiller had called. There was a phone number and the box requesting a return call was checked.

"Well, crap," I said. "What does *he* want?"

Rose looked over the top of her cheaters at me. I muttered a second apology and slid into my creaky office chair. I didn't want to call the state police office and risk being overheard, so I decided to wait until I could sneak outside.

The front door swished open and Dad came in, trailed by Mia. Gussy must have sensed her arrival, and he casually stepped out of his office, as if on an important mission.

"Good morning, all!" Dad bellowed. "Gonna be a hot one."

We all muttered return salutations.

"Oh, hello, Mia," Gussy said. "I was wondering if you and I could review some things."

She smiled brilliantly and said, "Of course, Gussy. Just let me get my stuff put away."

Rose scowled mightily and made a small, derisive noise. There was no sign of Raymond, which was good from the standpoint of Gussy's wellbeing, but not so good for me because I wanted to talk to him about putting a camera facing the front of the mod where I usually parked.

As I was booting up my computer, my cell phone dinged. I tapped on the message and saw it was Nikko. Wow, a phone call *and* a text all within the same day.

I just got a call from Spiller, Nikko texted.

I got a call, too. Haven't called back.

Don't bother. He wants us both to come in tomorrow. I work til 3:30 so he said come at 4.

Why?

Don't know. Could be a lot of things.

I did an emoji of poop.

Nikko did an emoji of a laughing smiley face.

I texted, *See you at noon at your dad's office.*

I waited for some XXs and OOs or maybe a heart, but nada.

We're popular with the cops, he finally said.

That got no response from me.

24

I swung the pimpmobile into the parking lot at the Sheriff's Department. No matter how much I monkeyed around, I was straddling the line between spaces. I didn't think it was illegal, per se, just rude to hog two spots. I got out of the truck and hit the lock button on the fob. It was hard to remember since I had never locked any of my previous vehicles. The new truck would honk at me if I got out and tried to walk away without locking it. It also honked at me if I tried to leave my purse in the car with the fob in it. And it honked once or twice just to mess with me.

I grabbed the aromatic pizza and headed to the front door. Just as I was getting buzzed in, Nikko pulled up and parked. He got out and came over to me, carrying a bag.

"Hey, Kat, you're parked over the line," he said, holding the door open for me. "There might be a penalty for that. Of course, being a woman driver and all, well…."

"Bite me," I said.

"Oooo, are we in a bad mood?"

"I'm never in a good mood on days I have to go into the office. Rose wants me to go up in the sweltering attic and arrange things back to the way they were before I rearranged them."

"Sounds like you're being hazed," Nikko said.

"With Rose, I'm in a constant state of haze."

A deputy manning the front desk buzzed us through, and we walked down the hallway to Sheriff Olsen's office.

"I smell pepperoni!" came a voice down the hall.

"Dad is part bloodhound," Nikko said.

We walked into the office, which sported its usual disaster décor.

"Hey, Pop," Nikko said. "When did the tornado go through?"

"Shut up and bring that pizza over here," the sheriff said. "Hello Kat. Why do you put up with this guy?"

"Who says I put up with him?" I said, laying the pizza on a pile of papers on the desk.

"Smart girl. You got napkins?"

I pulled a wad out of my purse, and the sheriff flipped open the pizza box. Nikko pulled some cans of pop out of the bag he had brought in. We greedily dug in.

"I got the phone," Sheriff Olsen said. "At first it was in evidence with the staties. Then they gave it to us because they didn't find anything particularly helpful. We have a box of the victims' personal effects, so it went there. Hope we never have to prove a chain of custody because it's toast. Anyway, let's finish eating, then you can scroll through the photos. Like numbnuts here probably told you, you can't take the phone, but you can look at pictures and send them to your phone. The couple was not on the up and up, I can tell you that. They had false ID, and their so-called hippie look seemed to be a ploy to deceive. But until we can find out just what they were up to, we probably won't know if their deaths were accidental or otherwise. Spiller and I are tracking down some leads. Anyway, it looks like the phone belonged to the guy, Theodore Hilman—that's his real name. There was another burner phone, but that didn't have a camera."

"I really appreciate this," I said.

"No problem. Pizza is superb, by the way."

After we had polished off all but a couple of slices, Sheriff Olsen opened a desk drawer and rummaged around. He pulled out the phone and slid it across the desk.

"You probably know more than me on how to do things, so have at it," he said.

I turned the phone on and saw it was at about 50 percent power. I opened the camera and began scrolling through the photo gallery. It looked like a couple hundred photos, with pictures of the VW camper along with a few photos of a man and woman who may have been the dead couple when still alive and without their hippie attire. But since I never really saw them, other than being toted out in body bags, it could have been their Uncle Lou and Aunt Tillie for all I knew. There were a lot of photos of scenery, historic-looking buildings, Lake Superior, road signage, and a shot of a pasty doused in ketchup. Typical photos of a road trip.

Then it got interesting.

"Hey, guys," I said, "look at this."

The three of us crowded around the phone, and I enlarged a photo of what looked like some kind of ancient tablet, maybe made of stone or clay. It had a series of crude pictures and several lines of some hieroglyphics along the bottom of the object. Another photo was of something that looked like a Sphinx sitting on a box, and another of a necklace with a large pendant on it, also crudely inscribed.

"I think these must be some kind of artifacts," I said. "Could be that the hippie couple was into studying ancient things. Maybe they were at a museum somewhere. I can tell you these aren't objects from the Peshekee Historical Society Museum."

"They look Pre-Columbian," Nikko said. "Or knockoffs. Who knows? They could be stage props or priceless relics."

"My, aren't you Mr. Academia," I said.

"I took some ancient history in college," Nikko said.

Sheriff Olsen gave a derisive snort. "Along with partying one-oh-one."

I looked closer at the tablet. "Hey, look, I think it's telling the story of the creation of man, you know, from the Bible."

"Yeah," Nikko said. "That's Adam and Eve. You know, where Adam met his downfall because of Eve."

"Always blaming women," I said.

The sheriff gave a snort.

"Anyway, what I really want to see is if they took photos of some pages from Helvi Paavola Huntington's journal," I said, scrolling through more photos.

"Who's Helvi whatsername?" Sheriff Olsen asked.

I explained the homestead saga.

"Oh, right," the sheriff said. "Nikko said you were researching the homestead at Wildwood, and you think the hippie couple was also doing some research of your place?"

"Elsie—the volunteer at the museum—said they also looked at Helvi's journal. We're not sure what they were looking for, but there are missing pages."

"So, you think they stole the pages?" asked the sheriff.

"Not really," I said. "I think they would have taken photos of things in the journal that interested them. That's what I've done, or did, until Elsie cut me off. Removing the pages would have been unnecessary."

"Unless there was something to hide," Nikko said.

"And as I mentioned, first Elsie banished me, and now has invited me back to the museum. I think she's a little, well, high-strung." *Or wacko*, I thought.

I continued to scroll through the photo gallery, and the sheriff finished off the last two pieces of pizza. He pulled a box of breath mints out of the drawer and popped a couple into his mouth. He held out the container and we all took a mint.

"Ma will smell the pizza on your breath a mile away," Nikko said.

"Well, at least it's not booze," the sheriff said.

"Hey! I think I found something!" I shouted. "Here's some photos maybe from the journal."

The three of us huddled around the phone. I enlarged a photo and began to read. I felt a grin spread across my face.

"Looks like you're having a eureka moment," the sheriff said.

"This is it, photos from Helvi's journal. *I knew it!* It's gonna take me a while to make an album and send it to my email. Then I can bring them up on my laptop and read them."

"Okay, well, I have to get back to work," the sheriff said. "Go ahead and do what you need to do, and then call dispatch and ask them to have Sergeant Haapala come get the phone."

"Will do," I said. "And thanks again."

The sheriff nodded and left the room. Nikko came over and stood behind me while I worked with the photos. He put his arms around me, making me fumble the phone.

"Hey," I said. "Kinda busy here."

"Sure, but I do believe you owe me a debt of gratitude."

I thought for a moment. "Okay, your—ah—assistance entitles you to one free riding lesson."

"Hmm, I guess that's a fair deal," he said. "When?"

"How about tonight around seven, after it cools down?" I said.

"How about I come around six and I'll bring dinner and some beer."

"No alcohol. You need your faculties."

"Oh, well, yes we want my faculties to be in order."

He bent over and kissed me on the neck, sending a tingle into my hair follicles.

"Gotta go," he said. "Duty calls. Good luck with your photo session."

* * *

"It's called the forward position—or the two-point," I barked as Nikko lumbered around the riding ring aboard Rusty. "Lean your butt out of the saddle, pivot at the knees, and ride off your lower leg. Arch your back a little, knuckles on each side of his withers."

"How the hell can I remember all of that?" Nikko bellowed.

I was giving Nikko the promised riding lesson. There's something to the advice of not trying to teach anything to one's "significant other." While Nikko had excellent athletic ability, riding a horse was not so much about power and strength as it was about flexibility and finesse. One might say that you need to almost become *part of the horse* to have things flow amicably and avoid inflicting excessive, albeit unintentional, suffering upon the schooling horse. Luckily for Nikko, he was riding Rusty, who was tolerant.

"It will come naturally!" I bellowed back. "*Eventually*. Do a couple more times around in the position. You are practicing for when you actually start to jump."

"My back is killing me."

"Quit whining. I thought you jocks worked through the pain."

Nikko sat back in the saddle and pulled Rusty to an awkward halt. "That was in high school. I'm older now."

"Oh pshaw!"

"Pshaw? What are you, my grandma?"

I ignored the insult. I had the upper hand and Nikko hated that. "Okay, now take the forward position at the trot."

"You're kidding."

I put my hands on my hips and gave him a look. Okay, maybe I did act like his grandma.

"Fine," Nikko said. "I'll do as you say, but I won't be in any shape for any lovin' tonight, so don't expect any."

"I'll live. Quit talking and get moving."

He urged Rusty into a trot and awkwardly took the two-point position. They bobbed around for a while. I swear Rusty added a little extra bounce in his gait. *Take that, human!*

"Okay, sit back and let's see you at a posting trot."

Posting was created to enable horse and rider to travel a fair distance at the trot without the trauma of constantly banging on the horse's back. The rider uses the upward thrust of the horse's trotting gait to rise slightly out of the saddle, then lowers his or herself gently on the offbeat. So instead of being at odds with the horse's movement, the rider merges with it. Western riders jog-trot their horses, which tends to be slower than the English trotting gait, and thus smoother and easier to sit. Either style requires learning to feel the horse and flow with the movement.

Nikko transitioned into a fairly competent posting rhythm. Rusty plodded around the ring, probably letting his mind tune out the annoying human and maybe thinking about something pleasant, such as rolling in the dirt or chewing on a fence board.

A truck pulled up and Susie Koskinen got out and walked over to the riding ring.

"How's it goin'?" she asked.

"Okay—hey, heels down and chin up!"

"How's your hottie?" Susie said.

"My hottie?"

"Uh-huh."

"I call him my friend who is a boy. You're on the wrong diagonal!"

"Does he know that the diagonal is the outside shoulder—he's supposed to go up when it's forward?"

"I've told him like a zillion times," I said. "Rise and fall with the shoulder by the wall!"

Nikko looked down at the horse's shoulder.

"You should feel it."

"What?"

"Halt!"

Nikko pulled harshly back on the reins and Rusty skidded to a stop. "Why am I stopping?"

"Just seeing if you were paying attention," I said.

Susie was giggling.

"When do I get to try jumping?" Nikko asked.

"Maybe next time," I said. "The last thing today is to learn to fall off."

"*WHAT?*"

"Quit saying *what.* You need to learn to fall off the horse and also hang on to the horse after you fall. It's an essential skill."

"You have got to be kidding."

"I gotta see this," Susie said.

"I'm not kidding," I said. "We'll do it at a walk."

Nikko urged Rusty into a walk. "I better not get hurt," Nikko said. "I have to work tomorrow."

"You should have thought of that before you hooked up with me," I said.

"Yeah, you got that right," he said.

"Okay, now loosen the reins; kick your feet out of the stirrups."

Nikko obeyed.

"Now bend over; grab the horse around the neck."

Nikko grunted a little but again did as told.

"Now slide off the horse on the near side and push *away* from him, and jump off. Try to land on your feet—remember to bend at the knees—and hang onto the reins with one hand."

Nikko slid off, fell backwards and landed on his keister. Rusty jerked the reins free and trotted off to a patch of grass growing under the fence.

Susie snorted with laughter and said, "You ain't gonna have him for your hottie much longer."

"Aren't," I corrected. "Aren't going to have."

"You're kinda bossy," she said.

Nikko got up, dusted himself off, and glared at me. Susie and I watched him retrieve Rusty and lead him over. "Yeah, she's bossy *and* mean."

"I'm not mean, just strict. By the way, you flunked falling."

Susie laughed again. "An F in falling."

Nikko scowled at her. "Don't you have somewhere you need to be other than being a royal pain in the—?"

"Okay, okay. I'm gonna take Shadow for a ride. Hey, Kat, FYI, Miss Moss said things are going great with the bid for the horse camp. I'm, like, so excited!"

"Like, me too," I said. Now I was talking like a valley girl.

"See ya," she said.

"Are we through here?" Nikko snapped.

"Be sure to cool him off and give him a rubdown."

"Why? He'll just roll in the dirt. And I'm the hottie, not him. Maybe I need to cool down."

I looked at him.

"That's right. I heard Susie call me your hottie."

"Her words, not mine."

He grinned and grabbed me behind the neck, dipped me backward, and planted a kiss, all the while hanging onto Rusty's reins.

"Put that in your pipe and smoke it," he said as he walked off leading the horse.

≈ 25 ≈

After Nikko left, I finally had time to boot up my laptop and start reading the photographed journal pages. I had already seen the first one, which mentioned the unearthing of something *not found in nature* while digging postholes. The next page expanded on the find.

Ruthie is so excited about the strange object that William and Luke dug up. I speculate it is likely something buried years ago by the Native people who still inhabit the area. The item resembles a slate, such as the children might use at school, but of a softer earthy material, and contains crude pictures and writing that even William found puzzling. It seemed to be telling a story, perhaps of the creation. I told Ruthie we'd take it into the Mercantile where many Native people shop and perhaps one could identify it. Ruthie promised to take very good care of the find because she was sure it was special.

The description of the tablet the Huntingtons dug up at the homestead sounded similar to the tablet artifact in one of the camera photos. I wished that Helvi had drawn a sketch for comparison.

Before I could read the next page, my cell phone whinnied at me. The readout said 4HR. I answered and it was Marjorie VanderVeen, the director of the foundation.

"Hey Marjorie, how are things going?"

"Pretty good, Kat. How about with you?"

"Next time you come by, plan to spend a couple of hours chatting and I'll fill you in. I can say for sure that things have not been dull."

"Well, I *do* plan to come at the end of the week, if possible."

"Time for an inspection?" I asked.

"Oh I suppose, but actually I'm hoping you can take in another rescue."

When it rains, it pours, I thought. But of course I couldn't turn Marjorie down.

"What have you got?"

"A Shetland pony mare, at least ten years old. Severe neglect."

"I think we can handle it," I said. "I have good help. Has it been in quarantine?"

"Uh, no. Here's the deal: The pony has been locked in a dark barn for several years, standing in manure up to its knees. It is severely foundered and nearly starved to death."

I felt my face burn. I tried not to get emotional about the horror stories. Ponies are very susceptible to foundering. It's a condition where the animal likely has suffered from a painful hoof condition called laminitis. Imagine pounding your fingernail with a hammer and multiply the pain about 1,000 percent. That is what the horse goes through. Then the damage to the hoof causes the horny portion to deform and often grow out of control, sometimes into ski-like curls that completely cripple the animal.

"We did have the hooves worked on a little after the rescue," Marjorie said. "And the pony had an IV for dehydration and some antibiotics. She's stable now but will need a lot of TLC and a good farrier to work on her hooves. The reason it's kind of last minute is she's currently in a temporary situation near the bridge, and I need to move her out within a couple of days. It makes more sense to head up your way; you're the closest rescue, and this poor little thing shouldn't travel any farther than she has to."

"Okay. When are you thinking?"

"How about Friday afternoon?"

"We'll be ready," I said. *Somehow,* I thought.

"Excellent! Thank you, Kat. Of course we'll be compensating you."

"That always helps," I said. "Safe travels."

"Yup," Marjorie said and disconnected.

My laptop was still on but had gone into sleep mode. It was getting past my bedtime, and now I had to get some things ready the next day for the new arrival on Friday. Also, I was not going to make my minimum hours at the office if I didn't at least go in for part of the day. I sighed and shut down the laptop. I was pretty sure the page I read describing a tablet was not something Native American. Maybe if it was pottery or a tool, that would make sense, but the tablet artifact did sound like what Nikko described as pre-Columbian. If it was, that could be significant. The implications were enormous. Maybe an ancient civilization—here in the U.P.? It seemed unlikely. I expected I'd be looking for an expert on the subject, once I learned more. But that would be for another time. I stumbled into my bedroom, threw my clothes on a chair, and fell into bed.

I was asleep before my head hit the pillow.

* * *

After a few hours at the office, I hurried home to work out a plan to quarantine the new pony. I also had to remember that Lieutenant Spiller had requested the honor of my and Nikko's presence that afternoon. I set the alarm on my phone to make sure I didn't lose track of time.

Marjorie from 4HR hadn't mentioned a name for the pony that was to come under my care. As a young girl, I had a series of picture books about Peaches the Pony. I also had a Peaches the Pony stuffed animal and a ceramic statue of Peaches. I had cherished my Peaches Pony years and read the picture books over and over. Peaches was a precocious pony that got into mischief on occasion. She always learned a lesson, which was lightly veiled as a lesson to her human readers. Things such as obeying your parents, caring about others, sharing—the usual. I still had the collection of books and the stuffed pony. I remembered breaking the ceramic version of Peaches and being devastated over the loss. But the other treasured items were safely stashed in my closet, along with a high school yearbook, senior picture, college diploma, and other memorabilia that I couldn't part with.

I decided to name the rescue pony Peaches, after my beloved childhood idol. Then I had a second aha moment. I had been wracking my brain over what to do for Jeannie's family. Mom said the Usitalos had more casseroles than they knew what to do with. I could donate to Brianna's college fund, but she was only six, so that wasn't going to help a little girl who had lost her mother. I smiled and set off to rummage through my closet. Maybe Peaches the Pony books and a gently used stuffed animal would comfort the child, if only a little.

* * *

The lieutenant had us wait for him in a small conference room. I had gotten there a little early and killed time by wandering around the windowless room. I figured it was the briefing room for the troops before they started a shift. It had a more "lived in" look than Lieutenant Spiller's sterile office. Chairs were a mishmash of castoffs. There were coffee rings on the table along with an empty donut box and an assortment of empty pop cans and Styrofoam cups. One wall had a couple of computers set up, probably for writing reports. A whiteboard was wiped clean except for a scribbled message in the corner stating *Spilljoy Was Here!*, along with a rough sketch of a stick person complete with badge and gun. Clearly an effigy of Lieutenant Spiller. I debated whether to wipe it off, then thought better of it. I pulled out my phone and took a picture. I wasn't sure why. The only other thing of minor interest was a bulletin board displaying HR stuff and a hodgepodge of clippings, flyers, business cards, and pushpins.

Nikko came in next, wearing his CO uniform. I was wearing business casual—very casual. He smiled and walked over to me, then pulled me into a kiss. It was a nice way to say hello, though I wondered if we were being recorded. Police departments tend to have a lot of security cameras.

"Glad we both beat Spiller in," Nikko said. "He hates to be kept waiting."

"Who doesn't?"

Nikko moved over to the table and looked in the empty donut box.

"Kind of a cliché, isn't it?" I said. "You know, cops and donuts."

"Kinda," Nikko said. "And not a crumb left."

We heard the door open and turned to see Spiller stride in as if he were entering the Oval Office. He was carrying a laptop. He nodded and we nodded back. Spiller frowned at the empty donut box. He grabbed it along with empty Styrofoam cups and pop cans and threw them in a nearby wastebasket. If he saw his Spilljoy portrait on the dry erase board, he showed no reaction.

"Shall we all sit down?" he asked. "I'm sorry if I'm a little late, but I just got some new information."

We all sat. Spiller opened the laptop and tapped at some keys.

"So, I suppose you're both wondering why I asked you here," he said, not looking up from the computer screen.

The line was straight out of a Mickey Spillane novel.

We nodded.

"First off, I'll just be using the laptop to type some notes from our meeting. This is not a formal record, but just for my recollection. I'm trying to piece some things together, and talking to you is just routine."

"Okay," I said.

Spiller looked up. "As you know, I requested the drone that you, ah, found be returned because the owner was demanding it. Or I believe it was a piece of equipment that person was actually leasing. In any event, he—or she—wanted it back."

I nodded. "You got it, right?"

"Yes. Apparently you had an agent deliver it," Spiller said. "Interestingly, the person demanding it has not come in to claim it."

"Raymond is a coworker, not an agent. But yeah, he brought it in for me as a favor."

"Which I appreciate. The claimant of the unit was doing some surveying of the area, which was sanctioned, but we all get a little...unsettled when drones fly over, so the fact that it was obviously shot down is not something I'm going to pursue."

"I think we have a right to know why something like that is going on," I said. "It spooked my horse, and I was injured in a fall."

"I agree," Spiller said. "And I'm sorry about your accident. But, unfortunately, little regulation exists for drones, except in the case of airplane flight patterns, military bases, and so forth."

"What exactly was the thing surveying *for*?" Nikko asked.

"I was told a survey was being conducted in a search for artifacts in the area."

"Artifacts?" I said. "Like what?"

"The person wouldn't say. While looking is one thing, I did caution him that if they intended to dig up Native American artifacts or other relics, they needed to go through the proper channels."

"Who, exactly, did you tell this to?" Nikko asked.

"It was a man named Alex Varga," Spiller said.

I jerked upright in my seat. "Varga?"

"Yes," Spiller said. "According to Sergeant Witz, who investigated the arson of a certain vehicle at your premises, you pointed out some veiled threats from this Mr. Varga. That's one reason I brought you in today. As I said, I'm trying to put things together on this."

Nikko said, "So, Varga is looking for some sort of artifacts."

I said, "He offered to buy my land—actually, *insisted* on buying part of my land, which, I'm thinking, probably contains something related to his drone search."

"It would seem so," Spiller said. "I concur with Officer Olsen that it involves some kind of artifacts."

"Native American things?" I asked. "And if so, who *is* Varga—a grave robber or something?"

"His credentials," said Spiller, "show him to be a curator of the Dumbarton Oaks Museum in Washington, DC."

"And you're sure he's legit?" Nikko asked.

"Yes, I verified his credentials."

The lieutenant typed a few keys, then turned his computer screen toward us and showed an official-looking ID from the museum. Varga's photo was on it.

I said, "Okay, first off, Varga gave me his business card a while back, and it mentioned nothing about him being connected to any museum. And why didn't he just tell me that and what he was doing?"

"I am not certain," Spiller said, "but there may be a couple of reasons. One would be that he wanted to keep things quiet in case a major discovery was involved. Perhaps he was concerned that making it public knowledge would result in a slew of fortune seekers muddying things up. Plus, you might demand a piece of the action or at least a sizable sum for your real estate—much more than a landlocked parcel of land would normally go for. The second possible reason relates to the information I just received about the dead couple. We already knew they had false IDs, and we were able to track their real identities with fingerprints. What is new news is that they were former employees of the museum where Varga works. Their names are Theodore and Laureen Hilman. He worked in the mailroom, and she was Varga's administrative assistant. It's always possible Varga was in cahoots with them. Or at the other end of the gamut, he was hunting them down."

"In cahoots?" I said.

"They were suspected of a theft from the museum via the mailroom."

"What did they steal?" I asked.

"This is some more information I just got," Spiller said. "It's very strange, but the shipment of stolen items were replicas of a famous pre-Columbian excavation that ended up being a hoax."

"So, they were knockoffs of knockoffs?" Nikko asked.

"Right," Spiller said. "The replicas were going to be used for an interpretive display about an extensive archaeological hoax that actually occurred in Michigan at the turn of the twentieth century. Apparently, it's quite a story involving two men—" He paused and looked at his computer screen "—James Scotford and Daniel Soper."

"I wonder why anyone would steal something like that," I said.

"Maybe they thought the pieces were authentic," Nikko said.

"Possible," Spiller said. "Except that Laureen Hilman was privy to enough information that she likely would have known they were indeed simply replicas. Plus, if the items had been authentic or even potentially priceless artifacts, they wouldn't have come regular UPS; they would have been privately transported with a lot of security in place. In any event, the FBI is involved. The stolen pieces do have value."

"Kind of like *Antiques Roadshow*," I said.

Nikko and the lieutenant looked at me.

"Who doesn't watch *Antiques Roadshow*?" I asked. "You know, where they say it's a *good* reproduction of something priceless, and has some value as a curiosity for collectors."

"That may be a motive," Spiller said. "But seems kind of risky to steal something of minimal value, which is still a serious crime when a museum is involved. Plus, they gave up two good jobs and became fugitives from the law."

"So, were the feds on their trail?" Nikko asked.

"I think the trail was cold, plus it wasn't a great priority, and the Hilmans easily slipped away before the paperwork of the missing shipment caught the problem. They were on the run, obviously disguised as the aging hippies in a VW camper, which is a pretty good disguise. They draw a lot of attention to themselves but pose as something entirely different than who they really are. Then, of course, their bodies were found by you two in the Crystal Lake Wilderness."

"So, what I'm hearing," said Nikko, "is that this case was growing cold. What about now that the couple is dead?"

"The deaths are being investigated by us and the sheriff. If we find the missing museum pieces, we will let the feds know. So far, they haven't turned up. Probably stashed in a bus locker somewhere. Eventually maybe they'll surface. Meanwhile, the feds and local law enforcement have gone through the Hilmans' things with the proverbial fine-tooth comb."

"So what turned up?" I asked. "I mean besides the hemlock in the tea tin?"

Spiller said, "They found the couple's counterfeit ID and maybe some research papers. Their fake names were Jason Martinez and Emily Bentley. They had forged passports and Michigan driver's licenses. We didn't find anything else, such as charge cards or health insurance cards. There was significant cash in the van, which was stashed under the dining table seat cushion. I think well over five grand."

"So, are you still ruling the Hilmans' deaths as likely accidental?" Nikko asked.

"Not so much now," Spiller said. He stood and began pacing.

"Would it have been Varga who hunted them down," I asked, "and somehow staged the whole thing? You know, to make their deaths look like an accident."

"Possibly, though it would just be speculation," Spiller said.

"I mean if he was tracking them down legitimately, why not just have them arrested?"

"Another excellent question for which I have no answer."

Spiller sat back in his chair and typed a few notes on his laptop.

"Did you interview him about it?" Nikko asked.

"Unfortunately, I have not had the opportunity."

"Why not?" I asked. "Is he under some kind of special protection because he's foreign or something?"

"No," Spiller said. "No foreign immunity applies to Mr. Varga, and I assure you that I'd very much like to talk to the man. I have a BOLO out for him. However, he seems to be missing. I had his business card, but he doesn't respond to my phone calls, texts, or emails. The museum claims he's still on special assignment and hasn't been in contact for a while. We've even tried to get a ping on his cell, but no luck. And he never showed up to claim the drone, which was strange since he was so insistent about getting it back. I have some concern over his disappearance. I believe you, Miss Wilde, may have been the last person to see him, or at least speak to him, and I'd very much appreciate it if you'd let me know if he gets in contact with you again."

"Okay, sure," I said. I was silently hoping that Varga *wouldn't* contact me again.

"So you met with Sheriff Olsen?" Spiller asked.

"Yes," I said.

"Something about journal pages and photos? Ollie contacted me, just to make sure I was okay with it."

"Right. I'm doing a little research on the homestead, but now I seemed to have stumbled onto something a lot more significant than I thought."

I explained the missing pages in the journal.

Nikko asked, "Just out of curiosity, what did the items look like that were stolen? I'm interested in archeological history."

I gave Nikko a puzzled look and said, "Go figure."

"I would have loved to spend my life digging up pot shards, but there isn't much of a career path in it, so I focused on criminal justice, and now I get to chase Russian boars through the forest."

Spiller looked at Nikko for a moment, then apparently decided not to ask about wayward swine. He cleared his throat and tapped some keys on his laptop. "I believe they sent some JPEG photos of them that they got from the organization that crafted and shipped them. I just got the email and haven't had a chance to read it or look at the photos. Okay, here's one of them."

He brought up a photo of a tablet, complete with a series of pictographs. I pulled my phone out and brought up my photo of the tablet I had copied from the Hilman phone. I emailed it to Spiller. He opened it and put the two photos side by side. We moved in for a closer look.

"There, look," Nikko said. "There's Eve tempting Adam in the Garden of Eden."

"Ding ding ding!" I said. "We have a winner!"

"Looks identical," Spiller said. "Possibly a depiction of the story from Genesis, or the creation of man."

I looked at him.

"What? You don't think I know the Bible?"

"No," I said. "Of course not. I—ah...."

Spiller ignored my babbling and frowned, "I can't believe we missed this. I thought one of the detectives went through the phone. Unfortunately, probably whoever it was—and I'll find out—was more focused on calls, texts, emails, and maybe internet search history."

"There were a lot of photos on the phone," I said. "I mean a lot, and they seemed like ordinary vacation pics, including touristy historic sites. It might have been easy to miss if someone scrolled through quickly."

I brought up the other photos relating to the artifacts. The Sphinx sitting on the box or wall also matched a photo Spiller had. He had another photo of a slate tablet with a series of pictographs that clearly depicted the biblical flood, complete with a crude sketch of the ark. The pictures looked as if they were drawn by a kid in first grade art class. Spiller also had a photo that displayed multiple pieces from the collection, including more tablets and boxes that resembled mini-sarcophagi. He didn't have a photo of the necklace with the amulet. It was always possible the necklace wasn't part of the collection of missing museum pieces.

"I can't believe that they would keep incriminating evidence on their phone," Nikko said.

"Maybe they were hoping to pass the things off as authentic on the black market," Spiller said. "They'd need to do that electronically and would need the photos. I guess the deceased couple are now deceased suspects. We'll need to put that phone back into evidence. Hard to interrogate the suspects now that they're dead."

"And just to add another monkey wrench into the works," I said, "I think you should know that the homestead family dug something up that may match the description of the stolen tablet, or at least be similar from the standpoint being pre-Columbian. But, of course, there is no photo, not even a drawing, only a vague description."

"Maybe no connection to the Hilman heist," Nikko said. "Could just be a coincidence."

"You know what they say about coincidences," Spiller said. "Sure would like to talk to Alex Varga right now. His disappearance is very concerning."

"And, just for the record," I said, "maybe I should tell you about the latest."

Nikko frowned and looked at me.

I told them about the brake line in the loaner truck.

Spiller took a deep breath and leaned back in his chair. "I suggest you make a police report, Miss Wilde, either with us or the sheriff's department. Then law enforcement can send someone out to Mike's Auto for a look and a statement."

I nodded and Nikko reached over and took my hand.

"And Miss Wilde, I think it would be wise to exercise extra precaution in your activities and routine until we get to the bottom of things."

He didn't have to tell me that twice.

26

I took my laptop with me onto the mod porch so I could look at more journal pages while waiting for the new rescue pony to arrive. I booted up my computer and brought up the next couple of journal page photos.

William and Luke finally got the rest of the postholes dug. They said they didn't know that many rocks existed in all of God's green earth. They fashioned a fine pen for the milk cow we'd be getting and enlarged the horse's shed for both animals to share. With fresh milk and eggs from our laying hens, I can finally do some proper baking. I decided to celebrate our blessings by making a cake, but I was in need of some goods. William readied to ride our horse to town to fetch our new cow. I saw my opportunity and gave him a shopping list. He laughed at me saying I made him my tote boy. I told him to hush if he wanted a piece of my apple cake.

Just as William was leaving, our Ruthie hurried out of the cabin clutching a parcel. She had wrapped the tablet in a piece of cloth and asked her papa to see if anybody knew what it was. William is always tender toward his children and said he reckoned he could. Ruthie got very serious and asked if her papa could please also bring her a peppermint stick. She mentioned that she had been good with her chores and her prayers. William smiled and said he'd see what he could do. Ruthie and I both knew he would buy all his children a special treat.

I smiled, thinking how the Huntington family didn't seem to dwell on their hardships, but enjoyed the blessings of apparent good health and a loving household. I heard a vehicle approach and saw a truck towing a horse trailer mincing its way up Horse Camp Road. I shut my laptop and took it back into the mod, then went out to greet my new arrival. Clay had heard them coming too, and he came out of the barn to join me.

The truck and trailer pulled around. Marjorie VanderVeen climbed out and stretched the kinks out of her back. Clay and I joined her, and we all shook hands.

"Thanks for taking the pony on such short notice," Marjorie said.

"No problem," I said. "Clay has a stall ready, but I expect the pony will need to be outside for a while after her trailer ride."

"Yeah, good," Marjorie said. "No need to quarantine her. She was cooped up alone in a horrible situation but not exposed to things like the horses we get from the auction barn. The pony has been checked out, and like I said, given some preliminary rehabilitative care for her hooves and otherwise despicable condition. For sure her hooves and teeth are going to need extensive work. Just be sure to get receipts."

Marjorie opened the back of the horse trailer and went inside. After a couple of minutes, a raggedy animal minced its way backward down the ramp and stumbled onto the parking lot.

"Meet Honey," Marjorie said.

The pony was indeed a horror show. Her feet were still terribly misshapen, and her coat was long, dull, and patchy. She was a black and white pinto, though the black was dull to the point of being more charcoal gray. I already had Spud the farrier scheduled for next week, along with our vet, Dr. Jukkila, to help work out a recovery plan for the pony. As was typical of the Shetland pony breed, she had an abundant mane whose weight pulled the crest of the neck askew. In spite of her pathetic condition, the little mare lifted her head, pricked her ears forward, and flared her nostrils, taking in her new surroundings.

I went up to the pony and stroked her muzzle. "Hey there, sweetie, you're safe now." I turned to Marjorie and said, "I'm going to rename her Peaches after a childhood book series, if that's okay."

"Change noted," Marjorie said. She pulled a clipboard with some paperwork out of her truck, scribbled a bit, and handed me a wad of papers. "This puts things in order. We'll be electronically transferring the first payment to your account in the next couple of days."

"Great, thanks," I said, stuffing the paperwork into my pocket.

Clay said, "How about I give the little lady a tour of the place. Let her see the other horses, have a drink, and maybe some hay?"

"Sounds great," I said. "Thanks, Clay."

He led Peaches off and I turned to Marjorie. "How about some coffee or tea?"

"Sure, but just a quick cup, and I really need to use your bathroom!"

After Marjorie left and Peaches was settling in, I decided to take another quick look at the journal page photos. I sat at the kitchen table and flipped my laptop open. Jupiter sauntered in and looked at me, then looked at the clock.

"You've got at least a half hour before dinnertime," I said.

"Yow!"

Aunt Lin came through the kitchen and went over to the fridge. "Sorry I didn't come out to meet your friend," she said. "I was in the zone—meditating. I've been feeling some strange vibes lately."

"No problem," I said. "It's probably me giving off the vibes. I've spent way too much time hanging out at police stations."

Aunt Lin pulled a bottle of her chilled tea out of the fridge and turned to look at me. "I sense that you are full of angst. My special tea will calm you and help you focus."

"Sure, okay," I said as I booted up my computer.

Aunt Lin filled a glass and put it in front of me. I absently took a swallow. It tasted like grass and mint. "Thanks."

"I'm headed out now," Aunt Lin said. "Raymond and I are going to some kind of ceremony his people are doing. I'm truly honored to be invited."

"Uh huh," I said as I brought up the next journal page. "See ya, and say hi to your sweetie."

"He's not my sweetie! He's my soulmate."

"Say hi to your soulmate for me."

The next journal page of course talked about the new cow. Everyone was very excited. Livestock was a big deal, and now the Huntingtons had a horse, a cow, and chickens. I speed-read until information relating to the tablet caught my eye.

Ruthie jumped around barely able to control her excitement. She asked William about the tablet even before she asked about her peppermint stick. William handed me a parcel with the goods I requested and returned Ruthie her tablet. He told her it stirred up a fair interest at the Mercantile, and that there happened to be a man there, Ezekiel Adams from the mining school, stocking up on supplies. William said the man showed curiosity about Ruthie's find and wondered if he could visit with us after he had some time to do research. We expect he'll come by if he finds a reason.

I took another sip of Aunt Lin's tea and had to admit it was growing on me. I looked at my watch. Time to start chores. Jupiter was still staring at me, lest I forget he was a priority.

The next day was Jeannie's funeral. I wondered what to wear. Was the protocol still black or could I get by wearing my blue dress, which was my only dress? I had a pair of low heels I hadn't worn since I worked at the hospital as a grant writer. And I likely would need a slip under the dress, and a bra that wasn't made for riding horses. I knew I didn't own a pair of pantyhose, so pasty white would be the fashion of the day, unless Aunt Lin had something I could borrow. I also needed to dig around for a gift bag to put my *Peaches the Pony* books and stuffed animal in for Brianna. Nikko had promised to meet me at Shute's Funeral Parlor about an hour before the service. We'd probably just do the visitation and then I'd head to the museum to meet with Elsie and see what she had up her sleeve. I wasn't getting my hopes up that she had anything significant to share. I was beginning to think the Huntington tablet would remain a mystery. Speaking of mysteries, I wondered if Nikko had any updates on the cut brake lines.

* * *

The parking lot was already jammed when I pulled the pimpmobile into Shute's Funeral Parlor. I finally found a spot in the back of the lot that wasn't actually a parking spot, but more like a gravel driveway to a maintenance building. Good enough. I backed in, marveling at the two backup cameras that guided me perfectly into place.

It looked as if the visitation line was stretched outside onto the porch and down the steps. I hobbled over in my impractical pumps, carrying my gift bag containing the *Peaches the Pony* treasures, and joined the queue. I heard someone call my name. I looked around and saw Nikko standing in the doorway, waving. I wasn't a line cutter by nature, but one could have a place saved, couldn't they? Nobody made a fuss when I joined Nikko inside a small vestibule.

"Let's go find a place to sit until the line goes down," he said, looking me up and down. "I don't think I've ever seen you wear a dress. You look nice."

"Thanks. You clean up pretty good too. I like the paisley tie."

"Have to keep my *hottie* image up. Anyway, follow me and we'll see if we can wrangle a couple of chairs."

"Sounds good to me." My feet were already killing me and the pantyhose Aunt Lin lent me were digging into my waist.

We worked our way through the crowd into the Serenity Room where Jeannie was reposed for the viewing. I could see she had an open casket, and I couldn't imagine staring down at her young face and proclaiming that she looked *so good* or *so peaceful*. I wondered who would have done her hair and makeup. Likely she would not be pleased, whoever it was. Jeannie's parents were standing just past the casket, and the line of visitors moved slowly along, with each person first looking at the abundance of flower arrangements, then solemnly at Jeannie's remains. Next, they moved to Mr. and Mrs. Usitalo, muttering words, hugging, sobbing, and triggering unimaginable grief in the parents. Then they moved on and some took seats while others moved toward the exit.

Nikko and I looked around and found a couple of seats along the outside wall of the room. As we moved toward them, I spotted Brianna sharing a couch with a woman off in a corner. Three young boys were exploring a potted plant in the corner.

"I'm going to go give Brianna this gift," I said to Nikko. "Please save me a seat."

I worked my way over to Brianna. She was wearing a pretty yellow dress and had a bow in her hair. On her lap, she held a game of some sort, but showed no interest in playing it. I approached her and her big blue eyes stared at me, wary. Was I another grownup going to tell her how wonderful her mother was? Tell her all about God and heaven and other promises that were too complicated for her young mind to grasp?

"Hi Brianna," I said. "I'm Kat."

"Hi," she muttered, looking down at her hands. She held a shredded tissue; little pieces littered her lap and the floor by her feet.

A woman sitting next to her looked at me and said, "Hello Kat. Thanks for coming. I'm Jeannie's Aunt Denise. Those three kids over by the potted plant belong to my son and daughter-in-law who are around here somewhere. HEY, boys, no digging!"

"Nice to meet you—both of you," I said.

Brianna continued to focus on her tissue.

"Hey, Brianna, I brought you a little gift. Something I liked when I was about your age."

She looked up, her worrisome expression dropping a little.

I pulled the picture books out of the gift bag. "They're books all about a pony named Peaches," I said. "And also there's a stuffed pony here. It's a little worn because I loved it so much. Sometimes when I was sad, I hugged Peaches and felt better."

Denise looked up at me and smiled. "Isn't that nice, Brianna?" she said. "Maybe I can help you read those books. Look at that pony. Isn't it cute?"

Brianna took one of the books and looked at the cover. She said, "I love horses. My favorite TV show is *The Saddle Club*."

"Oh, that's a good one," I said, though I'd never heard of it.

I handed Brianna the bag with the other books and the stuffed pony. She pulled the pony out of the bag and hugged it. The shredded tissue fell out of her hands and the game slid off her lap. She started to cry.

Oh damn! I thought.

Denise hugged the child. The three boys abandoned the potted plant, and came over to try to comfort Brianna.

Denise looked at me and smiled and whispered, "She has not cried yet. It's okay."

Of course, I started to cry. One of the boys handed me a box of tissues from a nearby table. I pulled a few out and stumbled away to find Nikko. He looked at me and actually stood to wait for me to sit. His mother had trained him well.

"Are you okay?" he asked.

I nodded and blew my nose. "That poor kid. I opened up the girl's floodgates with my Peaches the Pony move."

"Maybe not a bad thing. I'm kinda surprised they brought her here."

"Probably trying to help the kid deal with the reality that she's now motherless so the healing can begin."

"You sound like a shrink," Nikko said, handing me a crisp, white handkerchief.

"Thanks," I said, blowing my nose again. "I didn't know guys still had these things."

"My grandpa always said a gentleman carries a handkerchief. You never know when you'll need it. Ma buys me a fresh package every Christmas."

I nodded and said, "I'll wash it."

"Keep it. I've got a drawer full. Well, the line has gone down if you want to pay your respects."

I took a deep breath and nodded. We joined the line and worked our way up to the flowers, casket, and devastated parents. I couldn't bring myself to give Jeannie more than a glance. I struggled to make eye contact with the Usitalos, who looked traumatized beyond description. Then Nikko and I moved off toward the exit. I fought the urge to hurry, even run, and maintained decorum during my exit. Once outside, I gulped in fresh air. Nikko put his arm around me. Several men and women stood around on the porch, clearly the funeral personnel waiting to carry out the logistics of the day with the procession to the cemetery. The hearse and several dark sedans stood in wait at the portico. The staff all wore dark suits and nodded grimly at us. I'm sure I was a spectacle, but nothing they hadn't seen a million times.

Nikko walked me to my truck. Before I clambered in, I took off the dress shoes and pulled some tennies out from under the seat.

"That's my girl," he said. "Always practical."

"The pantyhose go next," I said.

"I can wait."

"Fine," I said, squirming out of them.

Nikko smiled as he watched.

"Oh, grow up," I said.

"I'm hoping you brought an entire outfit you can change into here in the parking lot. I'll stand guard."

"Hah! Just the shoes and pantyhose today," I said, slipping my bare feet into my tennies.

Nikko helped me into the truck, giving me an unnecessary boost.

"Always copping a feel," I said.

"I don't know what you're talking about," he said. "Anyway, I'm going to head over to my folks' and get Tobey, then go home. Ma's helping with the funeral lunch at the church and Pop's at work. Tobey shreds things if he is alone too long."

"I'm gonna run home and change into reasonable clothes before I head off to the museum of horrors," I said.

"Wanna come over later for dinner and stuff?"

"And stuff?"

He smiled.

"Maybe after chores," I said. "I'll text you."

"I can cook some burgers on the grill. Ma gave me some potato salad left over from a giant batch she made for the Usitalos."

"Okay, sounds great. I'll let you know for sure. We got a new rescued pony and I want to make sure it's doing okay."

"I'll heat up the grill," he said. "You know, get it hot."

"Just stop."

27

The first thing I did when I got home was shed my blue dress, slip, and scratchy bra and put on utilitarian underwear along with jeans and a tee. I wandered into the kitchen and opened the fridge to root out my hidden package of bologna. I found it with a sticky note attached. *This is loaded with chemicals. Chikan salad is in blue bowl.* I had tried Aunt Lin's "chikan" salad. It was a vegan replica of real poultry that failed miserably in the flavor and texture department. Kind of like eating a sponge that had been moldering in the dish drainer for a while. Even Jupiter wouldn't eat it. I slapped some ketchup on a couple slices of bread and added two slabs of bologna. Next, I dug out one of my diet colas and popped the top. I sat down at the kitchen table, opened my laptop, and pulled up the final two photos of the journal pages. I wanted to read them before I headed over to the museum to meet with Elsie.

I took a bite of sandwich and chewed as I read.

Mr. Ezekiel Adams from the mining college did come out to our home. He was quite distinguished and polite. We invited him to have a meal with us. The children were all enraptured by Mr. Adams and Ruthie brought him the tablet for him to inspect. Mr. Adams said he believed the item could be from a lost civilization. He was quite certain it was not a product—he called it an artifact—from Indians. My eldest daughter, Sarah, was overly enchanted by Mr. Adams. He showed interest in her as well, and I will say he took her hand in a rather forward gesture and posed her with a lot of questions pertaining to her interests and plans. William was not pleased with this, though I thought it quite natural for a girl—almost a woman—to be curious about the world outside of our homestead. She has spoken often of wanting to attend teacher's college when she turns eighteen.

Mr. Adams shared a meal with us, claiming it was the best stew he had ever eaten. This pleased me, and I will admit I was charmed. He also offered to pay two dollars for Ruthie's tablet and said he'd send it off to a place for further study. Ruthie was allowed to make the decision. She studied on her options and finally agreed to accept his offer. Mr. Adams soon departed, but not until after he once again took Sarah's hands and spoke to her.

That was the end of the entry. I clicked on my last journal page photo.

The next day, Sarah was gone. We believe she left very early in the morning, taking a bundle of her belongings with her. She left a note only saying not to worry, that she would send us word when she settled, that Mr. Adams was going to help her in the furtherance of her education. William and I are heartbroken. Sarah is only sixteen and still a child in my eyes. Her father set off on the horse to search for her and hunt down the scoundrel who sweet-talked her into running off.

This turn of events in Helvi's journal took me by surprise. The daughter, Sarah, was wooed by a man who only stayed for dinner. Somehow, the two made arrangements for her to run off with him. Unbelievable! Right under her parents' noses. I thought about the journal page of the family tree, with Sarah's line seeming incomplete. And a baby boy with no name. I could only imagine how the story played out, because there was no more to the story. As far as I could tell, the journal ended there. If I were to finish the story, I'd say that Sarah came back home, pregnant from the charming Ezekiel Adams, and both she and the infant died during childbirth. A tragic story in an otherwise inspired homesteading saga.

I shut my laptop and went to the barn to check in with Clay. He had Peaches in the wash rack and was giving her a much-needed bath. The pony appeared to be delighted, with her ears flopped sideways and her head drooped against the crossties.

"How's she doing?" I asked.

"Peachy," he said, smiling.

"What, you don't like my name for the pony?"

"Doesn't matter to me. She's doing fine. Real nice little animal, especially for a pony."

Ponies had a reputation for being on the cantankerous side. Often parents were advised to get their youngster a small horse instead of a pony. Uncle Phil had a pony, which I rode only once. It spooked for no apparent reason and bolted for the barn, smashing my kneecap on the door frame in the process.

"Well, I'm headed out for an appointment," I said. "Then I'll be at Nikko's later, but I'll come back to help with chores first."

"No need," Clay said. "I can handle the chores if you don't want to come all the way back out here. That is, if you trust me," he added with a smirk.

"Of course I do. It's just—"

"Just poking some fun. I know I owe you an explanation about things—when we have time."

"I know," I said. "I've hardly had a chance to land for a minute to catch my breath."

"Sure," he said, turning back to the pony.

"Guess I better get going," I said. "Tomorrow—I'll take you for breakfast and we'll sort things out."

"Maybe you better make it for lunch," he said, smiling.

He was right. I'd never make breakfast if I stayed over at Nikko's, which was a possibility.

"Hey, Clay," I said.

"Yeah?"

"Thanks for everything. Really."

"Sure, no problem."

* * *

When I pulled into the museum parking lot, I saw Frankie using a shovel to dig up a section of sod. Maybe he was going to plant a historic garden. I went to the front door and saw a closed sign. Just as I turned to leave, the door swung open and I was greeted by Elsie, who had ditched the pioneer woman attire and was wearing lavender polyester pants and a lively floral blouse to match. She smiled and gestured for me to come in.

"I didn't think you'd be closed," I said.

"Oh, well, I don't want us to be disturbed, so I closed a little early today."

"You have something to show me?" I asked, wishing I'd declined her invitation. It had already been a long day, and Jeannie's funeral, especially seeing Brianna, had drained me.

"Yes, dear. Please come into my office and I'll explain."

I had always thought the reception desk in the museum served as the office, but I was led back to a dark hallway with three doors labeled Restroom, Maintenance, and Office. Elsie used a key to unlock the office door. She flicked on an overhead light and we went in. Dust motes floated around and the room had a musty, basementy smell. I surveyed the tiny office, which was crammed from ceiling to floor with bookshelves and cluttered tabletops containing papers, photos, and unidentifiable sundry items. A fake potted plant sat in one corner and a mini fridge with a microwave perched on top took up another corner. An ancient-looking oak desk dominated most of the cramped, windowless space.

"Have a seat, my dear. Can I offer you tea or maybe some water?"

"Water would be great," I said.

Elsie opened the mini fridge and pulled out a pitcher of water in one of those fancy water filter jugs. "I don't like the city water—all those chemicals. And, of course, plastic bottles are terrible for the environment. This filter is supposed to clean out the chemicals." She poured water into a real glass and handed it to me. No Styrofoam or plastic here.

"You would get along very well with my Aunt Lin," I said, taking the glass and drinking. "Tastes a little sweet."

"Oh yes, I put a little lemon and a touch of sugar in the water, and sometimes cucumber or strawberries if I have any. I call it my spa water."

"Very tasty," I said. "So, I'm all ears about new information for my homestead research. And, by the way, did you ever find out what happened to the missing pages of Helvi's journal?"

"As for the missing pages, I'm afraid I haven't figured that out, but don't worry, I know you didn't do it. While I do keep the journal locked up, the keys are sitting in my desk drawer out front. We do have people come and go," she said absently. "I am curious if you had a look at those pages before they went missing."

"Well, no," I said. "Not really. I just flipped through a lot of the journal. However, I did, ah, gain access to them—the missing pages—through the dead couple's phone. Like me, they apparently photographed some of the journal pages. Interesting that the missing pages seem to correspond to the photos they took."

Elsie studied me for a moment, then said, "I see. Yes, well that is interesting. I guess it didn't occur to me they would have photos. And may I ask if you found anything you consider...significant?"

I decided not to play my hand yet. "Oh, not really," I said. "Just stuff about some fellow who was wooing their daughter and such. They got a new cow. You know, things that were monumental in those days."

I had awkwardly tiptoed around the artifact Ezekiel Adams had apparently come to own. And as far as someone randomly stealing pages from the journal, it seemed unlikely. In my mind, the finger pointed right back to Elsie, though I wasn't sure why she would remove pages when she could have simply taken the whole journal out of circulation. When circling back to the artifact that Ruthie Huntington found and apparently sold to Ezekiel Adams, Alex Varga and his drone came to mind. If Varga requested the journal, Elsie kept that bit of information to herself. At least I didn't think she mentioned anyone else besides me and the hippies interested in the homestead. Or maybe she did. My memory seemed a bit fuzzy. Hell, I was having major brain fade. My mouth felt metallic and I was incredibly thirsty. When I went to pick up my glass of water, it slipped from my hand and banged on the desk, slopping a little.

"So sorry," I muttered, snatching a wad of tissues from a dispenser on her desk to dab up the puddle.

"Not a problem, dear," Elsie said, grabbing a roll of paper towels to finish the job. "Shall we proceed now?"

"Sure," I said. "Whatcha got?"

Elsie sat back in her chair. "Very well then, this is what I wanted to show you," she said, reaching into the desk drawer and pulling out a file. She laid it on the desk, opened it, and turned it toward me.

It was a photocopy of a newspaper article or maybe something taken offline. Some kind of gobbledygook with a headline stating, "Mormonism's Encounter with the Michigan Relics."

"Mormons?" I said. "I don't understand." I let out a huge yawn. "'Scuse me. Been a long day."

"Yes, I imagine," Elsie said, pushing the article closer. "You see, it was something that originally took place back around the turn of the last century in Lower Michigan. Basically, it was an enormous hoax involving archaeological forgeries. I won't bore you with the details or expect you to read this whole article, but I thought you might understand why I have been forced to do some things. To protect everything."

As I processed the information, my mouth felt increasingly detached from my brain. Like a drunk trying to act sober, I concentrated on my response and managed to ask, "Hoax?" Only it came out more like *hoak.* It was stifling in the little office, and I was feeling hot and clammy at the same time.

"Quite a scandal."

I vaguely wondered if this hoax Elsie spoke of related to the stolen replicas that the hippy Hilmans were involved with. And then the journal. Of course it was. But how, exactly? The room was awfully stuffy, and Elsie had lit a scented candle. I hated scented candles; they always gave me a headache.

"A straw horse!" I blurted, as if having an epiphanic moment.

"I beg your pardon."

"We'll huff and we'll puff!" I bleated, as if that explained my train of thought. "You know and we'll blow the ho' to hell!" I giggled, feeling very clever with my deranged Three Little Pigs analogy.

"You look a bit pale, dear," Elsie said. "Would you like more water?"

"Sure," I said, trying to engage my tongue, which felt like a slab of cement. "Um, you shad shometing about protecting thingsh?"

"That's right," Elsie said, looking at me over the top of her glasses, just like Rose did when she disapproved.

"From wha'?"

"More fakes, more hoaxes, disrupting our ways, and more exploitation!"

"Explo-ta."

"I made a big mistake with them," Elsie said.

"Who—ah, whom? No who?"

"The so-called hippies. I had no idea things would make such a mess. My goodness, I won't try that again. Well, anyway, my Frankie saved the day."

"Hooray for Misher Frahk!" I slurred.

"Oh my, it seems you are a bit out of sorts," Elsie said sardonically.

So tired.

"Well, I guess we're done here," she said. "Hopefully, we can continue this conversation and you will see things my way."

"Hokey dokey."

"I don't believe you're in any condition to drive."

"Pimpmobile!" I blurted.

"Frankie will take you home."

"He likesh my hair!"

"Yes, it is quite...interesting. I'll go fetch him."

I had a brief cerebral moment before slipping into oblivion. *Oh hell! It's the water.*

28

A fiery horse galloped across the blazing sky, its mane and tail a stream of flames. I shouted for it to stop, repeatedly hollering *whoa*. I felt an overwhelming sense of doom, as if the fire would consume me. Then I was riding the horse toward a cliff. I tried to jump off, but my legs wouldn't move. We were flying, floating, and the horse started to dispel, like a dying fire turning to embers, then coals, then only a ribbon of smoke. Then nothing but ash. And I was falling, arms flailing, my silent screams lost in a foggy abyss.

I jerked awake and heard someone yelling. Maybe it was me yelling. Someone else was talking.

"Good morning, sunshine," intoned a male voice. "I believe you were having a bad dream."

"Huh?" I looked around. Though the room seemed like an office, it wasn't the one at the museum. There was a man sitting in a chair backed against a wall. I was sprawled on the floor.

"What the hell?" I said as I struggled to sit up.

"Welcome," said the man. He sounded familiar. He had an accent. I knew that voice.

Varga.

"I'm of course being sarcastic," Varga said. "We are not in a good or welcoming place."

"Where...?"

"Excellent question," Varga said, standing up. "Here, take the chair. There is only one."

He helped me to sit in the lopsided office chair.

"Mind the wheels," he said. "Don't let it scoot out from under you."

I rubbed my eyes and shook my head, trying to clear the mud out of my brain. Varga looked a tad worse for wear. He sported several days of beard growth, and his hair had sprung loose from its coif. His white shirt looked soiled, and the crease was long gone from his khakis. Varga had a crusty scab on his forehead. I suspected I wasn't the picture of fashion myself. Plus, I clearly had been separated from my purse, which held my phone among other essential items, such as a couple of much-needed aspirin.

"Mr. Varga," I said.

"In the flesh."

"I was drugged," I said. "I'm so *stupid*! The water was obviously spiked."

"Well, my dear, you were lucky," Varga said. "A thug with a very large handgun got the jump on me down by the waterfront. He ordered me into my car, and when I didn't move fast enough, he shoved me and I bashed my head on the door frame. I was out cold for a while. The man hijacked my car with me in it, and I ended up in these lovely accommodations. I believe I may have a concussion; not that I'm expecting any medical attention."

"Who…?"

"That Neanderthal son of the woman who runs the museum."

"Frank Tuttle," I said. "But why?"

"Why? I think probably Mrs. Tuttle ordered him to. I suspect she is deranged with some concept that she must preserve a happy place that lives in her head. That my—and now your—nosing around are a threat to the delusion of her relevancy."

"You sound like a shrink," I said. "Man, my head is pounding. I wonder what she gave me."

"Whatever it was, it appears to be wearing off. I imagine she sedated you with something from a stash of prescription drugs. What dotty old lady doesn't have valium in her medicine cabinet, perhaps along with some psychotic drugs that her son keeps on hand."

"Yeah, valium maybe," I said, rubbing my forehead. "Or LSD. What a trip. There was a horse…. Anyway, so here we are being held captive by a psychopath and/or sociopath. I suspect our future is not looking too rosy."

Varga sighed. "So, there is good news and bad news."

"There always is. Give me the good news."

"The good news is that we are not tied up and can roam freely around this very secure office. There is an air conditioning unit stuck in the wall, which makes the temperature bearable. In addition, it has a small washroom through that door where we can get water and use the facilities. *And* I found a box of granola bars and a bottle of excellent scotch in the desk drawer."

"Okay, and it is good not to be wrapped up in duct tape. Been there, done that. So we are in some kind of office. Again, where and why?"

"Well, that brings me to the bad news," Varga said. "I've been here for a few days—truthfully, I have lost count. There are no windows and so I'm losing track of day and night and the bum stole my watch. It was my father's. But anyway, the batty museum woman and her idiot son have seen to our incarceration, apparently to remove us as a threat to whatever the woman purports to be protecting."

"They can't keep us here indefinitely," I said, standing and trying to get the crick out of my neck. I looked around the room, which was at best utilitarian. A ghastly overhead fluorescent light cast an anemic glow, with an occasional flicker and buzzing. The décor of the place—or lack thereof—reminded me of the offices one finds occupied by auto mechanics who never quite get the grease off their hands or remember to wipe their feet. I suspected there might be no soap in the washroom or seat on the toilet, which at some point I would need to explore.

"With your permission, I will continue with the news," Varga said. "If things had gone off without a hitch for the Tuttle duo, I would have been reduced to a very compact glob of humanity crushed within the chassis of some hapless vehicle."

That got my attention.

"Best I can tell, we are being held captive at a scrapyard where Frank Tuttle works. It is not just a scrapyard, but also a chop shop. We are in the building where the chopping takes place."

"Chop shop?"

"Right. They steal cars and dismantle them quickly, then sell the parts to make something new. It happens a lot in the big cities. Apparently, rural setups are on the rise. They actually reduced my Mercedes to pieces very quickly, I am told. But I believe the demise of my vehicle isn't why I was assaulted and kidnapped. It was just an ancillary benefit to the whole endeavor. You know—that woman's unhinged concept of protecting the time capsule she's living in. Or at least part of her is living in."

"So, you and she chit-chatted?" I asked.

"Oh, indeed. I was looking at the homestead on your land. There may be something of great value there, or not. Mrs. Tuttle seemed so eager to help."

"Aha," I said. "She never mentioned your visit. Only the hippie couple who died."

"Hippie couple?"

"Right, you know, they were former employees from your museum."

"Ah yes, the Hilmans. There's another story to tell—eventually."

"You might recall when you first visited me at Wildwood—right after the storm—that you gave me a business card that said you were some kind of consultant—nothing mentioned about the museum where you worked."

"Yes, well, I do have a separate card for me personally that I use sometimes. I have a second vocation—or sideline as you Americans call it—as an independent business consultant, so it is genuine. I didn't want to tip my hand at that point about Dumbarton Oaks Museum's interest in your land when we first met, for reasons I've cited before. I was hoping my bogus story of a family connection to the land would serve the situation best. Kind of like the police who misrepresent their personas to catch those who are committing misdeeds."

"Undercover," I said.

"I beg your pardon?"

"Cops that, as you say, misrepresent their personas, are said to be working undercover."

"Like a stealth weapon," he said.

"Sort of," I said. "Anyway, just curious, did you ever look at Helvi Paavola Huntington's journal?"

"Yes, I paged through it and saw what I was looking for."

"And...?"

"The discovery of an artifact unearthed at the homestead located on your land."

"The last few pages were removed. I don't suppose that was your doing?"

"I may as well be truthful," Varga said. "I did use a small razor knife to carefully slice out the pages relating to the potentially authentic artifact. It was rather an impulsive act on my part, and went against my soul to deface such a thing. However, I was hoping that by removing them, the whole piece of the story would remain a secret, at least until I had time to further explore things. My concern was to avoid the potential of your raising the price of the land, plus perhaps turning the town into a circus. I have seen it before, so I tried to keep everything quiet."

"But I had already looked at the journal," I said.

"True, but I wasn't aware that you and I were going down the same path."

"What about the Hilmans? They also looked at the journal and took photos."

"I didn't know about that until after I realized they were dead. And I wish I had taken photos too. I'd left my phone at the motel and used very poor judgment as a result."

I looked at Varga. He did have a motive to kill the Hilmans.

"And the unfortunate thing," he said, "is that Mrs. Tuttle caught me in the act. She went quite off her rocker, snatched the journal away from me, and kicked me out of the museum. Her demeanor was beyond bizarre, and the change was exceedingly abrupt. While I understand her being angry, it was as if a different person emerged and went into a frenzy. Such behavior may be an indication of mental illness, such as dissociative identity disorder or DID for short. In lay terms, multiple personality disorder. I now believe that is what my father suffered from, though he was never formally diagnosed. It can result in memory loss when a person switches from one personality to another."

"Like in a movie I saw," I said. "It was about someone who had been abused by her mother and the father did nothing. *Sybil!* Yeah, she switched from one personality to another. I guess it was based on a true story."

"Often caused by trauma of some sort," Varga said. "Childhood abuse before age six, a loss they can't cope with, and so on. I suspect Elsie Tuttle has a dark history."

"She was like Dr. Jekyll and Mr. Hyde with me as well. I think she envisioned some kind of humanoid invasion at the homestead. I believe she wanted to convince me to keep things secret, but maybe decided I would be corrupted by, uh, people offering to buy my land. You know, like you. Sorry if my mention of you might have made you a target."

Varga shrugged, then winced. His forehead not only had a nasty scab but also was purple and black with bruising.

"According to Lieutenant Spiller," I said, "you are responsible for the drone surveying the area. Care to tell me what that is all about?"

"Sure," Varga said. "As a representative of Dumbarton Oaks—"

"I think Spiller mentioned it as your employer."

"Right, it's the museum I work for. We leased a drone setup from a surveying company to search the area for artifacts. You see, Miss Wilde—"

"Call me Kat."

"Okay, Kat, and you can call me Alex, a tablet that was unearthed by the homestead family made its way over the decades to Dumbarton Oaks. It has been authenticated many times, and after some fundraising, we were looking to further explore a possible early civilization here in Upper Michigan."

"One of the Huntington daughters sold it to a man—Ezekiel Adams," I said.

"And it ended up moving about and eventually coming to Dumbarton."

"Is it Native American?" I asked. "And again, what's the deal with the drone?"

"The artifact is very early. Pre-Columbian. The drone showed some promising anomalies in the area of the homestead. But there are a lot of false hits, so we were just in the early stages of surveying the area. But, of course, the drone met an untimely demise, which by the way the museum will have to pay for."

"Why didn't you just come straight with me?" I asked.

"In retrospect, that would have played out much better."

"Though I hate to ask," I said, "you were saying something about being compacted?"

Varga nodded. "It seems things have gotten a bit off schedule because the vehicle compactor—a big crushing machine—broke down. Our friend Frank Tuttle obviously enjoyed telling me his grisly plans. He is a very disturbed man."

"But don't others who work here know we're being held?" I asked.

"I think the boss man might be gone. Tuttle is in charge, and as far as I can tell, nobody else is around. I did hear some racket yesterday and some talking that sounded Latino. Maybe they were chopping up the Mercedes. Even though I pounded on the walls and yelled, nobody came. Perhaps they couldn't hear me. And I imagine they might be here illegally, so weren't likely to come to my rescue."

I digested the information, feeling a sinking pit form in my stomach. The prospect of escape seemed dismal. The office only had the one door and no windows. The doorknob and lock mechanism looked heavy duty and likely could withstand an assault by Bigfoot.

At that moment, the door banged open and a smirking Frank Tuttle appeared.

"Well, I see that Ma's stuff wore off," Tuttle said.

It was the first time I'd seen Tuttle up close for a while. He was a mountain of tattooed muscle. He wore a T-shirt that positively strained at the biceps. His shaved head had a disturbing tat of a snake eating a woman's crotch inked across it. Most notably, however, he held a handgun pointed in my general direction. I wasn't much of an authority on guns, but it was big and shiny and menacing.

"You won't get away with this!" I said. I couldn't believe I had blurted out that timeworn cliché.

Tuttle looked at me and sneered. "You know, you were one of the girls that made fun of me. Not feeling so *cool* now, are ya?"

"Cool?"

"Yeah, back in high school. You and them snotty girls. Anyway, Ma said you needed to get taken care of along with Mr. Fancy Pants here," he said waving the gun toward Varga. "And we had it all figured out way better than with them two old hippies. Ma wanted it to look accidental, so she got some kind of weed 'long the river and made them tea. Boy, they was so sick and it messed up things. Aren't yous glad we didn't do that to you? Had to make sure them bodies were all nice and tidy before I drove them out into the sticks in that fuckin' camper. Thing don't steer worth a damn."

Tuttle's boastful confession at least cleared Varga of having any involvement in the Hilmans' murders. I gave Tuttle an icy stare and resisted the urge to mention that I knew he was talking about the water hemlock that had killed them. Elsie and Frank Tuttle obviously didn't take into account the violent death the toxin would cause, including major bodily purging. I surmised the Tuttles had their hands full cleaning up the couple and getting them back to their camper. Frank Tuttle had the muscle to do it. I remembered it was mentioned that the dead couple had been dressed in odd gowns or robes rather than regular day clothes. Maybe a couple of period frocks that Elsie had on hand. I wondered if Elsie Tuttle thought that whatever drug concoction she gave me via a water filter pitcher would have been a cleaner, more practical murder. But then I didn't die; I just hallucinated for a while and plan B—death by compactor—was on deck.

"Yeah, everyone gets their due," Tuttle muttered. "Yous and them other two girls."

"What other two girls?" I said.

"The mean ones."

"Who?"

"Oh shut the fuck up," Tuttle said. "You figure it out. Anyway, I got some good news."

"Really?" Varga said, his tone dripping with sarcasm.

"Yup. Got the part I need to fix the compactor. She should be back in business soon as I get things switched out."

Tuttle looked at me again. "It's gonna break my heart to chop up that pretty blue truck of yours. Now be a good girlie and tell me where th' fuck the fob is. It started fine when yous were in it, but now she won't go when I push the start button."

I felt the bulge of the fob in my front pocket. I resisted the urge to look down.

"Wudn't in your purse. Nice bit of cash, though, that yous won't be needing."

"Uh, should have been—well, I'm not sure. I usually keep it in the cup holder," I lied,

"Which cup holder?" Tuttle snarled. "Front, back?"

"Um, front. Maybe it fell on the floor or something."

"You better hope I find it," Tuttle said.

"They sometimes have an emergency key," Varga offered. He cast me a look and the corner of his mouth twitched.

"Sure, and where the fuck is that gonna be?"

"Well, often it's hidden in a fender, or sometimes the tailgate. Or perhaps under the bed protector. Or even within the door panel."

I couldn't believe that Tuttle was buying this line of BS, but I could see his forehead scrunch up, as if he were giving it a think.

"Oh, that's right!" I said. "I think the dealer mentioned something. Now let me see, was it a quarter panel? No, the taillight. No, that's not right either. Oh, shoot, that stuff your mother gave me has really messed up my head."

Tuttle glared at me. "I know a load of bullshit when I hear one. Ya know, it's too bad yous got all mixed up in this. You wasn't as mean as the rest." He smiled. "But I do like me a good fire."

Fire?

"The Jeep," I said. "And the cut fence."

The tampered brake lines! Was Jeannie one of the so-called mean girls? And what about the bent-up fence at the Jesson hunting lodge? Valerie Jesson was definitely a girl who could be classified as snotty *and* mean. Funny she had ended up wrangling wild pigs.

"I got me some work to do," Tuttle muttered, slamming the door when he left. We heard the lock click into place.

"Why didn't we jump him?" I asked. "Next time, we jump him."

"Sure," Varga said. "I'm sure he'll miss us with that cannon he carries, what with us being a whole two feet away."

"Which makes me wonder why he doesn't just shoot us."

"I suspect because guns leave a lot of evidence. If we're compacted into oblivion and sold for scrap, then melted down at a temperature rivaling the surface of the sun, there likely wouldn't be much DNA left to find."

"So, Tuttle isn't as dumb as he looks," I said. "Now that you've provided me with all the details of things, I feel *so* much better. At least now I'm sure you didn't kill the Hilmans, who you still need to tell me about. But back to Elsie Tuttle. I don't understand why she shared Helvi Paavola Huntington's journal with both you and me if she was so afraid of—whatever it was she envisioned. She seemed so pleased to share it with me, let me delve into the homestead's history."

"She did me also, at the beginning. I can only say her mind kept moving from one place to another—accommodating historian to—"

"A crazy bitch!" I supplied.

"—possibly personality two. Complete with deranged offspring."

"Where are the journal pages now?" I asked.

"She took them away from me, so probably somewhere in her office."

"We need to figure a way out of here," I said, looking around and up.

"Of course. But first, would you like a finger or two of scotch?" Varga asked as he pulled open a desk drawer. "It appears to be single malt."

"Sure, why not?" I said. "Now, tell me more about the two hippies...."

29

"She was my assistant at the museum for over ten years," Varga said. "Laureen was an ideal employee. Smart, reliable, creative, highly organized. She had my back. When I went to meetings, I had everything I needed. She was excellent at research, too. And I trusted her implicitly."

Alex Varga and I were both slumped against the wall of the dingy office, passing the bottle of scotch back and forth. I felt like a homeless person huddled under the Peshekee River bridge. The scotch had dulled my senses to the point where my lips felt tingly and my tongue was taking a siesta. Varga appeared to be unaffected.

"Granola bar?" he asked, offering me an oat 'n honey bar.

"Thanks," I said, taking it and tearing the wrapper off, then chomping down. I hadn't eaten anything since breakfast and was starved. Varga said he'd been there a few days, so he was probably thinking about cannibalism.

Frank Tuttle had not come for us yet, and we heard no sounds coming through the walls. Tuttle hadn't bothered to steal my Timex, which said it was 6:00 p.m. Nikko would be looking for me soon. I hoped. Clay would assume I didn't make it back to Wildwood for chores and probably wouldn't be expecting me until the next day. Same for Aunt Lin. Since the next day was Sunday, I wouldn't be missed in the office until Monday or Tuesday. My hope for rescue fell to Nikko.

I prayed that Tuttle hadn't been able to fix the crushing thing. I didn't know much—well anything—about scrap yards, but I did once see a video on recycling that showed cars being crushed flat as a pancake by a monstrous machine. I didn't think that Tuttle was looking to replace a washer or a couple of nuts and bolts, so I wondered if he could even handle whatever repair he faced. Maybe Amazon sent the wrong part or more likely sent the right part to the wrong place. Better yet, maybe Tuttle accidentally fell into the crusher and Varga and I would simply wait out someone finding us, if we didn't starve to death first.

"But then she got involved with a man from the mailroom," Varga said, tipping the scotch bottle and swallowing. "His name was Theodore Hilman, but everyone called him Teddy."

"Ah, twoo love," I slurred.

"Laureen was a fairly attractive woman," Varga said. "She was a bit overweight and far from glamorous, but quite smart and professional looking. She was the perfect assistant. Not married, no children, no family that I was aware of. Then Hilman gave her some romantic attention and she was besotted."

"You tal' funny," I snorted. "Beshotted."

"Are you okay?" Varga asked, looking at me. "I think maybe no more scotch. It's gone anyway."

"No more scosh!"

"I was fine with the relationship, although Laureen was well educated and Teddy was a mailroom clerk with not much hope for advancement."

"Dead end! Like at th' offish," I said. "Been there done tha'."

"Teddy manipulated Laureen. She was privy to a lot of information. As I said, I completely trusted her. I really don't think she would have compromised her scruples if she hadn't been turned down for a promotion."

"Ahhhh," I said. "The thick plottens. Disgrumbled."

"Right. I gave her an excellent recommendation for the promotion to Program Coordinator for Pre-Columbian Studies. She had the credentials and an excellent work record. She got passed over."

Varga took the empty scotch bottle into the bathroom. I could hear the water running. He returned with the bottle and handed it to me.

"It's water," he said. "Have a drink."

I took a couple of gulps and another bite of granola bar. I didn't feel so great.

"She should have had the job," Varga said. "They hired from outside. Brought in some fresh blood, as they called it. A young person right out of college."

"Soo unfair," I said, taking another swallow of water. I would have given anything for a cup of coffee. And a soft bed, and an escape plan, for that matter.

"Can't blame her for being bitter," Varga said. "Teddy Hilman was a snake and saw his chance. He suddenly showed interest in Laureen and the two got married after a brief courtship. Teddy easily manipulated his new bride into sharing information that he didn't have clearance on."

"Like shishp—shipments?" I said. I giggled. "Say that three times fasht!"

Varga studied me for a moment, then said, "Bingo. He worked in the mailroom where shipments come and go all the time. But he and others aren't privy to what is in the shipments. When something exceedingly valuable, delicate, or otherwise needing special handling is sent, it is usually hand-delivered by private means, not the postal service or regular carriers. The items he and Laureen pilfered were simply artifact replicas and came through regular parcel carrier."

"The knockoffs of the knockoffs," I said, feeling quite pleased with my improved diction.

"Right. They were created from photos of the original bogus pieces. You know the story?"

"Lieutenant Spiller told me shum—some."

"So, my office was arranging to create an interpretive exhibition of the artifact hoax that took place in Lower Michigan. We had replicas of the counterfeit pieces made, as I said before, by using photos of the original bogus pieces. Laureen shared the information with Hilman. The couple stole the replicas and then disappeared into thin air."

"But the things they stole weren't worth much, were they?" I asked.

"No, not as museum pieces go. Part of the motivation to do this exhibition was to build an awareness of scams. While most antique and antiquities dealers are on the up and up, some are not. Then there's the whole internet market. Fraud has risen exponentially."

Varga and I were quiet for a while. Either the couple was stupid or I was missing something, such as somehow Varga was—as Lieutenant Spiller suggested—in cahoots. I took another drink of water, then excused myself and went into the bathroom and threw up the scotch and granola bar. So much for a nice buzz. I used the toilet, washed my hands, took a pass on the grease-infused roller towel, and returned to the office. My watch said 7 p.m.

"My boyfriend should be looking for me by now."

"I think Tuttle is gone," Varga said. "Maybe we are good until tomorrow."

"What I can't get is why steal something of little value?" I said. "I mean, they gave up their jobs, went on the lam, then died. Of course they didn't plan on the dead part."

"There's a lot of irony in this debacle," Varga said. He stood and stretched his back, then walked over to the air conditioner and twisted the nobs. "I think this thing is on its last legs."

"Makes plenty of noise," I said.

"Anyway, the Hilmans wanted to bury some artifacts, and I wanted to dig some up."

I looked at him, trying to process the information.

"Laureen knew I was looking at potentially authentic artifacts being on your property around the homestead. She helped me track down the information, including the homestead on your land. I had the one relic—the one the Huntington daughter sold to Ezekiel Adams—with good provenance traced back to the homestead. I think what Teddy and Laureen Hilman did, or were planning to do, was to bury the replicas somewhere in the vicinity of the authentic piece. Laureen knew I was working on purchasing the land."

"But they wouldn't have any claim to things found on my land," I said.

"Or museum land, if you had agreed to sell. Public land, such as state forests and federal lands, are typically off limits for excavating historic and Native American artifacts unless the activity is sanctioned through the proper channels. However, museum property would enter into the realm of private land, where such finds may be considered finders-keepers, though typically only to the landowner. I believe the Hilmans planned to bury the items for a couple of months, obviously on the sly and far off the beaten path. I very much doubt they were going to have a public eureka moment, but rather do their business through the dark web. And the connection to the homestead property would lend credence to their claim."

"So, couldn't they just bury stuff anywhere, then dig it up?" I asked.

"They needed the credibility of your land. Even though they might keep things quiet, since they would have been trespassing, the black market would have found the claim more believable from a potential excavation site. The Hilmans assumed that the museum would acquire the land and start a dig. Laureen Hilman knew the plan. As I said before, she was privy to that information. The Hilmans likely planned to make it seem as if they did an illicit dig and thus uncovered rare archeological finds to sell privately."

"Okay. So they needed to have a connection with an authentic dig as you call it, to add credibility to their scam. Without that...."

"Buyers would be exceedingly skeptical," Varga concluded.

"Maybe that's why all the photos proving they were up here to begin with," I said.

"Very possibly. And they needed to have privacy, thus reducing the risk of being caught in the act. I have only the drone feedback and have not physically visited the homestead, but suspect it is very remote."

"True, but we do ride horses in the area occasionally. And come to think of it, Nikko and I saw evidence that an ORV—an off-road vehicle—had been back there."

"This is one of those big-wheeled machines?"

"Right. A great way to get back into remote areas. But don't people buying on the black market have ways to, I don't know, authenticate stuff?"

"It's true the items wouldn't stand up to authentication, but I'm sure the Hilmans had worked out a plan to get the money and run. The black market deals in these types of things regularly. Now with the internet, the opportunities are endless. Some buyers are very savvy, some not so much. And, of course, some of them are very dangerous people, and if they find they've been cheated, the seller better have a place to hide and an alternate identity to assume. The Hilmans' plans were full of flaws, and likely they'd eventually get nabbed, or worse. Turns out Mrs. Elsie Tuttle ended the whole game for an entirely different reason. The couple didn't bank on that when they tapped her for information. Nor did I, for that matter."

"Or me either," I said. "I was just curious about the woman who started it all, Helvi Paavola."

"A bit of a pickle," Varga said.

I mulled over the idea that Alex Varga somehow was not so much looking for more authentic artifacts as he may have been working with the Hilmans to set up an elaborate scam. He seemed to know a lot about it. I realized that while it was implied the offer to purchase the homestead was connected to the museum, I never saw anything official, and it occurred to me that maybe Varga was looking to buy the land himself—as he represented in our first conversation. This would give him free rein to dig up things and keep them. Maybe he could pull it off, even while working the legit side with the museum.

I looked at my watch. After 7:30. I thought of the movie, *The Princess Bride*, which I had watched multiple times. It was a slightly skewed fairytale wherein the damsel in distress, Buttercup, kept saying that her true love, Wesley, would save her before it was too late. It became too late—just a way to mess with the viewers who were expecting a rather predictable sequence of events. Eventually, good did prevail and Buttercup was saved from a frightful fate, but not in the expected manner. I wondered if my Wesley would save me.

Varga and I both jumped when the office door slammed open and Tuttle waved his huge, shiny gun around. He looked totally enraged.

"Can't find the fucking fob *or* key, bitch. I was gonna make things easy for you in the end, but now I wanna see ya squirm. You too, asshole," he said, pointing the gun at Varga.

"I presume the repair isn't going well either," Varga said.

"Fuck off!"

Tuttle stormed out. The door slammed and the lock slid into place.

"That went well," I said.

Varga and I sat silently, straining to hear anything, such as a car pulling away, or better yet, a car coming in, or *even* better, sirens. All we could hear was the annoying buzz of the fluorescent light and gurgling noise of the air conditioner.

"Damn, it's hot in here," I said. I got up, went over to the air conditioner, and gave it a hearty pound with my fist.

"Atta girl," Varga said. "Give it hell."

Just for good measure, I took the stance Aunt Lin had showed me in a quickie self-defense session. I shifted to one foot, managed to balance, then raised my leg and kicked the wheezing air conditioner with the fury of a pissed-off mule.

The unit gasped, then fell out of the wall and crashed onto the ground outside, leaving a gaping hole in the steel wall. The electric cord was still plugged into the wall socket, and the raw end that came out of the unit sputtered a little.

Varga looked at me, then went over to the hole. It was about twelve by eighteen inches.

"I'm too big, but I think you can squeeze through," he said. "I'll give you a boost."

* * *

"I told you feet first would work!" Varga said.

We had shoved the desk over to the hole in the wall. I climbed up on the desk, then put my feet and legs through the hole. The opening for the air conditioner was a sloppy gap cut through the steel, leaving sharp, jagged edges. Varga had sacrificed his suit jacket, which I sat on to protect me from being shredded like a cabbage. The big hangup in my egress was first my hips, then my shoulders.

"I think I dislocated a couple of joints!" I hissed.

A wooden support for the air conditioner was attached outside the hole, and I straddled that for a minute before flipping around and landing awkwardly on some gravel. I just missed hitting my head on the pulverized air conditioner.

"I'm out!" I said, stating the obvious since Varga was peering out the hole at me.

"Are you okay?" he asked.

"Yeah, just some major bruising and twisted joints."

"Try to come around and let me out. Watch to make sure there's no guard."

Varga made a good point. We weren't positive that Tuttle was gone, or for that matter, that he didn't live in some shack at the junkyard, though I suspected he lived with his mother.

I kept close to the building and worked my way past several bay doors to the service entrance. The scrapyard was an amazing array of enormous equipment, junk cars, piles of car parts, a mountain of used tires, and stacks of vehicles that had been reduced to metallic pancakes. Nearby was an enormous piece of machinery with large, horizontal metal plates. I assumed it was the unit that compacted cars into tidy rectangles of scrap.

What made my heart soar was the sight of the pimpmobile sitting across the parking lot next to a gigantic forklift. I worked my way to the service door, and just for kicks, tried the knob, but of course it was locked with an industrial-grade unit that bore a steel plate over the crack where the mechanisms would be located. I slunk around and peeked through a window. No sign of Tuttle. I glanced at the top of the building and doors, looking for security cameras and saw none. I soon found out why none were needed.

Two slathering, snarling dogs, probably Rottweilers, came streaking out of nowhere, displaying gleaming white fangs and a less-than-friendly attitude. I raced for the pimpmobile, yanked the door open, and leapt in just as the canine patrol flung themselves against the door. They jumped frantically around the truck, clearly enraged by my narrow escape. I heard toenails screeching against the powder-blue finish and saw a good deal of slobber on the driver's window. The inside of the truck was like an oven and I quickly reviewed my choices. I could die from the heat, which persisted even though it was nearly eight at night. Or I could be disemboweled by two junkyard dogs, or...I remembered I still had the magic fob in my jeans pocket and hit the start button. The truck purred to life, and I cranked up the air full blast.

My relief was short-lived when I realized a couple of things. First, I only had about an eighth of a tank of gas, so I couldn't sit in the truck indefinitely. Second, I couldn't merrily drive the truck off the lot and seek help because there was a formidable chain link fence complete with barbed wire at the top surrounding the scrapyard. Slats of some kind of aluminum privacy material were latticed through the chain link so that passersby were not likely to see me, let alone figure out my predicament. Of course there was a gate. Even from a distance, I could see an enormous chain and padlock in place and a battered-looking dump truck loaded with scrap parked in front of the gate, essentially derailing any thought of simply crashing the pimpmobile through the gate. If I got out of the truck to try to create an opening and squeeze through somewhere, I would become canine carnage.

The good news was the dogs had gotten tired, what with the heat and humidity. Their tongues lolled from dripping jaws, and both sat and glared at the truck. Eventually, they got up and wandered off to drink from a bucket, scarf some kibble from a bowl, and lay on a ratty mattress in the shade of a pile of twisted metal. I watched intently as the pooches seemed to drift off into doggie dreamland. I debated if it was safe to get out and check on Varga, maybe look for a window to get through. Or maybe I should look for bolt cutters to chop off the gate padlock and slip out on foot. Even if there were keys in the dump truck, I had no clue how to drive such a thing.

Then I heard a whinny.

It was the ring tone of my cell phone coming from within the truck. I pulled open the glovebox and center console and ransacked them, but no luck. The whinnying eventually ended. I searched the front seat floors, then climbed over the headrest and crawled around the backseat. I heard the muffled ping of an incoming text. I was sure I was getting closer. I groped under the seats and along the edge of the doors. I reached into all the pockets and cargo holds. The whinnying started up again. I was getting warmer. I jammed my hand down the crack between the front and back of the rear seat. Bingo! My hand felt the glorious rectangular plastic of my cell phone. It must have slipped out of my back pocket or from my purse during the process of my abduction. Since I had been comatose, I had no idea.

I looked at the display. Three bars, about 15 percent power and a bunch of messages. I punched in Nikko's number and he picked up on the first ring. I only got to utter one word: *scrapyard.*

≉ 30 ≉

The truck door jerked open. Someone grabbed me by my hair and yanked me out, headfirst. I landed on my shoulder, and it made a strange popping noise. The junkyard dogs were barking madly until a man shouted for them to shut up.

"Goddamn bitch! How'd you get out?"

Tuttle.

He jerked me up, and I yelped in pain, clutching my elbow to my body. My shoulder hurt like a son of a bitch. Tuttle grabbed my shirt and pushed me toward the building. I could smell a noxious combination of weed, sweat, and booze coming off him. The pimpmobile gave a beep and shut off, apparently sensing I was moving out of range.

"Hand me the fuckin' fob," Tuttle said.

"Lemme go. In my pocket."

Tuttle released me slightly, and I pulled the fob out of my pocket. As I was handing it to him, I twirled around, kicked him in the groin, and made a wild swing at his face with my good arm. Through some act of God, my punch neatly landed on his nose, and the added support of the fob made the blow significant enough to knock him back half a step and cause blood to spurt everywhere. Unfortunately, I also hurt my hand.

For a moment, Tuttle wasn't sure if he needed to clutch his crotch or hold his nose. He uttered some unflattering names and staggered a little, bending and howling. I took the opportunity to make a run for the truck. The guard dogs were instantly on my heels. I felt one grab my pant leg and the other attach to the seat of my pants. I saw Tuttle struggle to his feet and stumble toward me. My pace faltered under the weight of the attached dogs, and I could feel the pinch of fangs on my calf. I sensed Tuttle just a few paces behind. Even if Nikko figured out my one-word message, he wouldn't make it to the scrapyard before either Tuttle or the two dogs, or both, inflicted a lot of damage on me.

Then a shot exploded in the air. The dogs released my Carhartt jeans, yipped, and ran off. I continued my dash for the truck and had my hand on the handle when someone yelled, "Stop! It's okay!" It was

Varga. I turned to see him holding the gun over a crumpled Frank Tuttle.

"How unfortunate for Mr. Tuttle that he dropped his gun," Varga said. "While he was preoccupied with his testicles, I picked up his gun and got off a shot. I don't believe he's dead, but I suppose we should call an ambulance."

"But how…?"

"Well, I worked on the air conditioner gap for a while. Found some kind of giant pliers in one of the desk drawers and managed to make the hole big enough to fit through. Sorry I didn't get here sooner."

I leaned against the truck and started hyperventilating. "My phone—still in the truck. We'll call."

"Maybe no need," Varga said. "Looks like we've got company."

I looked over at the chain link gate and spotted the Olsen SUV. Nikko jumped out and yelled at me, "Are you okay?"

"I—I guess!" I shouted back.

Nikko opened the back of the SUV, rummaged around, and eventually pulled out a pair of bolt cutters. Tobey jumped out of the back, barking wildly.

"She needs an ambulance," Varga said. "So does this man. He's bleeding rather badly. I think I missed anything vital, but then, perhaps not."

Frank Tuttle was writhing around in the dirt, still holding his gonads. Even though he probably had a bullet in him, he had his priorities. The doggie duo were hunkered down back at their shady spot.

Nikko got the gate open, squeezed around the dump truck, and ran toward me with Tobey on his heels. The Rottweilers sprang into action and bolted toward Nikko.

"What the…?" Nikko yelled.

Then Tobey the Wonder Dog flew past Nikko and hurled himself at the Rottweilers.

"Tobey! No!" Nikko and I both yelled simultaneously.

All three animals rolled around in the dirt, screaming like banshees. Nikko rushed over to intervene. Frank Tuttle was curled into a fetal position, possibly going into shock. Varga still held the gun on him. I stood like a dope with my jaw hanging open, clutching my arm. I finally came to life, got my phone out of the truck, and called 911.

The snarling stopped and yipping began. The two junkyard dogs retreated. Tobey, hackles sticking up like a porcupine, strained at his collar that Nikko had latched onto.

"Is he okay?" I yelled.

"I think Tuttle's passed out," Varga said.

"No, I meant Tobey."

"Tobey seems okay," Nikko said. "He's a pit bull. All attitude and bluster."

The two Rottweilers had returned to their lair and were lapping water.

I heard sirens in the distance.

"The cavalry is coming!" I said.

"I'll see if I can move that damn dump truck!" Nikko said. "Call Tobey over."

I called Tobey and he obeyed, then sat on my feet, pant/clicking nervously.

Nikko went over to the dump truck and climbed into the cab. The engine growled to life, and after a wretched grinding of gears, the vehicle moved away from the gate. Nikko leapt out and swung the gate open, then hurried over to me.

I looked over at the forlorn Rottweilers. "I know it seems kind of stupid," I said, "but we can't just leave the two dogs once Tuttle is hauled off."

"We'll call animal control," Nikko said. "They'll have to be quarantined anyway. You have blood on your pantleg."

"Tuttle may be dead," Varga said, lowering the gun. "No, perhaps not. I heard a moan." He lifted the gun back into position.

I was feeling a tad weak-kneed. Blood had dripped down inside my pantleg, my shoulder hurt like hell, and I may have broken my hand. I felt as if I were melting into an amoebic puddle. The fiery horse from my earlier chemical hallucination reignited and raced across my field of vision. Then bright lights, talking, and someone put a mask on my face.

* * *

Something was beeping and someone was talking. I opened my eyes and eventually determined I was once again in the ER at Peshekee Memorial. Or ED, as they called it now, because it was not a *room* but rather a *department*. The plastic oxygen mask had been removed from my face, but I had the little oxygen doodads plugged into my nostrils. An IV was in my fairly good arm, while the arm attached to my messed-up shoulder was in a sling. The hand on the IV arm was encased in an ice pack and was basically numb. My nose itched like a sonofabitch, and I had no way to scratch it.

A person in a white lab coat was talking to someone in green scrubs. The green-scrub person nodded and left.

"Mah nosh," I muttered. It was supposed to be a plea to itch my nose.

"Ah, there you are," said the white-coat person. "I would like to say that it's nice to see you again, but that would be very disingenuous."

The speaker had a Middle Eastern accent and a lovely smile.

"Dr.—Zee?" I muttered.

"The one and only," he said.

I struggled to shift my forearm up to my nose to scratch it. Dr. Zee saw my dilemma and removed the ice pack so I could reach my face.

"Thanks," I said.

"So, this wasn't from a fall from one of your horses," Dr. Zee stated.

"Nope."

"Dislocated shoulders are pretty common with horse people. That and crushed toes and empty bank accounts. You probably remember me telling you my wife has horses."

"Uh huh," I said. "Arabians."

"Good memory. And I think the bump on your head is just superficial and you seem pretty coherent. Anyway, I understand you were assaulted, by both a human and a dog."

"Dogs," I said.

"Yes, we did have to put a couple of sutures in your calf. Of course, we need to know if the dogs were vaccinated for rabies. I believe the police have them in quarantine until they can see if the animals have had their shots. If not, they'll wait for any symptoms of disease, which is a ten-day period. If either are indeed rabid—and truthfully, it is very rare—we do have treatment for you."

I had heard about people getting the series of rabies shots and that it was no picnic. I prayed that wasn't something in my future.

"Your shoulder did dislocate but popped back. We'll do an MRI to see if it will heal on its own or needs surgery. No bones in your hand were broken, but there is significant trauma involved. It should be much better in a couple of days if you keep icing it, but you'll definitely need to have a follow-up appointment to make sure. The last thing we noticed was in your lab work. Someone may be in to talk to you about combining alcohol and drugs. Especially street drugs, such as we found in your system."

"I can explain," I said.

I told Dr. Zee about the funky water that Elsie Tuttle had given me that caused an incredible hallucination of a fiery horse.

"I admit to drinking some scotch when I was in captivity. I mean, what the hell?" I said.

"Captivity?"

"It's a long story. And complicated. When you said something about street drugs, what were you talking about?"

"The chemical name is lysergic acid diethylamide. Or LSD, among other names."

The curtain flew back on my cubicle and Nikko came in. He looked at me, then Dr. Zee, and nodded.

"Sorry to barge in," he said. "The nurse said it was okay. I got here as soon as I could. I was tied up with the police. Kat—are you okay?"

"More or less," I said, trying to scooch up a little.

Nikko came over and kissed my forehead. He looked around at the medical accoutrements surrounding me, then at my sling and ice pack. "I would hold your hand, but there doesn't seem to be one available."

"Dr. Zee, have you met my, ah, good friend Nikko Olsen?"

"I believe we met last time," Dr. Zee said. "I'll let the nurse know she can start the discharge process. Do you have any questions?"

"Yes," I said. "Tuttle?"

"Oh, the man who was shot?"

"Uh huh."

"He came and went. They took him off to Marquette. Due to patient confidentiality, I can't say much more. But I understand that he was the person who assaulted you."

I nodded.

"Alex Varga shot the bastard in the ribcage," Nikko said. "A couple of ribs are shattered, but he'll live to eventually stand trial for a laundry list of things, including murder, kidnapping, and unlawful imprisonment, assault, illegal firearm possession, and being an asshole. I made that last one up. There won't be any parole for him this time."

"What about Elsie Tuttle?" I asked.

"They're picking her up," Nikko said.

"And Alex Varga?"

"He was treated and released," Dr. Zee said. "I think he asked the nurse to give you a message."

"I also think the police have an interest in him, besides being a victim," Nikko said.

"Whatever is going on with Varga doesn't matter to me anymore," I said. "He may have saved my life. Tuttle was totally desperate. I mean, he took a long time to figure out I had escaped from the building. Then he dropped his gun. He was so incredibly strong. That is until I kicked him in the, ah, crotch."

Dr. Zee smiled. "That is a humbling experience for any man."

"Might have been doing drugs," Nikko said. "Some give the person incredible strength. This is something people don't understand when they see some video where it takes four cops to hold down one guy. Sometimes they don't even respond to a taser. However, Tuttle obviously underestimated you."

I smiled. Of course I had not come out of things unscathed, but I did prevail—with the help of Varga.

"The nurse should be in shortly," Dr. Zee said. "She'll arrange for the follow-up care. I hope I don't see you again in my emergency department anytime soon, Miss Wilde. Please do take care."

"Thanks for everything," I said.

Dr. Zee left, and Nikko pulled a plastic molded chair over and sat next to the bed.

"I heard the doctor mention LSD," Nikko said.

"Yeah, I think the water Elsie Tuttle gave me was laced with it. It tasted a little strange and was kind of sweet."

"They soak sugar cubes in the LSD sometimes. She probably got them from Frank Tuttle. Along with the chop shop at the scrapyard, he was probably peddling dope. His dotty mother is another case altogether."

"Two people are dead. Frank Tuttle told me all about the hippies. Wish I had been able to record it. He was so cocksure that he'd be rid of me and Varga, the pompous ass told me all about how his mother had Theodore and Laureen Hilman drink a toxic tea. *And* he bragged about burning the Jeep I had as a loaner. I also think he cut the wires on my pasture fence and messed with Cam and Valerie Jesson's game ranch fence, thus releasing the Russian boars."

"Some of which are still at large," Nikko said. "People are gonna start shooting them. But anyway, I don't entirely understand Frank Tuttle's motivation."

"Well, with the hippie Hilmans, it was Elsie who decided they needed to be removed. They, along with Alex Varga and me, were a perceived threat to her. Or at least one side of her. Varga thinks she's got a mental condition—I can't remember the formal name, but she may have had multiple personalities."

"I'm sure the police will look into her mental history," said Nikko. "Also, once you are up to it, we get to go to the state police post for you to give a statement. And, of course, Lieutenant Spiller has requested the pleasure our company."

I groaned.

We sat for a moment, listening to the slight hiss of the oxygen pumping into my nostrils and the occasional inflation of the blood pressure cuff.

"I'll be glad to get out of here," I said.

"You really gave me a scare," Nikko said. "When you didn't show up for dinner, I thought maybe you got tied up with a sick horse or something. I called the stable and Clay said you never came back after your appointment. After a while I went to the museum, but you weren't there. I was going crazy trying to figure out what the hell happened to you. I kept calling and texting and driving around, hoping to find you at the grocery store or broken down somewhere. Then you called and just said *scrapyard* before it disconnected."

"Tuttle jumped me, and of course, I lost the call. And I think I was having some kind of flashback from the LSD trip. I was pretty damn glad to see you."

"And those two dogs came at me," Nikko said. "That was a moment I won't forget."

"Tobey was awesome," I said. "Is he okay?"

"Yup, not a scratch. And he's had his rabies shots, so no worries."

"Wish I could say the same."

"I think they're trying to contact the local veterinarian to find out if the two Rottweilers had been vaccinated."

"Hope so," I said.

We sat and listened to some urgent noise out in the hallway. Someone shouted an order and called for something. I heard a gurney being quickly wheeled by. It was ghoulish, but I wondered what was going on. A heart attack or car accident maybe. Or a drug overdose. They weren't a rare occurrence anymore in Peshekee.

"Hope that nurse gets here pretty soon to spring you," Nikko said.

"Sorry to be such a pain in the butt as a, ah...."

"Girlfriend," Nikko said.

"Or at least a friend who's a girl."

"Or more."

Nikko leaned in to give me a pretty good kiss, considering he had to deal with the bed railing and a couple of tubes. I slipped the ice pack off my hand and reached up to pull him toward me.

"Your hand's cold," he said.

"I'm freezing," I said.

Nikko fought with the railing for a moment, then managed to drop it down. He sat on the bed and leaned in for another kiss.

I was starting to warm up when I heard my mother's voice talking to someone. The curtain whipped open and Mom rushed in. Nikko snapped up and managed to get tangled in my oxygen tube.

"Kathryn! Oh dear God, look at you! Nikko, what are you doing?"

"Oh, just trying to make Kat more comfortable," he said, finally disengaging himself from the plastic tube. He made as if trying to tuck the blankets tighter around me. I had to suppress a smile.

"Darling, the doctor out there just asked me *again* if you were prone to accidents as a child. If I weren't so worried, I'd be embarrassed as a mother who somehow failed to properly raise her daughter."

"Sorry. All I was trying to do was find out about the homestead on the Wildwood property."

"Your father will be here in a minute. We'll take you home."

"I'll take her," Nikko said.

Mom eyed him.

The curtain opened and a nurse came in with a clipboard that I assumed had my discharge papers. "Hi. I'm Natasha. Let's get all these things unhooked. Oh, I have this message for you, Kathryn." She handed me a folded-up note.

Hope you're feeling better. I'll have a final offer soon. Best, Alex.

Mom and Nikko were looking at me, waiting for me to share.

"Oh, it's just Varga wishing me well," I said.

The nurse removed the oxygen tubes, heart monitor, blood pressure cuff, and IV. She looked around the crowded space and said, "Who is going to help Kathryn get dressed?"

"I will," both Nikko and Mom said simultaneously.

"You can draw straws," I said.

31

Nikko and I lounged on the mod's porch, sprawled out in Uncle Phil's old, webbed lounge chairs. Nikko had offered to buy new furniture for the porch, but I couldn't part with Uncle Phil's old, rickety lawn furniture. Tobey lay nearby, making a rhythmic snorting noise as he drifted off into slumberland. We were waiting for Jeannie Usitalo's daughter, Brianna, to be brought out by her grandmother. Susie Koskinen was also going to come out, and the plan was to have Brianna get involved with horses as her young mind grappled with the loss of her mom.

It would be Susie's first real equine therapy experience. Our plan was to have Brianna unofficially assigned to the new rescue pony, Peaches. She could focus on bringing the pony back to good health, learn how to care for horses, and eventually start riding lessons. Brianna's grandmother said that the prospect of having her own pony to look after had brought a smile to the child's otherwise glum demeanor.

The weather had cooled and humidity was down. Aunt Lin had planted a couple of flower containers and put them next to the door of the mod. A soft, sweet smell drifted off their blooms, and a big bumblebee drifted from flower to flower doing what bees do. It was a perfect day to be outside. The great outdoors was something I hoped Frank Tuttle wouldn't be experiencing for a while. A lot depended on if they could prove he cut the brake lines on Jeannie Usitalo's vehicle, causing the fatal crash. While Tuttle had spoken freely—actually bragged—about his part in the murder of Theodore and Laureen Hilman, a good lawyer could argue he was caught up in protecting his mother and was an accessory after the fact. Still bad, but not as bad as murder one. Plus, there was the whole mental illness factor. Tuttle never admitted to me he'd cut Jeannie's or my brake lines. I could have kicked myself for not coaxing it out of him. I was positive he had done it. However, my preoccupation with my impending doom via a vehicle compactor had been my main priority. It amazed me how an old grudge against a bunch of silly high school girl bullies could fester and grow and, eventually, trigger revenge involving malicious vandalism, sabotage, and homicide.

Aunt Lin came out of the mod carrying a tray with some beverages on it.

"It's my special lemonade," she said. "I thought you two could use a cool drink."

We thanked her and each took a glass. Green floaties drifted around as I stirred the ice with a straw. I took a sip and suppressed my grimace.

"Raymond will be here in a while," Aunt Lin said. "He wonders if you want to keep the surveillance equipment up. If so, he wants to make some adjustments."

"Sure, if he doesn't mind," I said. "I appreciate being able to keep an eye on things. And Aunt Lin, I want to thank you for teaching me a few self-defense moves. I think the basic foot to the groin and nose punch definitely bought me some time."

"My pleasure," Aunt Lin said. "There's more where that came from. Lemonade that is. And a couple of other nifty moves as well. You know, in case Mr. Hot Stuff here tries anything."

Nikko chuckled.

"Be forewarned," I said.

"I'm going into town for a couple of errands," Aunt Lin said. "Anyone need anything?"

"Nope, thanks," I said.

"Okay. When Raymond gets here, tell him I'll be back in an hour or so."

"Will do," I said.

She got into her Subaru and drove off. Nikko and I took tiny sips of our unsweetened lemonade and had a contest about who could screw up their face the worst.

"We could dump it," Nikko said.

"I usually do, but it has to be handled carefully. A large wet spot off the edge of the porch is a dead giveaway. Plus, it kills the grass."

"How's your shoulder?"

"Good," I said, carefully moving my arm. It was still in the sling, but I could use it a little. No surgery would be needed, and the swelling in the other hand had gone down. "Now I know how Clay felt, dealing with only one useable arm," I added.

"Speaking of Clay," Nikko said. "How does he fit into all of this? I mean, could he be connected to Varga? You know, as a spy or influencer or even saboteur?"

"You've got to be kidding," I said. "That doesn't add up at all."

"Probably not, but I imagine his background check came in a long time ago, and you never mentioned the results. I've been waiting and wondering."

"Oh, well that. Things did come back, and I did have a question about one, ah, part of it. He and I are going to discuss it—eventually."

"What did it say—the report?"

"Well, it's confidential; I can't share. They're very strict about that. Employers shouldn't share results with irrelevant parties. It could lead to legal issues. It was in one of the many policy and procedure notices I signed. His past or present, for that matter, have nothing to do with stolen fake artifacts or anything else that has been going on around here."

"Uh huh," Nikko said, frowning.

"Besides, Tuttle confessed to most of the sabotage *and* the Hilmans' murders. Far as I'm concerned, Clay is totally exonerated, not that I suspected him of anything anyway."

"Probably," Nikko said. "Then there's Varga...."

"Yeah, well, he saved my life, so get him out of your sights as well."

Nikko continued frowning, then changed the subject. "How about the LSD tripping? Any more episodes?"

"You sound like the doctor. No, just the original one, and then the one when I passed out at the scrapyard. I guess I might *trip*, as you call it, for a while."

"Far out," Nikko said.

"Oh, just stop! It's not like I took the stuff on purpose."

"Yeah, I can dig it. Totally groovy."

"Don't forget Aunt Lin taught me some moves."

"Speaking of moves," Nikko said, leaning across his armrest, puckering his lips, and making smacking noises.

"You're a goofball," I said, sneaking Tobey a piece of cheese. "You could at least get out of your chair." I reached down and scratched my calf where the dog bite had been sutured. "Damn, these stitches itch like crazy."

"Means you're healing. Don't scratch them; you could get an infection. When do you get them out?"

"A week or so."

"Good news that the Peshekee Animal Hospital had records of the two dogs being vaccinated."

"Yeah. The doctor's office called and let me know. What will happen to them—the dogs?"

"Maybe Mike would adopt them—you know, our slightly sketchy auto repair and used junker car salesman. He doesn't believe they are vicious at all. Tuttle didn't own the dogs. Harvey Walsh owns the scrapyard and the dogs were his. Harvey has flown the coop. There is a warrant for his arrest involving the chop shop operation. Right now the Walsh Auto Recycling Center, which is its official name, is closed for business. Not sure where Mike's Auto is going to take the junk heaps he sells for scrap."

I thought about how close I came to being melded with one of those junk heaps.

Nikko said, "And I meant to tell you something interesting that Dad found out when he went to talk to Mike about Jeannie's brake lines and so on."

I was all ears.

"Seems that Mike said he rented out the ATV to the Hilman hippies. Of course they went by their false names and had fake IDs. I guess they had cash and no charge card, which Mike usually requires. However, cash is easy to forget to put on the books, so I imagine that's why he took it."

"I wonder about those ORV tracks we saw back at the homestead," I said. "And the marker ribbon."

"Could have been them, though I don't exactly know what they'd be doing back there. I mean, they allegedly stole a bunch of artifact replicas."

"Maybe they were also looking for the real stuff, like Varga," I said.

"And, apparently, Dad asked Mike if anyone matching Mr. Varga's description had rented the ATV, and that was a negative."

"So, maybe it was the Hilmans who were back there," I said. "We need to make another trip to the homestead. It'll have to be in that obnoxious tank thing of your dad's. I can't ride horses for a while."

"The Druggie Buggy," Nikko said. "Sure, no problem. What will you be looking for?"

"Inspiration."

"I have Thursday off. We could go then."

"Great, thanks. I'm going to the office tomorrow. Not sure what I'll do there, but it won't be any heavy lifting. First, I have to stop at the state police post to give a more detailed statement. I think I'm meeting with Sergeant Witz, not Spiller. There is a God."

"Spiller's not a bad guy," Nikko said. "I think he was kind of impressed at how you handled the situation at the scrapyard."

"I Am Woman!"

Nikko grinned. "Indeed you are. I'll get the trailer and the machine and be here around nine Thursday morning."

I watched the horses lolling in the warm sun. Big Mac and Peaches were sharing a paddock. They looked like a circus act with the Belgian, Mac, being about seventeen hands, or sixty-eight inches at the shoulder, and maybe 2,000 pounds. Peaches, a Shetland pony, and one of the smallest equine breeds, was a mere ten hands or about forty inches at the shoulder and was terribly underweight, probably lucky to be 300 pounds. She would need to put on about 100 pounds to be considered a good weight. The other horses dozed in the main pasture.

I sighed and said, "I feel so...bored and useless sitting around waiting for things to happen."

"What? You want to be kidnapped again?"

"No, twice was enough."

"What are the odds, eh?" Nikko said. "Of being held captive not once, but twice in the same year? First our duct tape debacle in the cabin last spring, and just a few short months later, an adventure in the scrapyard. And you're not even a super-spy or undercover agent."

"Just a gal trying to run a horse stable," I said.

"A plucky gal, though."

"I feel more like I've been plucked."

"So, what are your plans for the Alex Varga guy?" Nikko asked.

"Well, first off, I'm going to buy an expensive bottle of scotch and take it to him. I think he's staying at the extended-stay Marriot in Marquette."

"I'm not sure I like the sounds of that."

"Relax. I'll explain the scotch later. As I mentioned before, he probably saved my life. I assume he's going to hang around for a while until things are cleared up."

"Yeah," Nikko said. "I don't think the feds are looking at him in connection with the stolen fake artifacts the hippies were involved with. To them, the death of the Hilmans closed the case, except of course for the recovery of the objects. The local police will be conducting the investigation relating to their deaths. For now the Peshekee Museum is considered a crime scene and closed until further notice. But what I'm actually wondering is what you are going to do about Varga's reason for being here."

"What do you mean?"

"Are you going to sell that land to him?"

"I don't think so," I said, venturing another tiny sip of lemonade. I thought about Varga's note mentioning a "final offer." The whole issue wasn't about money, it was about doing what was right, and I wasn't sure what that was.

"It's completely up to you," Nikko said, taking another sip of his drink and grimacing.

"I'll be right back," I said. I got up, went into the mod, and returned with a can of pop.

"Here, would you pop the top?" I asked. "If we add diet pop to the lemonade, it makes it drinkable. I got a Dew because it's yellow and Aunt Lin will never suspect."

Nikko took the can and snapped it open. We split it between us and resumed drinking.

"That does help," Nikko said. "So, anyway, what if there are priceless artifacts at the homestead? Should they just stay in the ground?"

"I don't know," I said. "Probably not. I mean, it's good for these things to be shared with the world. You know, to help piece together the history of humans and so on. Yet it somehow seems sacrilegious to me to dig up stuff. I mean, what if it turns out to be some kind of burial ground?"

"Good point."

I took another sip of my drink. "I'm starved. I only had a piece of toast for breakfast." I got up again, went into the mod, and rooted around until I found some slices of cheese and a sleeve of crackers.

"Yow!"

Jupiter made an appearance and began snaking around my ankles.

"Okay, a couple of snackies, but don't tell Auntie Lin."

I went to the kitty cupboard, pulled out a bag of Kittie Yummies, and plopped a couple in Jupiter's food dish. He trotted over, circled the dish twice, sniffed, and delicately picked up one of the morsels. After a little humming, he scarfed up the other Yummy and trotted off, perhaps to cache for a future snack. For all I knew, he had a whole stash of Yummies somewhere.

I stuck the cheese and crackers on a paper plate and awkwardly carried it back out onto the porch.

"A snack," I said, handing the plate to Nikko.

Tobey's head shot up at the sound of the word *snack*. He stood, stretched, wandered over to Nikko, and assumed his begging position.

I watched a car work its way up Horse Camp Road.

"The first of our visitors," I said, shoving a cracker-cheese sandwich into my mouth. "Looks like Gussy's car."

The car pulled in and Gussy, Raymond, and Mia got out. Nikko, Tobey, and I walked over to meet up with them.

"Go ahead," Raymond said. "Fess up." He gave Gussy and Mia a stern look. "There are no tricksters in our family."

"What's going on?" I asked.

Gussy scraped his toe in the dirt and avoided eye contact. Mia cast her eyes downward, as if showing humility. But she had a small smile on her lips.

"We're waiting," Raymond said. "Mr. Gustafson...?"

Gussy cleared his throat, looked up at me and said, "We didn't mean anything by it."

"I'm going to need more info," I said.

"The ghost horse," Mia said.

I hadn't given the phantom horse in the campground much thought for a while. A car fire and fatal car crash of a friend, then being drugged, kidnapped, and tripping on LSD had distracted me, along with a couple of dog attacks and the prospect of being crushed like a cardboard box.

"See, I was just showing Mia—" Gussy said.

"Showing off," Raymond said.

"—showing Mia how the hologram worked at the campground. You know, Raymond had all the equipment and taught me some stuff, and I paid attention. Mia borrowed the equipment—"

"Without my permission," Raymond said, glaring at his sister.

"—and we went to the campground and got it all reinstalled."

"It was totally cool!" Mia said. "Gussy is so, like, totally amazing."

Gussy grinned from ear to ear. Raymond sighed and rolled his eyes.

"We didn't mean to scare anyone," Mia said.

"But when...?" I asked.

"Well, we came the back way along the two-track. Later in the evening, a while back."

"Told her Aunt Lucy that she was at the library. Studying," Raymond said.

Ah, the ol' I'm going to the library to study ploy, I thought. I'd pulled it a time or two.

"Anyway, we'll take it down now," Gussy said. "I'm really sorry if we upset you. I mean, you won't tell Mother will you?"

That would be a good one for the Nasty List. Where would she start? The unauthorized "borrowing"? Sneaking out with a girl? Lying? Scaring people? The whole episode would take the starch out of Rose's hairdo for sure. She'd probably take away her son's allowance for a month and feed him only bland meatloaf and boiled chicken.

"I won't tell Rose," I said.

Nikko was trying to suppress a smile. It was pretty funny that Gussy took great risks to impress a girl.

"Hey," I said. "Was that what you two were looking at—at the office? The hologram?"

"Uh huh," Mia said. "Gussy is sooo smart. He got it recorded, and we watched it on his laptop. We saw when you were back there with that lady and she freaked."

"Willie Moss," I said. "I had to dig myself out of that one."

Raymond glared at the two, who submissively lowered their heads.

"Not only will you two take down the equipment," Raymond said, "but Kat needs to determine some kind of punishment. Maybe a chore for you to do around this place to make up for the trouble you've caused. Something unpleasant."

The two nodded meekly. Gussy looked at me with pleading eyes. Mia continued to have a small smile on her face. She glanced at Gussy and winked at him. A blush materialized on his cheeks. Oh my, but she had him hook, line, and sinker.

There were a lot of unpleasant chores connected to horses. I thought about the manure pile that had morphed into a looming monster. We had finally gotten a used spreader and tractor, but now the pile needed to be forked into the spreader and scattered in a meadow behind the campground. At some point we'd get a conveyor that would eliminate a lot of the manual labor, but even a used one was pricey. Clay could drive the tractor and do the spreading, but getting the moldering manure into the spreader was a monumental task Clay didn't have time to deal with, and I, of course, had only one good arm at the moment.

"First off, I want you to leave the hologram equipment up. We'll figure out something fun to do with it once the camp gets going."

Gussy and Mia grinned.

"However, I do have the perfect task for your penance."

32

I recognized the Koskinen pickup bumping down Horse Camp Road. It pulled around and Susie Koskinen and Brianna Usitalo climbed out. Brianna was clutching the stuffed Peaches the Pony I'd given her. She looked small and anxious.

"Hi!" Susie said, coming up to us. "I had Mrs. Usitalo sign all the release papers and brought Brianna out to look the place over." Susie pointed at the scrubby-looking pony napping in the paddock. "Hey, Brianna, there's Peaches!"

Brianna looked over at Peaches and her paddock-mate, Big Mac. "She's dirty," Brianna said with a small smile.

"And we're gonna clean her up," Susie said. "Why don't you go over and get a closer look at Peaches and see what you think? Right now maybe just look; don't reach through the fence. I need to talk to Kat a minute."

"I'll take her over," Nikko said.

This made me raise my eyebrows. "Really?"

"Sure. Come on, Brianna. Let's go see the horsies."

Susie and I watched Nikko take Brianna's hand and lead her away. She looked up at him and seemed to be chatting him up.

"Horsies? What the...?" I said.

"Totally..." Susie said. "Totally odd."

"So you wanted to talk to me?" I asked.

"Yeah, um, I talked to Ms. Moss, and she said that most stuff is all good, you know, like in order and all. The workers are coming next week to start the tear down. Thing is, there's only me right now, and technically, if we start Brianna under the therapy program—even unofficially—we need at least two attendants. You know, mostly for our own protection. It would be good to have another horse person, not just like some kid from high school. I know you're pretty busy...."

I nodded. "We didn't plan on having any students before things were more organized. We should probably try to get someone besides Clay or me to assist you. That person should be committed to Magic Stirrup and not directly connected to Wildwood."

I looked over at Nikko and Brianna. Peaches and Mac were showing great interest in the twosome. Brianna pulled a carrot out of her pocket, and Nikko broke it into pieces. He showed Brianna how to hold her hand flat to present the carrot pieces to both horses.

I smiled and said, "Too bad Nikko already has a job. Apparently, he's good with kids."

"Yeah," Susie said, "like a big brother or something."

"So, I'll give a think on another instructor."

Then I had an epiphany and said, "Beatrice!"

"Huh?" Susie asked.

"You go and take Brianna around," I said. "I have a call to make."

* * *

I went into the mod and got my cell phone. I went back outside, sat on the porch step, and turned on my phone. Nikko came over and looked at me.

"You look serious," he said.

"Trying to remember someone's last name. Her first name, I think, is Beatrice, but nothing comes up."

"So, who's this Beatrice person?"

"She sold me her Stübben saddle last spring. She's a nice lady who had to give up riding because of hip problems, among other things, and needed the money for her surgery copay and whatnot."

"Okay..." Nikko said, sitting down beside me.

"She would be perfect! If she is still, you know, around."

"Perfect for what?"

"To be an assistant for the Magic Stirrup Therapy Camp," I said with a touch of annoyance.

"Of course. How could I not know that?"

"Sorry. It's just...wait, okay, here it is! It's *Bernice*, not Beatrice. Perry. Bernice Perry, and I have her phone number."

Nikko stood. "Well, good. I hope it works out." He looked across the parking area at Susie and Brianna. They had taken Peaches out of the paddock and were leading her toward the barn. "So, I'll see you Thursday."

"Sure, sorry," I said, standing. "I just hope Bea—er Bernice—is still active. She seemed so, I don't know, sad to give up horses."

"You really do care about people," Nikko said, pulling me toward him.

I was momentarily distracted by a tight embrace and lingering kiss.

We heard Susie and Brianna making "oo" noises. I looked over and Susie was grinning at us.

I pulled away abruptly. Nikko looked over at the two and said, "Don't you have anything better to do?"

The two giggled and continued toward the barn.

"I think Brianna's doing great," I said. "She's already opened up, and it's just her first day here."

"Yeah, she's a great kid," Nikko said. He gave me a peck on the cheek and headed out.

I returned to my phone and called the number for Bernice. It was still active, but nobody answered. I left a message reminding her of who I was and asking if she wanted to talk about a proposition. I gave both my landline and cell number and asked her to call. All I could do was wait.

* * *

My tardiness at the office was excused since I had been at the state police post giving a lengthy statement to Sergeant Witz. Blessedly, I didn't have to endure the so-called third degree from Lieutenant Spiller. Turns out I was going to be a primary witness to a lot of things. Elsie Tuttle was under psychiatric evaluation at a secure mental institution, and Frank Tuttle was being held without bond. Sooner or later I'd likely be doing a deposition, or actually testifying in court. Undoubtedly, Alex Varga would also be called upon as a witness. Of course, there was always the prospect of a plea deal with the Tuttles.

When I finally arrived at the office, Gussy's beater and Rose's sensible Buick were the only cars in the lot. Apparently, Dad was not in. If I'd expected Rose to throw me a pity party at the office, I would have been woefully disappointed. I had entered the office many times with various physical ailments throughout my employment with Wilde Accounting. That past spring, I had to use a cane for a while after having my knee wrenched in a tussle with the late Scott Summers, who had tried to claim Wildwood as his own. He became dead through no doing of mine. Rose's reaction was suggesting I adjust my morning schedule accordingly so I wouldn't be late.

This time, I was wearing my arm in a sling and had a slight limp from the stitches pulling at the laceration on my calf. I was a pathetic vision that should have earned a dose of grace from Rose—not that I was surprised when it didn't come.

"Good thing it's your left arm," Rose said, peering over her glasses at me as I wobbled in. "At least you can still do *some* work."

"Good morning to you, too, Grace—I mean Rose."

She looked oddly at me. *Freudian Slip?*

I went to my nook and threw my purse on the desk. I sat down and booted up my computer. A lot of emails had backed up in my absence.

"How's the newsletter coming?" Rose asked.

"Uh..."

My phone whinnied. I could feel Rose's judgmental scowl penetrate the air molecules. I looked at the display and saw an unfamiliar number.

"Kat Wilde speaking," I said.

"Kat!" said the voice. "I do hope this is a good time. This is Bernice Perry—the saddle lady. You called me."

"Oh, Bernice! So good to hear from you."

"Oh my, I could say the same. It was a delight to get your call."

"How are you doing?" I asked. "Are you healing from your surgery?"

"Very well, thank you for asking. I am doing splendidly. I think the doctors bought me a few more years."

"I am so glad to hear that. Anyway, I have no idea where you're at with things or where you even live now—"

"Oh, I'm just puttering around. Done with physical therapy and living in a monthly rental in Marquette. Now you mentioned something about a possible position with your stable? I'd love to hear more about it."

"That's great," I said, looking over at Rose, who was pretending not to eavesdrop. "Is there any chance you could come out to my place, Wildwood Stables, and we could talk?"

"Oh, certainly. Just name the day and time."

Bernice and I settled on a meetup and I gave her directions. I had a good feeling about Bernice. Susie was a young adult, Bernice an experienced senior citizen. Both would be excellent as staff for the Magic Stirrup Therapy Camp. I would need to contact Willie Moss and work out the details if Bernice was indeed interested.

I sighed and settled into my workspace. It would be interesting to try to work on a newsletter when I had only one hand to type with. At least the rotation of heavy boxes in the attic would be on hold. I contemplated my bank balance, which had become—if not completely healthy—at least off of life support. I now had three rescue horses and a pony for which I was being compensated. At some point, I was pretty sure Big Mac and Peaches would be excellent therapy animals for

Magic Stirrup. Rusty, of course, who was my gift horse from Dad, was as solid as a horse could get. Oscar and Emmy were not good prospects until they had some more miles put on them. I realized, once again, how blessed I was to have Clay working with them, patiently bringing them along. They were both show quality horses, even if their appaloosa spots never emerged. I wished I had never run that background check.

The front door swished open and Mia came in. She chirped good morning to everyone. Gussy, who had probably been watching out the window, casually emerged from his office and feigned surprise at seeing her. As if he hadn't given her a single thought.

"So, Kat," Mia said "when do you want us to, ah..." She looked over at Rose, who was watching. "Ah, you know, come over and help with that thing you need."

Of course she was talking about the manure pile reduction plan, which was penance for the ghost horse hoax.

"Let me check with Clay since he'll.... Anyway, maybe next weekend?"

"I can drive," Gussy said.

Rose's antenna was fully engaged.

"You two are awesome," I said. "So compassionate."

Let Rose try to sort that out.

33

I was in the barn trying to sweep with one arm, when I heard a car drive up. My bum shoulder was almost back to normal, but the doc said to baby it. Nikko pulled up with the Olsen SUV towing a trailer loaded with the Bobcat. He got out, went around to the passenger door, and got Tobey out. The pooch spotted me and, I swear, grinned from ear to ear and rushed over. Ya gotta love it!

"Who's a good boy?" I said, reaching down to scratch his favorite spot behind his ears

His tongue lolled and he engaged his major butt wiggle.

Clay came out, leading Oscar.

"Hey," he said to Nikko.

"Hey," Nikko said back.

Men were so chatty and warm.

"How's the colt doing?" I asked.

"Getting there," Clay said. "I'm going to just hang out with him today. I don't want him to think it's always about work and training. Today is going to be a little walkabout and maybe a nice bath and rubdown." He slipped the horse a treat.

"Good plan," I said.

Clay scratched Oscar on the forehead, then dropped his hand to his side. He looked at Nikko and me and said, "So, if the two of you have a minute, I think I can explain that blot in my past."

"You don't have to," I said. "I mean I really don't think it's important. Plus, well, maybe it's just between you and me."

"I'd like to tell the both of you," Clay said. "I know Nikko is just plain suspicious of me."

"No, well maybe," Nikko said. "Kat hasn't told me anything, but she seems to be troubled."

"Don't want that," Clay said.

"Maybe we should all go in the mod and have a chat," I said.

"Nope," Clay said. "This will just take a minute, and I don't want to keep you two from your date."

"It's not a date," I said.

"It's an adventure," Nikko said, smiling.

"Anyway," Clay said, "a couple of years back, I worked for a ranch out in Wyoming. It was a decent spread, but the owner had a different perspective than me on the value of horses and how to treat them."

I nodded.

"Long story short, Mr. Corbin, the owner, saw some money in rounding up mustangs. It was legal in some cases to round them up and sell them off when the herds overgrazed the land that was used for cattle and other domestic livestock."

"Sell them off?" I said.

"Wild horses?" Nikko asked.

"Yup. Totally feral, and born to roam free. Pretty hard to find them good homes, and that wasn't Corbin's plan anyway. He wasn't into rescuing the mustangs, just exploiting them."

"I don't think I like where this is going," I said.

"Yup. Meat. They cram them in trailers, some injured, foals separated from their moms, hot, dusty, thirsty, hungry, terrified. You get the picture."

"Damn," Nikko said.

"So, it's pretty simple," Clay said. "I let the animals loose one night. They were all jammed in a few corrals with no food or water, waiting to make the trip to Mexico where they'd be butchered."

"God!" I said. "Makes me sick."

"Ditto," Nikko said.

We all looked at Oscar and thought about the fate he might have had at the auction.

"So, I didn't try to hide it. I let the animals loose, and they had returned to their range miles away before Corbin even had his morning whiskey-laced coffee. I didn't deny it was me. I was proud to do it and would do it again. But I broke the law and got arrested for what they called attempted larceny. As if I'd taken the horses for my own use."

"Sounds ridiculous," Nikko said.

"Yup," Clay said. "It was a pretty trumped-up charge. Anyway, it got known to the public what I did, and while some folks didn't want to mess with Corbin, others didn't care for the man and there was some public noise about his nasty operation. Ended up they reduced the charge to malicious destruction of property, or MDP, fined me, and told me to get out of town. That's likely what's on my record. Corbin said I damaged his fence and so on. Bunch of bull, but I just wanted to get on with things and get the hell out of Wyoming. I probably should have paid a lawyer to try to get me off the hook. I never thought about the whole thing coming back to bite me."

I said, "I remember you mentioned that I'd have done the same thing. Back when we first talked about your background check."

Clay nodded.

"You were right. I would. In a heartbeat."

"So now what?" Clay asked.

"Now we try to find a way to get that so-called blot off your past," I said.

"Well, now, I don't think—" Clay said.

"Forget it, Randall," Nikko said. "Kat will be on it like a dog with a bone."

Tobey barked when he heard the word "bone."

We all laughed, and I reached over and shook Clay's hand.

"For now," I said, "you are golden at Wildwood. But since we will be having a children's therapy camp here, we need to get you squeaky clean."

"Yes, ma'am," Clay said with a grin.

Tobey barked again.

"Someone's impatient," I said.

"Ready to head out?" Nikko asked.

"Yes," I said. "Give me a minute to let Aunt Lin know, and I'll grab us a couple of snacks."

"No need for snacks. I have a cooler in the Bobcat."

Clay nodded at Nikko, who nodded back. Then Clay headed away, leading Oscar.

Nikko loaded the Bobcat and we piled in.

"So, how do you feel about Clay now?" I asked.

"You know," Nikko said, "I'd probably do the same thing too."

We looked at Tobey, who was positioned between us. The dog began his pant/clicking.

"Guess Tobes was a victim of bad people too," Nikko said.

"I try not to hate them," I said. "But I do."

Nikko put the Bobcat in gear and we headed out. It was another lovely summer day. Not a cloud in the sky, and a gentle zephyr of warm air floated through the Bobcat windows. The green of the trees was just a tad beyond peak and hinted of summer winding down. We bypassed the campground and took the direct route to the homestead. Dog breath aside, some might describe the atmosphere as companionable silence. I was thinking that Nikko seemed pensive and a little distracted.

"Penny for your thoughts," I said. "Still thinking about Clay?"

"Nope. Plus, my thoughts are gonna cost you more than a penny," he said with a grin.

"Really, and what would that be?"

"I'll let you know."

We pulled up to the homestead and got out of the Bobcat. Nikko snapped a leash on Tobey and helped him down.

"Tell me what to look for," Nikko said.

"Clues."

"Of what?"

"I don't know. I just know there are some answers to things here."

"To what?"

"Well, I do know why Varga wanted to buy my land. At least his story is plausible about exploring the potential of authentic pre-Columbian artifacts and all. I mean, as Varga said, they did verify that the relic has provenance leading back to the tablet that Ruthie Huntington sold to Ezekiel Adams."

"Okay, so are you thinking of digging up anything? There's a spade shovel in the Bobcat."

"No.... Well, maybe."

I went up to the chimney ruins, then walked the vague perimeter of the homestead cabin.

"Okay, so the cabin was here," I said. "But what about a shelter for the animals? The journal said the artifact was unearthed while digging a fencepost hole. Where would that be?"

"Hard to say," Nikko said. "Everything is grown over now. There is equipment—ground-penetrating radar, I think—that can help find things in the ground. Of course I have no idea where to rent one of those."

"Plus, there's so many rocks. If I were to let Varga have a go at it, I expect he'd get some sophisticated equipment. But actually, I'm still trying to figure out why the Hilmans—you know the dead couple—were back here in an ATV. I mean, I believe it was probably their tracks along with the flag marker that we saw when we first came out. As you said, Mike rented his ATV to them."

"Maybe to look for the real stuff?" Nikko said.

"Maybe. But neither your dad nor Lieutenant Spiller mentioned special equipment for finding underground objects among their possessions. Digging with a shovel would be overwhelming. Plus, they were trespassing, so if they just started randomly digging, it would be pretty risky. For all they knew, I might start shooting."

Nikko gave a quick snort of laughter.

"It could happen," I said, "if I had a gun."

I left the vestiges of the homestead structure and began a semi-logical search pattern by widening a spiral around the cabin area. Nikko went to the Bobcat and retrieved a small cooler, then went over to Helvi's spirit rock and sat down next to it.

"Let's have a snack," he said, patting the ground next to him.

I temporarily abandoned my search and sat next to Nikko. Tobey, hearing the word "snack," positioned himself so he was facing both of us.

Nikko dropped the leash and said, "We have food; Tobey's not going anywhere."

He pulled out a couple bottles of water and some bags of trail mix. We sat shoulder-to-shoulder while we munched on the trail mix and sipped our water. Nikko filled a Sierra cup with water and offered it to Tobey, who lapped noisily. I slipped a dehydrated orange thing to Tobey.

"That'll make him gassy," Nikko said.

"Better him than me."

Nikko put his arm around me and turned in for a kiss. Things escalated a little, but only so much as the hard ground, a rock digging into my back, and a canine chaperone would allow.

"There's something I need to talk to you about," Nikko said.

I looked at him. "This seems serious."

"It is. Not a bad thing. Just a shock or at least a major surprise."

"You found out that there's no Santa Claus?"

"There isn't!" Nikko said, feigning horror.

"Sorry to break it to you. So, what's the major surprise?"

"I might as well just say it," Nikko said, taking swallow of water. "It would seem that I might be—well, it's very likely—that I am a father."

I turned to him. "This some kind of a joke?"

"Nope."

I stared off into the woods. Tobey drooled and panted. Nikko gave a lot of attention to picking out M&Ms from the trail mix.

"Okay," I said. "This has been quite a day for confessions. Details?"

"Brianna Usitalo."

"Oh. My. God."

"I had no idea. I mean, I don't hardly remember Jeannie and me.... I mean...."

During one of my past hair appointments, I remembered Jeannie mentioning the old horse camp at Wildwood being a high school destination for drinking and making out. I tried to grapple with the irony of Brianna possibly being conceived back there.

"Why now?" I asked. "I mean, the child is like six."

"Well, here's the short version," Nikko said, standing. He began to pace back and forth. Tobey watched him. I watched him.

"I knew that Jeannie Usitalo got pregnant in high school. Everyone knew it. And I knew she and I had—hooked up. But, truthfully, Jeannie did get around a bit. Plus, she never said *anything*. But now that Jeannie is dead, things have changed. Jeannie's parents asked to meet with me, so we met. Mrs. Usitalo said that Jeannie believed me to be the father, but she didn't want to complicate things by making me own up to it. She and I weren't serious about each other, or even dating. Jeannie was insistent, I guess, on going it alone. She had a lot of guts."

"She did," I said. "I remember when she went onstage to receive her diploma and was about eight months pregnant."

"Her parents respected her wishes, but now things have changed. Mr. and Mrs. Usitalo are more than willing to raise their granddaughter, but they felt that I should know I was the biological father, and asked me to give things some thought. They are grandparents, so a little old to be raising a child. I think they're looking to me as possible backup. Meanwhile, I agreed to take a paternity test."

"And...?"

"I'm 99.99 percent sure to be the father."

"Would you have married her?"

"Maybe," Nikko said, "but we didn't love each other. I admit I was just a horndog in high school. Not proud of it, but there you are. We all have a past. I guess Clay can back me on that."

"So now what?" I said.

"Truthfully, I have no idea. I want to do what's right, but what is right?"

We sat silently for a moment. Tobey's head shot up and he sniffed the air. Nikko looked at me and said, "How are you feeling about this?"

"Well," I said, "somewhat knocked for a loop, for sure. But I guess it's more important to figure out what's best for Brianna than what's best for me—you and me."

"I agree, but what *is* best?"

"I'm not sure, but I will say for sure that Brianna doesn't need another shock in her life right now."

Tobey stood and looked off into the trees. I heard the chattering of a red squirrel, and Tobey launched himself into a chase.

"Tobes!" Nikko shouted. Come back!"

We both took off after the dog, stumbling through the underbrush and into a wooded area, calling Tobey repeatedly. I heard some rustling, then the wayward pooch burst from behind an enormous rock and ran to Nikko. Tobey was holding a live squirrel in his mouth. At least I believed it to be alive because its tail was twitching. It had a frozen expression of terror on its squirrely face, and its little legs stuck out like stiff twigs.

"Drop it!" Nikko commanded.

Tobey obeyed and reluctantly let his quarry drop. The squirrel lay on the ground for a moment, tail twitching. Then, as if jolted awake, it jumped up, gave Tobey a thorough scolding, and scampered up a nearby tree. It continued its tirade from a limb safely away from its tormentor.

"Good boy," Nikko said.

"Why was he good?"

"He did eventually obey. You're not supposed to punish them when they finally obey. Then they get confused."

Maybe Nikko would make a decent father, I thought. *But then, what about us?*

Nikko snapped the leash back on Tobey, who merrily looked around as if searching for more mischief. I regarded the woody landscape. Most of the white pine in the area had been logged over decades before, and rotting stumps appeared throughout the second-growth woods. I moved toward a stand of mature oak trees huddled in a grove, looking almost out of place. I gazed up toward the sky, which peeked through the limbs. Acorns would come later and provide a bounty of food for the wildlife.

The only other remarkable thing about the terrain was an enormous boulder—the size of a compact car—lurking in the shadows of oaks. I had never seen it before; it was quite extraordinary. I headed that way to check it out. The rock was probably glacial. I found the power of nature, moving multi-ton boulders, truly amazing. Nikko and Tobey followed.

"Will you look at that thing!" Nikko said.

Tobey began to strain at the leash a little as we approached the rock. It was moss-covered and actually had some plant life sprouting from its crevasses. The monolith appeared to be granite, though I was no geologist. I wondered how far it had traveled over the millennia and where it was first "born." Tobey pulled Nikko around to the backside of the boulder and showed great interest in a mound of dirt. He snuffled the way dogs do when something smells interesting to them. He dug at it with a paw.

"What have we here?" I asked, reaching down to pat him.

It was a very strange and somewhat unnatural-looking mound. Dead trees, erosion, and past glacier activity did form humps and mounds in the woods, but this one had a very raw appearance. And it was quite large, about three or four feet tall with a circumference roughly the size and shape of a small dome tent. While there was some leaf litter and twigs scattered across it, no foliage or moss sprouted from it. A couple of significant holes, nearly filled in with leaves, were nearby.

"What do you make of this?" I asked, pointing at the mound.

"A mass grave?"

"Don't even say that."

Tobey's interest intensified. He tried to dig with both paws, but Nikko pulled him away.

"Tell you what I think," I said.

"Yeah?"

"You know how on *Antiques Roadshow*—"

"On what?"

"*Antiques Roadshow*," I said. "I mentioned it before in Spiller's office when we were discussing replicas of priceless artifacts. It's the TV series where a troupe of experts go to different cities and set up a huge production for this show. People bring in various objects that might be family heirlooms, garage sale finds, memorabilia, antiques, artwork—you name it—and the experts examine the piece to determine if it's valuable. Sometimes it's a priceless object, other times fake, and sometimes just an average thing sold on the mass market. Everyone, even those who are disappointed, always says they had a great time. I always figured people who were totally pissed off and thought the experts wrong were edited out. Anyway, I remember one time someone brought a statue in that was sold to them as pre-Columbian. The expert said unfortunately the item was not authentic and that scammers often bury the objects in dirt for a couple of weeks to a few months in an attempt to make them look old, when they're really not. Among other things, they lack an authentic patina."

"Patina?"

"Yeah, the natural oxidation of things. It's hard if not impossible to speed it up. But to the average person, we don't know the difference."

"You say they sometimes bury things?" Nikko asked.

"Varga suggested it back when we were, ah, incarcerated. He said he was looking to dig something up and the Hilmans were looking to bury something. I was a little out of it, what with lingering LSD and blood alcohol possibly over the limit. Yeah, he talked about the very thing. But, of course, it was all speculation. And where to even begin searching?"

We looked at the mound.

"I think we may have stumbled upon the whereabouts of the knockoffs of the knockoffs," I said. "Or I should say that Tobey played a major role in the discovery."

"Good boy!" Nikko said.

Tobey wiggled his butt and continued to sniff around the mound.

"I wonder what he smells," I said.

"Probably the leftover scent of the hippie Hilmans. You know, *before* they died. I don't think we have any missing persons right now. Pitties aren't generally cadaver dogs anyway. Yet they do still share an incredible sense of smell like all dogs."

We both looked at the mound again.

"Now what?" I asked.

"I'll get the shovel."

34

Sheriff Olsen, Alex Varga, Nikko, and I were all seated around my miniscule table in the mod. The sun was past the yardarm, so we were having an adult beverage. Before we had gotten down to business, I had presented Varga with a bottle of expensive scotch, which he broke into and was enjoying on the rocks. The rest of us were drinking beer straight out of the bottle. Sheriff Olsen still wore his duty trousers, but had stripped off his uniform shirt and gun belt and officially declared himself off duty. Tobey lay snoring under the table, and Jupiter sat in the doorway, tail lashing to and fro, glaring at Tobey. Aunt Lin and Raymond were in her room, and I could hear the plink-plunk of the lyre. Based on the discordance we were hearing, I figured it was probably Raymond at the strings.

An object lay on a piece of newspaper in the middle of the table. It was straight on three sides, and rounded on the top, and about two-and-a-half-feet tall, eighteen-inches wide, and maybe three-inches thick. It had the beginning of a crack going through it. According to Varga, it was likely made of fired clay, like one would use to make pottery. It resembled a tablet such as Moses could have used to share the Ten Commandments. The item bore several sequential scenes, divided into squares marked by lines, and crudely etched into the material. Each square had a little vignette featuring God, rays of the sun, Adam and Eve in the apple orchard, a violent scene that looked like it involved a sword, and then a final square with an angel scolding someone. At the bottom were a series of scribbly symbols fashioned to depict ancient hieroglyphs. According to Varga, a proclaimed expert in hieroglyphics, they were totally bogus, as was the entire piece.

"I want to thank you again for the Glenfiddich Scotch," Varga said, taking a sip.

"My pleasure," I said.

Things weren't entirely chummy around the table. Sheriff Olsen and Nikko's view of the events leading up to the scrapyard showdown still had them eyeing Varga with suspicion. Neither was convinced Varga didn't have a connection to the hippie Hilmans' theft of museum property and the plan to launch an elaborate scam. However, it was beyond certain that Elsie Tuttle along with her "helpful" son had killed the Hilmans and attempted to do the same to Varga and me. Sorting out the museum theft would be left to the museum itself and the authorities connected to that investigation. While Varga hadn't been straight with me up front, he may have saved my life, and to me that was redemption with bonus points.

Sheriff Olsen cleared his throat. "So, Nikko told me how you inadvertently found the burial place for the fake museum stuff, but I'm a little fuzzy on the sequence of things."

I explained Tobey's assault on the squirrel and how the boulder and then the mound caught our attention.

"The soil was very sandy," I said. "Easy to dig. Looked to us like the mound was built by digging up dirt and piling it alongside."

"We stopped when we found what looked like a bone," Nikko said. "Part of a skull, probably. And it didn't appear to be an animal."

"You can tell that?" Varga asked.

"He's a trained professional," I said.

Sheriff Olsen snorted.

"I know animal remains pretty well," Nikko said, giving his father a poisonous look. "It was too big for a small mammal and shaped wrong for a deer or anything canine. Round, not elongated."

"What I think," I said, "is that the bone fragment was accidentally unearthed from one of the holes the Hilmans dug to get dirt for the mound."

"Give the girl a cigar!" the sheriff said, raising his beer. "I still say you should give up this horse stuff and get into police work."

A career in law enforcement was not on my wish list.

"Well, it's ghastly," Varga said, taking another swallow of his scotch. "Not Kat's career choice, but the unintentional disinterment."

"So the bone or skull fragment ended up in the mound," I said. "When Nikko and I started digging for the artifacts, this tablet thing was pretty close to the top. We debated what Alex would want us to do and decided to dig a little deeper. Then up came the bone. At first, we thought maybe just a deer or some other animal. And then I saw something on the boulder. Something not natural. Some faint writing on a flat spot that had moss and lichens growing over it. Nikko and I cleaned it off, and it was definitely an epitaph, like on a headstone."

"Could you make it out?" Sheriff Olsen asked.

"Yes," I said. "Nikko wrote it down for me on the little spiral notebook he always carries."

Nikko patted his pocket and smiled, then pulled out said notebook and handed it to me.

I read it aloud, "*Sarah Maija Huntington, May 10, 1906 Jan 17, 1922. Baby boy born still.* Helvi Paavola-Huntington's journal seemed to stop when the daughter, Sarah, ran off with that Ezikiel Adams. I believe she may have come home pregnant, and not even sixteen years old. I suspect she died in childbirth along with the baby. I always wondered what happened with Sarah since the Huntington family tree stopped so abruptly for her."

"And of course," Nikko said, "when we found the bone, we stopped, since it could be a crime scene."

"Just shoot me," I said.

Everyone looked at me.

"What?" I said.

"I know a bit about forensics," Sheriff Olsen said. "It seems likely to me that bone would have long turned to dust after over a hundred years."

"They have found ancient bones that are hundreds of years old," Varga said. "But of course in arid climates. And Upper Michigan climate is not conducive to preserving anything organic. Except...."

We were all ears. Varga took a dramatic swallow of his drink. The ice cubes clinked back into the empty glass.

"I'm getting a refill," he said, standing. "Can I get anyone another beverage?"

"Except what?" I said.

"Let me think," Varga said.

He replenished his drink and brought over three bottles of beer and placed them on the table. We all took a beer and twisted off the caps with a synchronized hiss. Raymond always lectures us white folks, saying we must learn to be patient. "You may miss something important," he'll say, "if you are always in a rush." That, along with a good set of brain cells, made him an excellent IT guy.

So, we waited.

"Unless," Varga continued, "the soil was alkaline. Or neutral. Maybe sandy soil that drains well."

Sheriff Olsen took a swig of beer and said, "The average embalmed corpse buried in a quality coffin could have decipherable bone remains up to about fifty years max. At least around here, what with the ground freezing, thawing, the snowpack, rain, and so on."

"And even less time if just buried in the soil directly," said Nikko.

"And not embalmed," I added.

"Did you notice the species of trees around the area?" Varga asked.

"Yes," I said. "It was quite remarkable that a good stand of mature oak trees—"

"Burr Oak," Nikko interrupted.

"—were there. Mostly, it's second growth around that area with aspen, poplar, and some spruce and balsam."

"Oak trees do thrive in alkaline soil," Nikko said.

"So," Varga said, "it's possible the soil provided a friendly environment for slowing the decomposition of a skeleton."

We were quiet for a moment, thinking about what may have been disturbed.

Sheriff Olsen was picking at the label on his beer bottle. "The alleged skull piece is at the lab. They're sending it somewhere to determine its genus and age, among other things. In the meantime, we need to consider it a possible crime scene, so no poking around for a while."

"I say it's the resting place of Sarah and her baby," I said.

Sheriff Olsen grunted. "Let's hope so."

"In any event," Varga said. "I believe we have solved the mystery of the location of at least one of the missing museum pieces. Of course, I wouldn't dream of trying to dig anything up right now."

"But what I still don't understand," I said, "is why the Hilmans chose that specific spot."

"Maybe it's as simple as it was a nice, sandy area and easy to dig," said Nikko. "And the boulder made it easy to find. I wonder if we were to look around, maybe even into Crystal Lake Wilderness, that we'd find other places they tried to use and had to abandon."

"There was no sophisticated digging equipment in the Hilman camper," the sheriff said. "Maybe a spade shovel, which is pretty standard camping equipment."

"When you are dealing with all the roots and rocks around the area and are using simple equipment," Nikko said, "it's damn hard to even dig a hole to plant a tree seedling. Believe me, I know."

"And if we continue speculating about the homestead mound," Varga said, "Laureen Hilman knew the vicinity was the location of a significant find already. It added credence to their plan. That said, it is very possible the Hilmans had various objects in various mounds. The one you discovered may be the tip of the iceberg. Perhaps the tablet you dug up was the only item in that particular mound."

"So multiple mounds," I said.

"If one mound became inaccessible for some reason, there would still be others," Varga said, "thus giving the Hilmans some insurance."

"Like diversifying," I said.

"I wonder," said Nikko, "how they would have kept track of where everything was, like with some kind of map."

"There were some research papers," Sheriff Olsen said. "Far as I know, no so-called map."

"It may be cryptic and easy to pass over," Varga said.

"Always possible," Sheriff Olsen said.

"Maybe they marked things with ribbons," Nikko said, "like the one we saw at the stream crossing."

"I wonder if it really matters at this stage," I said.

"A good point," said Varga. "I doubt Dumbarton will want to spend resources exploring thousands of acres of wilderness for some simulated relics. Cheaper to make new ones. Might be interesting if someone in the future inadvertently digs up one of the replicas and starts a whole new sensation."

We all chewed on our assorted speculations for a while.

"The Hilmans are dead," I said. "Their scheme died with them. In a way, Elsie Tuttle won the battle. She stopped something—well, something if not evil, then nefarious."

"Too bad she killed people in the process," Nikko said. "Not to mention abduction and imprisonment."

"There is that," I said.

The lyre plinking stopped and I heard Aunt Lin's door open. She and Raymond came out and looked around.

"Hmm, so serious," Raymond said.

"Super-sleuthing going on," I said.

"Ah."

Varga stood and took his empty glass to the sink, dumped the cubes, rinsed the glass, and put it in the dishwasher. He took the tablet replica and the scotch bottle, then looked at Sheriff Olsen.

"I assure you, Sheriff, that I'm fit to drive. Also, I'll take care of shipping the tablet to the museum. I don't want to try to take it on the plane. And, Kat, thank you again for quite an adventure. I'll be heading back to my motel, then catching a flight to DC in the morning. I'll be consulting with the museum board along with security and God knows who else about our next step in this debacle. Lieutenant Spiller has indicated that no charges will be brought against me for shooting

Mr. Tuttle. However, I may be testifying in the future, and while I'm not pleased at the prospect, it may mean we will all meet again. Perhaps you can get me on a horse. Can one learn such things on YouTube?"

"Maybe," I said. "We can see how it works out."

"Yes, and Kat, to reiterate the reason I came here to your lovely neck of the woods, the offer is *still* on the table."

"I'm thinking about it—the possible authentic artifacts at the homestead. I will never sell the land. If I do agree to an excavation, it won't be for profit; it will be because it's the right thing."

"An excellent response," Varga said.

"It's just that I'm not sure what is right."

Varga nodded at me and left. We heard his car start and drive off.

Sheriff Olsen left as well, probably following Varga as far as he could. Aunt Lin and Raymond took off to some kind of Native American cultural thing at the tribal community center, which I suspected involved Bingo.

Nikko looked at me and smiled. "Lots of things to think about—I mean, what's right."

"Yup," I said. I knew he was thinking about Brianna.

"I mean, should I let her know? Wait 'til she's older?"

Nikko came over and stood behind my chair. He kissed the top of my head. I stood up and turned to face him. I had at least made one decision.

"I'm with you no matter what," I said. "We'll work it out."

Nikko let out a breath and moved in for a kiss. I took him by the hand and led him toward my bedroom. Tobey raised his head, got up, and tried to follow. Jupiter hissed and blocked the doorway.

"Let the kids work it out," Nikko said.

"May the best species win," I said, shutting the bedroom door behind us.

35

"Kinda sad," I said. "Another piece of Uncle Phil's legacy gone."

Nikko and I had ridden to the former horse campground and future location of the Magic Stirrup Therapy Camp. It had been a while since I'd been in the saddle. I was finally able to ditch the sling, and while not actually cleared by my doctor to resume riding, neither was I forbidden. I didn't bring it up in my last checkup. Doctors are always in a hurry, which worked well for me. I was aboard Big Mac, and Nikko was on Rusty. Barring any drones flying overhead, Mac was as solid a horse as God put on earth. I was safer on him than I was getting out of the shower or using my can opener.

"Are you sure you don't want me to carry that backpack?" Nikko asked.

He was referring to the hiking daypack I was wearing.

"I'm good," I said.

We watched the workers from Kusch Construction disassemble and demolish the corrals, picnic tables, campfire rings, rotted benches, and, sadly, the listing remains of the outhouse. There were six guys in all. Two had taken off their shirts, and while I refrained whistling any cat calls, I did enjoy the scenery for a couple of minutes.

The metal pieces and decaying lumber were sorted into piles for recycling. One of the workers asked permission to take the outhouse riser and seat for his camp. The campground, originally created for fun and respite, was also a disturbing reminder of the murder of Scott Summers just a few short months prior. It would be a while before that memory faded. Perhaps the future young occupants would dispel the gloom and replace it with happiness and hope.

Nikko and I were on a mission and planned to visit the old homestead. It seemed more appropriate to ride horses than rumble noisily there in the Bobcat aka Druggie Buggy. We had gotten the word that the area was not a crime scene, and thus, we were free to visit. Quite remarkably, the piece of skull was determined to be quite old, possibly over a hundred years, and likely that of a newborn baby. That bit of news convinced me I was right about the boulder and adjacent area being a gravesite for Sarah Huntington and her baby boy. It couldn't be verified, but given the age of the skull, and the practice of early settlers burying family on their own land, it was a viable theory. The only evidence of wrongdoing was that the Hilmans had inadvertently dug into some human remains when making their mound for the fake relics.

The workers broke for lunch. The noise quieted and was replaced by bird twitters and the sound of a gentle breeze through the pine boughs. I heard the soft thudding of hoofbeats approaching, and turned to see Susie coming up the two track leading Peaches. Brianna was aboard the pony and clung to its mane for security. Willie Moss was walking alongside the pony, holding Brianna's leg. It was the standard procedure for escorting a child engaged in a therapeutic ride. Sometimes two people were involved in walking alongside the horse or pony.

Brianna could not have had a wider grin on her face. We didn't yet have a pony-sized saddle, so she was riding bareback. Her cheeks were pink, and her blond pigtails swayed a little with the pony's movement. She was wearing youth riding jodhpurs and boots, which Nikko had bought for her, but kept the gift anonymous. Already spoiling the child! When Brianna saw us she let go of the thick mane with one of her hands and waved. Nikko and I waved back. Susie waved. Willie waved. The workers, munching sandwiches and guzzling energy drinks, also waved.

"I guess we've all said hello," Nikko said.

Peaches and company pulled up alongside us, and Brianna reached down and vigorously petted the pony.

"Isn't she just the best!" Brianna said, as she ran her hands across the thick Shetland neck.

"She is," I said. "You look very nice up there."

"I wanna get down, though," she said. "I can't ride Peaches too much because her feet still hurt. I don't want to hurt her feet."

"Of course," I said.

Nikko and I both dismounted, and he handed me Rusty's reins. He went over to Peaches and helped Brianna down. She reached for his hand and he took it for a moment, then turned her over to Susie. I felt my throat tighten for a moment. *I won't get choked up!*

"Do you want to take Peaches over to meet some of the guys working today?" Susie asked.

"Yeah! They're all looking this way."

They were looking our way, but not because of Peaches or Brianna. Susie Koskinen was undeniably attractive—or "hot" as Gen Zers would say—in her four-way stretch riding breeches and tall black boots. The clingy tank top didn't hurt either, or the long blond ponytail cascading down her back. She and Brianna went over to the work area and chatted up the fellas.

"Things are finally moving forward," Willie said. "I think we can have a grand opening yet this year before we lose the weather."

"That would be fantastic," I said.

"I talked with your little girl there, Brianna. I understand that with her it's emotional, not physical. Lost her mother."

"Yes," I said. "Not really an official student of Magic Stirrup yet, but Brianna needed something to help her cope and Peaches needed someone to love her."

"Seems to be working out well," Willie said. "I take it there's no father."

The question hung heavily for a moment.

"Um..." I said.

"We are looking into it," Nikko said.

Willie gave him a strange look. "I see."

She might have figured it out. There was an undeniable resemblance, especially in the eyes, now that I looked a little closer. How stupid of me not to notice sooner.

"Let me know when you're ready to go," Nikko said. "I'm gonna go talk to some of these guys about some work on my house."

"Okay," I said.

Nikko led Rusty over toward Brianna, Susie, and the clutch of workers.

Willie walked closer to the demolished campground and looked around. "What a beautiful spot we have here."

"My uncle always thought so," I said.

"Perhaps we can name something here after your uncle, in his memory."

"I'd like that. So would he—and my dad."

"Maybe the community building," she said. "I have plans for a log lodge, to fit the environment. A nice stone fireplace, comfy furniture, kitchen, accessible restrooms, of course, and a deck with outdoor fireplace. There will be accommodations for the staff. Some will be bunking with the students and others in separate quarters. We'll need a mix of male and female personnel."

"Wow. I'd love to see the plans. I guess I just thought there'd be some cabins and maybe a firepit. I don't suppose you would have room in the plans for our ranch hand, Clay Randall?"

Willie gave me a sly smile. "Things have been upgraded. I got a private donation on top of the grant that will give us the funding. And it's possible that Mr. Randall could be accommodated, perhaps helping with maintenance, so long as he's agreeable to the necessary background checks and so on."

Getting Clay's record cleaned up moved to the top of my to-do list. "That would be great. I know he can't live indefinitely in that truck camper. Oh, and speaking of staff, I'm wondering if you had a chance to look over Bernice Perry's application for Magic Stirrup."

"Yes I did, and I called her. We did a video chat. She is a delightful woman with an amazing history. Did you know that she had a physical deformity as a child and many surgeries? Her parents got her interested in horses, and she swears they were her salvation. She's the poster child for equine therapy."

"I didn't know that! I knew she was having surgery when she sold me my saddle. I assumed it was the usual hip thing with aging."

"All part and parcel with her earlier problems. Anyway, I have recommended her for the position and have every reason to believe she'll be brought on. There'll be a background check along with program training, which we can get going on before the camp officially opens."

"That's great," I said. "Do you think we'll need more horses? I have probably five that will be suitable. Some of the horses are rescues and subject to adoption."

"Five is a good start. If you have a rescue horse that you'd like to incorporate into Magic Stirrup, just let me know. We'll look into its purchase. All horses used in the camp will have to be tested for reliability and so on. You and I both know there is no horse without its quirks. However, we want to be as conscientious as possible to have suitable animals."

"Absolutely," I said.

Nikko and Rusty returned. "Need a leg up?" he asked.

I nodded. I have altitude, but still needed help getting up on a seventeen-hand horse. I bent my leg and put my knee in the cup of Nikko's hand. We counted to three, and he boosted me into the saddle.

"Teamwork!" I said. "Thanks."

"My pleasure," he said as he mounted Rusty.

"Do we need to discuss anything else?" I asked, looking at Willie.

"Nope," she said. "I'll just see Susie and Brianna back to the stable then I've got to scoot."

"Nikko and I are headed out to a place to take care of a little business. I wanted to check things out here first."

"I'll be in touch," Willie said.

Nikko and I urged our horses forward, and we headed down the trail toward the homestead. Mac was leading the way, and Rusty had buried his head in Mac's tail. Very trusting. I wasn't going to lecture Nikko about the dangers of tailgating. He had mentioned more than once that I tended to be bossy around horses. When we arrived at the homestead, it seemed different. Everything looked the same, but a little bit of its mystery had been unraveled. While a major archeological dig was still uncertain, a piece of the homestead's history had come to light.

We dismounted, and I pulled the pack off my shoulders. We tethered the horses to a couple of trees and set off toward the boulder site.

"I think Brianna has taken a shine to you," I said.

"You think so?" Nikko said. "Maybe I'm just irresistible to women."

"That's what got you in this pickle to begin with."

"My irresistibleness?"

"Is that a word?"

"Am I—to you?"

"What, a pickle?"

"Very funny," he said, holding a branch back for me to pass. "I might just snap this back in your face."

"There's the oak trees."

"Burr Oak."

"What's the difference?" I said. "No wait, never mind. I don't need a botany lesson."

Nikko tugged at my waistband and pulled me toward him, then dramatically dipped me into an overly elaborate kiss. The backpack plopped on the ground.

"Oh, my, sir. You are being quite forward!"

"You ain't seen nothin' yet, my dear," he said, swooping me back upright. "I saw you ogling those construction workers. For shame!"

"Why, I don't know what you're talking about," I said, my voice dripping with a fake Southern accent.

"Hah! Are you sure you don't want me to carry that backpack for you? I mean, I am a gentleman."

"A little late for the gentlemanly offer. We're here."

We walked over to the boulder and mound. Nothing had changed since our last visit, except maybe a little more forest litter here and there.

"Thank you for making the thing I asked for," I said. "It's perfect, but I'm not sure where to put it."

"Wherever you put it, it will be right."

"Because I'm doing what's right?"

"And I've been thinking about that," Nikko said. "What's right."

"I think we're talking about two different things. But go ahead; tell me what right you're thinking."

"Brianna, obviously. And you. Us."

I brushed some twigs away from the front of the boulder. A good deal of the rock was likely underground. I noticed a strange notch in the rock, as if someone had drilled a rustic hole in it. I stood up and gave Nikko my attention.

"I think she should know. The sooner the better," he said.

"Have you talked to the Usitalos about it?"

"Yes, early on. They said they'd help. Brianna knows that most kids have a dad. And according to her grandma, Alice, she has been asking why she doesn't have one."

"A delicate conversation," I said. "You'll have to try not to talk over her head. She'll want to know a lot of things."

"She's a very inquisitive child. I have to think about how to explain. And I'm hoping...not to go it alone."

I looked at him.

"I need you."

Nikko had never said he needed me, just wanted me. And of course the "L" word had never been spoken by either of us.

"To help me. To be with me. I'm...it's...."

I wrapped my arms around him and could feel his body shake. He was crying. So naturally, I started to cry.

"Damn!" he said, pulling away. "Where did that come from?"

"They were very manly tears," I said, laughing as I wiped my eyes.

He laughed and I snorted. My nose was running freely.

"Here," he said, pulling a crisp, white handkerchief out of his back pocket. "Blow."

I blew. We both took a deep breath and looked over at the boulder and mound.

I pulled a wooden cross out of my backpack. "I think there may have been a cross or something here once," I said. "There is a kind of notch carved in the rock."

"Perfect," Nikko said.

I held up the wooden cross, which Nikko had made. It was hickory, which he said would last a while. It had been inscribed with a wood burner, then varnished and waxed. It was simple and beautiful.

"Sarah Maija Huntington, May 10, 1906 Jan 17, 1922. Baby boy, born still," I recited. "I wish I had the Huntington journal so I could insert this piece of her life—and death—into it."

I placed it into the notch in the rock. It seemed to fit perfectly. Next, I pulled a small bundle wrapped in a white cloth from my backpack. I unwrapped it and revealed the tiny partial skull of the baby boy. The last item in the backpack was a small, folding shovel that Nikko took.

"Where?"

"I think in the mound. Maybe there are other, ah, parts in there. Some may still be elsewhere, but I think the mound."

"What if we find more relics?" Nikko said.

"Leave them there. And any other, um, human remains."

He nodded and started digging. The mound soil was still loose and soft, making the digging easy. When Nikko reached the bottom, he encountered much harder earth. Thankfully, no more artifacts or bones were unearthed in the process.

"Here okay?" he asked.

I nodded, rewrapped the tiny skull in the white cloth, and dropped to my knees, then onto my stomach, and carefully lowered the bundle into the hole. I stood and brushed the dirt off my clothes. Nikko filled it in and we smoothed over the top.

I looked at the cross and gravesite of a mother who had died too young, along with a baby who never had a chance to live. Life was short and precious.

I turned to Nikko and said, "One righted thing can be checked off the list."

He drew me into a hug and put his chin on my shoulder. "I'll do it tomorrow. Talk to Brianna."

He pulled out of the embrace and held both my hands. Our eyes locked. "I'm terrified," he said.

I nodded. "Me too."

"Tomorrow."

"Yes."

About the Author

Straw Horse is Terri Martin's second novel in her Kat Wilde U.P. Mystery series. Martin's first of the series, *Gift Horse*, begins the story of a resurrected horse stable along with a few mysterious deaths, and a perplexing romance with a conservation officer. Martin also has an additional full-length novel entitled *Moose Willow Mystery*, along with three anthologies of humorous stories. She received the U.P. Notable Book Award for her middle-grade children's novel, *The Home Wind*, and has an additional middle-grade book, *Voodoo Shack*.

Martin started her writing career as a regular contributor to several Midwest publications. Her stories often reflect the culture and characters she has encountered during her twenty-five years of living in Upper Michigan. Terri and her husband enjoy watching the menagerie of freeloading wildlife from their home on the Silver River. While the winters are harsh, the soul never tires of the beauty of the Northwoods.

Martin has a master's degree in English and has taught college success courses, tutored English, and served as an aide for college composition classes.

Visit Terri's website at www.terrilynnmartin.com or email her at gnarlywoodspub@gmail.com.

The *Kat Wilde Mysteries* Begins with *Gift Horse*

Tucked away in Michigan's Upper Peninsula, the village of Peshekee has more to worry about than the long winters and steelhead fishing. Scandal and a suspicious death or two visit the rural village, setting speculation and gossip into motion. After her post-college career collapses, Kat Wilde finds herself living with the family cat in her parents' basement. With no other prospects on the horizon, Kat is offered a gift she can't refuse: inheriting her late uncle's failed equine venture, Wildwood Stables. There, she sees hope for regaining independence from a pity job at Dad's accounting firm. Attracting the attention of Nikko Olsen, a local woods cop, leads to unconventional romance and adventure. The discovery of a corpse, along with disturbing encounters at the old horse campground, launches a spate of entanglements that unravel as Kat stumbles onto family sins and secrets.

"I want to be Terri Martin's Kat Wilde in Gift Horse: the reluctant recipient of a run-down horse boarding stable whose spirit is exceeded only by her heart! Martin's *Gift Horse* is a pleasure ride, with enough bumps, turns and twists in the trail to keep the reader glued to the saddle -- right up until a very satisfying ending."

-- Nancy Besonen, author of *Off the Hook*

"Kat Wilde, a Gen Z woman trying to find a life in the rugged wilderness of the U.P., stumbles into an unlikely inheritance that reignites the fire of her forgotten youthful passion for horses. She is a down-to-earth heroine I rooted for at every turn, as she and new beau, Nikko Olsen, unravel the schemes of a murderer and impostor."

-- Victor Volkman, *Marquette Monthly*

A suspicious death in a game processing meat locker is just the beginning of bizarre events happening in the Upper Michigan village of Moose Willow. It all starts when a mysterious woman appears at the Methodist church during choir practice. Janese Trout and her best friend, State Trooper Bertie Vaara, team up to connect the woman to a growing number of disturbing occurrences around town includeing the disappearance of Janese's eccentric lover, George LeFleur, and an undeniable increase in Bigfoot sightings. Meanwhile, Janese faces a multitude of personal challenges as she grapples with a sagging career at the Copper County Community College, an elusive pregnancy test, and a controlling mother who inserts herself into every hiding place of Janese's life.

"*Moose Willow Mystery*, by Terri Martin, lets cozy mystery fans know they are about to experience something wildly different with edgy characters, a big dose of humor, and an insider's look at America's best-kept secret the mysterious Upper Peninsula of Michigan."
—Carolyn Howard-Johnson, award-winning writer of fiction, poetry, and the HowToDoItFrugally Series of books for writers

"Terri Martin manages to present the ordinary, the bizarre (of which there is a steady stream), and even the violent in a way that will open a hilarious glimpse into the world of a small town. With brilliant characterization, she takes the reader on a wild ride of murder and mayhem, so let me warn you. Don't start reading until you have the time to keep going."

—Bob Rich, PhD, author of *Sleeper, Awake!*

"Take a mini-vacation and read this delightful mystery! Laugh away the problems of the world (and cry a few times) along with the remarkable, talented characters in *Moose Willow Mystery*. A refreshing whodunit with plenty of mystery to keep the reader unable to put the book down."

—Carolyn Wilhelm, M.A., *Midwest Book Review*

Featuring Yooper Woodswoman Nettie Bramble!

Nettie Bramble lives with her ma in Upper Michigan in a cabin that's slightly off the grid. She claims to "subsist" off the land and prefers to do so without the benefit of hunting or fishing licenses. Nettie is bound to have a clash or two with the local woods cop, CO Will Ketchum, and the chronically cranky Judge Nightshade. Most places that Nettie goes, her "citified" nephews, Wanton and Wiley, tag along to muddle up her plans. Nettie will meet up with Church Lady Bea Righteous, as well as Tami and Evi Maki (thrice-removed cousins) in an erratic road rally with a cash prize that brings out the worst in everyone. No spoiler alert for the surprise ending in this collection of short stories featuring a strong dose of the Yooper way.

"Terri Martin writes fast-paced little tales peppered with humorous disasters following one after another... If you live in the U.P., you'll have heard plenty of fish tales and hunting sagas from your outdoor friends. Some of them may be whoppers, but none as big as the ones Nettie Bramble tells."

—Jon C. Stott, author of *Yooper Ale Trails*

"*Roadkill Justice* has to be among the funniest books I have ever read. Our heroine's ongoing battle with the law, the clever use of malapropisms and the caricature of a now-gone culture had me laughing several times on every page."

—Bob Rich, author of *Hit and Run*

"*Roadkill Justice*'s unlikely heroine, Nettie Bramble, is rough-edged but 'big-hearted, with 'sisu' to spare. Author Terri Martin does a fantastic job of capturing the spirit and the spunk of the Northwoods character in a plot that sweeps her reader along, like a fast-running trout stream, on a delightful ride filled with twists, turns, laughter and the occasional explosion."

—Nancy Besonen, author of *Off the Hook*

Learn more at www.TerriLynnMartin.com

Jamie Kangas struggles with turbulent emotions caused by the death of his father, who perished in a logging accident—an accident for which Jamie blames himself. While his mother works as cook in a logging camp, Jamie is run ragged as chore boy. The grinding dreariness fades when Jamie meets a Native American boy, Gray Feather, who carries a burden of his own. The two boys become close friends as they face the challenges of a harsh environment and prejudiced world. And as trees fall to the lumberjack's blade, Jamie hears the ghostly words of his father, warning of future catastrophe.

The Home Wind is a middle-grade children's novel (ages 9 and up), which takes place during the 1870s in a Michigan logging camp. Quality paperback, 198 pages plus discussion guide.

"*The Home Wind* is a beautiful novel for both middle grade readers and a wonderful a read for adults, too. Steeped in carefully researched historical events in Michigan's Upper Peninsula, *The Home Wind* is a delight. Martin's characters captured my heart and made the story come alive--two boys struggling to understand the world around them. This is also an important book for anyone interested in the history of Michigan's logging industry and in the Native peoples of Michigan. I highly recommend *The Home Wind*, and if you are looking for a gift for your middle reader, it's perfect!"

—Sue Harrison, author of *The Midwife's Touch*

"Martin's descriptions of the scenes and action make a reader feel as if they are right there in the middle of it all. Readers can't miss the symbolism found throughout the book and a wonderful way to learn about the past at the same time. This book should go far, and not just with young audiences."

—Deborah K. Frontiera, *U.P. Book Review*

Learn more at www.TerriLynnMartin.com

Join Iris and the Voodoo Shack gang as they investigate a mysterious death and an unsolved crime!

When 11-year-old Iris Weston discovers a ramshackle hunting cabin deep in Hazard Swamp, she and her friends decide it's perfect for a secret clubhouse. The gang dubs it the Voodoo Shack and meets there to swap stories and play card games. Ol' Man Hazard, the former owner, died under mysterious circumstances, and the kids speculate whether it was an accident, suicide or maybe even murder! The gang believes that cash from an unsolved crime may have been stashed within feet of the cabin. Even as things go badly awry, feisty Iris learns how to use her wit and independence to put things right, discovering what family really means in this adventurous and often humorous coming-of-age story set in rural Michigan in 1962.

"Set in the early 1960s, Martin's novel traces a girl's journey toward understanding the true meaning of love, family and friendship. Iris is an appealing character whose relationships with friends and family are realistically portrayed as she struggles to find her place."

—*School Library Journal*

"Martin has drawn on her childhood memories to create an engaging, feisty heroine, lively supporting characters and an easy-to-visualize early 1960s rural Michigan setting. And, although Iris doesn't solve all her mysteries, she finds the answers to the most important ones in this fast-paced story."
—*ALA Booklist*

"Readers fond of lightweight mysteries solved by spunky heroines will take to this fiction debut, though a heavy ballast of tragedy and near-tragedy keeps it low to the ground. Some of the dialogue and set pieces show a promising authorial gift for comedy. (Fiction. 10-12)"

—*Kirkus Reviews*

Learn more at www.TerriLynnMartin.com

www.ingramcontent.com/pod-product-compliance
Lightning Source LLC
Chambersburg PA
CBHW022004010726
47494CB00003B/878
* 9 7 8 1 6 1 5 9 9 4 6 5 6 *